OUR CONQUEST

OUR CONQUEST

GERT HOFMANN

TRANSLATED BY
Christopher Middleton

Fromm International Publishing Corporation
NEW YORK

Translation copyright © 1985
Fromm International Publishing Corporation, New York

Originally published in 1984 as *Unsere Eroberung*
Copyright © 1984, Hermann Luchterhand Verlag GmbH & Co. KG,
Darmstadt und Neuwied, West Germany

All rights reserved. No part of this book may be reproduced
or utilized in any form or by any means, electronic or mechanical,
including photocopying, recording or by any information storage
and retrieval system, without permission in writing from the Publisher.
Inquiries should be addressed to Fromm International
Publishing Corporation, 560 Lexington Avenue,
New York, N.Y. 10022

Designed by Constance Fogler
Printed in the United States of America
First U.S. Edition

Library of Congress in Publication Data
Hofmann, Gert.
Our conquest.
I. Title.
PT2668.0'376U56   1985   833'.914   84-28789
ISBN 0-88064-019-7

OUR CONQUEST

1

ONE day our little town came to be conquered, or, as mother says, *rolled up*, from north to south, cut off from all surrounding towns and villages. (No resistance, the streets and squares deserted, for it happened at night while we were underground, with rats and mice for company, in our various deep and damp cellars—or else we simply slept through it.) So there can be no more thought of our Edgar leaving us now: we'll all be staying put. Perhaps, for all the talk there'd been about it, our defense up on the Hoher Hain had been overlooked, or our troops were worn out, or there was confusion at command headquarters, or the attack, though anticipated for weeks past, came after all as a surprise. Constantly we'd been nodding to one another and shouting: Tomorrow we'll be conquered!—yet still our conquest hadn't come. For a long time we thought it never would come. Or else it'd be tomorrow, we'd thought, and at nightfall we'd put the chain on the door. And once again we're standing at the window of our children's room and gazing out across our habitat which, as we learn at school, has no distinguishing features. No mountain pastures, no dunes, no moors, no marshes, no heathland—we live in an indeterminate, almost characterless upland region, imperceptibly polluted and sooted by a few not-so-distant industrial centers, country, as father says, not worth one enemy bomb. In other places there are foreign workers by the hundred, even thousands of them, but here in our town there can't be more than a few dozen. So: Tomorrow will be the day of our conquest, we think, and we thrust deep into our pockets the white handkerchief that mother gives us, for surrendering with—but then tomorrow also passes. But it'll be tomorrow, we shout down into the courtyard weeks later, yet still our conquest doesn't come. And now, after three nights in the cellar . . . For with our Edgar among us—Edgar, who suffered a great misfortune several weeks ago and actually lives with his aunt in Herrnburg, but, because he's our friend, is staying in our garden shed for the time being as our lodger—we've spent three days and three nights huddled and snuggled together in the cellar of our villa, in the farthest corner of it, where usually the jars of jam are kept. For a long time all the signs have been indicating that the shooting will begin at any moment and that we're done for. How our conversation wilts! Cringing, heads down, shoulders hunched, we look at one another in the light of our candle. Or we look—our angled legs thrust far under the old horse-blanket—at the cellar walls, at the ceiling. Meanwhile our mother, who has quickly been burning one more flag behind the outhouse and has very dirty fingers, sits at the foot of the stairs to protect us, and she looks at the floor between her feet. Raising our eyes we picture what will happen if a bomb or shell falls on our villa. Which part of the ceiling will collapse on whom first, whom will it kill or mutilate first? Will it collapse first on top of our Edgar, sitting up against a pillar? Or on mother, because she's so close to the entrance? Or on us, who've sat down, without giving it a thought, beside our Edgar and simply stayed there, just because we didn't want to get up again? Our Edgar, for sure, is sitting beneath an iron crossbeam, which is so strong that mother had wanted us to sit there, but we gave the place to our Edgar. We're sitting beneath a plain section of the ceiling, which will probably be the first to give way. Definitely we'll be the first to die, our skulls will be crushed first. Then will come the graying skull of mother, with its thin and veiny temples, and then the tall, fair-haired, pristine skull of our Edgar. Yes, Edgar's place is the safest of all in our admittedly not very deep, not very safe cellar. But perhaps mother will be killed first, because she's sitting so close to the door, so that when the bomb arrives she'll spread her arms and stand in its way and at least save us. Can she really save us, when she stands in its way? Will she even have time to walk toward it and spread her arms? Anyway, we're sitting in the middle of the cellar, far from the perilous door, so that the bomb, if it comes out of the garden, will hardly reach us. Yet everything might turn out altogether differently. Since we're sitting in the farthest recesses of the cellar, we could easily suffocate, whereas mother, because she's sitting by the door, will always have enough air to breathe. All right, we're thinking, now we're going to be annihilated! But then, heralded by a sound, there's a sudden turn in events. Crouching beside us, certainly on a blanket, probably the gray one, wearing white socks and shorts that he's growing out of, our Edgar suddenly raises his narrow head, hears the sound, and at once explains to us what it is. As soon as we hear his explanation, we breathe a sigh of relief. Just a moment ago our skulls seemed to be contracting under the pressure of our conquest—and now, quite nonchalantly, the foreign soldiers are flowing in among us. Yes, here it is, our conquest at last, at last. In whispered discussions, forbidden but philosophical, our Edgar explains our conquest for our benefit and his own, and meanwhile he lies down between us, for, around midnight, we take him into our midst and stretch out on the cold floor, although a night spent on such a floor can be, of course, fatal. And toward daybreak, after a dream (we'll be coming back to that), when we've been completely conquered, amid a great amount of noise, if without a single serious shot being fired, we flex our limbs and sit up again, stand upright in the cellar and climb out—our Edgar first, swaying and with wobbly knees, to find mother waiting for us already at the back door, to tell us finally *who* has conquered us. Cautiously, hands shading our eyes, we stumble into the courtyard and look through the grill of the courtyard gate at the enormous foreign trucks squeezing down our alleys in the fresh morning light. How quiet it suddenly is, after the gigantic tanks, which naturally want to go on fighting somewhere else as soon as they can, have been waved through our little town, and after we ourselves have been conquered! For a long time even the birds—though we could be wrong about it—haven't been calling.

Even then, we know it's all over now and time for our *extermination* to begin, something mother has told us so much about. Perhaps they'll herd us together and shoot every one of us. After going back to our children's room and taking a long look at one another, breathing a long breath at one another too, we go to the window and look out, speechless. Doing so we forget, if only for the time being, about being shot. Instead, here's the world outside again, the railed courtyard, the street on which none of us dares to walk today. (Only very slowly, first in the gutter, then on the sidewalk, do we find the confidence to walk along our streets again.) Nothing else that's new can be seen today, not even Americans. Except that very far off, on the edge of the park, beside the fire hydrant, they're burning a heap of rubbish. We take a good look. And we've seen them pouring gasoline over the heap, once they're satisfied it's big enough, and simply setting fire to it. (On that heap there could have been things to eat, cans to lick clean, or things to drape around one's head and shoulders during bad weather.) The stink that fills our street is, of course, unimaginable. What's this stink? mother exclaims from father's room, where she's gathering up a lot of things that also have to be burned, but burned in the chimney stove, and while gathering them she listens for sounds below, hearing a knock sometimes, goes downstairs, in spite of her bad leg, and opens the door a crack to look out, but each time, this morning at least, she's mistaken. Ah, we say from the window, they've set fire to something. Then shut the window, mother shouts from the next room, they ought to be ashamed of themselves, making a fire on the street in broad daylight. And you get away from the window and play at something in your room. But what are we supposed to play at? we ask, because we've played all the games before our conquest, and today we'd prefer to see the heap that's burning. Ah, as if it mattered what games you play, mother says, quick now, sit down on the bed. But because we'd like to see something burning this morning we ask her if we couldn't at least watch when *she* burns something, but she won't allow that either, she says she's not burning anything at all, only tidying up, while we're certain something is going to be burned in father's room, she's only waiting until we're asleep. So that on the day of our conquest we don't see anything burning, outside or inside, even if, outside as well as inside, we *smell* a whole lot of burning. So we sit on our beds and mother goes away again. And when we've sat for long enough on our beds and the fire near the hydrant has burned out and the smoke has cleared and we're standing again at the window, now closed, our gaze wanders across the park and suddenly we see our theater. How could the fire have made us overlook our theater! We've studied everything, the tiniest details, but not our theater! Had it been shrouded in the smoke? But we should have noticed it *before* there was any fire or smoke. Now, anyway, we suddenly see our theater clearly *after* the smoke and we recognize too how much we miss our theater. The fact is that this theater has been closed since February and it probably won't be opened again so soon either. Our beautiful theater, what a pity! How many times we've walked around it, our hands in our pockets, morning or night, because we've missed it so! And rattled the doors, one after another. And how many times we've *thought* of it, because we can't go into it. Of course we'd also thought of it before sometimes, when it was still open. And we'd simply stationed ourselves at the door, when we had no tickets, hoping we'd be admitted all the same. (We were wrong.) And how many times, after looking for quite a long while at all the people going into the theater (everyone except us!), we've run around our theater when the show had begun, and finally run home to look across the park at it, as now, from our window. So as to dream of our theater, at least, lying in our beds, when darkness came and the performance was in full swing. And when father once gave us his tickets—he doesn't like the theater and calls it a bladder of a building—how motionlessly we sit in our theater then, with sweating palms, and gaze at our stage! What life there is on that stage, compared with our life! How the actors, when the curtain has gone up, suddenly leap from the wings as quite different people (also as nonpeople, animals, monsters) and with gestures, in costumes, sometimes also masked, step forward to the footlights, simulating a different world. Which then can also be clearly glimpsed, behind and between them. Lying in our beds we think ourselves into our theater as deeply as we can. Or on tiptoe, in the uncertain light, we gaze from our window toward its entrance. And once we've studied our theater sufficiently from the front, we walk all around it, our empty theater, trying every single door, in case just *one* might be open. (But not one is open.) Nevertheless in our thoughts we all do enter our theater, study the stage, the gallery, the plush seats, wine-red and gold. For a long time we stand at the window, looking across the park to our theater, and thanks to our theater-memories we forget about being shot. Nothing else happens during this afternoon, except that our Edgar collapses once and has to be covered by mother with a blanket and sprinkled with water. While we stand at our window and then toward nightfall yawn a lot and press our foreheads against first this pane and then that. The day of our conquest, spent cautiously, behind curtains, it's a long one, isn't it? Then comes the dark but much briefer night. According to strict regulations our town is plunged in a darkness that makes our first springtime nights still more confining, more closed in. Then the gloom, which extinguishes everything. With a sheepskin over our knees we crouch around a candle. Until eventually the moon—we'd entirely forgotten about it—mounts solemnly above our roofs and begins to steam in the sky. Shivering, we walk to the window and look up at it. And when, at that moment, in the park or beyond it, probably because of their barking, a few dogs are shot by our conquerors, who are certainly drunk, we shout: Listen, now they're shooting! And of course we're thinking that the shots aren't meant for the dogs but for us. And we think: Yes, they're starting it now. And we're convinced that this very night, beginning with our theater, our whole small, freshly conquered town will be exterminated. But then suddenly the shooting stops, and in the boundless parental bed where, for this night, we're allowed to snuggle down, our Edgar at first between us and then at our feet, we quickly fall asleep. Then the darkness that is outside is also inside our head, we fall out of one into the other, closing our eyes. No wonder we can't for a long time find things the way they used to be. Never before had our uphill and downhill streets been so bewildering. Wasn't our town more clearly laid out and actually so designed that the villas, like ours, surrounded by spacious gardens running down the slopes of hills, should be situated on its north side, and the narrow, squat apartment buildings, like the one that Edgar lived in, occupied by others, by unimportant people, on its south side? Now all that has changed. Because of the bombs that fell at seven in the morning on the eleventh, rapidly falling over the south side, that side no longer exists. We hardly recognize anything—the walls, the rubble, the ruins of houses through which we run and beneath which eighty-eight dead people are lying and, as mother tells us, won't ever be brought up again. Our town, where is our town? Never stopping, we run through our streets, not up and down, but always straight ahead and yet continuously in a circle. Until, with a few leaps, all of this in our dream, we've jumped through a gap in a wall out of our town, and, with dully beating hearts, outside in Wundenplan we collapse in front of our father's small whip factory, on the low wall overgrown with weeds, and we wake up exhausted. Yes, that factory of ours which puts us to shame, there it is again, reaching right into our dreams. Ah, if only father didn't have the factory, we think, and we want to get up, and we're stretching our limbs, but we sink back onto our wall again. We can hardly even walk a little up and down in front of our factory, which is lying ponderously, angular, pallid and flat, inside our skull. Well then, as so often, with tired limbs, this first night, we take a little walk around our factory, skirting its confines. We make one of our reconnaissances around the building we've been forbidden to enter, looking upward to the workshop windows that our father, fearing thieves, had quickly had bars put over. So tonight, facing these windows, most of which are open, so that the stench that always fills such a factory can go away, we walk up and down a bit, looking now at the ground, now furtively up at the windows. Yes, that's the tanning workshop and there's the vat room! And there too is the office where father sacrifices himself for us and, like ourselves, except that he's inside, clasps his hands behind him, pacing up and down, him too, with quick neat footsteps. The office: a high room crowded with brown desks and closets and black filing cabinets, frosted glass around three sides of it and closed on the fourth side by the foundation wall of our factory, it extends far into the tanning workshop. Here, in addition to father's really oversize desk, across which pens and papers are tirelessly pushed back and forth, there stands the somewhat smaller desk of our chief clerk, Herr Lange, who was killed in the Crimea. His half-filled tobacco pouch is said still to be in a drawer of this desk. And with a view across to father there's a standing desk at which gloomy Herr Diviora, with his one hand—the other has withered away—supervises the mail going out and coming in. But father alone is in charge here, deep into the workshops. He has shifted his desk so that when he sits at it and raises his head he can survey not only the spacious tanning workshop, but also the workshop where the leather is cut. Often there's a lot of commotion around this desk, father is in demand from all sides, but he'd prefer to sit quietly in his armchair, supervising the work in silence. Yet that's one of the wishes he can't make come true. The moment he sinks into his chair in the morning, loud voices and red faces are hacking away at him. They throng at his elbows, not to greet him but to reproach him and call him to account for the most abstruse things that have often slipped his mind. Thus, surrounded by customers, hemmed in by colleagues, sweating, hoarse, in need of air, he spends the best hours of his life. When evening comes, as at a whistle blast, they abandon him again. We picture him slumping into his chair, suddenly isolated at his desk. Long after work has stopped he sits in his box, utterly devoted to his firm, thinking about it. That's the moment at which we'd like to cheer him up, perhaps call out to him, but we're too timid. We stand by the door to the workshop, scraping at the dust with our feet, picture our father's back, his desk, his hand, but secretly, because we're forbidden to go inside, it's a good thing he doesn't see us. But except for us—we're standing behind him—father sees everything in his factory. Only one workshop he doesn't see into, because it's so far away from his office. It's the workshop where the vats are, in which the hides are boiled. We've never been into this workshop, but we've heard a lot about it and sometimes picture it, if not as it really is, then certainly as it might be. Father, who knows the workshop well, also thinks about it a great deal. If he wants to see it, he only needs to get up from his desk a little and stand on tiptoe, then he can look, whether he wants to or not, into the vat room, because the door to it, on his express orders, must always be open. Then he can see, if he leans forward a little, what's going on with his vats, which now are being looked after—nobody else could be found—by the Czechs. It's no surprise to us that he can't find anyone else for his vats, because it's not a nice place to be, the vat room. Here the fresh hides are boiled in a special concoction which is father's secret, and while they're boiling they're stirred around. Once a week, usually on Tuesdays, they're delivered by a big truck, covered with a gigantic gray tarpaulin, the truck honks incessantly, and amid a cloud of flies, the hides are delivered and dragged in bundles across the factory yard. The smells on delivery day are naturally terrible. They're probably the reason too why father always uses such a lot of scent. As if that were any help! And not only on him, on us too the smells settle, and on mother, who always wears loose clothing on Tuesdays. They even settle on our Edgar, who has nothing to do with our factory, as well as on our neighbors. On delivery day they shut all their windows and doors, cursing and holding their noses they vanish behind their blinds and curtains. It's obvious that the smells have made many people think of father as an enemy. Some of the neighbors no longer greet him, not even to return a greeting from him. A lot of talk goes on behind his back. Yet the smells aren't his fault at all, when you come to think about it. The hides are simply necessary, what can he do about them? One can only hope that when they're being unloaded a breeze will rise from behind the hills and blow through our factory yard, seize upon the smell and carry it far away into the countryside. As for the goodness of our leather, thus of our whips, that depends entirely, as father says, on the stirring of the vats. Not everybody is made for such stirring, of course, standing so close to a vat, in the vapor that constantly envelops it. A person who stirs can't afford to be fussy, for instance, and he mustn't have a fine sense of smell, he has to ignore many smells, but he also has to be quick on his feet. That's not so simple, considering how cramped the vat room is. It's also stuffy, the air in there, one quickly starts to sweat, the sweat runs into one's eyes and mouth, and the vapor, which is hot and dense, attacks the lungs and eyes. No wonder father is so concerned that somebody should not only stand by one of the vats and hold a stick out, but should actually be stirring also. For, since the Czechs have been in the vat room, so father tells us—most often in the evening, by the light of wax or tallow candles, freshly scrubbed we're sitting at a table and the smell father brought home has already dispersed, or we've absorbed it and no longer notice it—anyway, ever since the Czechs have been there, a lot of yawning goes on around the vats, and, instead of a lot of standing, more and more frequent leaning against the walls, beneath the windows. Briefly, the Czechs behave as if father had put them in the vat room only to watch, as if a vat could stir itself. Is it surprising that he has to leave his desk more and more often, rush into the vat room and put the stirring stick back into the hand of the Czech, who spends more and more of his time leaning against the wall? Such a remote vat room can't be ruled with fine speeches from a desk, with head-shaking from a glass door. No, father is compelled to stand up from his desk and leap into the vat room, to see that the sticks aren't being leaned on but also stirred with. Yes, the work in the vat room keeps father very occupied, no wonder it keeps us occupied too. No wonder, then, that toward daybreak we're dreaming of this work and would like to ask father about it, but that's not so easy. Mostly, before he'll listen to us, we have to tug for a long time at his sleeves and drag him with all our strength away from his thoughts, yet even then he doesn't say much. How often he thinks about the vat room work, how seldom about us! From our position—outside beneath the workshop window or at supper—we cannot, of course, understand what he's thinking.

We can't even understand what it is that propels him to his desk each morning, but who could? Perhaps Herr Lange could have, but he doesn't come here anymore. And to think that the bad vat room now has to be occupied by Czechs! That's all the dreaming to be done between night and day in our parents' bed, and now, to the hissing of a whip blow that strikes into our dreams, we leap, waking up, away from beneath the barred-over workshop window, and return, with a jerk of our head, to ourself. Ourself in a reality that is, as our Edgar says, different.

2

This hissing, a sound until recently to be heard sometimes in our father's factory, now shut down, follows us through the morning. Sometimes we quail, probably duck our heads too. Strange, because we've never heard a whip really hissing, at least not one that was aimed at us. Slowly now between twilight and daylight we peel ourselves out of the parental bed and go back to our room. And stumble—pale in the face, our Edgar stumbles ahead of us—to our window, with its view over our Laubgasse, our Meistersingergasse, our town park, and, in the distant landscape, our theater. We see: a new day has dawned. And that day will now be told about, as it passed into its night. We see a few white clouds, fresh paint, stationed in our sky, which begins immediately behind the apple tree, a few birds are back in the garden, chirping thinly out of the shrubbery, and overnight even the air in our alleys must have been renewed. Later—curiosity compels us—we go downstairs and walk into our courtyard. Narrowing our eyes—how dazzling the sun is!—we grope our way to the gate, but no farther. Stop, mother calls, she's not upstairs in father's room, where last night she took the books and pictures out of the cases and off the walls and burned them, but downstairs again, in her big smoky kitchen. From here, through the window looking out on the garden, she has seen us, she runs after us through the front door. Stop, she calls, much too loudly for the short distance and the still noiseless day, come back at once. With her warm housecoat wrapped around her body, she stands there, looking sleepy, but large in the doorway, and she's not only calling, she's even threatening us. And why is mother threatening us so early in the day, this morning after our conquest? Feeling a pang of guilt, we clutch our head with unwashed hands. That's it, we've forgotten again to put our cap on. The cap that father surprised us with, a year ago, coming home from a business trip, suddenly extracting it like a take-home present from the secret pocket of his briefcase and clamping it ironhandedly, as if for all time, over our head. Since then we've had to wear it when we go out, and not only in the wintertime, without the cap we're no longer thinkable. If anyone sees us in the Amselgrund, he'll see the cap, if anyone sees us outside the theater too, near the church, or tobogganing, drinking hot soft drinks, he'll always see us wearing the cap, which, if ever we forget it, is always at once brought back to us. An ugly thing, black, with earflaps, a thing we don't like to think about and keep losing too, but what's the use? It's found and given back to us every time, because nobody wants it. As if we wanted the cap! This cap is a pain to us, can't mother see that? We reject the cap altogether, we're honestly disgusted by it. So now: on the first morning after our conquest we stand at the gate and with hands on the grating gaze out on to the Laubgasse, and we want to see Americans at last, preferably black ones, but there's something not right about us. We think what it might be, then we notice: of course, no cap! Something mother at the kitchen window has already noticed too. What are you doing out there in the courtyard, without your cap too, she calls, runs from the window back into the house, snatches the cap from the hat stand, carries it through the spacious hallway and tosses it across the strip of grass to us from the front door. Ah, says our Edgar, who, having no cap, doesn't have to wear one. Then he takes a step back from the gate, so as to speak with mother. Ah, he says and sways back and forth a bit and points toward us and says: Because they've been in the cellar for such a long time. And since we've been conquered now, we'd thought we'd like to look around a little. Without a cap? mother exclaims and wrinkles her forehead. Yes, our Edgar says, because it's such a fine day. And is that any reason for going out without a cap, when it might rain anytime? mother asks from the door. And our Edgar, after glancing up at the sky and briefly studying the clouds frothing up above our park: Ah, probably they thought that if it's going to rain it'll be later. And they hadn't thought of going far, just around the house a bit. Around the house, around the house, mother exclaims and stamps with her good leg once or twice. The town is full of Americans, don't you realize? There, she exclaims, and raising her arm, which has been getting thinner and thinner recently, pointing through the grating into the Meistersingergasse, there go two more of them. And they've got weapons. Ah, Frau Imbach, our Edgar says, it doesn't matter if they've got weapons or not, and he doesn't even take a look at the soldiers—neither of them is black anyway. Who, besides, when they see us in the courtyard turn around and disappear in the depths of the Meistersingergasse. Well, now they've gone and you didn't even look at them, mother says. Ah, but we've seen them already, from the window upstairs, our Edgar says. Were they the same ones? mother asks. Well, they looked like it, our Edgar says. Anyway: on this undecided morning we want to go out, but mother, in her housecoat, is against it. What do you want to do in the town? she asks, and she looks at us instead of Edgar now. We wriggle a bit. Ah, look at everything, of course, we say and put our cap on, though not very firmly. And what do you think there is to be seen? mother asks, and because of her leg, she leans a shoulder against the house. Ah, we say, how can we know before we've seen it. Things that have changed since we got conquered. Ah, there won't be any changes, mother says, and she simply won't let us leave the courtyard, although we now have our cap on. So we stand for a while by the wrought-iron grating and push our legs through it, but only up to the knee, because the bars aren't wide enough apart for our knees anymore. Only our Edgar can still stick his knee between the bars, because his is thinner than ours, although our Edgar is older and taller than us. Then we climb around on the grating a little, first at an angle, then upward, pull our cap back and forth a little, and then, once we've climbed to the top, we climb down again to rejoin the others. Then we go back to the house, to which mother is still clinging, and say, because it has just occurred to us, that she must have misunderstood us, we hadn't wanted to go *into the town*, only *around the house*. Around the house? mother asks. Yes, around the house, we say, but she doesn't want that either. Just when everybody's glad to have a roof over his head, she exclaims, you suddenly want to go around the house, suddenly you want to go into the town. No, we say, not into the town, only around the house. And why do you want to go around the house, mother asks, why don't you stay in the yard? You've spent half your life in this yard and have always been happy. Ah, we say and scrape a little dust together into a mound with our feet, just because. Just because, she asks. Yes, we say, just because. And what do you want to do when you're in the town, she asks. Ah, we say, nothing at all, actually. Nothing at all, she asks. Yes, we say and keep making the heap bigger. And why can't you do it here, do *nothing at all* here, mother asks, and she points to the narrow strip of grass between our house and the wrought-iron gate—when we were smaller, the strip was much wider and edged with roses on one side. Here, she says, where at least there's a fence between you and the others. No, we say, we can't stay here. And we jump once on the gradually collected heap of dust so that a small cloud escapes. So you can't stay here, mother says. And what if something happens to you out there, even by mistake? she asks. Happens to us, we exclaim and watch the dust slowly settling again. Ah, we exclaim, nothing will happen to *us*. No, mother says and resolutely shifts her whole weight, which isn't much, onto her right leg, which she settles firmly on the ground. And when she has thought it over again, probably more forcibly, she again says: No. Oh well, we say, then we'll stay here. Yes, she says, you'll stay here. There it is: on this first day after our conquest our mother, who's feeling unwell again and can't depend on her head or her legs, forbids us to open the wrought-iron gate and leave the courtyard. We mayn't even go around the house, on the contrary, she puts her arms, which have grown so thin, around our neck and shoulders and leads us through the front door back into our fundamentally grimy and dilapidated villa. But mother, we exclaim, what are you doing? She doesn't answer but pulls us, having taken us by the hands, so that we can't escape at the last moment, deeper and deeper into our villa. Don't do this to us! we exclaim and try to brush her hands away, but with the strength of desperation mother holds us tight. And we let ourselves be pulled, even if we resist. First up the stairs, past the corridor window, its whole width packed with sandbags, then along the upper corridor, past father's sunny room where the picture of our father in uniform, no longer there, has made a patch on the wall. Until we arrive at the wide-open sunlit door of our children's room. But at this door everything changes. That's to say, mother stops to draw breath, lays a hand on her heart, and changes her mind, we can see it in her eyes. Mother, we exclaim, what's the matter? Why do you look like that? Ah, mother says, do whatever you like. And she lets go of our hands and shoulders and pushes us with her chilled, limp, disheartened arms far from her, almost as far as the stairs. But mother, what's the matter, we exclaim. Ah, it's all the same, everything's going to blazes, mother says. What's going to blazes, we exclaim, tell us, please tell us. Ah, mother says, young folks, old folks. And with her now free arm she points far across our courtyard. We stand facing her at the top of the stairs, shoulders drooping, chin down, cap on head, which is shaven so close that our Edgar sometimes calls it our *mongol pate*. So we can go? we ask. Do whatever you like, she says. So then: right beside father's room, the door to which is wide open, face to face with the desk which, since father left, has been draped with a gray cloth, face to face with his bookcase, in which the books are now somewhat sparse, in the mild air that's blowing through the house, mother has suddenly changed her mind. Yes, we may go around the house. And instead of holding us tight she pushes us away. Do we want to stay, of our own free will? No, it's too late now for that. Ah, why should I get in your way, she exclaims, and before we know it she's driving us downstairs again. What if we'd rather stay at home? we ask. No, she exclaims, get along with you. Of course, we could play outside in the courtyard, we say. No, no, she says, it's not big enough for you. But if you've got to go and can't stay at home a single day to see what happens, for your own mother's sake, who's got so many troubles she doesn't know what to do, then—she exclaims and tosses at us several far too large shopping bags that she pulls from a kitchen corner. Well then, there's *Butterschmalz*. What? we ask. *Butterschmalz*, she says. It's not certain, but probably there's *Butterschmalz* at the slaughterhouse. But the slaughterhouse, we exclaim horrified, that's in Wundenplan! Yes, she says, that's where the *Butterschmalz* is. But that's right at the other end of town, we exclaim. Yes, she says, in Wundenplan. But isn't it dangerous to go as far as that, right after we've been conquered? we ask. Yes, she says, that's where there's *Butterschmalz*. So then: on this Wednesday morning, around eleven, the weather being still uncertain, perhaps it'll rain, perhaps not, first we're not allowed to leave the courtyard, because that's too dangerous, and then, moments later, it can't be eleven thirty yet, we suddenly have to go to the slaughterhouse in Wundenplan. Because, while we were still asleep—we shake our heads at once, no, we hadn't been asleep, we'd been having our nightmare and were in the vat room, but mother makes a dismissive gesture. Well, when we'd been supposedly asleep and she'd still been standing at the window, the widow of Malz the plumber— last winter he'd died of suffocation, *on the home front*, while cleaning a boiler out—had come hobbling at top speed along the Laubgasse, with her deformity, and with a tin pail hanging from her, and she'd shouted to mother the news that there was, or might be, *Butterschmalz* at our slaughterhouse. And how come suddenly there's *Butterschmalz*? we ask. Because, mother says, some supplies had been stored in the locker plant there. Now we've been conquered they're to be shared out among us. People have been talking about it, saying there's a line already, but . . . And we need it, the *Butterschmalz?* we ask. Yes, we do, mother says. And do we have to go to the slaughterhouse, even if we hadn't wanted to go into the town? we ask. Yes, you do, mother says. But we only wanted to go up the street, to look at a few Americans, we say. But then in her kitchen, flooded this morning with sunlight, windows and door flung wide open, mother yells loud and shrill: I don't care what you want. If you must risk your lives and go into the town, you might as well ask for *Butterschmalz* too and do a few other things for me. But what else then? we exclaim—but mother's not telling us yet. Without saying a word she pulls the slaughterhouse money out of her housecoat pocket and presses it into our hands and exclaims that she hopes we hadn't forgotten to be obedient and to whom we'd made the promise to be so. No, we say, we haven't forgotten, and we fasten our eyes on the kitchen floor. Very well then, mother says. And she isn't one of those mothers who put up with it when her children answer her back, other people torment her quite enough as it is, and she has to take care of everything . . . Please, not another day like yesterday, that would be the end of me, she exclaims in far too loud a voice. But Frau Imbach, our Edgar says quietly, and now he has come into the kitchen, nobody's asking you for another day like yesterday. After all, we've been conquered now, and it's all over. Ah, conquered or not, mother exclaims, I know what I know. And I know, she says, with a fixed look at the kitchen wall, where the dishcloth is hanging, that something terrible is going to happen soon and nobody will help me. But what's supposed to happen? our Edgar asks, and while he's talking he takes one of the shopping bags from us. I don't know that either, mother says to the dishcloth, but last night when I was too tired to sleep again I had a very definite feeling that it'll be soon. And one isn't mistaken,

I'm certain of it, about such feelings. But Frau Imbach, our Edgar says, everything has happened already. It's not possible for anything else to happen. And besides, since last night everything has been quiet. Can't you hear how quiet everything is? he asks and stretches out a forefinger, having first quickly licked it, into the mild air of the kitchen, so that we'll all be able to hear the quietness. Ah, it only seems that way, mother says, after looking at the finger and hearkening to the silence for a moment. And then she looks past the sandbags into the courtyard and says that the quiet is deceptive. Ah, she exclaims, why did you leave me on my own with this great load to carry? But Frau Imbach, our Edgar says, your husband will certainly come back soon. You just have to be patient a bit longer. You'll make yourself ill, if you always think the worst. Why don't you lie down for a bit, while we go to the slaughterhouse? No, lying down won't help, mother says, after giving the idea a moment's thought. Besides, it doesn't matter what becomes of me, the main thing is for you to take care of yourselves. Will you promise me that you will? Yes, we promise to take care of ourself, we exclaim, and in the kitchen doorway we dance up and down a bit in front of mother. Well, our mother says to Edgar, at least I know that *you'll* take care and that I can depend on *you*. You won't let anything happen to them, will you, you'll bring them home safe and sound again? They're my only hope and all I still have. You'll do that, won't you, Edgar, you're the sensible one, you'll take care of them? But of course I'll take care of them, Frau Imbach, our Edgar says. We'll just go up the street a bit, only as far as the park. And to the slaughterhouse, mother says, don't you forget that. No, our Edgar says, we won't forget, you needn't worry a bit. Ah yes and before I forget, mother says and puts a hand to her forehead, because something else has occurred to her. Herr Henne has been killed in action, you've heard about that. Who? we ask, because we can't recall Herr Henne right away. Ah, the man who lives on Güterhofstraße, mother says and flutters her hand a bit. In January he was still writing letters home and now he's dead and his poor wife is alone, with nobody to care for her. And she's not in the best of health, and she must have run out of money, probably. So if you've got to walk into town and risk your lives, you could pass by her house and talk with her a little. What about? we ask. Well, mother says, you could ask her if there are any of her husband's belongings there still. And what might still be there? our Edgar asks. Something to wear, of course, mother says, her husband—God knows where he's buried—won't need it anymore. Something to wear, you mean? our Edgar asks. Yes, something of her husband's, she says. But you needn't say that he won't be needing it anymore, she certainly won't like to hear that. You must be a bit tactful, best don't talk at all. All right, our Edgar says, we won't say that her husband has been killed, we'll just ask if there's anything of his left. In any case, mother says and pulls a white envelope from her housecoat pocket, I've written her a few lines, you can give this to Frau Henne. My God, our Edgar says, when do you find time to do all this? When? mother says, at night of course, while you're asleep. But we weren't asleep, we say, we weren't . . . But mother makes a dismissive gesture. You even slept very soundly, she says, I heard it. And then, to our Edgar: Now you'll promise me, won't you, to go by Frau Henne's house and ask her if there's anything of her husband's left? Look, she says and tugs at our sleeves, you're growing out of everything. And Edgar, we ask, pointing at his sleeves, isn't he growing out of everything too? And, we ask, shouldn't we ask her if she has something for him? But mother doesn't concern herself at all with our question. Instead, she says we should *behave*, the woman had suffered a great deal. Up till recently she hadn't been able to believe it, because it had been so incomprehensible. And, we ask, does she believe it now? Yes, mother says, now she must be believing it. All the same, it won't be easy to persuade her to part with the suit. Perhaps too the downstairs door will be locked, because she might have retreated into her house and won't want to talk with anyone, but that needn't trouble us. It wasn't our fault that her husband had been killed, we needn't have awkward feelings about that, but should be insistent and shout from down below, until she comes down to us and opens the door for us. You know the one, she says, it's at the back where the shrubs are. Yes, our Edgar says, the jasmine. And, mother says, in case she should say no and not stir in her room, we shouldn't give up but shout and knock until she *had* to come down and open the door for us. She was certain there was still a suit there, and we must cadge it off her, especially since Herr Henne, who had hardly been home during recent years, had certainly not worn it often. Of course Frau Henne would tell us the suit was a thing to *remember* him by, but that mustn't trouble us. Tell her simply that you've got nothing left to wear, then surely she'll give you the suit. And Edgar, we ask, doesn't Edgar need a suit? but mother simply isn't concerning herself with Edgar this morning. What's more, she says, Frau Henne has no money, and that can be taken advantage of, for she needs money, even if it's worthless. All right then, don't let her put you off, but make sure she takes you upstairs and get her involved in a conversation, even if it gets on her nerves. And never you take any notice of how she has changed. But has she changed? we ask. Yes, mother says, people say she has changed. And where has she changed? we ask. Oh, how should I know where, mother says, I haven't even seen her. Anyway, people who've seen her say she's almost unrecognizable. Ah, our Edgar says, don't worry, we'll recognize her. In any case, mother says, act as if she were the same as always. All right, our Edgar says, we'll simply go up to her and say we're sorry for her, but not that she has changed, until we get on her nerves and she gives us the suit. And don't let her ask you questions, mother says. Ah, she exclaims and seems to be quite desperate. I hope I can depend on you. And I hope she hasn't taken it into her head to trade the suit for something. Ah, she says, if only I had another pair of legs and another head, then I'd do everything myself, instead of having to ask you to. Yes, yes, Frau Imbach, our Edgar says, we'll be thinking about the suit. And the slaughterhouse, she says.

Then, when we've left the house again—Edgar without a cap, us with one—mother sends Edgar back into the garden shed, to put another shirt on. But I haven't got another shirt, our Edgar says. For weeks he's been running around in the same white shirt, or it's a *smock*, which is now quite gray. You haven't got one? mother asks. No, he says. When did you last have a look to see? she asks. I don't know, our Edgar says, I've only got one shirt. Then have another look, mother says, perhaps you'll find one. But I've only got one, he says. Have a look, quick now, mother says and claps her hands a few times. Then when he's gone— he moves across the grass leaning forward as if blown by a wind—mother beckons us back into the kitchen and hands us our breakfast, a slice of bread with bacon fat, which we quickly swallow while our Edgar is in the garden shed looking for the shirt. And Edgar, we ask, when the good bread has slid into us via mouth and throat, but mother only shakes her head, for there's nothing in the house apart from what she's given us. (So on the first day after our conquest we'll have had breakfast, but our poor Edgar none.) Then when Edgar is back beside us, wearing his old shirt, mother thinks of something else. That if we're going to see Frau Henne we should also see Herr Schellenbaum . . . See Herr Schellenbaum too? we exclaim, in utter astonishment, interrupting her. Yes, Herr Schellenbaum, she says. But, we exclaim, he was going to hide. Not from the Americans, mother says, only from the Russians. And why not from the Americans, we ask, why only from the Russians? But mother won't tell us. Only from the Russians, she says, not from the Americans. But, we say, he lives somewhere quite different. That doesn't matter, mother says, and from the same housecoat pocket that contained the money for the slaughterhouse and the letter for Frau Henne, she pulls one more letter, which she probably also wrote last night, when we weren't asleep but in the vat room, even if only in a dream. Strange, all the things that go into a housecoat pocket. If the letter for Frau Henne was white, the one for Herr Schellenbaum is blue, and if the one for Frau Henne was, if anything, thick, the one for Herr Schellenbaum is, if anything, thin. Now watch out and don't go dreaming, mother exclaims and claps her hands loudly. She's afraid we might go into a dream and be lost to her. But we're not dreaming at all, we exclaim. So much the better, mother says. Right then, the letter for Herr Schellenbaum is thin, blue, and personal, it's important too, so we have to give him the letter personally, that is, so nobody sees. Not in his garden or on the street or on his balcony, but indoors, inside his house, best of all in his parlor. The room where the sofa is? Yes, she says, where the sofa is. And if he's not in his parlor but hiding? we ask, because we don't fancy going to Herr Schellenbaum's. No, we don't fancy going to the slaughterhouse or to Frau Henne or to Herr Schellenbaum, but if we were allowed to we'd rather stay altogether at home. Nonsense, mother exclaims and notices our reluctance and becomes almost angry, he's not hiding, he'll always be in his parlor toward evening. And all the same, what if he isn't at home? we ask. Then bring the letter back to me, mother says. All right then, she says and waves the letter back and forth, who should I give the letter to? No, better not you, Edgar dear, she says, because his shirt, which is actually an old working smock of his father's, has no pockets, and she prefers to give the letter to us. And when the letter is inside our coat, we brush over it a few times with our hand and make it crackle softly. And then we walk across the heap of roof tiles, the mound of slates, the hill of stove tiles, and the pile of roofing metal, all made of the tiles and slates that have fallen off our villa during recent years and which mother has arranged behind our house, beside the empty dog kennel—Hector has passed away—and thus kept in good order, the way it is in these times. Later, when there are people for them again, all the things will be stuck back on our villa. And don't talk about the letter, not to anyone, mother says and comes into the courtyard with us. The white one or the blue one? we ask. Both, mother says, but especially not about the blue one, it's meant as a surprise. For Herr Schellenbaum? we ask. Yes, she says. And at the slaughterhouse, in case there's a line, don't let anyone push you aside, but push back. Use your elbows, don't hesitate to, other people use theirs. Ah, she says, if only I had other legs, I'd get the *Butterschmalz* and do everything else as well. Yes, yes, we say and know that it's only a manner of speaking. Where could she obtain any other legs at her age? And then we're close to the garage, which, like the dog kennel, is empty, because the small car and the big one, both, have been commandeered. And we're about to go out onto the street, but mother won't let us yet. If you happen to go past the church and if it happens to be open, you can go in, if you care to, she says. Why? we ask. You can think, she says, about your father. Can't we do that here too? we ask. You might pray for him too, mother says. Only for ours, or for his too? we ask and point at Edgar, whose father is also missing, for a longer time than ours too. For both, of course, what a question, mother says, and she pulls a face, as if she didn't understand the question. Actually it's just an awkward question for her. For she doesn't like it when our father, who owns the factory and the villa, is mentioned in the same breath as Edgar's, who owns nothing at all because he was only one of our workers in the tanning workshop. On the other hand she can't simply say so, because our Edgar is standing again between us, with folded arms, but she has to pretend that it's quite natural if we pray for both together. All right then, we say, so we'll pray for both. Even if it won't help them much, our Edgar quietly says, and he blushes a bit. But it won't do them any harm, mother says, and she's snappy and short. All right then, the church, we'll go there, we say and lift our bags up in the air and effortlessly push open our wrought-iron gate. Doesn't the air on the far side of it feel different? And the slaughterhouse, mother calls after us, and leaning against the house she gazes toward us across the courtyard. Don't worry, we exclaim, brandishing our bags as soon as we're on the street. All right then, good-bye, our Edgar says. All right, mother says. Right, we say.

3

That's how it is: this Wednesday noon mother orders us to go to the slaughterhouse, and, if there's any *Butterschmalz*, to stand in line and buy as much as we can carry. Yet we hadn't wanted to go to the slaughterhouse, only around the house! Or else we had a quite different destination, one we hadn't mentioned but had had in mind all the time. With our depressing cap on our head we rush down the Laubgasse and think of our real destination and that it's time now to talk about it. Thank God the Laubgasse is so deserted today and nobody hears and sees us. Certainly people might be standing in the windows and looking down at us, there's hardly ever nobody looking down when, wearing our cap, we walk along the streets. Later—the big yellow posters our conquerors have pasted to the walls in our part of town. There's even a poster on the gate to Herr Direktor Schüssl's house—his youngest son has also been recently killed in action. It says that we aren't allowed to leave our houses at night and that we have to obey and that no infraction will be allowed but punished with *death*. With the shopping bags in our hands we stand facing the poster and read everything it says, and we resolve to go out on the streets at night sometime, as soon as possible. Mother can't see us now, so we take off our cap and toss it into our shopping bag, where it will stay for a long time. And now we'll ask Edgar where we're *really* going. To school? No. To the stadium? No. To the Hoher Hain? No, not there either. To the park, perhaps, to see if we can find the dogs that have been shot there? No, not to the park either. Hands in pockets, searching for something, our Edgar says: Let's go now. Where to? we exclaim, with one voice. To the Amselgrund, he says. Hm, we say, the Amselgrund? And our Edgar says yes, that's where. Aha, we think, so we're going to our Amselgrund, and it's no surprise to us, even though the situation there is as follows. On the eleventh our Amselgrund was destroyed, because it was mainly on our Amselgrund, instead of our town, that *terror-attack bombers dumped*, as mother says, their bombs, thus over the hills outside our town and south of it, the wooded hills, the slopes that roll into our gentle Mühlental, over our Rabenstein ruin, over the fields that were just beginning to be green. In six minutes it had all been *wiped out*, at least badly damaged. Briefly: where the Amselgrund had still been, in March, is now, in May, flattened, and what was green in March is now unploughed and black and no longer recognizable. So we slowly shake our head and ask: But isn't it too far? Not too far, our Edgar says. All right, we think and walk on. And ask: Isn't it too dangerous? But our Edgar doesn't understand us anymore. We're talking about the Amselgrund, we say. No, he says, not too dangerous. And then he stops and looks us in the eye and suddenly he wants to know what mother gave us while he was in the garden shed. Gave us? we exclaim, as if we didn't understand. Yes, our Edgar says, gave you. Ah, we say, so that's what you want to know. A piece of bread, we say. What with? our Edgar asks. Bacon fat, we say. With facon bat, he says. Yes, we say. And why, he asks, do I have to go into the garden shed, while she gives you your breakfast? Because you weren't meant to see, we say. But I know it anyway, our Edgar says. Yes, we say, but you didn't see it. Later, outside the villa of Dr. Grünfeld, who killed himself two years ago in a horrible way—with *nails*—we ask our Edgar whether we shouldn't go to the Amselgrund tomorrow instead, because tomorrow we wouldn't have to go to the slaughterhouse, but our Edgar, still thinking of our breakfast, says: No, not tomorrow, today. But if you don't want to come . . . Oh yes, we do, we do, we say. And as long as we're still in the Laubgasse, we ask just one more question: Where *exactly* in the Amselgrund shall we be going—into the part where the birch trees were, or the part where the forester's house was, because both parts, the birches and the forester's house, don't exist anymore. To where the forester's house was, our Edgar says, and he's still searching in his pockets. Aha, we say and nod to one another, and we know at once we're going to the Amselgrund to find the knife. Nevertheless we pretend we haven't understood, and we ask: And why to the forester's house? Ah, our Edgar says, you're asking why? For the knife, of course. Aha, we say, as if we hadn't been thinking of the knife for weeks. And our Edgar, going still deeper into his pockets and swaying a bit, because yesterday and probably the day before yesterday too he had nothing to eat, says: For the knife, yes. Good, so it's the knife, we think, and we nod and walk past the house of Frau Reißer, who has lost her husband, not, like Frau Wittke—she comes in later—in Siberia, but in Africa. And in passing we rap our knuckles on Frau Reißer's house and call out: Wakey wakey, time to get up! and then we bang on Frau Wittke's house with our fist and call out: Stay put, it's too late now! And we're thinking of the trees in the Amselgrund and how they'll soon be surrounding us, charred and spiky. When we get there, we ask, do you want to dig the knife up again? And our Edgar, who now at last finds in his pocket the cigarette butt he's been looking for and sticks it at an angle between his teeth, in between the teeth that will surely all fall out if he doesn't have something to eat soon, our Edgar says: Dig it up, yes. And take it home with us? we ask. And he answers, lighting the cigarette butt: Yes, take it home with us. Fine, we say, we'll get the knife. All right, we're thinking, all right, the knife.

This is the knife that our Edgar had buried in the Amselgrund at the time when people, with hands cupped to their mouths, were starting to talk about our being conquered and when he didn't want it to be confiscated and there was no place to hide it in his shed and it wasn't to be buried in the garden, because cognac and cutlery and the shotgun had already been buried there. (Nor could a knife like this one be thrown away, it was usable.) Naturally during our conquest, as we shuttled back and forth between living in the cellar and living in our children's room, we often thought about the knife. With which, when mother wasn't looking, our Edgar would cut for himself from the loaf a piece of the crust. So is the knife for cutting bread with? No, it can do more. What it's able to do still has to be *tried out*. On what? we'd asked our Edgar. You mean on whom, he'd said. On whom? we'd asked him then, but our Edgar had only shaken his head and said: Wait and see. Whenever he beckons to us to come over into his half of the cellar, we cringe against the wall of our half. And if he walks across to us, to show us the knife, we shrink back, without being able to escape from it, quite the contrary. For we brood on this knife, not only in the daytime but at night too we think of it. Eventually, with his knife in our thoughts, we fall into a troubled sleep. Hardly asleep we dream, naturally, of Edgar's knife, and when first light comes the knife is back in our room again. Take hold of it, he calls to us from the doorway, and he extends it toward us, but we shake our head. Are you scared? he asks, you can tell me, if you are. Yes, we say, we're scared. Until one evening he takes our hand and guides it to the knife and presses the cold knife haft into our hands. Our first contact with Edgar's knife—no, not much comes of it, we resist too much. Our hands are clenched, becoming fists, only the knuckles knock against the knife. Unmoved, even unmoveable, they rest against the haft. No, we won't touch the blade, however much he asks us to. But suddenly all that is changed from one moment to the next. Suddenly, during a deluge of rain, we feel secretly stirring in us a liking for his knife. Until one night we curl our fingers around the haft unasked. What amazing heat shoots through our limbs then! The next day we take it to the window into the sunlight and let it sparkle for a long time. Even the blade, in which we're mirrored, is now touched by us. Next Edgar teaches us slowly to ask him for the knife. Look, he says, there it is in my pocket, why don't you take it out? Come on now, at last you can learn how to handle it. And really we do learn fast. We learn that when we put our hand in his trouser pockets the trousers are agitated. We learn to tell his left pocket from his right pocket. We learn what he keeps in his right pocket, for instance the flat stone he puts into his mouth when he's hungry. In his left pocket there's a hole that leads to the knife. Here it hangs by a leather thong against his left hip, so that when he runs, the knife dangles between his legs. On both sides of the haft a splendidly inlaid swastika gleams, and that's another reason why it has to be buried. So it's good that it's buried now and nobody sees it, but bad that even we can't see it anymore, touch it anymore. For even if we hate the knife most of the time, we often long for it. One thing's for sure, that a knife like this one shouldn't lie in the earth and rot. But another sure thing is that the *Butterschmalz* shouldn't be forgotten on account of the knife. But unfortunately the farther we walk, the farther the slaughterhouse is from the Amselgrund. We'd never have thought our slaughterhouse was such a long way around. For instead of walking from the Laubgasse via Lange Zeile and the Theaterring and then, as in last night's dream, out of our town—and down the embankment—and to the river and the bridge and then on to the Amselgrund, we now have to go from the Laubgasse via Lange Zeile and the Theaterring, and then, since we have to go to the slaughterhouse, through Wundenplan. Only then can we finally arrive, much farther down, over the embankment down to the river and across another bridge, at the Amselgrund. The slaughterhouse, whichever way you look at it, is a long way around, but there's something else that's worse. What's worse is this: to go there we have to pass through Wundenplan, where bombs also fell on the eleventh, and which has also been partly *flattened*. We'd have liked best, of course, to avoid Wundenplan and make a detour, especially on account of our Edgar, who used to live in Wundenplan and lost somebody there. But nobody in our town can avoid Wundenplan if he wants to go to the slaughterhouse. Isn't that so, if we want to reach the slaughterhouse we have to go through there, we ask and point into Wundenplan. Yes, our Edgar says, and he sways a bit, we go through there. And from behind? we ask. From behind? our Edgar asks, and the smoking cigarette butt hangs from his mouth. Yes, we say, from behind. No, our Edgar says once he's thought it over a bit, not from behind, there's no way. Even if it's such a miserable walk? we ask, and pointing at the ruins we take a few hesitant steps into Wundenplan. No, our Edgar says, and he goes on walking, there's no way from behind. The fact is: it's difficult to walk in Wundenplan because no streets are left. The old streets and alleys have vanished under the ruins. Either they've melted away or they've been buried. Now that's bad, of course, but it's not the worst thing. Admittedly we have to clamber through bomb craters and over slopes of rubble, and we twist our ankles, but there's something else that's worse. Might it be the stench that hangs over Wundenplan, although it was destroyed some time ago? No, that's not so bad. Worse, no, the worst thing is that we know that people are buried under Wundenplan. Isn't that so, we ask, there are dead people here? Right, our Edgar says, walking ahead of us into Wundenplan. Eighty-eight, isn't it? No, our Edgar says, eighty-nine. Eighty-nine? we ask. Yes, our Edgar says, eighty-nine, and then we fall silent for a while. Dead people who can't be reached, isn't it? we ask, and now we're in the middle of Wundenplan, completely surrounded by ruins. Yes, our Edgar says, and he breathes into our face as we walk along, they'll be staying down there. To think that eighty-eight people (eighty-nine?), almost all of them from our town, are lying beneath Wundenplan for all eternity! They were taken unawares, people say. People say they were sleeping, eating, thinking about something, having a talk with someone, looking forward to something, being afraid of something, just at the moment when . . . No, we won't picture it, we'd rather think of something else, if anything else occurs to us to put the eighty-eight people out of our mind. And over these eighty-eight people we walk to the slaughterhouse, nose full of smoke, strutting along on this first day after our conquest. Very well then, we take a deeper breath, swing our shopping bags higher, place our feet more resolutely, and follow our Edgar more closely, as he blows his breath one moment from his mouth and the next from his nose. Many of them we knew, so mother says, even if only by name, so that when we want to picture them we keep mixing them up. People we thought were dead are then suddenly not dead, but come toward us up the street. But probably others we thought were alive are dead. Denkstein, Frisch, and Ziegel, whom mother never mentions, are the only ones we don't mix up, because they were our classmates. Do you remember Denkstein and Frisch and Ziegel? we shout to Edgar from behind. Yes, our Edgar shouts, not turning around, I remember them. Do you sometimes mix them up? we ask. Mix them up? he asks, how do you mean? Well, we say, like the others who turn out not to be dead. No, our Edgar says, I don't mix them up. So you think of them sometimes? we ask. Yes, our Edgar says, now and then. And what are they, when you think of them, alive or dead? we ask. Then they're dead, our Edgar says. No, he says then, alive. No, he says then, dead. Isn't that so? we say, and then we're silent again. The fact is that until the eleventh they were in our class and that their seats are empty now and everybody behaves as if they'd never sat there. Not once since the eleventh have we talked about them, although we talk about everything else. Yet we don't think about them much either. Whenever they suddenly cross our mind, we stamp our feet and force ourself to think of something else, until they disappear again. That's why we hate going through Wundenplan, because it forces us to keep thinking of them. Do you like walking here? we ask our Edgar and point at the rubble we're walking over. No, our Edgar says, lurching over the ruins with long strides, do you? No, we say, we don't like it either. Yet it has got better for us, it was worse right after the eleventh. At that time, when we'd had to go to Wundenplan—Edgar had been taken quickly to a rest center—we simply said no. Then mother had refused to listen anymore to this everlasting no and she'd taken us by the hand and simply dragged us in among the eighty-eight (or eighty-nine?) dead people. It will pass, she'd said, dragging us for the first time over Denkstein, Frisch, and Ziegel, and she also told us why. Because horror, she said, was a matter of custom and we simply hadn't got accustomed to Wundenplan being *flattened*. So that once we even had to lean over in the ruins and vomit. But that too will pass, like everything else in life, mother said, standing between us. If only we'll *pull ourselves together* and *force* ourselves to walk over the dead people, then we'd soon get so accustomed to it, a walk like that would be quite normal and we'd think nothing of it anymore. Nothing at all anymore? we'd asked. Well, less at first, and then nothing at all, mother had said. But isn't it always sort of sad to walk through ruins like this and away over *them*? we'd asked. Yes, it's sad, mother had said, and she'd nodded her head (it had gone gray overnight), but in time we'd forget it. For that's how people are: after a time they just don't think about it anymore. Not anymore? we'd asked. Not anymore, mother had said. And in fact after a time, for she was quite right, we thought less and less of it and got more and more accustomed to it, not entirely, not quite, but soon we would, so mother says. Just think how short the time is since the eleventh and how much we've grown accustomed to it! And to think how, when our horror was still fresh and we found out bit by bit who was lying dead beneath the ruins and we heard of our Edgar's great loss and which of *his* people lay under the ruins and couldn't be brought up out of them, we'd refused to go anywhere near the ruins or even to look at our ruins, still smoking, but preferred to keep our heads down and go all the way around them! And had preferred to avoid certain places in our town altogether, so we wouldn't have to go through Wundenplan, or over Wundenplan! Only weeks later did we begin, bit by bit, to go to Wundenplan again and touch something, look at something, here and there, bits of melted wire, all the charred wood. Even stones had melted in Wundenplan on the morning of the eleventh. All the things we took from the ruins and carried home with us! But now, because we've grown almost accustomed to Wundenplan being *flattened*, we don't touch things and carry them home anymore, we simply climb over them. Who knows what we'll grow accustomed to in time! Well then: on the way to our slaugherhouse, in the ruins of Wundenplan, to which we have grown almost but not quite accustomed, there's no trace of our conquerors, least of all the black ones, so that our English dictionary stays quite useless in our pocket. And once we've passed through Wundenplan, once Denkstein, Frisch, and Ziegel are behind us, then we see the slaughterhouse. There it is, we shout and climb up over our ruins, where they're heaped highest, and we take Edgar between us and ask him: Can you see it? And our Edgar, tossing the remnant of his cigarette into the ruins, says: How shouldn't I? but he doesn't look, not even once, in the direction of our slaughterhouse. Which is easily recognizable, far off, in the clear and slightly becalmed noon air. A detour, he says, this slaughterhouse, it has cost us time we'll need later. Ah, what should we need it for? we ask. But our Edgar isn't telling us yet.

4

Our slaughterhouse is located between the gasworks and Wundenplan and is much larger than you might think. All the same, it isn't easy to spot from a distance, because it merges with woodlands all around it into the flat area of Wundenplan. Who'd ever think such a small town had such a large slaughterhouse? You might suppose there'd be a lake here, a fish hatchery, a bathing beach, but a slaughterhouse? In fact it takes an effort even to picture a slaughterhouse here, and unlike Wundenplan it's still intact, because, as mother says, it was just *beyond the fringe* of the carpet of bombs intended for us. Out there, leading past our slaughterhouse, there's the endless Wundenplan boulevard which runs into our town, and it's on this boulevard that we're now walking. Since the sun is shining, though hesitantly, there's a little shadow, and since the sheds and warehouses on the right-hand side of the boulevard are no longer standing, we can see out of the shadow far into our ruins. But we can't see to the left, because our slaughterhouse is cut off from the world by a high wall topped with broken bottle glass, a wall that exudes an odorless liquid in the summertime but is typical at all seasons for that sort of an establishment. Yet once you know it's there, our slaughterhouse can't be missed. It covers such a big area that everything seems deserted, the stalls, the trees, the slaughteries. You can't forget the slaughterhouse, once you've seen how it spreads over this area, weathered, like a fortress, and crude. As we pass by, we tap on the high slaughterhouse wall, weeds growing halfway up it, our slaughterhouse, we're thinking, because it's already obvious to us that there's no *Butterschmalz* to be had outside the slaughterhouse. The footpath that's crowded with people whenever there's fresh lung or tripe is deserted. Far and wide—no people in line anywhere. But here's the gateway, and it's open. Let's go in.

When you get closer to it and eventually go into it, you see that in addition to its huge main slaughtery, actually much too huge for our town but now deserted, from which the loudest bellowing used to come and which has only two doors, although these doors are very wide, one for the living and one for the slaughtered animals, our slaughterhouse has seven or eight smaller buildings, for skinning, breaking, and hanging. In these the animals can also be slaughtered, if the main slaughtery is overloaded. Anyway, these smaller buildings spaced out over the slaughterhouse area are properly equipped, even if they're empty at the present time. So that somebody coming into our slaughterhouse on the first day after our conquest, if he didn't know the place, would obtain an entirely false impression. Dead! our slaughterhouse might seem dead! Yet it's only the immense silence enveloping it. Only our footsteps echo over the slaughterhouse pavement, through the slaughterhouse area. Aside from these footsteps and the cawing of the crows which, living in the Amselgrund, drift in great arcs over our slaughterhouse, there's not a sound to be heard. Which doesn't mean that our slaughterhouse is altogether inert. Rats keep scurrying past us across the Großer Viehweg—the Great

Cattle Path—or they scamper from one building to another, but softly, softly. Also the area is large, large as ever, perhaps, because of the sudden emptiness here, even more so, yet softly so. Also there are lots of flies. And the buildings, sheds, stalls, the receiving and slaughtering plants, are still there, though inactive. The Siechenfeld gate—the second gate is the Wundenplan one—which always used to be open, so that the wagons with fresh cattle could quickly pass into the slaughteries and be unloaded, is closed, the rails, two straight lines drawn across flat country, are gathering rust, and between the ties, across which the cattle used to be driven, weeds and grass are growing up again. The slaughteries themselves, from which vapors used to rise when cattle were being skinned, stand there dry now, and the two chimneys, towering up like landmarks, stare cold and smokeless into the sky described already. All life in the spacious inner yard, paved by our grandfathers, animal or human life, has been arrested, nobody walks across the yard now dragging an animal, with blows from a whip of ox hide, or carrying a slaughtered sheep into a building to hang it up there. All for nothing, we think, a waste of effort, to have come here, to have clambered over Denkstein. Yes, our Edgar says, your mother lied to us, there's no *Butterschmalz*. Only one hope is left: inside the main slaughtery there might be some, where the locker plant is, that's where the line could be. Why else should the Wundenplan gate be so wide open and draw into our slaughterhouse anyone who might be passing by?

Indeed, though God knows why, our slaughterhouse has always drawn people into it, it's known for doing so. If anyone is missing or has disappeared, in our town, the first place where people go to find them is the slaughterhouse. Mostly it's foreign workers, thus Czechs, who hide away there. But also writers of dud money orders, suicides, unmarried fathers, army deserters, and lovers with no prospects have been found here, so mother tells us. If you were to comb through the place, you'd get a surprise. In any case, our runaways don't go into the forests but into the slaughterhouse. Singly or in pairs, people escape from our town as soon as twilight falls, so we picture it, leaving the gasworks on the left, the Great Pond on the right, they hurry up the Wundenplan boulevard straight to the slaughterhouse. Naturally, as soon as a person's absence is noticed our townsfolk start a search, for we can't stand by and let anyone escape. In small groups, as soon as the sun rises, off we go in pursuit. Photos of escapees are passed from hand to hand, rewards are announced in loud voices, shrill whistlings summon dogs. We even go in search ourselves, if only in the park, where we don't find them, though we creep right in among the bushes. For while we're combing the park, toy pistols in hand—the adults have real pistols and are searching the Wundenplan forest—the escapees are crouching, bewildered by hunger and thirst, in some corner of the slaughterhouse, where they are found, perhaps weeks later. Many emerge of their own accord from the pigsties, without even being looked for, with hands raised over their heads, to surrender to the first German-speaking person they can find. Unless by mistake they've crept not into one of the side buildings but into the locker plant, in which case they're pulled out one morning, stiff as trees, tears frozen to their cheeks, and thrown onto one of the cattle trucks parked in the yard. Or else they find a halter to hang themselves with. No wonder our slaughterhouse is the first place that comes to mind as soon as someone can't be found. In any case, ever since our Czechs couldn't be trusted anymore, only a few of us go into the forest, and if anyone does, he never goes alone. Yet probably those Czechs have left us long ago and are back in their own country, or else they've been ferreted out and quietly taken away. Nobody's hiding here, are they? we ask our Edgar as we walk into our slaughterhouse, through the Wundenplan gate, which is oddly wide open, but our Edgar doesn't know either. Maybe nobody, he says, maybe somebody too.

So then: shopping bag held tight, letters deep in our coat pocket, we move shoulder to shoulder into our outsize slaughterhouse. To right and left are the low sheds, thrown together out of cement blocks, where the smaller animals are dismembered, sheds strung out as far as the Großer Viehweg, their iron-gray painted iron doors on rusting slide rails, difficult to open at the best of times, are shut. The sheds have dark windows, many-sectioned, dulled by slaughterhouse dust, and they have numbers. Set a little apart, numberless, the locker plant, out of which recently someone was pulled, frozen stiff, and where, if mother is right, the *Butterschmalz* is stored. *Butterschmalz*, of course, we think, and after taking a few more carefully placed steps into the slaughterhouse interior we knock on the door of a shed, but of course there's no response. Then we stand on tiptoe and try to see into the shed through one of the barred windows, the panes of which haven't been cleaned for years. And because of the bars we remember at once our dream and the windows, also barred, of our father's small whip factory. Generally the slaughterhouse reminds us of our factory, although we're wrong and there's no real connection. All the same, there's the feeling that if one only looked around for long enough there'd turn out to be a connection. No, we don't need to look, even. As if we needed to look around in order to know our slaughterhouse! Countless times during recent years we've wandered across our mouse-infested Wundenplan stubble field into the slaughterhouse, without ever having a thought of our factory. We've spent countless hours in our slaughterhouse without even considering such a connection. Do you remember? we ask our Edgar, and we look through a dirty windowpane, broken probably by a stone, into the shed before us, which previously was full of life, that's to say, full of bellowings. Whereas now it seems hollow, pallid, dull, and vacant, and thus dimmed. Remember? our Edgar asks us. Yes, we say, remember how it was. And we point through the broken pane into the shed that has been scraped empty down to its remotest corners. Yes, our Edgar says, I remember, though of course I wasn't here as often as you. Yes, that's so, we say. At this moment, probably not intended, an unusually dark cloud, never seen before and forgotten again in an instant, and certainly at a very great height, is conducted across the sky. We tilt our head back and look up at it. And thus, with the darkness of the cloud overhead, the sound of Edgar's voice in our ears, the bag containing the cap clasped in our fingers, and gazing upward, we tramp up and down outside the shed for a while. Yes, we know the slaughterhouse better than our Edgar does! Does he still remember coming sometimes to pick us up here? You stood by the wall there, we say. I know, our Edgar says. And sometimes, remember, we say, you pushed the shed door open a bit and looked in on us? Yes, our Edgar says, that's right. Until one of the butchers grabbed you by the shoulders and yelled at you, we say and laugh a bit, and suddenly an uneasiness comes between us, on account of this memory. Or our giggling when we mention now and again our father's factory, which we shall one day take over, whereas our Edgar will of course have nothing to take over, nothing being there for him. The fact is that our Edgar was often yelled at by the butchers, whereas we, because of our father, were never yelled at. Definitely too we laugh too much. And in recent times, because of this laughing, things have become more and more awkward between us. Because our Edgar doesn't respond much to what we're saying, we're left alone with our thoughts. Our slaughterhouse, we're thinking: because—and isn't it peculiar?—about three years ago, when our music school on Haydnstraße was filled overnight with soldiers who were wounded and dying, we came over here to continue our piano lessons. Yes, we could hardly comprehend it, almost believed it was something we'd thought up, but for three years we had piano lessons in this slaughterhouse. (Edgar didn't have piano lessons, in the slaughterhouse or anywhere else, because there was no money.) When one thinks—one can't do so without clutching one's head in one's hands—that the wounded and dying soldiers were laid out in the wooden paneled rooms of our music school (founded in 1834) on the Haydnstraße! And to take us out of those rooms and stick us into the slaughterhouse, just so that our music lessons could continue! Just to fulfill our parents' wish to develop our supposed—though hidden or buried—musical aptitude, to extract from us the latent sound! Certainly people were confused at that time, there was widespread chaos, but all the same, all the same! And to send us with our piano into the slaughterhouse, was that the right thing? When one considers—and again one clutches one's head in one's hands—that it was art-loving, benevolent, intelligent, and supposedly *human* people who hit on the idea of moving our lessons to this place! Of course, we often wondered what they might have been thinking of, and for a long time found no answer. Until recently it occurred to us that they probably weren't thinking of anything at all, but were certainly proud of their idea to open up the slaughterhouse for us. And us? Ah, we were just children. And we had to accept the decision and go quietly to the slaughterhouse with our piano music. Instead of letting our musical aptitude perish, canceling our education, putting the piano, along with all the other now superfluous pianos, in the attic of our music school and letting it fall apart into its elements, the keys, the hammers, and the strings. But no, the lessons had to be, no matter when or how or where. And our piano had to be hammered on, in no matter what circumstances. As if in our town, if people had searched more carefully, another place might not have been found finally to accommodate our piano and us! But it was alleged that all other buildings were already occupied. It was alleged that the slaughterhouse was the only place left, it alone proposed itself, since the volume of slaughtering had declined. So that our piano and our stool and our metronome and the two closets with piano music and music books, along with the portraits of composers, one day in June—it was warm, we sat around at home a lot and were still not eating meat—were loaded onto the Schenker removal truck and rolled and shoved all the way from our music school on Haydnstraße into the Municipal Stockyard and Slaughtery Company on the Wundenplan boulevard. We ourselves were lured into the slaughterhouse under the pretext of looking on while our piano was set up. And indeed we watch, while the crows circle incessantly overhead, how first our stool and then our piano and our music closets are lugged into the shed by the movers, who sweat a lot as they work. That's it! Then we enter the shed, smiling awkwardly, to see our piano in its new surroundings, among the meat hooks. That's it! And the stool, because it's too low for us, is quickly rotated by the movers, so that if we should ever want to play the piano we can reach the keys. The shed itself isn't altered. That's to say, the ridged cement floor is the same, the drainage gutters, the rods for the hooks, the hooks themselves—for the bodies, animal bodies. The cattle scales, on which we're forbidden to stand, also remains in the shed, except that it's pushed to the back, so we won't always have it under our eyes while making music, and it's covered with a black curtain. (As if we didn't know *what was covered* by the curtain, as if we weren't constantly, while making music, thinking of *what's underneath!*) And this is where we've been coming, since that day in June, our music under our arm, first without the cap, then with it, twice if not three times a week, to take our lessons, except during holidays. The drains in the corners, the rods sticking from the wall, we sit down under the barred window at our piano and, ready to make music, hold our hands over the keys. Or because the stool is still occupied and Denkstein has to play first, we stand with our legs apart under this window, with the warm slaughterhouse air blowing through it. Yes, how often during better times of the year, when the window wasn't shut and frosted outside with the sky beyond it, we've stood, preferably on tiptoe, in our nostrils a little smell, which, like a memory, issues from the shed walls, motionless in our new *music room*, waiting for our turn to come. While a classmate, Ziegel perhaps, sits on our stool and artfully extracts his scales from the keyboard. How often too, immersed in the art before us, we've been brought back by a bleating or bellowing from the yard or a neighboring shed, back to ourself, out of the art that was meant to be into the slaughterhouse that is. Or, with legs crossed, one hand, usually the right, clinging to a meat hook, we've waited for our piano teacher. Who, many years ago, in Plauen (Vogtland), so mother says, almost became a pianist and now, in a dark dress closefitting like a sheath, her eyes full of memories, rushes toward us in the shed, always at the last moment. How often, sitting on the stool, while our instructress paces up and down behind us, we've become victim to the flies on hot days. During the short breaks she allows us, and those only with reluctance, we whack at the flies with our music book. And we smell the smell of the walls and then speak about what we smell. What? she asks, our instructress, who seldom listens, and she looks at us, as if from far away. The walls, we say and point at them. Yes? she says, and what about the walls? Ah, we say, we can smell it. What can you smell, she asks and arches her eyebrows. The smell of death, we say. And when she has gulped once and hesitated and asked us who told us about that, we say: Nobody, we smell it by ourself. While from outside through the window, if not through the very walls, at about this time, there comes a tapping sound. We hold our breath, freeze, wait for our feelings to return, our speech—until that tapping stops, lost in the distance, unless, for this too is possible, it comes closer to our shed and comes to a halt outside it. When this happens, it's as if fingers of iron were scratching on our door, it is pushed forcefully open, and a butcher's face, a shadow across it, looks in. Yes? she says, and our instructress shows that she feels intruded upon. Ah, says the butcher, it's only me. Yes, and? our instructress asks and stands bolt upright behind our stool. Ah, the butcher says and grins a bit, I only wanted to say good evening. Good evening, our instructress says. I was just passing by, the butcher says, and he slips cleverly into the crack of the open door. Well? our instructress says. I was passing by the door, the butcher explains—he can't think of much else to say. Well? our instructress asks again, and she takes up the ruler that's lying on the piano lid and is meant for our fingers. With a few fresh animals, the butcher explains and scratches his neck. And I plucked up the courage and pushed it open, the door. Well, and . . . why did you push it open, our instructress asks and tugs at her blond hair-knot. Because I was telling myself, the butcher says: Have a look in! I've taken off my butcher's cap, see?—just like you wanted. I've wiped my feet too, on that patch of nibbled grass. They go on guzzling to the last moment, point is to fill their bellies. Well then, I pulled myself together and now I'm here. And then, because he feels comfortable in his door crack: It's on account of the music you make here. Does it disturb you? our instructress asks. Oh not at all, the butcher says. If I thought you might have the impression your music disturbed me, right away I'd . . . , he says and pauses a bit. Tear off my ears, he then says. Should I? he asks and takes hold of an ear. So it doesn't disturb you, our instructress says, her poise unshaken, quite coolly. But how could it disturb me, the butcher exclaims and stamps his feet. What else have I got, when I'm passing by with my cattle outside? What I mean is, he says, how strange this meeting is, you and me and here! And he makes a gesture pointing around the whole place, as far as that's possible. What do you mean? the instructress asks. I mean, the butcher says, what wonderful music you make, anyway it's beautiful to me. Because of the bellowing I usually hear all the time, the sound of it is of course especially beautiful in my ears. Makes you want to tear the door open in the middle of—hm—a bar and stick your head into it, or else take a chair and sit yourself down into it. But you can't do that, there's too much else to be done. And it has to be done, if one person doesn't do it, then another person has to. But don't think we don't notice your music on that account. Even my cattle, when I take them to be slaughtered, are quite strangely touched by it. Then we stop in our tracks, gasp a bit, put our ears to the door of the shed, and think our way, deep, into the music. Pity you can't see us, when it takes hold of us that way. Was it a tango this time? he then asks. No, our instructress says, a tango it was not. Pity, I hoped it might be a tango again, the butcher says. I like tangos quite especially, you see, I can even whistle one. And he sticks his head farther in, points his lips more sharply, and begins, before we know what's going on, to whistle a tango. And then, when he can't complete it: Well, he asks, how was that? Lovely, our instructress says. Yes, the butcher says, that's the best I can do with it. And what else do you want, our instructress asks—she thinks from dawn to dusk about our making progress. As for that, the butcher says, I wanted to ask if you'd like to go for a bit of a walk with me on Sunday. No, our instructress says and strikes her own fingers with the ruler. Oh well, the butcher says, just as I thought. But even then, a pity. And you kids, he suddenly shouts, turning to us, what are you goggling at, what's so funny? Us? we say and look all around. Yes, you, he says. But we weren't goggling, there's nothing funny, we say and huddle closer together. Making fun of me, that's what, he shouts. But we weren't, we say, we're laughing at you. Trying to make a fool of me? the butcher shouts and stands up, as tall as he can, in his door crack. As if I didn't know the difference between being made fun of and being laughed at. What are they really doing here? he says, turning to our instructress. They're students of mine, our instructress says and lays her hands on our shoulders. Oh well, if they're your students, then I could have been mistaken, the butcher says. Are they good at learning to play? Oh yes, the instructress says. And what music have they learned to play? the butcher asks. The music on page seventeen, our instructress says and points to our music book. So, this thingummyjiggery, the butcher asks, and he leans over, as low as he can into our shed, so as to get a better view of our music. Yes, the instructress says. And have they understood it? the butcher asks, and when our instructress nods he shouts: Then make them play it. And when we've played a few bars, with wrong notes first in the higher and then in the lower registers, he asks: Is that all? Yes, we say. And to learn that you had to sit around here for hours and drive the lady to despair? the butcher asks. Yes, we say. We are, we say, bunglers on our instrument. Yes, he says, I can tell that. And then he quickly asks the instructress if everything is otherwise all right. Yes, *alles in Ordnung*, the instructress says and claps her hands three times, as a sign that the conversation is now at an end. Yes, then I'll be going now, the butcher says, and his gaze wanders over us one last time, as he says: Well, goodbye! and as he leaves, whistling his tango, he shoves the door shut from outside. His boots become quieter again, finally there's no sound of them. And we, as well as the instructress with the ruler in her hands behind us, breathe again and sit for a long time at our piano, without touching it. Certainly since we've been making our music the cattle have been driven into the sheds at the back. Certainly the slaughtering has been done in the mornings, so that when we arrive for our lesson the crudest part is over, but all the same, all the same! Why was our piano, which we almost loved, brought here of all places, why were the portraits of composers hung on these walls? And to our Edgar—slowly now we're emerging from our thoughts—we say: Do you remember? and we walk on. Remember? our Edgar asks—he's quite pale and soon he'll be transparent—remember what? How we always shouted: Why don't you come in? But our Edgar, who's dragging his heels behind us, doesn't remember anything. And, he asks, did I, he asks, ever go in? and he pulls from his pocket another cigarette butt, which he also lights, unless we're entirely mistaken. Yes, we say, but only once. And kicking a stone ahead of us we say: In any case, you opened the door. And we stop and remind him how he pushed the shed door open and looked in, when along comes a cattle driver and grabs him by the shoulders and pushes him up the Einfangstraße, back to the slaughterhouse gate on the Wundenplan boulevard. And throws you out, we exclaim and laugh again, yet our Edgar, cigarette butt in mouth, can't remember anything. Really, he asks, did he really throw me out? You really don't remember? we ask. No, our Edgar says and shakes his head, did he really? But of course, we exclaim, of course. And how the butcher always came, because he wanted to talk to the instructress and hear us play, don't you remember that either? we ask. No, he says, not that either. And he stops and stands there in an attitude typical of him: straight legs, knees pressed back, finger to his cheek, eyes narrowed to slits. That's how he stares across the slaughterhouse terrain, close beside us, but unreachable. Edgar, we shout and nudge him in the ribs. Ah, he says, let me be. Yes, we later say, perhaps you're right. Perhaps you never did join us, you weren't allowed to. But then it occurs to us that we've already told him about the whole incident—the butcher, the instructress, and ourself—exactly the way it happened, and we tell him so. No, our Edgar says, you never told me, not me. Strange, we say and let everything around us go quiet for a moment, and we see clearly both scenes before us, the butcher arriving and us telling our Edgar about it, but probably we've only imagined them again. Then we've only imagined it again, we say. Probably, our Edgar says. His head, in the cigarette smoke, is blond, his hair piled up somewhat, so that it forms a little hood, which he calls his *thinking cap*. And now he has almost shut his eyes, so as to see better. Yes, our Edgar sees less and less every day, even in the clearest light. What goes on *behind* his eyes is also odd, of course. Odd, we say, and because the area in front of the locker plant is deserted too and definitely there's no *Butterschmalz*, we decide to leave the slaughterhouse right away. And telling you all those things, we quickly add, did we imagine that too? Probably, our Edgar says. It's a fact that we often used to be tired during our lessons and did a lot of imagining, and perhaps in doing so we exceeded the truth. Also it's a fact that our Edgar really had no reason to visit our slaughterhouse. He took no lessons, because there was nobody to pay for them. Because Edgar's father . . . Yes, we remember him, though not very clearly. We've seen him a few times, mostly from a distance, except once, when he stood suddenly before us, arms held in to his sides, to give us some advice about our Edgar, but on that occasion we felt so awkward that we were looking up at the sky. Eventually, one Sunday morning—a surprise to everyone— there was the search at Edgar's two-room apartment on the Gießereistraße, at which nothing was found, to be sure, but various things were broken, a pendulum clock, for instance, due to carelessness on the part of the officials. The fact is that, as mother says, Edgar's father is *a man to be relished with caution*. Because, for instance, when home on leave from the front he tells illicit jokes, we don't know which ones. Also, when he's supposed to be going back to the front, his feet won't fit into his boots anymore, the boots have to be hurried to the shoemaker's before the train leaves, cut open and enlarged and sewn up again, so that Edgar's father can rejoin his regiment, where he's not very popular either. So that last fall he was transferred to a penal battalion, which is meanwhile said to have been badly mauled. Wasn't it? we ask, his battalion was rather mauled? Yes, our Edgar says, but not entirely. And hasn't he written? we ask. No, our Edgar says, he doesn't like writing. And how long is it, we ask, since you saw him? About two years, he says. Do you remember him still? we ask. Why should I? our Edgar says, he'll be coming back. Like ours, we say and look up at the sky, which is steadily closing in. And as the clouds quietly move past overhead we tell how our father was back home once in December and how he wrote later too, and that we remember him well, down to the tiniest details. And while we're saying this we do remember him, quite precisely, and that he has a narrow nose and hairs on the backs of his hands, when at mealtimes—we're eating meat now, if there is any—he rests his hand by his plate and drums with his fingers. Strange that mother seldom talks of him. As if, now that everything's over, there was nothing more to be said about him. Only very seldom does she want to talk about him and she takes a breath, then after all she doesn't, but talks about something else. This makes us think that he too could have been killed, but of course that's not so. There are four reasons why he should still be alive, whereas our Edgar's father is dead. — First reason: he's not, like Edgar's father, in a penal battalion, but is supposed to be helping a bit, for the moment, digging trenches on the far side of Görlitz. Second reason: he has a factory, even if it's small and a bit run-down inside and scratched on the outside. For this reason alone he has to come home, for who else could manage this scratched and flat and small but still basically intact factory? Third reason: yes, Edgar's father is dead, because it doesn't depend so much on him and as a mere leather cutter he can easily be replaced. The fourth reason, probably the most important one, escapes us at the moment. Yes, we say, our hands stuck in our pockets, because we don't want to show our Edgar how much they're trembling, our father will come home soon. We saw him last December, didn't we? But, our Edgar says, he was wounded. But not badly, we exclaim. He had a bullet wound, even then, our Edgar says. Yes, we say, but only in the leg. Quite high up, though, wasn't it? our Edgar says. No, we say, more in the middle. The fact is that, as mother says, ever since his father has been missing, our Edgar has got not only his father's haircut, but also his hair. Meanwhile for quite a long time his movements have been his father's, even if nobody noticed. Can't your father be easily replaced? we're about to ask, but then we don't ask it. Instead, on this first day after our conquest, the sky lowering but brightening, the raincloud blown away, in our municipal stockyard, until recently active with slaughtering and breaking, even if it now looks as if it had been scraped empty, we've walked up and down a bit, capless, talking of this and that and forgetting things and imagining things. And then, just as we're crossing for the last time our Great Cattle Path, up till last winter incessantly licked and grunted at and gnawed by our animals, and passing for the last time the stalls we've emptied by more and more uninhibited eating over the past few years, just when the wide-open Wundenplan gate is standing before us and we're about to leave our slaughterhouse, one of the big shed doors beside us, No. 5, thus on our left, is almost inaudibly pushed open from inside, a black hole opens in the lengthy corrugated iron building, and out of this hole step two men, one tall and one short. Naturally we cringe with fright. And think: Well, so our slaughterhouse wasn't quite deserted after all. And we're wondering what these two strangers are doing in the shed and if they live in it or have slept there. The small man, wearing a dark suit, with padded shoulders, almost festive-looking, is a *gentleman*, perhaps the slaughterhouse director himself, while the tall one, dressed in white with an almost whimsical scattering of red stains, is probably nothing but a butcher, even though he's not at the moment carrying a knife or a cleaver. Probably, at their business in the shed, they hadn't counted on seeing us. When they do see us, they're visibly shaken, probably they go pale too. Whether or not we go pale, we don't know, but presumably we do. And we stop and hold hands and stand close together, so as to form a more united and protected front against the men, if only for a moment. A mistake, to have gone to the slaughterhouse so soon after our conquest.

5

Hey! What are you doing here? the slaughterhouse director shouts at us, if that's what he is, he shouts it from far off and walks toward us waving at us a curiously shaped and faintly colored fist, while the butcher immediately lowers his head and leaps back toward the shed door, making to close it in our faces. Ah, we say, and while we're speaking we huddle very close together, doing here? We're just looking around a bit. And did you see anything? the director asks while the butcher has gripped the door with both hands and is rolling it shut, only a narrow crack is left, so we can't see anything in Shed No. 5, only a few ghostly objects lying around on the flagstones in the darkness, which we take to be bodies (of animals) that have been forgotten about or overlooked. Nothing, we exclaim, we haven't seen anything, if you mean in the shed. And we haven't seen anything at all really. The slaughterhouse is empty, isn't it? None of your business whether it's empty or not, the slaughterhouse director exclaims at once, and he positions himself, breathing with difficulty, he's so astonished, with his legs apart before us and starts, the way elderly gentlemen do, to pluck at our coat a bit, which, because of the nights spent in the cellar, has some wrinkles in it. And then, while he's plucking, we discover something about the director that we hadn't expected. That's to say, we notice that his left hand, the colored one, isn't made of flesh and skin and bone but of a much firmer material, probably wood or iron. And his wooden or metallic fingers are fitted into a black leather glove, with which he keeps on going up and down over us. His other hand is, if anything, even more horrible, for it's half alive. The slaughterhouse director's second hand, which isn't gloved, but is exposed, is so mutilated that only two fingers have remained intact. These two fingers, we can't tell which they are, jut forward from his wrist like the prongs of a fork. They're sheathed in a smooth skin like pigskin, which is crimson on the outside and more like pink on the inside. There aren't any fingernails. Strange, the director's hands, especially the one with the prongs, but we can't study them for long, because at once he goes on speaking. So let's get it clear from the start, he says and puts his hands behind his back, where he probably slots them into one another. I'm the one who asks the questions, right? Will you ask us a lot of questions, then? we ask and cling close to our Edgar, who, as most often at moments like this, has stepped between us. But there you go asking questions again, the director exclaims and brings his half-alive hand from behind his back, passing the longer of the two prongs, clearly visible before us, through the air. Sorry, we say, we didn't mean to ask, the question just came. We only wanted to know if there'll be many questions, because we have to be moving on right away. But we don't really have to know, if you don't want to tell us. Well, you'll soon see how many questions I've got, the director says—he seems accustomed to giving orders and probably has command over the whole slaughterhouse terrain. You'll answer yes or no, nothing else, is that clear? Where would we end up if everyone suddenly wanted to ask questions? Yes, we say and look at the ground, which is paved, because we're close to the gateway. Then we look over to where the butcher is, who has now drawn the sliding door shut, but still seems to be busy with the padlock, which, however much he hammers at it, simply won't shut. Perhaps something has got stuck in it, we shout over to him. What? the butcher says and puts a hand to an ear. Perhaps flies, we shout, or spiders. Or it's simply rusted, because it hasn't been used for such a long time. Excuse us for telling him that, we say, turning to the slaughterhouse director, but your friend obviously needs someone to help him with the padlock. Then the director yells: Quiet! and suddenly he's quite red in the face. He's managed till now quite well on his own with other things, he yells, all right? A padlock like that is no problem for him, even if it's blocked with dirt from every fly in the world. Isn't that so, Müller? he asks. Yes, sir, the butcher shouts back, I've managed well enough with other things. And you can manage the padlock too? the director asks and seems to be really a bit anxious now. I'll manage it, the butcher says and bangs the padlock a few times with his fist. Excuse us, we say, we only wanted to help. And I told you no questions! the director yells. And if I say no questions, that means there'll be none, just answers with yes and no. Nothing but that? we ask. Right, the director says, nothing but that. Well, we say, then we made a mistake in saying anything more. You see, generally we don't talk much and hardly ever ask questions. Well, I hope that's so, the director says and puts his hands away again, and slowly he calms down a bit. And then, when he's more calm, he exclaims: Well then, what are you doing here? Didn't you know that entry is strictly forbidden, he asks and points all around with his pigskin hand. And especially at a time like this. No, we say, and is it especially forbidden at a time like this? Of course, the director says, because nobody knows what the situation is. And what situation do you mean, when you say that nobody knows what it is? we ask. Ah now, what sort of a question is that? The present situation, of course. As if it wasn't as plain as the nose on your face, he says and brings out his right hand again, so we'll understand better, holding it flat before us, while the butcher in the distance seems not only to be hitting his padlock, which still refuses to snap shut, but also to be sniffing at it, even licking at it. For instance, the director says, nobody knows if the war's over or not. But of course it's over, it's been over since yesterday, we exclaim—louder than necessary, so he'll finally know. We've been conquered, didn't you know? But the slaughterhouse director merely shakes his relatively large head and says it hasn't been decided whether or not the war is over, that's a question for people other than him and us to rack their brains about. Isn't that so, Müller, he asks the butcher, who after his last effort has been able at last to turn the key in the padlock and his back on Shed No. 5. Yes, nobody knows, the butcher shouts back. Then he listens up at the sky for a moment and says that there's no shooting at present, though the situation could quickly change again. And then, hardly a moment after the hands had appeared, another strange thing happens, or rather, we notice it now. From under the shed door, which the butcher has locked at last after so much effort, a dark liquid is flowing and slowly spreading behind and around his boots. This happens in such a way that the butcher is soon surrounded by the liquid, although he doesn't notice. Naturally we'd like to ask what that liquid is, and where it suddenly came from, but then we remember we're not allowed to ask, and so we prefer not to. Certainly the liquid is dense and dark, but where's it coming from? From a bottle? A barrel? Is it running out of a machine? Out of a person? An animal? We can't tell. Did you hear what I said? The situation can change again, whereas entry into the slaughterhouse terrain is never permitted, the director shouts—he too hasn't noticed the liquid yet and he's thinking we must be dreaming, because we're so quiet. Didn't you know that? he asks. Yes, we say, we knew, but we didn't believe it. And why didn't you believe it, the director asks, and he raises his eyebrows. Because, we say, the gate was so wide open, wider that it ever was before. So we simply thought that it wasn't not permitted anymore. Ah, how can anyone be so stupid, the director exclaims and knocks his two prongs against his head a few times. As if it made any difference whether a gate is wide open or not. If it says that entry is prohibited, the gate could be nailed shut, as far as you're concerned. So if you thought you could do as you please, just because we've been conquered, then you were wrong. If it said "No Entry" yesterday, it still says the same today. And for all eternity, he adds after a moment, because he hadn't thought of it right away. Well, for all eternity, we say, and because the phrase is so strong we draw our foot around in the dust a bit. Yes indeed, the director says once more, sticking his prongs up in the air, for all eternity. Oh well, for all eternity then, we say. Well, so I'd hope, the director exclaims, and to calm himself down he blows much more air than usual out of his nose, across the Great Cattle Path. Instead of which, you broke in here. But we know that, we exclaim, and we're already getting a bit bored, because the slaughterhouse director so often repeats himself. It was, we say, a misunderstanding that won't occur again. Yes, yes, we know all about such misunderstandings and such promises, the director exclaims, and he takes a few steps around us, just so as to be moving. But such misunderstandings, he suddenly yells, shouldn't be allowed! What you may think about it doesn't interest me, I'm interested in one thing only: did you come through this gate—he's pointing at the wide-open Wundenplan gate—yes or no? Well, we say, we did but only very briefly. We only wanted . . . Stop! he interrupts us and even stops his ears with both hands, the flesh one and the metal one, so as not to hear us, you came through this gate, there's nothing more I want to know. Not even that we only wanted to see if there was any *Butterschmalz* here? we ask. No, that doesn't interest me either, the director says, the other thing's enough. And with both hands he gathers together into one great lump everything that doesn't interest him, even if one can't see it, thrusting it then far away from him, once and for all, with an energetic shove. And while the butcher is now standing, with his slaughterhouse boots, in the middle of the dark liquid flowing from Shed No. 5 and, without knowing it, splashing around in it a bit, the director starts to make a quite unnecessary speech right into our faces. One does everything one can to save our town from calamity and one leaves the gate open and even hoists, though in peril of one's life, a white flag . . . A white flag? we ask at once, where did you hoist it? Oh, behind there, the director says and points in some direction or other. But we never saw a white flag there, we say, yet the director insists that one is there. One hoists, behind there, a white flag, he exclaims, and one puts one's best suit on, so as to look smart, in case one has to hand over the slaughterhouse keys to the Americans, and what thanks does one get? Instead of Americans, suddenly these ragamuffins come marching in. Admit, he exclaims, that you've been snooping around everything. Oh, I could . . . and suddenly in his rage he grips our shoulders with his prongs, so that tears come not only to our eyes but also to his. Don't squeeze so hard, we exclaim, we weren't snooping. And nobody saw us either. Or . . . ? we ask and move our shoulders actually to make the director's prongs slide away, but he has clawed them into us so firmly that they stick. Listen, you're asking questions again. You asked: Or? As if I hadn't explained to them that it's me who asks the questions here, the director says, turning to his butcher, who at this moment notices the liquid he's standing in and jumps with a long bound onto dry land. What are you jumping for, Müller, the director asks when he sees the butcher suddenly jumping in the air. Ah, because of that, the butcher says and points at the liquid. The director, as he now looks and catches sight of the liquid, forgets for a moment to squeeze us with his prongs. What's that? he asks and points at the ground. Ah, the butcher says, something running out of the shed. And how come something's running out of the shed, the director asks and looks first at the liquid, then at his butcher. Didn't you promise to wipe everything up? But I *did* wipe everything up, the butcher exclaims and scratches his head. Then what is that? the director asks and points at the patch. That, the butcher says, is a puddle. And what is a puddle doing here in the middle of the yard, the director says. Ah, the butcher says, I must have overlooked it, now it's running out. Overlooked, overlooked, the director exclaims and stamps his feet with annoyance, one doesn't overlook such things. A thing like that, when people see it, makes the worst possible impression. If I say: Wipe it up! then it gets wiped up and I mean everything, Müller! Yes, Herr Moder, the butcher says. And while he stands with drooping white shoulders spotted here and there with red, helpless before his puddle, the director turns back to us, meaning to squeeze us again. Yes, he exclaims with his fork fingerbones sticking out hard and white, what are we going to do with you? You've seen the puddle now too. Actually we ought to hand them over to the Americans, but where are they? They've been to the town hall, to the gasworks, to the post office, only they haven't been here yet. Yes, we say, we don't know where they are either, we're wondering too. Are you? What do you want with them? the director asks. Ah, we say, actually we just wanted to take a bit of a look at them, especially the black ones. Take a look at them! the director scornfully says, and he starts to squeeze again. The best thing would be simply to put these ragamuffins in prison and let them stew a bit. Prison? we exclaim, horrified. Yes, the director says, but probably it's full. And then there's the danger that the Americans would send them home again, making the whole thing out to be a trifle. In some matters the Americans are said to be so broadminded it makes your head ache to think of it. But why prison? we exclaim, we were only looking to see if there was any *Butterschmalz*. Any what? the director asks, and for a moment he forgets to torment us. Ah, *Butterschmalz*, we say. And then, if they were to interrogate us, the Americans wouldn't understand us at all. You see, we've brought our dictionary along, the most important words are marked too, but our American isn't nearly good enough for us to explain everything, we say and let a corner of our dictionary poke out of our pocket for a moment. For instance, we don't even know what *Butterschmalz* is in American. Ah, what would it be, it'd be *Butterschmalz*, of course, the director says and tries to pronounce the difficult but entirely German word in a way that's as American as possible. Yes? So you can speak American? we exclaim and remember that a day ago at this time it wasn't even certain who'd be conquering us. And so well too, we say, that you know the American for

Butterschmalz! Oh, it's all the same whether one knows the American for *Butterschmalz* or not, the director says, and he makes a dismissive gesture. They'll be able to tickle out of you what they want to know and what you're refusing to tell me. For I can't simply let you go, unfortunately. Certainly you'd have found nothing better to do than spread the whole story around, so that before long all the young people wouldn't know the meaning of the word obedience. As if we didn't know the good old truth about the bad apple that spoils the whole basketful. We don't, we don't, we exclaim. And we move our shoulders up and then down again, so as to wrench them clear of the director's prongs once and for all. We've told you the truth, we say, even if you don't believe it. Ah, the truth, the director says, and first with his genuine hand, then with his false hand, he traces a line through the air, your appearance here has made things very unpleasant for me, and at present incalculably so, God knows how I can cope with it. No, no, he exclaims, while the butcher opens the shed door again and groaning and cursing brings out a long broom of the kind that's common in slaughterhouses the world over, and starts to sweep the liquid back into the shed, punish, punish! And why do you have to punish us, we ask, we only came through the gate and walked around a bit outside the cow sheds. And except for the puddle, we've seen much less than you probably think. How should you know what I think you've seen? the director asks at once and thrusts his head a little toward us, the better to hear our answer, while the butcher behind him continues to sweep resolutely. However, since the puddle doesn't stay in the shed but keeps running out again, he tries to spread it more evenly outside the shed door and, if there's enough of it, to make the whole yard equally wet all over. We look across. What could it be?

Certainly it's not water, it's too dark for that. If only one could dip a finger in and sniff it! And what's more, the director is now convinced we know what he thinks. But of course we don't know what you think, we exclaim, how could we? We only think we can make a guess, at least a rough one. But even if we had seen something we certainly wouldn't talk about it. So then you did see something, if you didn't mean to talk about it, the director infers—in an apparently quite logical way, but in reality quite wrongly. Not at all, we say, and during the pause that the director now makes we glance all around the slaughterhouse, which on this first day after our conquest is probably quite especially deserted. What we see is awful, of course. That there should be such a forsaken bit of the world in our neighborhood! Look, these terrible cow sheds, and here, the awful pig house. And those two rails there, rusting, because the cattle train doesn't come anymore! And behind, beyond the slaughterhouse wall, which at this point isn't topped with broken bottle glass but covered with barbed wire, our poor Wundenplan, *flattened!* Ah, if only we could get out of the slaughterhouse and be, if not in the town, then at least in its ruins! But the prospects are poor, we aren't even being understood. Ah, we exclaim, all we meant was: *if* we had seen something, we wouldn't speak of it. In fact we haven't seen anything to speak of. Yes, so you say, the director says, and what are you looking around for now? Ah, we say, we're only looking around because the place is so forlorn. Look at that tree over there, isn't it terribly sad? Which one? the director says, and he isn't believing us. Ah, that one, the one that's so black, we say and point at a bare tree with its bark gnawed off, beside a shed. And all the crows that are here. And you're not waiting for anyone else? the director asks and looks us in the eye. Nobody else, we say. And how am I to believe you're not waiting for anyone and haven't seen anything? the director asks and walks around us a bit. Yes, of course it's difficult, we say and sigh a little. If you don't believe us *simply so*, we don't know how. Well then, simply so? the director asks and looks at us sternly. Yes, simply so, we say. Even though we could give you our word of honor, anytime. Your word of honor? the director asks and wrinkles his forehead. Yes, we say, but probably you wouldn't accept it. That's right, the director says after a moment's thought, I wouldn't accept it. Who's to guarantee that your word of honor is true, and that you're not cheating? Yes, we say and can't help sighing again, nobody can guarantee it, of course, one just has to accept it oneself. Either one accepts it or one doesn't. No, the director says, after passing it through his mind again, this time probably from the opposite side, I can't accept it, unfortunately. And if we swear to it? we say. By whom? the director asks. By anyone you want, we say. All right, swear by . . . , the director says and thinks about it. By . . . , he says and thinks about it again. Ah, he says, for he still can't think of anyone for us to swear by, let it pass, I can't believe you. You yourselves didn't believe it when you saw "No Entry" here. Yes, but that's quite different, we exclaim, the gate was open—and we're amazed that the slaughterhouse director can put two such different things together. Yes, different for you, not for me, the director says and points with his ironlike hand at the broad and probably also padded chest of his suit. Just as I can hear what you say, you can read what's written. This "No Entry" sign, he says and points over his shoulder to where the sign probably is, you did read it, didn't you? Yes, probably, we say—although we can't remember. And you really can read too? the director asks. Yes, we can read too, we say. Perhaps we did read it, only we forgot right away, because we thought it didn't apply anymore. And why, the director asks, why shouldn't a sign like that apply just because the gate is open? The "No Entry" sign is a hundred times more important than a gate like that, which in most cases has been left open just by accident. And to make sure that we don't only keep hearing it, but also see it, he suddenly grips us by the neck and pulls us—we almost forget to raise our feet—across the entire yard, in former times so diligently licked by our cattle, to the Wundenplan gate. The sign really is there, on an iron pole, with the words "No Entry" on it, followed by the complete wording, printed much smaller, of the slaughterhouse regulations. Right now, the director says and stands bolt upright by the pole, what's that? Yes, we say and nod, that's it. Right, he says, now read it. Yes, we say, that's what it says. Read, you must read it, the director shouts and pinches our neck as if in rhythm with a reading. But we've been reading it all the time, we exclaim, rolling our head back and forth beneath his sign. Isn't one allowed to read silently? No, aloud, the director exclaims, so that we can all hear. Everything on the sign? we ask. Yes, he says, everything. All right, we say, then we'll read it aloud. Then, partly in chorus, we read our way, just because the slaughterhouse director wants us to, into paragraph 1 of the General German Slaughterhouse Regulations, which, however, doesn't apply one bit to our case, so that we frequently pause and soon stop altogether. Well, what's up? the director asks, while the butcher, under whose broom till now the yard has been softly rustling, puts his broom against the cow shed wall and walks over to us, positions himself behind the director and, so as to hear everything better, props his chin on the latter's shoulder. Strange, how this chin with the long teeth rests on the director's shoulder! Shall we go on reading? we ask. Yes, the director says, go on. But now it's just the cattle-driving regulations, we say. And is that too difficult for you? the director asks, and joining his prongs as a signal to make us continue reading, he waves them back and forth in our face in a rhythm of their own. No, it's not too difficult, but too long, we say—for the small print, as on all billboards in the world, takes up most of the space. Too long? the director asks. Yes, we say, too long. Well, all right, the director says. In any case, it says "No Entry" and when it says that, then entry is forbidden, especially to slaughterhouses. For a slaughterhouse like this one, empty or not, is no place for you. But we know the slaughterhouse, we're about to exclaim, for the director has obviously never heard us making music here, but no, we don't say it, we prefer to keep quiet. Yes, now you see where it gets you if you don't abide by the rules, the director says. I can only hope that if you ever get out of here you'll have learned something and will respect rules and prohibitions for the rest of your life. Excuse us, but is there any danger of our never getting out of here? we ask politely, and again we look around in the apparently limitless area, where it must be noon at least. Yes, the director says, that danger exists. And is the danger great? we ask and with our sound hands indicate the possible size of such a danger. That, says the director, is something one can't yet say. Isn't that so, Müller? That's so, one can't yet say, the butcher says—he still has his teeth, something horselike about them, on the shoulder in front of him. And what'll you do with us? we ask, but then the slaughterhouse director shrugs his shoulders, he doesn't yet know. The important thing for him seems to be that he has *got* us, that we don't escape, for if he has stood hitherto beside the pole, rather than beside us, he now takes a long stride toward us—what long legs, probably long-haired too, the slaughterhouse director has inside his dark Sunday trousers!—and he places his artificial hand once more on our shoulder, while the butcher sticks out before him the chin he's no longer able to rest on the shoulder, and walks around us, laying also a hand on our shoulder, but on the other one. So are we under arrest? we ask. That, the director says, you'll be seeing in a moment. And why is he holding on to us too? we ask, pointing to the butcher. It's his business whether or not he holds on to you, one can't argue with him about it, the director says. He'll have his ideas about it, even though one doesn't always know what they are. And if he's hurting us? we ask and even cry a bit or at least try to, although we don't really succeed, because no tears come. For the butcher, who's a rough drudge of a man, is not only holding us tightly but also taking the opportunity to give us a good pinch. Since as a breaker and slaughterer he has in his large, red, undamaged hands naturally much more strength than the slaughterhouse director in his artificial one, he also pinches much more vigorously, something the director doesn't, however, understand. Don't cry like that, he keeps on saying, what good is it? There's nobody around to hear you. Nobody at all? we ask and look around. No, nobody at all, the director says. And outside? we ask and point to the wall and over the wall. Nobody there either, the director says. And if we scream? we ask and look up at the director. Here? the director asks, astonished, and he points over his godforsaken terrain, which is no use at all to anyone wanting to scream. All the same we say: Yes—scream very loud. Well, you can scream, of course, if you want to, loud too, the director says after a moment's thought, but nobody will hear that either. Go on, scream a bit, if you think it'll help, he says and gestures with his artificial hand once again over the slaughterhouse terrain and right over the wall, where, beyond the rubble, our town begins. Does a scream make any sense in such a situation? Shouldn't one rather save the breath that such a scream costs? Well then, we say, so we won't scream. We'll scream some other time, when someone's listening. As you please, the director says, it certainly wouldn't have helped you. You'd only have blown the air about, but there's air enough here. Now don't press so hard, Müller, he then says to the butcher, or else they'll get bruises and that won't get us anywhere. If you think it was enough, the butcher says, standing high over us in the pallid slaughterhouse air. Yes, the director says, enough. Thanks, we say as we feel the pressure of the butcher's hand gradually lessening. Should we perhaps run away, slipping through the hands of the butcher, who, even if he's got long legs, is somewhat older than us? Simply as far as the gate and as quickly as possible out through the gate? But then the director, who has probably guessed our thoughts or secretly thought them himself, is already on the way to the iron gate and pushing it shut with his foot. Hey, what are you doing there? we exclaim when we see the Wundenplan slaughterhouse gate slowly closing behind us, doesn't the gate have to stay open? Ah, we know what we're doing, the director says, we don't need any advice from you, thanks. But we're not giving you advice, we say, we just don't want to be treated like murderers and locked up and so horribly pinched. Whether or not we lock you up and how much we pinch you, you must leave to us, the director says, we know what we're doing. Even if we haven't done anything? we ask. Whether you've done something or not, the director says, it's a fact. So we can't go yet? we ask. See for yourself, the director says and points at the now closed Wundenplan gate, there's no question of your going now. So now we'll be punished? we ask. You'll see that too, soon enough, the director says and plucks a bit at our coat sleeve, while the butcher stands behind us and his breath is warm on our neck. In any case, now comes the interrogation, the director says and looks around for a shed, since the yard is far too large for such an interrogation, and soon he finds one. Let's go, he says, Shed No. 12. But that's the pig house! we exclaim. Yes, the director says, that's the pig house. But then, we exclaim, but then . . . Quite right, the director says. Prisoners, we're prisoners!

That's how it was: shortly after our conquest, sometime around noon, instead of concluding our study of the Slaughterhouse Regulations by chasing us, with a few flappings extracted from his wrist, quickly through the open gate back onto the Wundenplan boulevard, the slaughterhouse director drives us through the springlike air farther and farther into his slaughterhouse. Doing so together with the butcher, as if they had an agreement about it, he herds us so close together, us and our Edgar, who, because he doesn't know the place, prefers to let us do the talking, that we feel Edgar's breath around our necks and ears. Thus we go from the pole with the sign on it across the paved yard, first down the Einfangstraße, then down the Great Cattle Path, to the pig house. Meanwhile the butcher is brandishing his long broom, probably from force of habit, high over his head, and the slaughterhouse director, having nothing to brandish, simply waves his arms. So we're really going to the pig house? Yes, he shouts, now move, move! And he leaps ahead of us, with long strides, to set a good example, while the butcher, to keep us hopping, makes rhythmical clicking sounds at us from behind with his tongue. Naturally with such an escort there can be no thought of escape. No doubt about it, instead of having such thoughts we're being heaped with reproaches. As if on a day like this there's nothing more important to do than arrest these ragamuffins, the director shouts, for instance. And: Ah, what's to be done about you? But you should do nothing with us, we shout at the back of his neck as we run along. You only have to let us go, instead of getting so worked up. And if you've put anything on the floor in there—we're racing now past Shed No. 5—something nobody's supposed to see, you needn't worry about it. We haven't seen anything, or at least we haven't recognized anything. What are you saying, the director shouts—we're only making him more agitated, instead of calming him down, as he shouts it over our heads to the butcher—which shed was it where we put something on the floor? Ah, only Shed No. 5, we say, where something was running out—because the butcher can't say it, he has to keep on clicking his tongue. And what did we put on the floor? the director asks his butcher, but the latter simply goes on silently running. Ah, we say, it's all the same, we're telling you, we didn't see, it was too dark. And then this gentleman here—we point at the butcher—shut the door right away, so what could we have seen? And him, we say, pointing at our Edgar, who while running is pale and stays close to us, he even *couldn't* have seen it, he's almost blind. Aren't you? we say to our Edgar, without glasses you're almost blind? Yes, our Edgar says and hurries along beside us, without glasses I'm almost blind. For instance the cow shed, we say and point across the Great Cattle Path. Look, Edgar, over there, see the cow shed? A cow shed? our Edgar exclaims, where is it? I don't see one. Did you hear that? we say to the director, he doesn't see the cow shed. And the sky? we say and point as we stumble along fleetingly up at the sky, do you see the sky? The sky? our Edgar asks and looks up, no, I don't see it. And the earth? we ask, and while running we look down, can you see where you're putting your feet? The earth? our Edgar says, and he too looks down, no, I can't see it either. Did you hear that? we shout, he can't have seen anything. He can't even see the earth, and he can't see the sky either. Ah, it makes no difference whether Müller shut the door in time or your friend is blind, the director exclaims and drives us on from the right side. And at this very moment he's passing, with his shiny shoes, through the liquid, we don't know what it is. Look at that, see what you've done, isn't it terrible, he exclaims, but he isn't pointing at the slaughterhouse pavement, no, but at his own mouth, out of which, in annoyance at us, something too is running, even if it's only spit. Meanwhile the butcher, driving us from the left side, does nothing but brandish the broom and click his tongue and shout: Giddyup, Pegleg! and Yeeho, Squinteye! Ah, why are you being so strict with us, we exclaim, but neither the man with the broom nor the director sees the point. Ah, the director says, we only want to ask a few questions and look a bit into your pockets. But there's nothing to be seen in our pockets, we just have time to shout, and then it's too late: as at a distant command the butcher, still clicking his tongue, starts to roll up his sleeves, so that he can rummage deep into our pockets during the interrogation, the moment we reach the pig house. Meanwhile, the slaughterhouse director pulls a big key ring from his trouser pocket as soon as we've come to a halt outside the pig house, he quickly finds the right key, unlocks the pig house, rolls back the door, and pushes us through the gap. Hand in hand we walk in, eyes tight shut, so as best to see nothing. Damp slaughterhouse darkness dripping abundantly from thick smooth walls and gusting through everything! Our horror, as steam enshrouds us in the pig house, the moment we open our eyes! Our disgust as it spreads in white waves over our hair and hands! And penetrates coat and trousers to find the skin. We'd never have thought there'd be such a fog in the pig house. Even the director's glasses are immediately steamed up, his hair bedewed. Ah, we exclaim, what a lot of steam in here! And why? we ask. Because we've made everything spick and span, the director says. But why did you think there was so much steam in here? he asks after a moment. Ah, we exclaim, we hadn't thought at all, there hadn't been time to think. Then you were probably going to think there's such a lot of steam because we meant to hide something here? the director asks. But no, we exclaim, not at all! Well, and we don't mean to, the director says and puts his keys away, all we've done is clean the place. The filth that was here, nobody would have believed it, even if one described it. Ah, you needn't describe it for us, we'll believe your filth, we say. In any case, the director says, it was suffocating, that's why we cleaned the place. The apparatus had been cleaned, the floor scoured, the walls hosed down. That's to say, he says after a pause and points to the butcher, he cleaned everything and hosed it down, I supervised him. He even had to polish the cauldron, the director says, pointing over his shoulder to the back, where the cauldron probably is. And he's glad that everything's clean and we're finally in the pig house, where he'll interrogate us, for he's pulling the door shut behind us, so that the cauldron, which was just then starting to shine in the steam beyond the pens, is hardly visible anymore. Ah, to be outside again, in the freedom of our Amselgrund, even in the ruins of Wundenplan! But they won't let us go now, it's unthinkable. Instead, there'll be the interrogation.

For the interrogation we're hustled back into the corner

behind the big slaughtering slab, so that we're kept in full view and can be hit at once with a single question. There we have to keep our hands behind our back to make our pockets freely accessible. We're strictly forbidden not only to ask questions but also to make remarks or utter exclamations during the questioning. And we're not allowed to clasp our hands behind us, because that would make things seem too relaxed. But the slaughterhouse director, who, to get himself concentrated before he questions us, walks with his head bowed up and down before us a few times, is not only allowed to ask questions and utter exclamations, he's also allowed to clasp his hands. Yes, presumably he could even link his fingers, if he had any. Also he's permitted to smoke while interrogating us, although with his hands that's not so easy, of course. Because the artificial left hand is useless for smoking, while the right hand has only two prongs, between which the butcher, after inserting a cigarette in his own mouth and lighting it and taking a few puffs on the director's behalf, has to clamp it. Is it clamped, Müller? the director asks. Yes, the butcher says, it's clamped. Are you sure? the director asks. Yes, I'm sure, Herr Moder, the butcher says. Right, now, who sent you here? the director asks, turning to us and cautiously moving the prongs with the cigarette around in the air. And because he means to interrogate us in as comfortable a position as possible, though standing, he leans one shoulder against the stone wall, the wall against which, in earlier times, though a bit farther down, the animal carcasses used to lean. Meanwhile the butcher comes around behind us, so that, standing and not saying a word, he can plunge his hands right and left as deeply as possible into our pockets. Well, it was like this, we say, and we too make our talking position as comfortable as we can in this difficult situation. Our mother sent us, because she thought there was *Butterschmalz* in the locker plant. *Butterschmalz!* the director exclaims and turns almost menacingly in the direction of the locker plant. Yes, we say, somebody called out to her, when she was standing in the upstairs window. Called out to her? the director exclaims, and he gets ready to smoke. Yes, we say. And who, the director says, called out to her? Ah, we say, it was Frau Malz. And your mother believed the thing about the *Butterschmalz*, the director asks and puffs briefly on his cigarette. Yes, we say, Frau Malz was carrying a pail. Then your mother naturally told herself that Frau Malz was going to the slaughterhouse. *Butterschmalz*, the director says and turns to the butcher, do you know anything about *Butterschmalz?* No, the butcher says, I don't know anything about *Butterschmalz*. Nor do I, the director says and slowly shakes his head. Hm, we say, we thought too that it was only a rumor. Then why did you come here, if it was only a rumor? the director asks. Because she sent us, we say. And why didn't she come herself, the director asks. Because she doesn't leave the house anymore, we say. That's why she got a headache and went to bed. And to make our point clear we clutch our own provisionally still healthy head, but of course the director must have understood us anyway. In any case he asks no more questions about our mother. Instead, he points to our Edgar and asks: Who's that? That's our Edgar, we say, while Edgar himself remains mute and lets us say who he is. And what's he doing here? the director asks. Ah, we say, he came with us and looks after us, but the director finds this hard to believe. And why doesn't he talk more, if he's looking after you? he asks. Ah, we say, he hasn't had anything to eat. And why not? the director asks. Because he hasn't got anything, we say. And then: Besides, what's there for him to talk about? He's almost blind, you know. All right, and you maintain that you came here to buy something, the director says and traces with his cigarette hand a sloping line on the wall, so that we can picture better the empty slaughterhouse terrain with a slight slope, probably, going up to the pig house. Yes, we say, *Butterschmalz*. And stick our heads closer together again, as instructed, so that he can keep us more easily in view. And if there really had been any such thing here, the director asks and guides his cigarette hand to his mouth again, what would you have done with it? We'd have taken it home, we say, and mother would have cooked something. Cooked something, the director says, and he's meaning to put his cigarette back between his lips and puff on it, only it slips out of his prongs, in spite of all the trouble he takes, and falls on the grill in the floor. Goddamn, the director exclaims. Oh my, the butcher says. Now, we say, it's on the floor. It doesn't matter, the director says, Müller will pick it up for me. Won't you, Müller? Would you be so kind? Of course, Herr Moder, the butcher says. And he extracts from our pockets his hands, bony and black-haired, and he stoops and gasps a bit, and having retrieved the cigarette and cleaned it a bit with his fingers and blown away the dust from it, if there was any, he puts it back into the director's narrowly opened mouth. Thank you, Müller, the director says and gives him a nod, and the butcher, before returning to our pockets, gives a little salute, putting a hand to where he has no more hair. And now? we ask and point to the cigarette that's drooping from the director's lips. And now what? he asks. We're thinking: What will you do with the cigarette now, we ask, will you clamp it between your prongs again? Whether I'll clamp it somewhere? the director asks and puts his false paw to his ear. Yes, in there between your fingers, we say and point. You mean here? he asks and raises up his hand. Yes, we say. The director gulps down two or three deep breaths to calm himself and says: Where I clamp my cigarette before, during, or after I smoke it is my own concern. And Müller's too, a bit, but no one else's, is that clear? Yes, we say. All right then, he says, do I have your permission to go on smoking? But of course, we say. Right, he says to the butcher, we can proceed. Very well, Herr Moder, the butcher says. And since the director can't for the moment think of anything else to interrogate us about, he asks the butcher: Well, Müller, what have you found? And he stretches his hand out, the artificial one, so that the butcher can place in it the contents of our pockets. Here you are, Herr Moder, the butcher says and places everything in it, piece by piece. Thank you, Müller, the director says. And then, when the hand has been filled, he shakes it a little, and we all peer into it. No! We never thought our pockets could be so full. And we're surprised ourself that among the many things extracted by the butcher there's nothing to arouse suspicion. Careful, our trousers! we exclaim because he's intending to get back to them for one more search, and our trousers—not to mention our Edgar's—aren't by any means new and could easily get torn. Ah, the director says, do you think we're interested in your trousers? It's your pockets and what's in them that interest us. But there's nothing in them, we aren't thieves, we exclaim. But the director isn't even listening. Well, Müller, what have they got on them? he asks and turns to the butcher, whom he seems to trust better than his own eyes. Ah, it's a pity, but not much, the butcher says, and he starts, while the director in his impatience flips his cigarette up and down a bit, to pick up again one by one each of the things he had extracted from us and placed in the hand before him, and to lift it up and pronounce its name aloud, all the way down to the flat stone our Edgar needs when he's hungry. I couldn't find anything else, he says. And did you go all the way down, the director asks, trying to take the cigarette out of his mouth again and clamp it between the prongs. All the way, the butcher says, but I'll try again. And they don't have any weapons? the director asks. No, the butcher says, at least I didn't find any. Weapons? But of course we haven't got any weapons, we exclaim in horror, and while still exclaiming it we realize that our arrest is obviously due to a terrible mix-up. Obviously we're being mistaken for other people. Obviously since last winter there have been a few boys between Wundenplan and here who perhaps resemble us externally, perhaps wear the same cap, and go around the slaughterhouse a lot, perhaps even look over the wall, even if they don't climb over it, and throw stones through windowpanes, make messes on the walls, now and then kick down a pen or tamper with the valuable slaughtering machinery. And now these two gentlemen are confusing us with this gang. They might even think we're the Coat-Slitter Gang which everyone hereabouts has been feverishly searching for but still hasn't caught. But we're not the Coat-Slitter Gang, we can swear to it! For months we haven't been on the streets after dark and we've spent practically every night in our cellar. Yet the gentlemen, because they don't know us personally, think the Coat-Slitter Gang is us! Isn't that so, you think we're someone in particular? we ask. Yes, we do, the director exclaims, we do. Someone you've been looking for, a long time probably? we ask. Yes, looking, we've been looking, he says. For a gang, wasn't it? we ask, and we stand as one before him in the pig house, ganglike enough, with drooping arms, shoulders too, even heads. Possibly, he says, anything's possible. Yes, we say, that's what we thought when you came out of the shed.

You think we're the Coat-Slitter Gang, don't you? The what? the director asks and puts his prongs with his cigarette to his ear. And you're the slaughterhouse director, aren't you? we ask. Possibly, he says, anything's possible. Then you came, didn't you, we ask, from Chemnitz not long ago? Yes, he says, from Berlin. In November, wasn't it? we ask. Yes, he says, in January. And because your hands were injured a bit, we say, you were appointed here? And how do you know all this? the director asks. Ah, mother told us, we say. And because you haven't been here so very long, you thought we were the Coat-Slitters, didn't you? But we aren't. The director has now raised his cigarette once more to his mouth and he blinks at us through the smoke in some bewilderment. The Coat-Slitters? he asks. Yes, we say, but you've been mistaken about us. Mistaken? the director asks, and very cautiously he moves his prongs to his mouth. Yes, we say, and if you weren't, then the other gentleman must have been. And we point over our shoulder to the butcher, who's oldish, but could also be any inspector or his assistant. Anyway, he's standing behind us with his hands in our pockets, although there's nothing left in them, least of all weapons, of course. When he hears that he's been mistaken about us, he pulls his arms from our pockets immediately and shakes his fist at us. How could I be mistaken, I'm four or five times older than you, he exclaims. I've never been mistaken about anyone, man or animal! But I'm also not so old as not to know whom or which I'm dealing with. Herr Moder, he says, turning to the director and placing his liberated hand on his heart, as true as I'm standing before you in this pig house, I'm not mistaken about them. How many times have I seen these rascals through this or that window, when I happened to look up from slaughtering, peering over the wall! If I took no action then, it was because

I wanted to catch them red-handed. And now that we've caught them red-handed, I'm supposed to be mistaken about them! What cheek! Excuse us, we say, we don't mean to be cheeky, but there must be a mistake. We've never once in our life peered over the slaughterhouse wall, simply because it's too high for us. And there's broken glass on top of it too, so we'd hurt ourself. And besides: if we'd really looked over the wall as often as he says, there'd have to be other witnesses, but there aren't, there can't be. Quiet! the butcher shouts, who naturally hadn't expected we'd ask for more witnesses. What do you mean, asking for more witnesses when I've seen you myself? With these eyes, he shouts and invites all our attention to his eyes, rubbing them savagely. Herr Moder, he meanwhile exclaims, if I see them with these eyes, have I seen them or haven't I? Yes, yes, Müller, the director says, but don't get so worked up. And is that enough or isn't it? the butcher asks. Yes, yes, Müller, the director says and taps him lightly on the shoulder, just calm down now. But it's some time before the butcher does calm down. Ah, he keeps calling, ah. And in the short time during which he's been busy with his eyes, hitherto so clear, if somewhat watery, he's managed to rub them quite red. Stop that, Müller, you'll do yourself some harm, if you're not careful, the director exclaims. Ah, the butcher says, I'm stopping it now. But with all I've been through recently, to let myself be told by these ragamuffins, who've done nothing whatever the whole time, that I'm mistaken about them, I won't stand for it. And he jumps around a bit more on the ridged floor, in his rubber boots, which have cuffs at the top, so that the slaughterhouse director has to call out sharply: Müller, that's enough now! Only then is he quiet again, but just at that moment, when he's standing still and not rubbing anymore, but putting his hands back into our pockets where they were before he erupted, our Edgar suddenly starts to sway. Yes, our Edgar, who till now, because he doesn't know his way around here, hasn't said anything and has accompanied us silently all the way to the pig house, seems to be feeling faint again, or at least he has to lean against us. Then as if copying the butcher, he even rests his chin on our shoulder and shuts his eyes, while leaving his mouth wide open, since he needs a lot of air. What's he doing? the director asks, and he looks at our Edgar. Ah, we say, he's swaying. And why is he swaying? the director asks, and suddenly he's not standing there so steadily himself either, for he hangs on to a meat hook, from which hitherto only animals used to hang when drained of blood. Ah, we say, why's he swaying? Because he's feeling faint. Faint? the director asks, and he raises his eyebrows. Yes, we say, because of his head. What's wrong with his head? the director asks. Ah, we say, he has a tumor. A tumor? the director exclaims. Yes, we say, but only a very small one. And where does he have the tumor? the director asks. Ah, we say, somewhere inside there, nobody quite knows. And is that why he sees so little? the director asks. Yes, we say, probably it's that. Oh dear oh dear oh dear, the little fellow has a tumor in his head, the director exclaims excitedly and seems most inclined to hang with both hands now from the meat hook, except that in his artificial hand he's still holding the contents of our pockets. Yes, we say, and it makes him feel faint. And then? What happens then? the director asks, while the butcher too looks baffled and gazes down from high above upon our Edgar's blond head. Ah, we say, then he collapses. And then? asks the director, who wants to know everything. Then, we say, he feels sick. Sick? Well, he should sit down at once, the director exclaims, for he doesn't want our Edgar to throw up in his freshly cleaned pig house. It'll certainly help him, if he sits down, won't it? he asks and looks around for something our poor Edgar could quickly be sat down on. Yes, we say, sitting down wouldn't be a bad idea. And what happens if he doesn't sit down, the director asks—he's worried because he can't see a chair for Edgar, either near the cauldron or in the pens, even though the steam has now gone away and we can easily see everything that's there, cauldron, hooks, knives, and the flat bowls for the blood. Well, we say, if he can't sit down he'll throw up. Throw up? no, not here, we've cleaned everything here, the director exclaims and shakes his head vigorously. The best thing will be for him to go over into the corner, he can sit down there, he exclaims and points to a calf-killing slab. Our Edgar, when he sees the calf-killing slab and hears that he's supposed to sit on it, goes paler than ever and whispers: Not on the calf-killing slab. Not on the calf-killing slab? the director exclaims. Yes, we say, not on the calf-killing slab. All right then, not on the calf-killing slab, the director exclaims. Yes, we say, better not. Otherwise he'll throw up and make everything dirty again. Dirty? No, that's impossible, the director exclaims and points to the flagstones which, especially in the grooves, are very difficult to scour. Yes, of course it will be dirty, there's nothing to be done about that, we say, first comes the faint feeling and then he throws up, that's the way it goes. But not in my pig house, better get him out of here, the director exclaims and stands up straight by his freshly hosed wall. And he lets go of the meat hook, so as to point with his extended prongs through the empty boiling room and right past the killing pens, into the yard, into the open air. And outside, we ask, where should we take him outside? I don't care, the director says, just get him out of here, out of my slaughterhouse. So then we'll have to leave?

we ask. Yes, he says, go away, right now! And don't we get back what we had in our pockets? we ask and point to the contents of our pockets, which the director, perhaps unknowingly, still has in his artificial hand. What? he asks. Ah, yes, he says, of course. And hurriedly he gives us everything back. Quickly we stuff everything back into our pockets. Right, now get him out of here, before he faints, the director exclaims and points at our Edgar. Ha! he exclaims, a tumor! And he shakes his head and takes us by the shoulders and turns us around beside the meat hook, to push us this time not deeper into the pig house, but, with equally vigorous thrusts, out of the pig house again. Herr Moder, the butcher calls and walks a few paces alongside the director and stoops, as he walks, toward him, so that it looks as if he's going to bite his ear, though all he does is talk into it. And he speaks so softly that we can hardly understand what he's saying, at least not everything. We understand only single words like "seen" and "good eyes" and "wall" and "window" and "bolt machine" and "Great Siechenfeld Gate." But whatever the butcher may be whispering, the director only shakes his head. No, Müller, he says, no. So I shouldn't search them anymore? the butcher asks and passes his hand over our trouser leg. No, Müller, the director says, we must let them go. What's going on, we exclaim, can we go now? Or should we wait till he makes everything dirty? It won't be long now, we say and point at our Edgar who's resting his blond head on our shoulder and—his mouth is wide open—breathing noticeably hard. Then the director shouts: Be off with you!—and gives a loud hand clap. All right, we're going, if you insist, we say. And pass through the sliding door again, into the yard, where it's bright and airy, whereas the animals, once they had gone into the pig house, never came out again alive. Outside, on the Great Cattle Path, we brush the pig house air well and truly off our coat and trousers. Also off our shoulders, where the two gentlemen squeezed us so hard. Yes, even the cap, although it has been in the shopping bag the whole time, we brush it against our knees. Well, we say while doing this. Well, the director also says, and standing once again before us with his legs apart he points at our Edgar and says: And now, quick, take him home! Ah, we say and make a dismissive gesture, he hasn't got a home. Is that so? the director says, and why not? Ah, we say, he used to live in Wundenplan. And then more softly: On the Gießereistraße. Well, if he lived on the Gießereistraße, the director says and is somewhat ill at ease, then take him somewhere else. Take him to his mother. Ah, we say more softly still, but she's dead. Oh, the director says—and in the light of nature, perhaps also because of what we're saying, he suddenly gives the impression of being much smaller in size, also faded. And his father? he asks softly. He's a soldier, we say. Unfortunately his battalion was mauled. Very well, the director says, then take him to some place where he can wait till his father turns up again, he can't stay here. Take him, he says and then reflects for a moment. Ah, he says, take him wherever you want. All right, we say, and we grasp our Edgar by his armpits, we'll take him into our garden shed, then he'll have some fresh air. And *Butterschmalz*, we ask, isn't there any really? *Butterschmalz*, the director says, and because he too wants, once and for all, to be rid of the bad pig house taste, he spits on the ground vigorously a few times, there isn't any. And now, he says, it's high time you got out of here, so he won't collapse on me, but slowly, nice and slowly, so nobody will notice, here, through this gate. Through the

Wundenplan slaughterhouse gate, we ask? Yes, the director says, the Wundenplan boulevard. And then, he says, walk nice and slowly down the road. The Wundenplan boulevard! we exclaim, loud and in chorus. Yes, the director says. All right then, we say, *auf Wiedersehen*. All the director says is: Be off with you! We put our cap on our head and shake his hand, pressing on it a bit, and we take a few steps. And then, when we stop again, meaning to shake the butcher's hand, the slaughterhouse director shouts: No! You needn't! And be off with you, but fast —and he pushes us out through the gate, into the open air.

Where, between us our Edgar, rapidly recovering in the fresh air, we slowly walked down the Wundenplan boulevard and then somewhat more quickly into our *flattened* Wundenplan and told ourselves that Frau Malz had probably told our mother a lie. Or it's also possible that mother hadn't heard her properly. Or else the wind had blown away from mother the essential words. But how should we explain this to mother, in her present condition? In any case, hardly arrived in Wundenplan we can already hear her reproaches. That we were weakly cheated out of the *Butterschmalz*, instead of following father's example, who doubtless would have conquered some for us at one stroke. But mother, there wasn't any *Butterschmalz*, the slaughterhouse was deserted, we say, if only to ourself, for now there wasn't a soul in the slaughterhouse, only a few rats. Nonetheless, we now have a pang of conscience about not being a better replacement for father, although during the past year we've grown such a lot and already have such big long hands and feet, noses and members. Whereas for his mother our Edgar had always been a good replacement for *his father*. Ah, always

Edgar, always Edgar! Ah, and always father! Yet, come to think of it, we do now have the slaughterhouse behind us. And what's this coming toward us, the whole length of it, we can still hardly see it, a patch of green, hoisted in the air a bit, isn't that the park?

6

WHERE we find under a lilac bush with blossoms wilting the dog that had been shot to death. This dog we stumble on, our Edgar having taken us by a shortcut through the Kellerwiese, is lying all alone under his bush. Perhaps he fled here, just after being shot, perhaps this is where he wanted to die. In any case, it's not so easy to spot him. As we come closer we'd like to think he was something else, best of all a stone, crusted a little by weathering, a little *transformed*. But when we've come closer and look down on him we see that it isn't a stone but, especially because of the head, a dog, and a dead one. And this head, which makes the stone into a dog, is where the bullet went in. How strange, a dead dog in our town park! Around which, hands in pockets, we walk a few times, trembling at the knees. Is he dead? we ask our Edgar, who's stroking the head with his delicately jointed fingers. Dead, our Edgar says. And why is he dead? we ask. Because he's been shot, he says. And where's he from? we ask, since like everything else that's dead the dog interests us very much. It must be one of the dogs that were shot last night, our Edgar says. Do you recognize him? we ask our Edgar, because presumably he knows all the dogs in our town. No, our Edgar says, do you? We stoop closer to him, study him carefully. No, we don't either, we say, but we're not sure. Possibly we've seen the dog, even if we don't know where. Could it be Botho Primus' new pet? Since when, our Edgar asks, has Botho Primus had a new dog? Since his son was killed in action, we say. Nonsense, our Edgar says, what Botho Primus has is a cat. No, no, this dog must be from Rußdorf, he says and points a foot at him. And why Rußdorf? we ask, why not perhaps Siechenfeld? No, our Edgar says, he's from Rußdorf. Unless he's from somewhere quite different, he adds, and just happened to be passing by. And got stuck here? we say. Yes, our Edgar says. And pushes the dog a bit with his feet, rolling him over and back again, so that we can see him from underneath and perhaps remember him, but we aren't looking anymore, we're looking away, because the dog makes us sad. Instead of looking at him we look at the lilac blossoms that surround him. And study—yes, lilac time is over—their formerly fulsome and white, but now shrunken and rusted-looking umbels, beneath which the dog, who'll remain a stranger to us, got ready to die. Are you allowed to do that? we ask as Edgar rolls him over with a foot. Why shouldn't I be? he asks. And your sandals, we say and point to them, because they actually belong to our father and, as our mother says, are only *on loan* to our Edgar. Yes, our Edgar says, what about them? Ah, we say, because they don't belong to you. Ah, our Edgar says, your father certainly won't need them again. Then he wipes the sandals a bit on the grass. When we think that our father used to wear them on his walks! No, in this respect we're different. We stand there quietly, touch nothing, roll nothing over and over, all we do is drink everything quietly and anxiously in. Wasn't there something—without our knowing what it was—keeps pressing on us and didn't we want to think about it? Didn't we? we ask our Edgar. Didn't you what? he asks. Shouldn't we? we ask. What do you mean? he asks impatiently. Wasn't there something we should be thinking of? we ask. And what were you wanting to think of? he asks. Ah, we say, we've forgotten what it was. And you, we ask, do you remember? No, our Edgar says. I don't either. All right, we say, then forget it. Well then, our Edgar says and turns away from the dog. Fine, and now the park.

If our town spreads southward into our forests and toward Wundenplan, our park is more in the center of it. And if our town, especially the northern half, has already been warmed by the sun and dried by the winds on this first day after our conquest, the park is still damp. So that yesterday's rainwater trickles down the gently sloping paths toward anyone coming into the park from the direction of the slaughterhouse. Also the ground to the right and left of the paths is still soft, and the trees, mostly firs, but also pines and oaks, stretch out their branches, black and dripping, into the air. Over them clouds, firm and round, from one eternity to another. Not knowing what we want to think of, we leave the main path and walk diagonally into the park and through it. And we grope through our coat to feel the letters for Frau Henne and for Herr Schellenbaum. And following the zigzag perimeter which curves here and there back into the park, we soon arrive at the flimsy house that Herr Schellenbaum owns on the far side of the street and which is distinguished from neighboring houses only by the color of its roof. We can already smell the smoke that's coming from these houses and is carried to us by a gust of wind, for today too, far into the night, people here are burning a lot of things. Yes, this is where Herr Schellenbaum lives, actually we could give him the letter now. Perhaps he's standing in his window and waiting for us already? Do you think we should go to Herr Schellenbaum now? we ask, and we're about to stop, because we're level with the Schellenbaum house. Later, our Edgar says and pushes us onward. And what if he's waiting for the letter? we ask. First, our Edgar says, we go to the Amselgrund. And what if . . . , we're about to ask. No, our Edgar says, later. And what . . . , we ask. No, he exclaims. In short, you could hear our First Herr Schellenbaum! lifted on a warm breeze, moving for a while over the damp leaves, while our Edgar's No, him later! floats very close behind it. All right then, later, we say and walk past the Schellenbaum house and think, as we look across toward him, that we can see Herr Schellenbaum standing in his window frame, waiting for the letter. He, Herr Schellenbaum, had once been the stoker in our father's small whip factory. With his flower-pattern suspenders he liked, while shoveling coke, to wear a pink singlet, which left the muscles exposed, but which always got soaked at once with sweat. How often these singlets, which his wife is incessantly washing, hang on the line in the backyard of his previous house and simply won't get dry because there's so little breeze thereabouts! We've also been in his cellar or boiler room, from which, with the pipes overhead, he keeps the vats boiling, and we've been able to observe from the cellar window the legs of clients above us. Behind Herr Schellenbaum, along the cellar wall, long iron poles hang in a row, with these he pokes his boiler hole, and when he pulls them out, redhot, he can swing them effortlessly through the air. Yes, father could always depend on Herr Schellenbaum, even if, like Edgar's father, he's to be relished with caution. Because, for instance, while employed by the Emmanuel Wolff Company, he unscrewed all the brass parts from the boilers he stoked there and sold them in Leipzig, so people say. What did he unscrew? we ask. Ah, it was nothing, mother says. Which parts did he sell? we ask. It's only a rumor, father says, and I'm asking you to be quiet now. Herr Schellenbaum can also be *bestial*. At least, it's said that he was once looked for by the police for *monstrous bestiality* and he'd certainly have been arrested if father hadn't let him stay in the boiler room. Weeks later, once his bestial side had been forgotten again, he crawled out from behind his boilers, hungry, thirsty, and needing a shave. When he went up the stairs and out into the factory yard, he put his hands over his eyes, the light hurt him so much. Then with a slight grin he mixed with people again. And from that day on—we celebrated him as a hero—he embarked on a *brilliant career*, as mother says, and *rose so high* that we all became giddy. Duly he gave up his stoker's position and sat down at a desk and used to appear before us on the street in the evenings wearing high black boots which his poor wife had to polish with pig's fat. So we're wondering, since we've been conquered now, how we should behave when we approach Herr Schellenbaum with the letter, which, though this is almost incredible, we've almost forgotten again. What does occur to us, instead of the letter, is the Czech Grave. Of course! That's what we'd been going to think about: our Czech Grave, which we'd only forgotten because mother had asked us to. How many times, mostly at breakfast, mostly from the window, she's asked us if it isn't time we forgot those *taradiddles in our head*. Which *taradiddles?* we'd ask—spoon in hand. You know which, she'd say. You mean, we'd ask, but then she'd interrupt us because she didn't even want to hear us say "Czech Grave," not even in a low voice. Yes, that's what I mean, she'd say. Ask about it? we'd ask. Yes, she'd say. Where it is? we'd ask. No, she'd say, whether it exists. So forget about it?

we'd ask. Yes, she'd say. One thing's certain: our Edgar doesn't forget it, but carries it around in his head all the time, and right at the front of his mind, presumably. And there probably is some sort of Czech Grave hereabouts, even if we don't know where. But if Edgar's right it's on the way out of our town, perhaps in the Amselgrund, and Herr Schellenbaum, as well as father, is certainly involved in the matter. For it's certain that one night in May Herr Schellenbaum dug a hole in some place unknown to us, put into it a Czech who was suddenly dead, and shoveled earth over the grave again in a big hurry. Which Czech? we'd ask our Edgar. Ah, one of yours, he'd say. And why do you think he was one of ours? we'd ask. Because I know it was, he'd say. Yes, of course, we'd say, tapping a finger on the tabletop impatiently, but how did you find out? Yet our Edgar wouldn't tell us that. Because I know more than you, because I'm older, was all he'd say. Yes, for the time being, we'd say, but not for long. Ah, he'd say with a dismissive gesture, I'll always be older than you, even a hundred years from now. A hundred years from now you'll be dead, we'd say. So will you, he'd say. And which Czech did Herr Schellenbaum put into the hole, we once asked, one from the vat room? Perhaps, our Edgar said. As we know, they live by the Frohnau boulevard behind a barbed wire fence in a few huts, which one isn't allowed to go near, and out of which, when no wind is blowing, there comes a smell of boiled potatoes and potato peelings. Yet out of curiosity we've been near to them, sheltering behind our Edgar, and we've looked at the Czechs through the barbed wire. With thin limbs, cross-legged, on a warm evening, they were squatting on our soot-sprinkled uplands earth, and yawning. Or leaning upright against the wooden walls of their huts, they drew their felt boots back and forth across the ground and stared back at us with red-lidded eyes. Our Czechs, we thought. And leaning against one another, probably hand in hand, certainly with mouths wide open, at nightfall, with the sun going down, we've stood by the camp fence, although we've promised mother not to go to the Czechs. How wide and deep it is, the trench that runs around the huts! Also, because of the many consonants, we don't understand their language, whereas they can almost always follow our sentences. Often too, mostly shoulder to shoulder, we've strolled along the trench, first to show them, then to throw them little apples we've had in our pockets, from our Golden Pearmain tree. Which they've then cleverly caught, raised to their mouths, and, with one bite, immediately devoured. To think that among all the things that bewilder us, we were forgetting our Czechs, of all people! And that of the many things we forget, it's our Czechs who now come to mind. Briefly: on the first day after our conquest, nothing but *taradiddles* in our head, as mother said, who'd like to stand constantly at the window and hear someone knock on the door, we're walking on the neglected side paths through our town park and wondering whether to go to the church first or to the Amselgrund, where, to be sure, not only our Edgar's knife is, but also perhaps our Czech Grave. Shall we go first, we ask, to the church or the Amselgrund? I don't know, our Edgar says, what do you think? We shrug, we have no opinion, we'll still do what Edgar tells us to. For a long time we think that our Edgar wants to go to the church first, and we prepare for church-going, but before we reach the Hot Drinks Stand we see that we're mistaken. We'll go to the church last, if we go there at all. So as we walk through the park, looking at the ground, the damp leaves and the uprootings of our trees, over which we have to jump, we're thinking of two things: whether we'll find the knife again, and where the Czech Grave is. Did Herr Schellenbaum dig it, perhaps on the far side of the Amselgrund, outside our town, perhaps north of Rabenstein, where nobody ever goes? Or did he go with the Czech, that night in May, perhaps far beyond Rabenstein and into the next county, to dig the grave there with his garden spade? Questions, nothing but questions! So that, with the spring wind shaking the crests of the trees high above us, while walking and jumping we thought and also called out to one another across the wet leafy ground that we'd surely never find the grave, but the knife, it was certain, would soon be coming our way, that was one thing we knew about. Because well before our conquest we've wandered through this region with our Edgar in the lead, who was wearing our father's sandals on his feet already at that time and carrying the knife between his thighs, in search of the Czech Grave, though never finding it. Yet, as our Edgar says, the Czech *can* very well be buried here. But where, where? we exclaim and stop to catch our breath a bit. Ah, our Edgar says and points vaguely around, somewhere hereabouts. For he doesn't know either *exactly* where the Czech Grave is. But father just as certainly does know where it is, if such a grave exists, though when we ask him he won't say. There isn't one, there isn't one, he exclaims and shakes his large head. Yes there is, there is, we say, there must be one, we know there is. Ah, father says, and wearily he makes a dismissive gesture, what do you know? Well, quite correct, he's right about that, actually we don't know anything, but the fact is we think a lot about our Czechs. And that, without knowing why, we remember very well all the Czechs we've ever seen flitting through our factory or squatting by their huts, and we talk about them a lot with our Edgar. We'd also like to talk about them with our father. Please, we call—usually before we go to bed—and we hang on to him, where is there a Czech Grave here? For there must be one, Edgar told us there must. Stuff and nonsense, father exclaims and pushes us, to be rid of us, toward our bed. And: Edgar, it's always this Edgar! I think, he exclaims and goes quite red in the face with annoyance, that I'll have to give that boy a talking-to. Why, we ask, because he always says he wouldn't like to be in our skins when it comes? When what comes? father asks and puts his hand in a pocket. Why, we ask, wouldn't he like to be in our skins? When what comes? father asks. Ah, our conquest, we say. Then father gives a laugh. Our conquest, he says, is that what he said? Yes, we say, yesterday. That boy's incredible, father says and clenches a fist. Have you heard what Edgar has been telling the children again? he calls through the open door of the children's room to mother, but because she has another headache mother will be lying down and probably won't hear him. One thing I'm sure of, father says and turns back to us when mother doesn't respond, this Edgar is going to be up to his neck in it one day with all that talk of his. And what's the neck he'll be up to in? we ask, but father won't tell us that either. Ah, why should I spend all this time discussing such things with you, he exclaims and walks up and down before us a few times. I don't want this Edgar coming into my house anymore and saying things like that. Like what? we ask, but again father doesn't answer, he only says: Things. And he talks about the many other children who always invade his house when he's not there, and that children's birthdays are celebrated with dozens of candles. What's so fascinating to you about this Edgar? he exclaims. Why do you have relationships that aren't only useless to you but also eventually get you into trouble? Somebody like this Edgar, that's for sure, isn't suitable company for you children. Do you understand that? he asks. Yes, we understand, we say. Well then, father says: So what's your idea in inviting him? he asks and lets a little air escape from him, especially through his nose. Ah, we say, no idea really. So why invite him? father asks. Ah, we say, he comes anyway. Yes, that's what I thought, he comes anyway, father says and pulls our blanket back. You've even been in my study again, you may as well admit it. And with downcast eyes we do admit it. But, we say, it was only for a moment. Haven't I expressly forbidden you to go into my study or let anyone else go into it? father exclaims and stamps his small feet a bit. Haven't I told you that the papers in my desk aren't for children? And to sit in my highly sensitive leather chair too! Admit that you sat in the chair, he exclaims. Yes, we say, but it was only for a moment. And what did you go into my room for? father asks. Ah, we say, we only swiveled around a bit in your chair. Swiveled, he exclaims, so it'll be broken again in a week or two. Did this Edgar sit in my chair? Yes, we say, but only for a moment. Ha, I thought so, father exclaims, and now he really gets worked up and calls him all sorts of names, which, because they come from Latin, we can only partially understand. A fine friend you've found there, he exclaims finally. But we didn't find him, we say. Well, father exclaims, did he fall out of the sky? No, we say, we only mean that we aren't his friends. So much the worse, father says, if he isn't even your friend. But he is our friend, we say, it's just that we're not his. Did he say that? father asks. Yes, we say. And why aren't you his friends? father asks. Ah, we say, we can't be his friends at all. He doesn't want to be mixed up with us. Did he say that? father asks. Yes, we say. Well, friend or not that boy won't enter my house again, father exclaims, and he pauses to catch his breath quietly for a while. And what's the neck he'll be up to in? we ask when the pause is finished and father has enough breath again. His own, mostly, father says. Then he doesn't say anything more. Also he won't tell us whereabouts in our neighborhood the Czech Grave is, but exclaims: Stop this now, stop! But you can tell *us*, surely? Us! we say and sit up in bed. Stop now, there's no such thing as a Czech Grave here, father shouts so loud that his voice carries into the garden and as far as our still unoccupied garden shed. If ever one of the Czechs you're so interested in disappears here, and that can happen, he has run away, understand? And where to? we ask, because we don't want to go to sleep yet, but would like to go on talking, even all night long, though father doesn't, he wants to go back to his desk. Ah, where to? Home, of course, he exclaims and throws his arms up in the air. But then we want to know where the Czechs who suddenly disappear have their home, and father exclaims: No, enough. And we see that tonight again he's not going to tell us where our Czech Grave is, but is already far from us in his thoughts and at any moment he'll be thinking of his factory again, sort of sinking into it. Quickly he kisses our cheeks, then blows the candle out, and at once we're plunged not into the room's twilight which we love so much, but into the room's darkness, which we fear. We know that this darkness is out there in our garden too, if only we could look through the black packaging paper that darkens the windows, we don't like to think of this darkness in the shrubs, the trees, the park, the Hoher Hain, in the villages around, even in the sky. Father, we call from our bed, but he doesn't answer. Instead, blackened by the darkness, which, it also occurs to us, also penetrates the Great Pond, father, now totally absorbed by his factory, stands for one more moment in our children's room, into which a faint light falls from outside, and he looks down at us for a last time. And then, although we call out Leave it open! he closes the door. What a long time it takes us to gain confidence in our darkness! To tell *our* darkness from the *outside* darkness above and below. And to see our way in our darkness when we step through it in our thoughts, and to sense at least (we won't be sure till morning) all the things that surround us in this night. And where those nearby things have their place, what colors, shapes, and purposes they have. Outside the window and the door there's still a whispering, at first indoors between father and mother, then in the garden among the leaves and the grass. Then we tell ourself: Now we'll go to sleep, and then we've slept. And when our room-things stand around us again in their colors, we've forgotten the darkness and, with it, the Czech Grave. Only when we see father turning to us, as he did last night, except that his hair is now brushed smooth, and when he asks if we *slept well*, do we remember it: this admittedly ghastly grave we dreamed about in the night, side by side, even though independently of one another, as being in this or that place in the Amselgrund, and toward which we walked, not reaching it, and we begin all over again. Father, we say, can we ask you something? Yes, he says, what do you want to ask? Can we, we ask, ask *everything*? Yes, he says, but make it quick. And even if it's what we wanted to ask yesterday but then weren't allowed to? we say. Hm, father says, why weren't you allowed to? Because, we say, we were just starting to when you blew the candle out. All right, father says, there aren't any candles now, but to our question whether the Czech—you know which one, we say, since he doesn't think of him right away—was one from the vat room, he only shakes his head, and in a voice that's much too loud for the bright light, he forbids us once and for all, morning or night, to ask him about the Czech or even to think of him. These people are here, he says, to work and not for anyone to waste time on, with endless talk about them. Is that clear? he asks. Yes, we say. Not even to think? we ask later when breakfast is ready, and we sit down at the table. That's right, not even to think, father says. But what if he simply pops into our head, we exclaim. No, father says, not even to think. And because there's no more gasoline to be had, father bicycles to his small factory, which has been declared necessary for the war effort, and where everything is waiting for him on the corners of his desk. No, we can't hope for father to tell us anything, father keeps his silence. And when he's away and we try to ask mother about the Czech Grave, she doesn't want to tell us either, and because it's a warm day she waves us quickly away to the back door. And exclaims: Can't you even be considerate enough to let me be ill in peace for a day? Czech Grave? Ask whoever you like, there's no such thing here, she exclaims and whisks us off to school. So might the grave have been something dreamed up in Edgar's narrow blond head? Definitely, even if it's not in the Amselgrund it's in our head and can't be removed. Our Edgar cautiously put it there one September night in our backyard, near the outhouse, because before that September night we hadn't thought of any Czech Grave. Definitely: with hesitant footsteps and following the furrows, our eyes always fastened on our terrain and the folds in it, since that time, waking and dreaming, we've been wandering in a region where, during the summer, we'd still lightheartedly gone eating all the blackberries off the bushes and then lain down with scratched hands beside one another in the tall tickling grass, looking up at the clouds, although there are vipers there. And as we approach the exit from the park, where the gate hangs crooked from its hinges, we run slap into Frau Kohlhund from the Schlotterstraße.

Guten Tag, Frau Kohlhund, we say and pull our cap out of our shopping bag and put it quickly on our head, for our first thought is: The cap, we're not wearing the cap! And on a day like this we're supposed not to be capless. Bareheadedness on our part, if mother should see it or someone tell her of it, comes in for severe punishment. So that naturally we startle, because Frau Kohlhund tells mother everything. Really bad luck, this meeting with her in the park on the day after our conquest! *Guten Tag*, Frau Kohlhund says, and out she steps, sprinkled with pine needles, from under a stunted pine tree. Over her shoulder she's carrying a sack. Presumably she's going to buy something or she's going begging. Her right arm, which has been useless since the eleventh—she tried to extinguish her kitchen closet—hangs loose at her side. Has she recognized us, we're thinking, for obviously the poor woman is half-blind even with her glasses on. And us with the cap on our head, we look the same as every other boy. Because the cap, with the thick earflaps that we'd very much like to tear off, is worn by everyone and gives even our face the obtuse and blinkered look our father wants us to have. This cap, how stupid it makes us, we're thinking, and we give Frau Kohlhund a friendly nod. Hesitantly, in the damp park, with the empty sack hanging in folds from her shoulder, she comes closer to us. What are you doing out here on a day like this? she asks and with her good arm pulls a twig away from her face. Well, that's what mother asked us too, when we told her we wanted to walk around the house a bit, we say, and we sigh a bit. Aren't you afraid of walking through the park on your own? Frau Kohlhund asks, and she decides to come to a stop facing us. She has probably recognized us too, because she beckons us closer, so that she can inspect our head. Afraid? we say and step into her orbit, swinging our shopping bag, why should we be? We haven't done anything wrong. And besides, our mother sent us. And where did she send you? Frau Kohlhund asks, and she looks at our head, because she's not yet certain that we really are wearing the cap. Ah, to the slaughterhouse, we say. To the slaughterhouse? Frau Kohlhund asks, and why there? Because, we say, we were supposed to ask if there was any *Butterschmalz*. *Butterschmalz?* Frau Kohlhund asks, how come? Ah, we say, somebody shouted to her about it from the street when she was standing upstairs in the window, but they were wrong, you see we've been there. Yes, I've been thinking there isn't any *Butterschmalz* at the slaughterhouse, Frau Kohlhund says, and she cackles a bit, enabling us to see some parts of her set of false teeth. If there really had been any *Butterschmalz* at the slaughterhouse, I certainly would have known about it. Certainly, we say. So you went to the slaughterhouse for nothing? she asks. Yes, it was a pity, we say, and we pull at our cap a bit, to make sure she sees it. So at home you haven't got anything left to eat either? Frau Kohlhund asks—recently she has become very thin and, as our mother says, looks like a hat stand. Over her bones, which stick out everywhere, she's wearing a flowered dress, although an old woman like her, when she walks through the park in May in our part of the world, should naturally wear an overcoat. Ah, we say, we really don't know for sure if there's anything there or not. You'll have to ask mother, she'll be able to tell you. Yesterday evening there was half a loaf of bread left. Wasn't there? we ask our Edgar. Yes, there was half a loaf yesterday evening, I saw it myself, our Edgar says—whom Frau Kohlhund presumably doesn't know, because he comes from the

Gießereistraße. I've got nothing left, nothing at all, Frau Kohlhund says and pulls her sack from her shoulder, meaning to swing it about a bit, but of course not so high in the air as we swing our bag. Her dress, though it's definitely not a warm day, isn't even buttoned up at the neck. Definitely she's not only thin, definitely she's freezing cold too. And then she takes one more step toward us, stretches out her arm, and asks: Look, have you ever seen anything like this? Like what? we ask. Ah, Frau Kohlhund says, an arm like this. You're freezing cold, aren't you? we ask and glance at the arm. Ah, she says, I don't mean that, I don't feel anything anymore, either in my arms or in my legs. No, I'm so thin. You can take hold of it, if you like. Take hold of it? we ask. Yes, she says, so that you'll know. Naturally we don't want to, at first, naturally at first we say no. And since she's not so close to us, we walk once around Frau Kohlhund. Later we ask: And why should we take hold of it, Frau Kohlhund? and we swing our bag faster. Ah, she says, so that you'll have felt what's left in time of an arm like this. And through the damp air she stretches out to us the arm that was singed on the eleventh, if not all burned away. And she pulls up her sleeve a little, to expose the arm somewhat and make it worth taking hold of, and now we see the arm entirely. The arm burned and singed on the eleventh, reddened by the flames, and which still hurts her, so mother says, is really very thin, very skinny. Quite fleshless and dried, the arm pokes from the sleeve of her flowered dress. All right, we say, if you insist, we'll take hold of it a bit. And then we really do take hold of Frau Kohlhund's arm, to do her a favor, since it's all the same to us. With our fingertips we stroke it a little, very gently, while Edgar really takes hold of it and even presses it a little. Naturally we're astonished, feeling how thin Frau Kohlhund's arm is. Not only is the flesh on it starved, also the muscles and sinews have shrunk, if not the bones themselves. Notice, she says. What? we say. How skinny it is, she says and wonders about it herself and chuckles a bit to herself, because we're so astonished. And what's more, she says, it's getting skinnier all the time. In the last few months it had got skinnier, even though there'd still been something to eat, just beans and oatmeal. Up till last Saturday, she says and chuckles a bit more, but now there's nothing left at all. Nothing at all? we ask, and we're feeling ill at ease to be standing like that before her. Yes, nothing at all, she says. And to prove that there's nothing left, she takes her sack from her shoulder and turns it inside out before us. Empty, we say. Yes, she says. That's why I'm walking around again this noon. Yes, we say, there's nothing left in it. And it won't be easy to get anything to go into it, Frau Kohlhund says, for I've been to everyone who might have something. And I've got nothing to trade, I've looked everywhere. I've already traded everything except one thing and I'm depending on that. I'll ask so much for it that I'll have enough for a few months. And when those months are gone? we ask. Then, Frau Kohlhund says, I'll put on my prettiest dress, the one with the dots, and my high boots and make myself very elegant and I'll lie in bed and wait in my prettiest dress and high boots until I've starved to death and they can carry me to the graveyard. Hm, we say, let's hope you'll find someone who'll give you something for a few months, so that for as long as possible you won't have to dress up and lie in your bed. Is it valuable, the thing you've got? Yes, Frau Kohlhund says, and it's heavy. That's why I can't carry it around so as to offer it to people. Because it's too heavy to carry around? we say. Yes, Frau Kohlhund says, it's my sewing machine. How could I walk through the villages carrying my sewing machine, tell me that, she says. Yes, we say and sigh a bit, that wouldn't be so easy. Don't you need it yourself, though? Yes, I do, but I need something to eat even more, Frau Kohlhund says, she who has traded all else and is standing there in her last, flowered dress, one that's not buttoned up at the neck, under the stunted pine tree, and is talking to us about her sewing machine. Don't you know somebody who needs a sewing machine that's in good condition? she asks, and through her thick glasses she searches our faces. No, we say, sorry but we don't. And you haven't heard of anybody? she asks. No, we haven't heard of anybody, sorry, we say. Or, we ask our Edgar, have you heard of anybody who wants a sewing machine? No, our Edgar says, I haven't either. A pity, Frau Kohlhund says. And your mother, might she need one perhaps, if it was cheap? she asks. No, we say, she's looking for something else. What's she looking for? Frau Kohlhund asks, just in case I've got it, I'll gladly see if I have. Ah, we say, she's looking for a suit for us, because we're getting slowly older and haven't got any more clothes to wear. But she'd have nothing to trade for it, at most a letter, which she wrote last night while we were sleeping, or so she thought. Ah, Frau Kohlhund asks, what should I do with a letter, eat it perhaps? And I haven't got a suit anyway, least of all one that would fit you. Why doesn't she give you a suit of your father's, since after all he's been killed in action. Ah, we say, he hasn't been killed in action, he's just missing. Hm, I thought he'd been killed in action, Frau Kohlhund says—presumably she has mixed our father up with someone else. I thought someone outside the baker's told me about it not long ago. No, no, we say, he's missing, not killed in action. Well, Frau Kohlhund says, whether he's missing or killed, surely one of his suits is still there?

You can shorten it and take a tuck in the sleeves, then it'll fit, you don't have to do any trading to get one. Ah, we say, it's a pity but father's suits won't do because mother is superstitious. She thinks he won't come back if she gives us his suit. Hm, Frau Kohlhund says, she may be right, I haven't got one anyway. But if ever you hear of someone who wants a sewing machine, you could tell me. We'll do that, Frau Kohlhund, we say, but now we must be getting along. And where are you going? Frau Kohlhund says, because she'd like to go on talking with us a bit more. Ah, we say, we thought we might look at a few Americans, but we haven't found any yet. And why do you want to look at them? Frau Kohlhund asks us. Ah, we say, just because. They say there are black ones, we'd like to see them. And Edgar here has another reason, but we mayn't talk about it. Well, if you mayn't talk about it, we needn't think about it either, she says. Have you had anything to eat today? she then asks. Ah, we say, not much. And when will you eat something? she asks. When we get home, we say. Have you got such skinny arms too? she then asks and hangs her sack over her shoulder again, so that her hands will be free. And because she's an *inquisitive old woman* she takes hold of our arms. For a long time she stands before us under the stunted pine, with her thin, gray, wind-tousled hair, with which she jumped out of bed this morning, instead of brushing it, and came straight into the park to feel our arms with the short fair hairs on them. Hm, she says, they're skinny all right, but not as skinny as mine. And then too, you'll be growing bigger. Ah, we say, actually we didn't want to, but perhaps we'll grow a bit still. And we gently take our fingers and arms out of her hand and pull, so as to distract her, our Edgar closer from behind the trunk of a beech tree where he's gone, and we point to his arms and hold them up to the light and say they're much thinner than ours, because he, just like her, has had *nothing at all* to eat. So he's got nothing at all to eat, Frau Kohlhund says. That's it, we say, nothing at all. And where are his arms? Frau Kohlhund asks—probably she can't see our Edgar properly and is looking everywhere behind us and in front of us for his arms. Here, we exclaim, and we pull our Edgar out from behind his beech tree. Does he belong with you? Frau Kohlhund asks. Yes, we say, sort of. And was he there all the time, she asks, or did he just arrive? He was there already, we say. And isn't there anybody else here? Frau Kohlhund asks, and she looks around. No, we say, there's nobody else. And where has he been all the time, Frau Kohlhund asks, if I didn't see him? Here, we say, behind the beech tree. Hm, Frau Kohlhund says, and when did you say he last had something to eat? He won't tell us, we say. Why not? Frau Kohlhund asks. Ah, we say, because he feels awkward about it. And me, Frau Kohlhund asks, would he tell me? No, we say, he wouldn't tell you either. Not even roughly when? she asks. When *roughly* he last had something to eat? Ah, presumably it was roughly yesterday or the day before, we say. Aha, Frau Kohlhund says, and what did he eat yesterday or the day before? A piece of bread, we say, he got it from us. And what's his name? Frau Kohlhund asks. Edgar, we say, he lives in our garden shed now. And what's he doing in the park here, if he lives in your shed? Frau Kohlhund asks and begins to feel Edgar's arms. He was with us at the slaughterhouse, we say. Did his mother send him with you? Frau Kohlhund asks. He hasn't got one anymore, we say. And his father? Frau Kohlhund asks, has he got a father? No, we say, not at present, but he'll certainly come back one day and then he'll look after him. Well, let's hope so, Frau Kohlhund says. After she's felt our Edgar's arms very carefully, she says: They're really very thin, his arms, nothing to be done about that. And you shouldn't be allowed to run around in the park like this, considering all the things that happen here. What things? we ask. Ah, Frau Kohlhund says, there are deserters wandering around and escaped prisoners and workers from the east and other bandits. They're just waiting to get their hands on someone. And Czechs? we ask, are there Czechs wandering around here too? Yes, Frau Kohlhund says, Czechs too. Because we've been conquered they thought they could do what they liked and of course they could too. Did you hear the shouts this morning? she asks. When? we ask. Around six, she says. No, we say, we were asleep. Well then, Frau Kohlhund says, if you're always asleep and don't hear the shouts, naturally you can't know what happens here. But we don't always sleep, we say, often we're awake, really we are. And sometimes we just pretend we're asleep, but really we can hear things. Last night, for instance, we heard the shots, but they weren't at all dangerous. Just a few dogs got shot, we've seen one. Yes, if only they'd shoot at dogs and nothing else, Frau Kohlhund says and tugs at her sack a bit. And then they've got other weapons too, ones that you don't hear. They caught someone over there two days ago, she says and points over to where the Biberbach runs, Beaver Stream, which from time to time we can hear though we can't see it glittering. And what sort of a person was it they caught? we ask. Ah, just someone, Frau Kohlhund says. And I won't say anything about the two they caught at the slaughterhouse. Hm, so they caught some people at the slaughterhouse, we didn't know that, we say. Yes, Frau Kohlhund says, one can't know everything, if one sleeps so much. And what did they do with them? we ask. Ah, Frau Kohlhund says, I just don't want to know, it's no business of mine. And even if I did know, I don't think I'd tell you. Me, though, I wouldn't go to the slaughterhouse, not for all the *Butterschmalz* in the world. Yes, we say, it's surely better not to. Hm, Frau Kohlhund says, well, that's behind you, you needn't think of it anymore. Even though I was astonished that a clever woman like your mother sent you to the slaughterhouse. But give her my best regards all the same and tell her I admire her for doing all those things on her own and that I'll come by soon in case she's got something for me. All right, we say, we'll tell her. In any case I wouldn't go in this direction, if I were you, Frau Kohlhund adds and points toward the Amselgrund. And why not? we ask. Because in this direction too, she says and knocks a bit with the knuckle of a forefinger on Edgar's shoulderblade, something happened a few days ago. What? we ask, but Frau Kohlhund won't tell us. A terrible thing, she won't say more, something that certainly won't have been removed yet but is lying around somewhere under a heap of leaves, probably. Before one knew where one was, one might stumble on it and might eventually be made responsible for something one had nothing to do with. Also there were unexploded bombs lying around. If you say so, our Edgar says—obviously, beside his beech tree, he doesn't believe her any more than we do and he wants to go to the Amselgrund, whatever her advice is. Well, you do what you like, but I wouldn't go in that direction for anything in the world, Frau Kohlhund says, and she's meaning to walk on, but then we have another question for her. If we might ask you, we say. Ask what you like, Frau Kohlhund says, I'm an old woman who doesn't know anything and to whom nobody listens anyway, but you can always ask. Well then, we say, this is the question: Where is the

Czech Grave hereabouts? Because we know there is one, though we don't know where. A Czech Grave, Frau Kohlhund says, no. I don't know anything about it. And she settles her dress down a bit and grips her sack more tightly and gazes, as if she were counting us, once more over our heads, and she says rather abruptly: Well, I'm off now. So are we, we say, *auf Wiedersehen*. And we nod, because she doesn't shake hands, and we walk past her and take a few steps and then, when we turn around, because she hasn't even said *auf Wiedersehen* and we want to see if she's also going, we see her still standing under the stunted pine and raising an arm, the bad one, in the air and shaking it at us. Naturally we're rather astonished, no, we're terrified by the sight of this threatening limb, which is not unrelated to the rigid branches above it and almost seems to be copying them. And she's calling out: You rascals! You rascals! Ducking our heads quickly, looking across the bushes, we call out: What? But she only calls back to us: You rascals! Yes, Frau Kohlhund, we say, and ducking our heads even lower we run, with a pang of guilt, we don't know why, toward the park exit that won't be under her eye or reached by her voice. And when we arrive at the gate—how crookedly it hangs from its hinges!—we look around again: there she really is, as if stuck in the ground beside her stunted pine, with her arm raised in the air. And she's uttering a long, coiling sentence, phrase by phrase, interrupted again and again only by her need to take a breath, a train of thought clear and angry in its fashion, perhaps a curse. But unfortunately the steady wind now fanning out through the park carries it away from us, piece by piece, across the smutgreen meadows. With long strides, almost stumbling over one another, treading on one another's heels, anyway in close order, as if we wanted to leave only one set of footprints behind, we leap to the park gate and tear the cap from our head and throw it into our bag and run, just as our Edgar does, bareheaded out of our park and into the Amselgrund which prolongs the park to the south and is the next stage of our day.

7

In the Amselgrund we quickly find the hole with Edgar's knife in it. And sure enough it's in the place we've been thinking of, all the time, a slight rise in the ground, that's to say, under a maple tree that's straight and high-crested, though its upper parts have been disheveled by bomb splinters. Here's the hole, we exclaim on the first afternoon after our conquest, in the middle of the Amselgrund, and we raise our arms. I'd shout even louder if I were you, our Edgar says, so that everyone can hear us, and he's probably thinking of the workers from the east and deserters and other bandits who are all around. Ah, there's nobody here, we say—but rather more quietly. Well then: as we're finding the hole, somebody may be watching us. Maybe from up there on the hill, maybe out of the bushes. Well then: careful! careful! And after we've made a thorough search of the maple tree's surroundings, without finding anything, and after we've sat down around the place, our Edgar starts to dig in the earth, partly with a branch, partly by hand. The earth is light and loose, so it's not difficult, he digs deeper and deeper, while we watch his hands. And then, when suddenly he winks at us and stops digging and with his elbows wipes to right and left his damp forehead—any strain, even the slightest, makes our Edgar sweat—we know: he's got it. Have you got it? we whisper. I don't know, our Edgar says, but I've got something. And then, when he has pulled the knife out of the dark earth and filled in again the hole in which it had been lying all the time and has drawn the knife from its sheath and wiped it and thoroughly inspected it, he exclaims: Yes, that's it! And to recover somewhat from the excitements of the search and the strains of digging, he stretches out on the damp earth and closes his eyes for a while. How sharply and threateningly his knees stick out from him the moment he's squatting. Was it such a strain for you? we ask. Let me be now, he says, let me be. All right then, he says later and opens his eyes again. All right, we say. Why not sit? he asks and points to the ground with his right hand, scratched now by the stones and earth and underbrush. Why? we ask, are we staying here? Yes, our Edgar says, we'll stay here for a while. And what shall we do? we ask. Talk, our Edgar says, and other things. And where should we sit? we ask and look around. There, our Edgar says and points to a moss-cushioned place which, even if it's not dry, is also not wet, and so we promptly sit down there. And leaning against one another lightly, our legs drawn up, for quite a long while without saying a word, on the moss that has been assigned to us, we sit among last year's decaying leaves, surrounded by yellow and brittle grass, scorched still from last summer, in our tattered Amselgrund. Yes, bombs fell here. But even before that the region we were born into was wild and forsaken, especially toward the south. Especially in summer our whole territory looks burned to the ground, but there's a good side to it. Because people don't come here, and probably to this day they don't. There, now we're sitting, we say and push our legs out into the leaves. Well then, our Edgar says. Well, we say. And then we rapidly take in one more mouthful of air and blow it out again. And then the knife, buried for so long, is held up before us by our Edgar, its edge is tested in the light, and in the following way. First he holds out the sharpened—and how sharp it is!—double-edged blade in the dull sunlight and lets it glitter, as best it will. Then comes the cutting test. We're allowed to search for a blade of grass, long and firm, in the patch beside us, and to pluck it out, then we have to stroke it over the blade of the knife, while our Edgar, sitting between us, holds the knife out vertically in front of us. As expected, the knife is still as sharp as before its burial, for the grass is cut in two the instant we pull it over the blade. When our Edgar sees how sharp it is he gives a long whistle, free, beautifully looped, dividing in two at a certain point but finally coalescing and firmly connected again, for the production of which he hollows his cheeks, so for a long time it looks as if he has no teeth and no lower jaw either. Then he says: All right now! and he chuckles contentedly and brushes his free hand from front to back over his head. Fine, isn't it? we say. And then, as in the cellar when we're being conquered and everything is touch and go and suddenly there's the noise that he explains to us, he's all at once lying between us, we can feel his warmth. Right, he says and pulls the box with the matches out of his trouser pocket. Right what? we ask. Right, this, he says and holds the box in the air. Right then, we say. And we heap, the way he taught us last autumn, a few twigs and branches in front of us on the ground, squat closer, strike a match, and hold its flame into our little heap. And then, as the wind softly moans—but *we* can hear it—and while the wood catches fire, he begins: Do you remember, he asks, looking at the ground between his legs. Remember what? we ask, so as to draw the matter out a bit, for of course we know what he wants us to remember. Ah, you know, our Edgar says and looks up at us for a moment, as if annoyed. Ah yes, of course, we say and try once more to distract him from *that night*, and we do it as follows. Why, we ask and look him in the eye, and we've wanted to ask you this for a long time, why do you take your head into your hands so often? Do I often take my head into my hands, our Edgar asks and takes his head into his hands. Yes, pretty often, we say. Ah, you know why I take my head into my hands, our Edgar says, it's because I've got a headache. Like our mother? we ask. Yes, our Edgar says, just about. But not all the time? we ask. Yes, he says, all the time. Ah, have you got a headache again now? we exclaim and click our tongues. Yes, our Edgar says, now too. And where, we ask, does your headache come from? Ah, our Edgar says, from the weather. But the weather isn't anything special today, we exclaim and look up at the sky, where everything is as usual, only a bit heavier, a bit thicker. And besides, we say, we haven't got a headache, although it's the same weather for us. Well, our Edgar says, perhaps it doesn't come from the weather, but from something else. If it doesn't come from the weather, we ask, should we rub your head a bit? Ah, our Edgar says, that doesn't help. Yes, that's what we thought, we say, because you've *always* got a headache. Even at night you've got a bit of one, haven't you? we ask. Yes, our Edgar says, at night too. Can you sleep then? we ask. Ah, our Edgar says, I could sleep all right, it's just that I don't go to sleep. If I could go to sleep, then, he exclaims, then . . . Then what? we ask. Then, he says, I'd sleep. But not for long, he adds rather quietly, after he's thought about it for a while. For, if I do sleep, *if* I do, he says, I wake up again right away, or I have dreams. Do you? we say, and what do you dream about? Ah, our Edgar says, always the same thing. That I'm lying in the shed and can't sleep. And you dream that? we ask. Yes, our Edgar says, if I can sleep. Well, we say, we dream too, but not about sleeping. We always go to sleep at once too. We sleep the whole night, mostly till about seven thirty. And you, how long do you sleep, if you do go to sleep? Ah, our Edgar says, till four perhaps. Only till four, we exclaim and laugh a bit. Yes, our Edgar says, then I'm wide awake again. Only till four, we say and shake our head, and then what do you do? Ah, our Edgar says, what do you think I do, the headache comes again. Your headache, dammit, we'd quite forgotten about it, we exclaim and slap our knees. And what do you do to stop it? Ah, our Edgar says, what do you think? Perhaps I take a drink of water. At night? we ask. Yes, he says, at night. Water, we exclaim and pull a face. Yes, water, our Edgar says. And does it help? we ask. No, our Edgar says, of course it doesn't. So drinking the water is pointless? we ask. Yes, our Edgar says, probably. To think that he always drinks so much water in the mornings and also that it's pointless, because the water doesn't wash away the pain that's in his head, but that the pain in his head floats lightly and safely on the water! Briefly: we laugh again, for quite a while, because we'd far prefer to talk about his headache than the *other thing*. But if it doesn't go away, we say, then your headache is incurable. Yes, our Edgar says, that may be so. But if it's incurable, we say. Yes, our Edgar says, that may be so. Briefly: our Edgar will have his headache for a long time, won't he? we ask. Yes, our Edgar says, probably. Then, because his headache is incurable, we suddenly can't help laughing so loud that all the birds that have been singing till now are suddenly silent and even our Edgar, instead of keeping his head still, can't help laughing with us. For a long time we sit around the knife hole and laugh about Edgar's headache, jerking our shoulders. And then when our laughter ends and can't be prolonged any more, just so he won't start talking about the *other thing*, we take up the subject of Edgar's headache for one last time, of what mother says about it—she says you have it because you don't get enough to eat, we say. Perhaps, our Edgar says. Can't you find something for yourself? we ask. Where could I? our Edgar asks. Is it because nobody gives you anything? we ask. That's it, our Edgar says. And you haven't got anything to trade? we ask, although we know of course that he can't have anything to trade, because the house in which everything was has been not only *flattened*, but also it has completely disappeared from the street, the town, the country, and the world. No, our Edgar says, I haven't got anything to trade either. Funny, we say, we've got both, something to eat and to trade. Well, our Edgar says, be glad of it. And then he's silent again and looks at the earth in front of him, meaning now to remind us of the night, but we don't let him. So your father and mother didn't put anything aside for you? we ask, interrupting his silence. Ah, what could they have put aside, they hadn't got anything themselves, our Edgar says and yawns. They only had you, hadn't they? we ask. Yes, our Edgar says, only me. Well, we say, our father and mother didn't only have us, they had various other things too. That's why they put aside something for us, bit by bit. Ah, your people, when they put something aside, it's easy enough, our Edgar says. But didn't yours put anything at all aside for you? we ask. How could they? our Edgar shouts, how could they? And then, after he's calmed himself down again and thought for a moment: Perhaps earlier, perhaps my mother did, but always something small. Half a loaf is the most they could put aside. Not more? we ask. No, he says, not more. And did you know where she put it? we ask. Ah, our Edgar says, she hid it. From whom? we ask. From me, of course, our Edgar says. So she was afraid you'd steal what she'd put aside? we ask. Yes, our Edgar says. And did you steal it? we ask. Whenever I could, our Edgar says. We laugh again. So you robbed your own mother? we ask. Yes, our Edgar says. And you simply admit it, just like that? Yes, he says, surely it's quite natural? Natural? we exclaim. Yes, our Edgar says, why not? So if you could, you'd rob her again? we ask. Naturally, our Edgar says. And your father, if he came back, would you rob him too? we ask. Naturally he's coming back, our Edgar says. Of course, we say, although we don't think he will, and if he came back you'd rob him? If I was hungry, our Edgar says. And us, we ask, would you rob us? Naturally, he says, if you wouldn't notice it and if I was hungry. And are you hungry now? we ask. Naturally, our Edgar says. And he pauses again and seems to be wondering how hungry he is, and then we ask him about that. How long is it *really* since you ate anything? we ask, you can tell us, don't worry. Ah, he says, several days. So you ate nothing yesterday? we ask. Yesterday, he says and thinks about it, when was that? Yesterday, we say, when we were conquered and then stood in the window upstairs and looked across to the theater. Ah yes, our Edgar says, and he remembers, yesterday. And then, after a slight pause: No, I ate nothing yesterday. And the day before yesterday? we ask. The day before? he asks. Yes, the day before yesterday when we were in the cellar, we say. Ah, our Edgar says, forget it, why bother? How should I know when I've eaten and when I haven't? But don't you remember? we ask. Ah, our Edgar says, sometimes I do, mostly I don't. And that, we say, isn't the only thing you forget, is it? No, our Edgar says, I forget quite a lot of things. Funny, we say, we remember everything. What we eat and drink and where we go and what we say and think, or mean to think or say, even if we don't always, because something gets in the way or someone else says or thinks something. And you remember all that? our Edgar asks. Yes, that's what we remember, we say. Even what you only *mean* to think? he asks. Yes, we say, that too. Why? he asks. Ah, we say, because otherwise it would be forgotten and somehow missing. Where from? our Edgar asks. Ah, we say, from the world. Even what you only mean to think? our Edgar asks. Yes, we say, that too. Even what we forget is missing. That's why we do remember it, basically, too, in any case it's always coming back up. Strange, our Edgar says, with me nothing ever comes back up. If something's forgotten, it stays forgotten. And then he closes his eyes and we don't say anything, and he opens his eyes again and we ask if perhaps his forgetting comes from his having a headache. Possibly, he says, possibly. And he asks us if we never had one and we say: No. And feeling giddy? he asks, don't you ever feel giddy? No, we say, we never do. Not even when you lie down flat, like this? he says and shows us, and he lies down flat on the grass and at once he has to put a hand over his eyes because he at once feels giddy. And we lie beside him in the grass, without closing our eyes, and look up into the sky and say: No, not even then. Strange, he says, and now he makes a really long and deep pause, actually one that can't be bridged, and we're beginning to think he's falling asleep or simply fading away or somehow otherwise disappearing, perhaps into the earth. At least, we think he's forgotten *that night*, but then, sure enough, he remembers it and comes back to us in the daylight and back to the night again. Well then, he says, and at once we now see that he's remembering it and forgetting his giddiness and his head, and how the night is there again. Well then, that night, is what he says. Ah yes, we say, that night. And we drill our fingers into the earth under us, but not very deep. And we'll concentrate now for quite a while on that night, in which father is presumably involved, although, when one thinks about it, it was quite some time ago. To tell the truth, we'd completely forgotten again about that night. Was there really such a night, yes or no? We don't know, we brood on the night, push it aside and, if Edgar wants, have to pull it back closer again. And have to ask our Edgar, because we remember so little or nothing at all about it, to tell us about that night. For our Edgar, though he does forget everything else, knows all about *that night* and he can tell us what in that night was seen, heard, said, not said, done, and not done. Yes, even the noises of that night, the wind roaring outside the house, across the roof tiles a clattering that never was explained, mother's slip of the tongue that suddenly appears and we distinctly hear it, and later it never comes again, all this our Edgar with his arms around his knees can accurately reproduce. For that reason we exclaim, while we look into a new match flame that wraps itself around a twig and will now either shoot higher or at any moment go out: Ah yes, that night! But, we say and finally admit it, we've forgotten everything about that night, unfortunately. So, with Edgar between us, we invent that night, all of us together. Right, we remember the night. That's to say, there was a night, if only because in our town there was so much talk of it at that time. Even in school, if not from the teacher's desk, certainly in the corridors, there was talk of it, and if not talk, then it was whispered about, there were rumors. Some people pretend there are no rumors, others spread them, others again, like father, oppose them. Father, who stands on the fringe of the rumors and whom people would like to push deeper into them. No wonder he starts to get thinner and thinner, or, as mother says, to *lapse from the flesh*, as if he were no longer eating enough. Or as if what he ate weren't being properly digested and ran straight through him. Look, he says to our mother one evening and pulls up his sleeve, look how thin I'm getting. Often too he's nervous, he walks about in his room a lot, locks a lot of things in his desk, lights one cigarette from another, forgets to stub them out, doesn't talk to us anymore or talks much too much, in too loud a voice, and his face, especially around the mouth, when he's talking, looks frozen, even in warm weather. When he looks down to us with this new face, looking as if he had something evil-tasting in his mouth that he had to keep pushing around as he speaks, his eyes around the pupils look out of kilter, as if he weren't perceiving us properly anymore. Our Edgar, on the other hand, who sees, hears, perceives, everything, naturally knows everything, for instance about the night, whereas we've forgotten again even the little that we knew about it. Well then, our Edgar exclaims and makes his knife flash. Yes, go on, we say. What about? our Edgar asks us. Ah, we just say. And after a while: that he'd better tell us what happened that night. Me? our Edgar asks. Yes, you, we say. All right, our Edgar says and stretches out a bit beside the knife hole, whereupon something about him, probably a bone, makes a slight crack. And then, while from far off, like thunder rumbling, a few single booms of artillery fire can be heard, he tells us what sort of a night it was. Between us in the prickly, singed grass, his head, with the night in it, propped in the hollow of a hand, and his gaze on the flame, he tells us everything. For instance, how father, hat on the back of his head—he'd been at the factory—finally, finally comes home, completely exhausted, with Herr Schellenbaum in civilian clothes two or three paces behind him, and at once sweeps us—we've already got up and are sitting side by side on the kitchen windowsill—into the hallway and up the stairs into the children's room, which he locks behind us— you remember? our Edgar asks—with the children's room key. So it was morning already? we ask. Yes, our Edgar says, night was over. Then was the night really a morning? we ask. Yes, our Edgar says, do you remember? Yes, we say, of course we do. Although actually we don't remember the morning and the key and how father pushes us into our room. And we see: no, the twig isn't burning, the twig doesn't accept the flame. And so as not to get burned, we drop the match and crush it with a stone. So that the Amselgrund, already so tattered, won't catch fire. Take a new one, our Edgar says. Yes, of course, we say. And we take a new match out of the box and strike the match and try finally to get the little heap of twigs to burn. Well then, our Edgar asks, so you remember? Yes, we say, obviously we do. What? he asks. Well, we say, and now we really push forward into the free region of memory and see our room before us, already we're standing with one foot in it. Yes, we're in pajamas, while our Edgar, because he has nothing else for the night, is wearing his gym singlet and shorts. Isn't that so, you haven't got any pajamas? we ask. That's so, our Edgar says, looking at his hands, bending and twisting his fingers. Really, our Edgar is a contortionist, a snake man. And shoes, we ask, have you finally got shoes now? No, he says, I haven't got any shoes. But that's not the point, he says. Yes, we say, you're right. Then what is the point? our Edgar asks. The other thing, we say. And then, clapping a hand flat against our forehead: Yes, now we remember, we exclaim and are still holding the new match, already burning for a while, to the twig. But since, one way or another, we still don't remember, Edgar bit by bit tells us the following. How, when father has locked us in, still wearing pajamas and with an ear to the door, we stand in the children's room, then walk to this or that corner of it, then finally to the window, roll up the blackout paper, and see the ascent of the sun as it climbs from the glimmering roof of our theater. Do you remember? our Edgar asks us—now leaving large gaps between his words, so that everything will come to mind. Yes, the sun, we exclaim and describe with a free hand a circle over the Amselgrund earth and picture the sun. But since we're already rather tired, it's the sun the other way around, the wrong one. Not one, that is, rising over the theater roof, all red, but one that's setting. Instead of making the sun rise, as Edgar wants it to, we make it set, the way it is in us. And then, after father and Herr Schellenbaum have spent a long time in the bathroom whispering and muttering and washing and scrubbing and rinsing, and have splashed water over the walls and the mirror, and also haven't bothered about the floor, father opens our door again and we all of us—our Edgar too, since he used to sleep on our sofa now and again even in those times—come together for a big breakfast. Do you remember the breakfast? our Edgar asks us and watches our flame wrapping itself around his bit of twig. Yes, we lie, of course we do. At that breakfast—we all had a big plate of fried eggs before us—not much was said, Edgar tells us, because of Herr Schellenbaum. Herr Schellenbaum who had never before passed a night together with father and had never sat at our breakfast table! Where he now sits beside us, as if it were the most natural thing in the world. Herr Schellenbaum, how he suddenly laughs until the ash drops off his cigar, he doesn't even scoop it up but lets it lie there, so that bit by bit it's trodden in. And gives us, with a black ribbon to hang from, a whistle which we promptly lose, presumably while trying to stand on our head beside the outhouse. Herr Schellenbaum: the spread of his fingers, red from washing, around the black coffee cup that mother places before him, the opening of his big hands over his bread. Did he sit, our Edgar asks, beside you or between you? We don't remember, we say. He was sitting between you, our Edgar says. Yes, we say, now we remember. And not once during the whole breakfast, as Edgar reminds us, did he turn toward us, but acted as if we didn't exist in that high, cool room that smelled of fried food. True, he said this and that—the word "earth" kept cropping up—but never to us. Also Edgar remembers how every remark we made was *shouted down* and how, from right or left, he is constantly jabbing at us. And then he knocks out of our hand the piece of bread we're about to shove into our wide-open mouth so that it shoots across the kitchen floor and vanishes under the cooker. Our Edgar also remembers—in spite of his weak memory he has remembered a lot about that night— how Herr Schellenbaum does not with so much as a single syllable apologize for the knock, and also does not go and look for the piece of bread. Altogether, during this breakfast, we felt very lonely. Their heads full of the past night, the *grown-ups* had crouched over their plates, to shove their eggs deep into their throats with their bread. And now this, our Edgar says, while we're trying to remember everything and finally to set fire to the little heap of twigs in front of us. This: our Edgar decides—we don't know why and are striking a third, a fourth, a fifth match—that this night in May was the night of the Czech Grave. Why he has such suspicions about that night we don't know, and our Edgar, if he has any reason, doesn't want to tell us what it is. He also doesn't tell us how we ourselves—through father and mother—are involved in the Czech Grave, but perhaps that'll come later. Certainly we'd have forgotten long ago about our involvement if Edgar weren't always drawing it out of us with his questions. Or putting it into us, we think and see with great joy how the heap of twigs is all at once catching fire. Yes, this time the match flame wraps itself more tightly around the twig and drives flames out of it, yes, this time one twig sets fire to another. Look, we exclaim, it's burning. Our Edgar who has been lying angularly on a level lower than ours, as it were on a more down-to-earth air level, now wriggles his way up to us. How bony his arms and legs are, how pointed his elbows! And his back, where the ribs are, how feebly it bends! He's starving, we think. Whereas we live off the sacks of powdered peas kept in our attic. You're always hungry, aren't you? we ask and study his ribs. Then he brandishes his fist in our face and shouts: Silence, you rascals! The fist, when he unclenches it, has long and delicately jointed fingers, which are strong, as we know. When he presses down on the back of our neck with them we sink to our knees and beg to be forgiven. The backs of his hands are covered with a down of fair hairs, and his smile . . . Lots of people have hairs on their hands, but not his smile. Which (the hairs) we've sometimes been allowed to stroke with our fingers—a horrid but genuine passion, for instance in the ditch when we're on the way to Herrnburg, under the granite cross. Then our Edgar sits on a patch of grass and says: All right, if you want! Or we twiddle behind his ears, where the hairs are even downier, or rub our noses on his shoulders, or make folds in the skin on his throat, or pull his face into strange shapes, or study the curves and flutings of his forehead, sometimes putting them there by squeezing with our fingers. What are you doing with me? our Edgar asks, lying by then on his back and groaning and looking at the granite cross. Ah, we say, just pressing a bit. Why? he asks. Ah, we say, just because. And what if it hurts me? our Edgar asks. Ah, you can take it, we say and stroke the hairs on his hand. As we do now, not under the cross but in the Amselgrund, and we'd kiss them if he'd let us, but he won't let us. Not now, first the other thing, he simply says and pushes us back and tucks away somewhere for the time being his hand with hairs that smell of the sunlight. And he crouches gingerly over the flame—probably he's feeling giddy—and, while pushing a few hairs back from his forehead, he holds the point of the knife for a long time into the flame. Motionless, perhaps immovable, we watch as the flame licks at the knife, wraps itself around its point, occasionally mounts higher, sometimes encircles almost all of of it. Meanwhile, because he's afraid somebody might come, or because he's looking for the Czech Grave, our Edgar takes a quick look now and then behind him or up to the Amsel hill. Well then, after we've pushed here and there a few dry pine needles into the flame and made the fire last longer and have *drawn the matter out*, he suddenly shouts: Enough! and now the knife point, even if it hadn't glowed red-hot, was purified of all foreign bodies. And as the flame subsides and the ashes continue to glow a little, our Edgar wipes away the soot that's on the knife with his handkerchief, which then, together with the box of matches, goes into his pocket. Right, he says, now the knife had been purified and could be *used*. Yes, we say and sink to the ground. All right, then, our Edgar says, looking around once again, but there's nothing to be seen far and wide, we're alone, not a sound to be heard from Amsel hill or from over the still-uncultivated fields and the meadows lightly smutted by the spring rains. Yes, except for the distant rumbling, of which we can't tell whether it's the war *still* or *once again* merely thunder, there's not a sound to be heard in the Amselgrund on this first day after our conquest. So our Edgar now makes us take our trousers off, because this time the knife has to be applied high up. All right, we toss them behind us into the blackberry bush. The underpants we're wearing are short. Then, after studying us in our underpants and saying Well, Well several times, our Edgar comes back to the question of our guilt. We bow our head, we cringe. For instance, he says, that night. May we? we ask and raise a hand as if we were on a bench in school. Yes, if the question isn't too long, he says and is very curt. What if he doesn't come back? we ask. Who? our Edgar asks. Your father, we say. Then I'll go away from here, our Edgar says and points into the countryside to show what he'll be leaving. But how can you? we exclaim, it's not possible. Yes it is, he says. But, we exclaim, you were born here. So what? our Edgar says, then I'll get myself adopted. Adopted? we exclaim. Yes, he says. And who by? we ask. Ah, he says, who knows? By an American. And how will you find one to adopt you? we ask. Ah, our Edgar says, I've already started looking. Simply on the street? we ask. Yes, he says, perhaps I'll find one who wants me. And if it's a black who wants you? we ask. All right, he says, then it'll be a black. Oh well, there's not much to keep you here, we say after thinking for a while about his mother and *flattened* Wundenplan, and that nobody here takes care of him except our mother and she doesn't much want to. Only it won't be easy for him to find someone who wants him, because he's so terribly skinny and certainly something has snapped in his head. Or I'll simply go away, he says, because he sees we're having doubts. And where will you go? we ask. Our Edgar thinks a bit and says: Into a forest. Into one like that? we ask and point to the disheveled tree trunks in the distance. No, he says, into another one. In a forest that wasn't *damaged* one could hold out for a while, as long as one had just a wool blanket and a knife and something warm to wear. And what will you live off? we ask. Ah, our Edgar says, you don't need much in a forest. If you're hungry you simply go to the nearest village and get a few spoonfuls of soup and a drop of milk. Do you think they'd give it to you? we ask. If you lend a bit of a hand with the harvest, our Edgar says, why not? But there's no harvest, we say, they haven't planted anything. One day they'll do it again, our Edgar says. Yes, perhaps, we say. And now, he says, do you know everything you wanted to know? Yes, we say, just about. Right then, he says, and now he's silent again and thinking again about the night. And since we don't know what *really* happened that night, our thoughts about what could have happened are unobscured. Specifically? our Edgar asks and holds out the knife toward us. A fight, we say and reach out for the knife. Yes, one of many, our Edgar says, but he's holding the knife back still. A fight into which father was drawn that night against his will, we're thinking. A battle, something being done beside a vat, we imagine, anyway in the vat room which we're well acquainted with. How often we've wondered how father can send people into a room like that and make them stir, people still so young they're hardly out of school, of course, and who yawn a lot and are always sleepy and never get enough food, fresh air, and exercise from father, but have to stir the vats, with mouths wide open, ready to collapse at any moment, while we're going to school after a good night's sleep. And of course we've wondered if father will be punished one day terribly for keeping people—such young people too—in the vat room, perhaps he'd be punished by being put into a room like that and forced to stir. So that when we happen to pass by our father's small whip factory we don't only hold our nose, like everyone else, we also shut our eyes, because we don't want to see anything, something that our Edgar, who's walking between us, always notices, of course. Why are you shutting your eyes? he asks. Yes, we say, that's right. Do you want not to see the factory? he asks. Yes, we say, that's right. And pay no attention to him but walk on and keep our eyes and ears and nose shut. Now, our Edgar says when we've walked past, we've passed it now. Thanks, Edgar, we say and open our eyes (ears, mouth, nose, brain) again. Our Edgar, who knows we can't bear the sight, noise, smell, *even the thought of the vat room,* and who now pushes us into the vat room with his questions! Then we're no longer in the pinewood hollow on the brittle grass, but in the vat room, and instead of looking between the scorched trees we're looking around among the heaps of hides. And discover: yes, this is a terrifying place! And see: no, even more terrifying. For not only is the ceiling damp and low, whereas the sky here is high and dry, also the floor we're standing on, like the floor of a slaughterhouse, is all slippery from the vats boiling over. We can hardly take a single step between the vats, in our imagination, without falling over. Whereas the Czechs, who come, like our hides, from Dippoldiswalde, even have to run between the vats, in obedience to the wishes of our father, who directs everything from his desk. Because the Czechs are now back in our heads again, driven there by Edgar. With red-lidded eyes they totter on weak legs over the slippery floor. Admit, our Edgar exclaims, that your father never gave them a moment's peace. Yes, we admit, probably that was so. And that he made them run for him, right up to the last moment. Yes, we admit, that's correct. Just see, our Edgar says, shaking his head, what sort of a father you've got. Yes, that's right, we're thinking. And we remember how, when we ask him again about the Czech Grave one Sunday morning, he holds his fist—which is scented—under our nose. Until, during that night in May, there was an *incident* in front of one of the boilers. Perhaps, instead of stooping over one of the vats, a Czech will have backed away from it. Suddenly, instead of leaning over the concoction, he's leaning against the wall. Isn't that it, we ask, didn't he lean against the wall? Which wall? our Edgar asks. The Czech, we say, don't you remember? No, our Edgar says. Strange, we're thinking, he doesn't remember the cracked, tall wall, smeared gray by vapors from the vats, the wall you're not allowed to lean against. Then it occurs to us that he can't remember it because the wall was only in our thoughts. And that we've only been thinking we've shown him the vat-room wall against which the Czech is leaning, for in reality we've never even been into the vat room. Isn't that so, we ask, we've never been in the vat room? That's right, our Edgar says, you haven't. And you, have you ever been in the vat room? we ask. Get on with it now, he says. Naturally father has been watching everything from his desk, as Edgar informs us, and he dashed out of his enclosure at once and in mid-dash gestures to the Czech to get back to the vat, but the Czech doesn't move, he shouts something that father can't understand, on account of the many consonants in the Czech language. All father hears coming from the Czech language, the Czech tone, is back talk. So it was a misunderstanding, we're about to exclaim in relief, but we don't exclaim it, we only ask: And? and? Well, our Edgar says, you know the rest or you can think it. And he holds out the knife to us. This time he doesn't withdraw it, but, well, he gives it to us. Right now, the knife! How cool it is in our hands! Naturally we shudder. Then, after passing our fingertips across the flat surface of the blade a few times, not across its edge, we pass the ball of our thumb across the edge, not over the surface. As we do so, our thumb isn't cut open, no blood comes rushing out, but all the same there's a small cut. Then, after putting our thumb in his mouth and licking it, our Edgar says: Well now! and he crosses his arms and leans back in the grass. We ask: How many times? Six times, our Edgar says. Six times, we exclaim and cringe. Yes, our Edgar says. And he sinks deeper into the grass and searches for a support for his elbows, so as to have somewhere from which to launch the gestures he'll be making. And we—we've taken a deep breath—take firmer hold on the knife and, with a determined lunge, stab it into our thigh, to punish ourself. Oh the pain! And oh this blood! And, among the old scars, the many fresh wounds. Briefly: while our Edgar, who wants to have a good look and share our experience, raises his head a little, we stab last February's scars on our thighs four times, then it's five, then six. Briefly: we're wounding ourselves now. Briefly: it's more than a whim, for we know why we're doing it. Briefly: it's because of father, who has never been punished, whereas Edgar's father and mother are buried, have disappeared. Briefly: it's because of father, who, as our Edgar says, on account of the other Czechs who stood around him that night in the vat room and clearly heard, every one of them, the back talk, has to make an example of one of them. An example? we ask. Yes, our Edgar says. And what, we ask, did he have to do? Ah, our Edgar says, he had to show them. And, we ask, did he show them? Naturally, our Edgar says, and we go on stabbing. Although we remember nothing, can't remember anything at all, because we didn't hear the threat, we've never been in the vat room. All the same we know that our Edgar is right and that pain is necessary, and we try to picture exactly our father's crime. The truncheon, we're thinking, which first appears in our small factory at about this time and is put behind the glass door and bewilders, frightens us, the moment we see it. And which father, when he sees the Czech leaning, takes into the vat room that night, probably to show it to him. But father also has a pistol now, he has shown it to us himself. In case anything happens, he said, so that if ever we want to dream, we can dream of the pistol now too. Which, so as to be *ready for use* at any time, lies in the top drawer of the desk. In any case, the Czech body lying, in our imagination, on the floor feels extremely fragile, no, broken, and must be removed at once. In any case, when everyone is standing at the vats again and diligently stirring, father returns quietly to his enclosure—nobody notices that something is up with him—and in a loud voice gives orders for the Czech body to be *taken away*. And who took him away? we ask our Edgar, while we very coldly study our small wounds. That, our Edgar says, you'll know for yourself, after all the hints I've given you. Us? we ask and point at ourself, which, since we're so entirely alone in the Amselgrund, is a foolish thing to do, of course. Who else? our Edgar says, you're not stupid. No, we're not stupid, we say and think of mother who says we're *bright as buttons but slow coaches*. And we throw the knife from us, onto the moss, but then Edgar says: Would you mind giving me my knife back, if you don't need it anymore? But it's there, isn't it? we exclaim. Where? our Edgar asks, I can't see it. There, we say and point at it. No, our Edgar says and stretches his hand out to us, I want it placed in my hand. Yes, we say, of course. And we lean over and pick it up again and press it into his hand. There, we say. Ah, our Edgar says, my knife. And after sniffing at it and wiping the blade with his handkerchief, he pushes it back into its sheath and sets it down beside him. Then he sinks back into his old position, on his more down-to-earth air level. And we reach gingerly for our trousers and —our wound!—slip into them. Well then, we say and sink down beside our Edgar. Our Edgar—when he's feeling high-spirited he performs a dance step, sometimes even two. This makes us feel the dance that's in us too. Or else like a conjurer after doing his trick—probably the trick wants to come out of him—he stretches out both hands, turning them palm upward in front of us, so that we can take a good look at his palms, which are very rosy. Or else he waves his calves back and forth when he's lying on his stomach between us with his chin in the hollow of a hand. Our Edgar, who, as we can see from his trousers, keeps his iron comb in a flat case. And on the outside of his trousers he places his fingers with nails outlined black like obituaries, and now he drums them on the case a bit. Then we must have fallen asleep for a moment—presumably worn out—because later we felt as if we were waking up again, though to the same rise in the ground, the same forest. Then it occurs to us that we've given our Edgar his knife back but haven't yet thanked him for it, and we're about to say Thanks, Edgar, but it's best we don't say anything.

8

And then our way back. If we'd had to go uphill on our way to the Amselgrund, on the way back we go more downhill. And if on the way there we'd still been able to walk, now we hobble, yes, we limp. True, bleeding of that sort stops soon enough, the blood is easily wiped away, but still we had our deep wounds. Admittedly they can't be seen, because they're inside our trousers, and a person not well acquainted with us, who didn't watch closely the way we walk, wouldn't be at all likely to suppose that there were any such wounds. Probably he wouldn't suppose anything about us at all, but he'd be wrong. Even if nobody knows it, we're carrying six open wounds around with us. And against those six deep wounds our much too tightly fitting trousers rub as we hobble back, so that even when the blood isn't flowing, there can be no healing of the wounds. And at every step—we're walking in the gutter, our Edgar on the footpath—we wince, wring our hands in pain. It's a good thing it'll be dark when we reach home. We can't bear the thought that someone might see us hobbling or ask about our wound. All right? our Edgar calls to us, waving us on. Yes, we're coming, we exclaim.

Past the brewery—where in January Herr Prollius, half-blind, had his crash course in antitank gunnery—our way back slopes downhill to the river and becomes steadily more slanting, steeper, but soon we reach the embankment and walk over the bridge. We'll be able to look at the water again, spit into our river. Which, because it rained so much during our time in the cellar, is very turbulent and soupy and brown. Altogether, on our way back the ground is seldom level, mostly it goes up and down. Then the silence of the abandoned quarry that towers up on our right. Then the trunk of the oak tree that was torn out of the earth last fall by what mother called a *twister*—at first we mean to jump over it, but then, though we're already set for the run-up, we only clamber over it. Then the wheat field inhabited by mice, which we know from plucking the ears off the stalks. There's nobody else on this Siechenfeld boulevard leading into our town (and out of it), it's dusty, unpaved, flat, and since last year weeds have sprouted everywhere. Yes, the weeds are coming back. And the rats are back too. Their scuffling, like the sputter of small fires, off the dry, narrow footpath that runs alongside the boulevard. Like phantoms they flit around the allotment huts, gnawing at them from underneath. The new refugees are supposed to live here, except they haven't arrived yet. A dark limousine shoots past the Polytechnic, aiming straight ahead and honking continuously—never a moment's peace in this town. We can't see if it's Americans or just Germans. Never a moment's peace for us either, it's always one thing after another. We've only just reached the line of poplars when our Edgar exclaims: And now the suit! The what? we exclaim. The suit, our Edgar calmly says, and he leaps on ahead. Ah yes, we exclaim, the suit. Which we'd almost forgotten, but that's how we are. First we forget the knife, then the Czech Grave, and then, on the way home, we also forget the suit. Yes, we'll have a hard time growing up, mother's quite right. The moment it's possible for us to get a suit, via Herr Henne, we forget it, whereas our Edgar, who usually forgets everything, has the suit safe and sound in his head. Yes, what a long time it's been since we had a suit! It has been ages since we slowly grew out of the last one and finally, because it was too tight all around, took it off for the last time and folded it up and passed it on to our long-haired cousin in Pommerania. Was the suit blue, was the suit green? We don't know anymore. Because at least since last year time doesn't *pass* anymore, it just *flies away*, as mother says. For instance, this afternoon, how it has flown away and has actually gone already, although we're still in the middle of it. Hasn't it? we ask, isn't this afternoon over already? Our Edgar, nodding the head with this question in it, asks: How could it be over? We're on the Siechenfeld boulevard, so we're right in the middle of it still. Yes, of course, we're on the Siechenfeld boulevard, we say, but all the same it is *actually* over. Actually? our Edgar asks. Yes, actually, we say. Ah, it's deceptive, our Edgar says, it isn't over. Do you think there's something more to come? we ask. Yes, our Edgar says, that's what I think. I don't find it's passing at all, he says. And why, we ask, doesn't it pass, in your opinion? Because everything always stays the same, our Edgar says, without wasting much time thinking. But how should everything be the same, we ask, everything's always otherwise. But what it consists of is always the same, our Edgar says. But this afternoon, look, we exclaim, just look. And we'd like to prove with words and ideas, ideas that are only words too, of course, that this first day after our conquest is unique, but we can't do it. And so we simply point to the line of poplars before us, gently moved by the wind. Well? our Edgar asks. There, we say. Trees, he says. Poplars, we say. All right, he says, poplars if you like. You see? we say—because our Edgar simply doesn't want to understand us. And really this afternoon has only just begun. In the yard, we say. Ah, our Edgar says, that only seems to be so, in reality it doesn't pass at all. Now I know you don't believe me, he says, but it will be eternal. Eternal? we exclaim—shocked—but how do you mean? Yes, our Edgar just says, but that's something we don't ever find. Well then, we exclaim, be more precise about it, be quite precise now. How long, we ask, have we been out? Our Edgar, having no watch, turns around while still walking and looks at what's left of the sun and says: About five hours. And how long, we ask and point ahead of us, have we still got to go? Perhaps two more, our Edgar says. And then the day will be over, won't it? we ask. Yes, our Edgar says, then it'll be over. But why can't you see, we exclaim, just a while ago it was still before us! Yes, just a while ago is just a while ago, and now is just now, our Edgar says and waves us on. Our Edgar, who'd be better off in the shed, lying on the *superannuated couch* and breathing deeply, instead of moving with us down the Siechenfeld boulevard, with his transparent cheeks and his hollow, dark-rimmed, moist, and increasingly dull though still gray eyes. Strange too, the long, narrow skull, almost pointed at the back. Are you a longhead? we ask. Yes, our Edgar says, I am. So are you a Viking too? we ask. No, he says, I'm not. And us, we ask, are we longheads? and we brush a hand over our head that curves quite differently from our Edgar's. No, our Edgar says, you're not. And not Vikings either? we ask. No, our Edgar says, not that either. If we aren't, what are we? we ask. Well, our Edgar says and allows a moment's breathing space, you're something else. Yes, that's so, but what are we? we ask. You're . . . , Edgar's hands flutter in the air for a long time but he still doesn't say it. And our head, we ask, what does our head make us? Ah, if you're not longheads, then you'll be roundheads, he says. And how is it we're a roundhead while you're a longhead? we ask. You'll have to ask your mother about that, our Edgar says, it's a family thing. But let's walk faster, we're thinking, before the day is over and our time ends, regardless of what Edgar says, and we hobble along faster. Near the lime kilns where the barrage balloon unit was stationed up till a year ago, a little breeze approaches us, pushed by low clouds. But we don't look up, we look down at ourself, where our wounds are. We don't see them, of course, but we know where they are. And in connection with our wounds we think that a new long suit, which we'd be able to pull right over them, isn't something to be scorned. The suit, with only our hands and, higher up, our neck with our head peering out, would draw all the attention. And we picture how we'd walk along the Theaterring or Adolf-Hitler-Straße in our new suit, past the shop windows, which are still intact, though they've been emptied, and how for a long time we'd study ourself in the suit—but study the suit too—because we've discovered that in shop windows, when they're dark and the light falls favorably, we look much better than we do in real mirrors or in reality as it usually is. Since father went off to dig trenches, we've grown much bigger, with broader shoulders, longer arms. As we stand on the Güterhofstraße facing Frau Henne's house, we're thinking we'd look good in black.

Frau Henne, widowed three weeks ago, hears us calling right away, but first she wants to see us, from upstairs, before she'll come down the three floors and open the front door to us. For she can't be certain that we really are us, can't think what we might possibly want. So we have to step away from the front door back onto the street again, before she can identify us quickly in the fading light. Waving long, thin white arms and leaning far out of the window, she directs us away from the side of the house into the middle of the street. Are we far enough like this? we ask. Yes, she calls, far enough. Can you see us like this? we ask. Yes, she says, I can see you like that. But when she takes a really good look down at us from her altitude, she utters a long cry, puts a hand to her forehead, and shouts: Go home at once! But, Frau Henne, we call, heads tilted back, we've really got to speak with you. No, she shouts, go home at once! But why? we ask and look upward where the widow isn't so distinctly visible anymore, and if we didn't know who she is we probably wouldn't be able to recognize her. No wonder it's hard for her to identify us, not knowing who we are, especially since darkness in cities begins in the streets. And then it occurs to us too: The cap! which we haven't put on, but still have in the bag. Is it because of the cap? we call. You needn't worry at all about that, we call, we've got it here. And we're reaching for it. But the widow doesn't understand us or won't believe us or simply can't see the cap from so high up in the twilight. But now, having waved it back and forth a few times, we put the cap on our head. Yet the widow looking down at us emerges farther and farther from her window and calls out: The cap has nothing to do with it! Don't you know what danger you're in? No, we call, what danger? And we look around but don't see any. But yesterday, the widow calls—she's probably, like mother in the kitchen, still only half-dressed—there was still shooting here. Ah, we say, that was only at dogs, we were there. And anyway the war's over, we call. And tell her, as we've told the slaughterhouse director and old Frau Kohlhund, that the shooting has stopped and we've been in the park without anything happening. But the park is full of soldiers, the widow calls. No, we call, it's quite deserted. Only Frau Kohlhund happened to be there, she had to go out begging. No, no, we call, nothing will happen to us. And we swing our bags around a bit and hop back and forth a little for the widow, as best we can with our wound. Then once more we tell her that we've got to talk with her. Ah, I don't want to talk, the widow calls. Because she's so high up in her narrow window she seems shrunken as she looks down on us, and she really has changed a lot externally, at least from a distance. And what if it's important? we ask. Important? she calls, what could possibly be important? And what if it's a letter? we say and look down the empty street. Then we confuse what mother said was for Herr Schellenbaum with what was for the widow. We can't tell you from down here on the street who the letter is from, we call, only indoors, best of all in the room with the sofa! But I haven't got a room with a sofa, the widow calls. Well then, some other room, we call back. And what sort of letter is it you want to give me, the widow calls—she has probably changed inwardly too and has taken the news of her husband's death very badly. For instance they say that when the message came and she had it in her hand, she stood there with the message, right where we are standing, at her own front door, and held out her other hand flat and suddenly pressed on all the buttons of the bells in the house and rang the bells of all the tenants at once, for a long time, to ring all the neighbors out of their rooms and apartments and kitchens and into the dimly lit stairwell. And when all the neighbors were standing in the stairwell and looking down at her from their various floors over the banisters, with sleepy faces stretching far forward—it was still early—they say she held up into the stairwell her fist with the message in it and called into the stairwell: Yes, you knew him, now he's dead, my Hans. And now we're standing where she stood three weeks ago and she's leaning out of the upstairs window and refuses to come down and open the front door. There'll be no opening of the door for an errand like that, she calls, which you can't even explain to me properly. Are you alone, at least? she then asks from her window, which she has flung wide open. We're alone, we call and do a bit more hopping. And what's your letter about? I've got to know that, at least, the widow calls, and she props her elbows on the windowsill, something to do with my husband? I don't know if you heard but it didn't take them long to kill him too. Yes, we call, we knew, but we didn't want to say anything, so that you wouldn't think of it so often. Ah, I think of it, the widow calls and rears up in her window, as if she wanted to see across to the tile factory, where in March they shot someone for being a deserter, only we don't know who. Well, she calls, have they found something of him? Or has someone come back who knew him and wants to talk some more about him? No, we call, nothing more's been found and nobody will have come back either, who could tell you some more about him. So what are you bothering me for? the widow says, and as she's speaking she wraps around her neck a long black shawl, which hereafter flutters far out over the street, on the least breath of wind. But we can't do anything about that, we call and swing our bag, we can't do anything about anything. To begin with, we didn't want to go at all, we're not allowed to tell you why, because everyone will hear. And we look all the way down the Güterhofstraße to the end of it, where it's blocked by rubble. And we really have the impression that people, especially at the topmost windows, rapidly being illuminated one last time by the last rays of the sun, are looking down on us and hearing and seeing everything, extracting everything from us, even our very last thoughts. Should we go away? we ask, but then the widow calls out: No, I'll open up.

So we arrive on the third floor where she lives behind a brown door—many rooms on the lower floors and all the rooms around the central courtyard are occupied by refugees from Warthegau, who, as we climb the stairs, stick out their heads in the doorways. And before we step into her corridor, which is stuffy and seems to have been turned soft by all the upholstered furniture that's been brought in from the side rooms, we spend a long time wiping our sandals on the doormat. Especially our Edgar has to wipe for a long time, because of the dead dog. The damp marks in this corridor! The crumbling, peeling stucco! The ceiling with its stains of wet! The air so thick you could cut it with a knife! On the toilet door, the scabby crust, trying to sweat out something spicy! The widow, gasping after her ascent of the stairs, we recognize her at once, although she has changed a lot, even when we're close to her we notice it. Her mouth hastily made up, the front-door keys in her hand, wrapped around her body a housecoat, out of which, above and below, something finespun peeps, she walks ahead of us. Her pale nose, her chin somehow hurt, her ashy voice! Contrariwise our head, heavy with looking upward, hard to quieten! We think she's taking us into the room on the right, but she takes us into the room on the left. Here, amid yellowed wallpapers, at a polished table, we line ourselves up, but Edgar at once breaks out of line. For no reason at all he walks to the window, now shut again, and he'll stay there at the window for a long time, swaying slightly, looking down at the Güterhofstraße, in which we were just now standing, and he'll be trying to fathom, from above, the place we're no longer standing in. Yet there's nothing to be seen in the Güterhofstraße apart from a few trees full of crows. So what do you want of me, if you've got no news of him? the widow asks and points at the table with the chairs. No, we'd rather stand. And take off our cap. Yes, we'll stay here at the table, we say and point at the table, because we're thinking there'll at least be a bit of furniture between the widow and us. Well then, the widow asks, who sent you? Well, our mother, of course, we say and try to swing our bag around in the room a bit, so it won't be completely useless. Your mother, just as I thought, the widow exclaims and laughs a little, from her throat, which is white and already quite furrowed. And why didn't she come herself? She's not feeling well, we say. Since when? the widow asks and poises attentively for our answer. Oh, we say, she's always been unwell. But particularly since we were in the cellar so often and then got conquered. That gave her a headache and she had to lie down, she's taking aspirin now. Aha, the widow says, so she's taking aspirin while she sends you out on the streets and lets you risk your lives. Well, we say, she takes aspirin while we're at home too, she's worried all the time. Well, if she's worried, it serves her right. She's been spared long enough, not like other people, she says and probably means herself. So what's going to happen to you, now you haven't got a father? Ah, we say, but we've still got one. Have you? the widow says, I thought he'd been killed in action. No, we say, only missing. And when did he last write? she asks. In January, we say. Like mine, the widow says. And since then? No, we say, not since then. But he'll come back. Funny, the widow says, I thought he'd been killed in action. Like my husband, in February. No, we say, he'll be coming back. And if he doesn't, what will become of you, the widow asks and looks at us over her shawl, which is restful now. Ah, we say, we don't ourself know what will become of us. And what plans have you got for the factory? the widow asks, and she draws a deep breath while we look around the room a bit. Well, you see, we say and scratch our head. And all at once we're picturing the factory so that we can think about it better, and how forlorn and elongated it lies in the hollow beyond Wundenplan. Ah, we say, something will become of it, actually we have no plans. Haven't you? Won't it be opened again? the widow asks—at one time she worked in our leather cutting workshop, though only briefly. We don't know if it'll be opened again, we say, perhaps it will, perhaps it won't. Well, if it stays closed that's no great loss, but it'll go to wrack and ruin, the widow says, and she grins. If what they say is true, it's pretty much gone to wrack and ruin already on the outside. And I wouldn't fancy thinking what it looks like on the inside. Nor would we, we say and sigh a bit, in the vat room for instance. Have you ever been in the vat room? Me? the widow exclaims, what would I ever be doing in there. Oh, we say, nothing of course. Probably you've never even heard anything about it. That's right and I don't want to hear anything about it either, the widow says quickly. What I saw and heard in the leather cutting workshop was enough. No, she says, don't count on me, I'll never go into that factory again. In case your mother wants to know it, tell her: no. Tell her that, you understand? the widow suddenly shouts and clenches a small fist which she places to her heart, as we can well see. As you say, Frau Henne, we say, and we're shaken by the small fist and the up-and-down of her voice but we follow her moves closely, even if we look sometimes toward our Edgar and through Edgar's window. Where, above the trees in the Güterhofstraße the hitherto blue sky is gradually taking on a gray tint and the crows are shifting silently from one poplar tree to another. Yes, it's almost time to talk about the suit, but will the widow let us? So your father, she says, after he'd been lying low for as long as he could, they got him all the same? Yes, yes, I know he'll come back, but still he's missing, she adds with a sort of gratification and pushes—probably she's counting on a long talk after all—a chair into position, on which, in due time, she'll probably sit. Yes, he's missing, we say. Or did he simply run away? she asks, has he simply crept into a hiding place somewhere? We don't know anything about that, we say. Hm, she says, anyway he won't be sitting at his desk for a while. At which desk, we ask, the one in the factory or the one at home? And because we believe she means the one at home, we say that he couldn't sit at that one in any case, since mother had covered it with a dark cloth reaching all the way to the floor, he couldn't sit at that desk even if he wanted to. With a cloth? the widow asks. Yes, we say, with a dark gray one, almost black. Well, we say, he's not sitting at a desk, either here or there. And when did you last see him? the widow asks. In the winter, we say. And was he well then? she asks. Yes, we say, he was well then and in January he wrote another letter. And so you believe he'll come home safe and sound? the widow asks, and finally she sits down on her chair. We don't know if he'll be safe and sound, but he'll be coming back, we say and trace with our feet the outline of the strip of carpet which has probably been in front of us on the floor all the time, except we notice it only now. Hm, the widow says, if they didn't manage to get him at the last moment, perhaps he really will come home. We shrug our shoulders. Yes, perhaps they got him, perhaps they didn't, we're thinking. And we're thinking: We saw this coming, how difficult she is, this widow, how difficult! As if we could know anything about father! We don't even like thinking about him anymore. And not liking it at all, we piece together out of the widow's questions her picture of our father, which is quite a different one from ours. And to prevent our picture from being utterly destroyed by hers, we start to rehearse in mind a few sayings that he left behind for us. First, because we remember them well, we rehearse a few of his morning sayings. At once he's standing beside us with his mustache and speaking of a trip to Hohenstein-Ernstthal, which he's supposedly planning. And beneath his Sunday hat, into the little car's engine noise—the hood is open—he sings the wayfarer's song. After the morning sayings, which are quickly rehearsed, come the evening sayings. They're longer and rather impatient, but still we remember them. Our father—who always sends us out into the fresh air, into the park and the garden, because at home, he thinks, we dream too much! Our father—who'd like best not to eat any meat and sausage, only raw fruits and vegetables! Our father—who, if everything goes wrong, can start again from scratch and who, because he believes in Karma, will see us again, if necessary, in the other life! There's only one saying that we can't remember, one that he always said and that concerns *Us and The World*. For a long time we search for this saying, we almost despair of finding it, but then father's rhythm comes through and we say that saying as well, inaudibly of course. Later we lean against the wall, cross-legged, we're tired and worn out, we hold a hand over our mouth, while the widow moves *her* hand restlessly back and forth over the tabletop. Our Edgar has turned away from us and is looking in among the roofs, with his forehead against the window crossbar. He doesn't say anything but he hears everything, thinks of everything, even if he's swaying. Whereas we're busy forgetting father, and this is how we forget father. First, we forget how in his stiff dressing gown he comes to us in the children's room and sees us standing at the window. And how he calls to us—we can easily hear his voice—to go to bed now, to close our eyes for the day. Then we forget how he walks toward us, how he stoops over us, draws the covers up to our chin, and kisses us on the cheek. And then he blows the candle out and walks back to the door. Father, we call, are you going already? Wasn't there anything else you wanted to say to us? Something else? father asks, and he already has one foot outside the room. When are we going to Hohenstein-Ernstthal, you know, the trip? we say. But then it's evident that father has given up the idea of a trip, or at least put the trip off. No, there's no time for a trip to Hohenstein-Ernstthal. Then why did you mention a trip at all? we ask and sit up in bed once more, to hold on to father, but then it turns out that father hasn't only given up the idea, he's forgotten it. But it was only yesterday that you were whistling like that, we say, how can you forget? Nonsense, father says, and if I was whistling it was for a quite different reason. And what reason? we ask, but father won't even tell us that, and at any moment he'll have vanished. Don't go, please, we exclaim. See you tomorrow, father says. And the moment he's gone, we forget him too, to pay him back. First we forget his hair, thin but soft and still growing over his ears, his thick eyebrows which he can arch up into the roots of his hair when he's disappointed with us, his clear sharpish voice, his footstep outside our door. Where, instead of thinking about us, he has quite different thoughts in his hard, round, enormous head, on which we were only just now knocking our fists in play. What's in his head is not The Trip! The Trip! but The Factory! The Factory! So that instead of thinking about him, while we're in Frau Henne's room, we have quite different thoughts in our much more fragile, much more easily injured, much more breezy heads. What we're thinking is not Father! Father! but The Suit! The Suit! But we're not thinking of one of father's suits that hang in the wardrobe in our parents' room, which, mother says, we'll only go into over her *dead body*, but of Herr Henne's suit that's no longer needed. Now for Herr Henne's suit, we're thinking, now, quick, we'll ask about it. But when the widow is so sad, is it all right simply to ask her for the suit? Yes, she says and lays her two hands before her on the table, hard hands, their backs ribbed with veins, it's not your fault, but there's a certain day I remember only too well. And I'm not the only person here to remember it, she exclaims, and some spit flies from her mouth. Is it a day or a night that you remember? we ask. Actually, she says, it's a night. A night in which month? we ask, was it a night in May? What? the widow asks—she's thinking, as we speak, of something quite different. Was it a night in May? But the widow doesn't want to talk with us about the night. Ah, let's forget it, she says. It's good that we're getting tired now, always that night, we're thinking, and suddenly we're so tired that we yawn a lot. Yes, it's only boring for you, the widow says and points into our wide-open mouth. You're too young to remember, she says. No, no, we say, we're not bored at all. Yes, you are, the widow says, yes, you are. But there are people here who aren't bored by it and who remember everything, she says, and probably she means herself. And she knocks, no longer with her hand but with her fingertips, a few times rapidly on the table. Tell your father, in case you should see him, that people know everything still, she exclaims. But how should we get to see him, he's missing, we say, and with our suddenly weary feet we trace a few deeply absent lines across the strip of carpet. Then tell your mother, the widow says. Has she talked about me a lot? No, we say, not much. Not at all? the widow asks. Yes, not at all, we say. Well, the widow exclaims, hasn't she at least mentioned me sometimes over all the years? Actually she hasn't, we say. And we're somewhat ill at ease that our mother shouldn't have mentioned the widow. But in fact nobody at home ever talked about her. Well, the widow says, it really doesn't matter whether she mentioned me or not. Tell her simply that nothing has been forgotten, she'll know what I mean. Yes, all right, Frau Henne, we say, we'll do that. But here, before our conversation (conversation?) can get even more fumbling and meaningless, further away from Herr Henne's suit, deeper into Frau Henne's hatred, our Edgar jumps into the breach, rushes to our aid from the window. With legs apart, his narrow skull thrusting forward—what a beautiful head!—the skull jutting far forward into the room, he moves between the widow and us. And then, turning on his hips to speak right into her face, into her eyes, he says: That it's true our mother seldom spoke of her, but that she knows all about her misfortune and is also very upset by it. And that she, our mother, like the widow herself, had been ready for anything, but not for that: Killed in action, he exclaims, killed in action! But that our father too—he says "their father" and points at us—let's not fool ourselves, he says, will not . . . And then he lowers his voice, so that we shan't hear what he's saying. But then the widow, who is sitting down and has collected her wits again, interrupts him: Who's this? she asks us. This, we say and look up, is our Edgar. And where did he come from? she asks. Ah, nowhere actually, he's always there, we say and shrug our shoulders. But he must have come from somewhere, the widow says and raps on the table a few times, insisiting on a proper answer. Well, we say, originally he comes from the Gießereistraße, but at present he's living in our garden shed. Then he's a friend of yours, the widow asks us. We look at our Edgar. Yes, we say, he's a friend, but probably we're not his friend. Aren't you? the widow asks us. No, we say. And why aren't they your friends if you run around with them? the widow asks our Edgar, but all he does is shrug his shoulders. And so you simply brought him along, perhaps because he's your friend? she asks us again. He simply came along, we say. And why then does he say your father won't come back, if he's your friend and goes around with you? the widow asks. Ah, we say, he doesn't mean it like that. Then why does he say it, if he doesn't mean it like that? she asks. Ah, we say, because of his mother. And what about his mother? the widow asks us. Ah, we say, she was on the Gießereistraße on the eleventh. Oh, the widow says. Yes, we say. And where was he on the eleventh? the widow asks. In our garden shed, we say. That's why he thinks his father will come back and ours won't, for justice's sake. Nonsense, the widow says, certainly yours will come back, and his probably too. People like your father always come back, she exclaims, the ones who don't are people like my husband. And why do people like our father always come back? we ask, but the widow won't tell us, instead she pauses, for once. Well then, he'd like to try to talk with her sensibly now, our Edgar says from his side of the table, once the pause is over. Well then: she's wrong. For our ("their") father, however much she might reproach him— we bow our heads a bit—wouldn't be coming back and nobody was counting on that. Or do you? he asks us so suddenly that we cringe. Us? we exclaim and point at ourself. No, we say, we don't. You hear that, Frau Henne? our Edgar exclaims and waves his forefinger. Ah, you're all in it together, you're only tricking me, the widow says, and she shifts her chair back a bit. Sometime or other they'll all come back, she says, all except mine. Then, having meanwhile placed a hand on the table, though he's still standing, and pulled himself along with it a little, our Edgar asks the widow if she's comfortable in her chair. Ah, the widow says, I'm comfortable enough. If she wasn't, our Edgar says, she could pull her chair up closer to the table. No, the widow says, I'm quite comfortable. Right, our Edgar says, this is the situation. We knew how she felt. What a loss! Also we'd known her husband, even if only by sight. Yes, that's true, our Edgar says, because for a moment the widow can't remember. Did he use to walk home every midday from the post office, past the pharmacy, or didn't he? Then the widow has to put a hand to her forehead and admit: Yes, that's right. You see? our Edgar exclaims—who is now carrying his knife again between his legs, so that we're wondering how he manages to keep it there. Well, Herr Henne, who's no longer with us, and that's . . . Yes? Frau Henne asks. And our Edgar, who usually can't think of anything to say, says that's a *fact*. Well: had her husband left anything, this or that, which he'd not need now? he asks and walks beside the table a bit closer to the widow, while in the rapidly darkening room we've positioned ourself as far as possible from her, against the wall, with its patchily torn and stained wallpaper. We look at the widow out of the corners of our eyes, then look at our Edgar, gazing at his eyes and mouth. Briefly: our ("their") mother, who has a headache, sends her best regards and would like to know if there was anything of her husband's left to *wear*. For look, our Edgar says and points at us and now we're looked at for a long time. Naturally one hung on to everything left from a happier time, on the other hand it would only be lying around, if the person in question had died. And that is why, the widow asks—after a pause during which she allows our Edgar's words to sink deep into her—that is why you've come to see me? Yes, that's why, our Edgar says. Ah, the widow just says, ah. And then she admits: Yes, some things are still there, but by no means as many as people say. The wildest rumors had been going around, especially on the Theaterring, where *the rich people* lived. May one, our Edgar asks, be quite specific? Ah, the widow says, ah—while our Edgar is already elevating his chin a bit to put the question. Is there, he asks, an overcoat? No, the widow says, that's gone now. Are there, our Edgar asks, any shoes left? They've gone now too, the widow says. And shirts, our Edgars asks, are there any shirts left? Yes, she says, but they've been promised to someone. Then is there, our Edgar asks and pauses for a moment, while in our embarrassment we look up once at the ceiling and down once at the floor, perhaps a suit? Yes, the widow says, there is a suit still. Aha, our Edgar says and reaches into his bag, as if he had the letter, although mother wanted the suit for us and gave us the letter. Ah, the widow exclaims, raising her arms, you want to have his suit, ah. And that's why your mother sent you out into the midst of such dangers, she says and shakes her head. If that's why you've come, I'm sorry but I must disappoint you. Everything has gone, you see. But the suit hasn't? our Edgar asks, and now he moves *his* hand over the table a bit. Ah, the widow says, if it hasn't been given away, it's been tidied away, so as to put it out of my mind. And where, our Edgar asks, has it been put? It'll be upstairs in the attic, the widow says, behind the lattice screen. Then our Edgar raises his right hand, as if he were in school, and he says: That doesn't matter, as long as one knows where it is, one could get at it. Couldn't one? our Edgar asks us. Yes, we say and wipe some of the sweat of our embarrassment from our forehead. We could get at it. But then the widow makes a dismissive gesture and says there are still all sorts of other questions. Such as? our Edgar asks. For instance, she says, the question whether the suit would even fit us. For such young people as us, with everything still *before* us, a suit that belonged to someone with, after all, everything *behind* him . . . You mean it's too big for them? our Edgar asks. Yes, the widow says, too big. Her husband had worked at the post office, she says, and had had a lot of walking to do, so his arms and legs were long, everything full size. I'm afraid, she says and takes a good long look at us, that the suit will be too big for you. One can't be so sure, our Edgar says and shakes his head. Look, he says and points at us, look at them. And we, exhausted as we are by our cellar nights, by our conquest, by the encounters at the slaughterhouse and in the park, by rambling through the Amselgrund, by digging out the knife, by the widow's questions, by the exchanges between Edgar and her, we hoist ourself up erect, with bleeding thighs, against the wall we're leaning on, we straighten our shoulders, throw out our chest, raise our head as high as we can, and look down at the widow. No, if she'd pardon him for saying so, our Edgar says, but still he remembered Herr Henne very well, and no, he certainly wasn't any taller, he says and points at us. If he had been, believe me, he says, I'd tell you so. And then, he says, while she closes her eyes to place the dead man in spirit side by side with us and to compare the breadth of our shoulders and the length of our limbs, we would also be growing. Ah, that's just talk, the widow says and makes a dismissive gesture, today everything has changed. Today nobody grew anymore, she says, today everyone stayed as they are. No, no, our Edgar says, not them. And we, tall against the wall, shake our head: No, not us. Well, the widow says and sighs a bit, because all at once everything's too much for her, and it's all the same to her whether we'll still be growing or not. What she had to decide was whether she should dispose of the almost unworn suit at all. Our Edgar asks at once if it's a winter suit. No, the widow says, that one has gone already. Is it, our Edgar asks, a brown suit? No, the widow says, that one has gone too. Rather, the suit she's talking about, which was *dark blue* and had *only a slight pattern* in it, was hardly known in the town, her husband had hardly ever gone out in it. Life, the widow says, simply never offered him an opportunity to put his suit on. True, she'd always told him: Tomorrow you'll put the suit on, but then he'd never been able to, for one reason or another. Twice or three times, on days home from the front on leave, he really had in the course of time slipped into the suit that was otherwise kept wrapped in protective paper always, and had walked up and down before the wardrobe mirror, had tugged at the suit, the fit of which wasn't *one hundred percent perfect*, to make it sit right, and then had always been very contented with himself and with the suit, but then, so as to conserve the suit and save it up *for later*, he'd always taken it off right away again and left it on a hanger beside the mirror. Then he'd bring a chair and sit down before it and for a long time look at himself and the suit. And, as he'd confided to her, he'd picture how it would be to *go out* in the suit, on a Saturday, into a restaurant. Sometimes, picturing himself appearing quite unexpectedly, wearing the suit, in a better-class restaurant, he hadn't been able to suppress a *chuckle*. While all this was going on, he'd usually smoke a cigarette, sometimes two. But whenever she'd gone over to him or sat on his knee and said: The suit's for wearing, Hans, not just for looking at! he'd only shaken his head and said: No, it still belongs in the wardrobe. Only twice, each time in spring, but in different springs, he'd gone so far as to take a walk in the suit, both times *arm in arm* with her. Once, as she recalled, just around the house, and once to the arcades. The ones by the theater? our Edgar asks. Yes, she says, the arcades by the theater. But then they'd been seen, if at all, by hardly any people, at most by a dozen. Apart from that, he'd never worn the suit outside, though he'd been very fond of it, and she was still very fond of it, he'd only looked at it indoors and saved it up, like everything else, *for later*. But she wasn't like that herself. If she'd had her way, he'd have worn the suit much more often, but he didn't want it so. No, he'd always said: I'm saving it up. Until she'd got so angry at him for *not ever once now* wanting to wear the suit, that she'd exclaimed to him one evening outside Reese's, the confectioner's (still open at that time), into which he'd been about to walk in his old suit: Yes, now I see, you'll never put the suit on, just because I keep on asking you to. I can see the day coming—and you'll never have worn the suit once. Then he'd given her his word that when he was next home on leave he'd wear the suit for a long time and *among people* too, and after the war he'd wear it *all the time*, to make good his omissions and finally, as he put it, to *take full advantage of the beautiful suit at last*, which, besides, she had given him as a present, but now everything had turned out otherwise. Now he'd never wear the suit, which they'd always taken good care of together, brushing it with the clothes brush from Bad Tölz—a souvenir. And all at once she stands up, and after we've left our wallpapered wall and overcome with weariness collapsed on chairs at the table, she walks with stiff, hesitant steps, as if wading through her deep memories of the suit's beginnings, out of the room to fetch the suit, yes, to fetch it *from upstairs* too, where all that miserable refugee junk is, she shouts out to us over her shoulder. And it seems it wasn't difficult for her to forge her way through to it, for in a moment she's back again, the suit over her arm, and she lays it on the table in front of us. We've hardly sat down, but now we jump up at once and see: what a wonderful suit, good material, the cut, buttons, lining, everything. And something at once obvious: really the suit has hardly been worn. In its silk-paper covering it will have been hanging or folded, well protected, in a closet sequestered in the attic. True, it's creased here and there, perhaps it has a few folds where it should be smooth, but all in all the suit is amazingly substantial, if somewhat starchily formal, on account of its sheer quality. Well now, this is the suit, the widow exclaims, running her hand over it. We bow deeply over it, heels clicked together. Yes, she says, take a good look, because I'm not going to sell it. May I? our Edgar says, and he too steps closer, to bow over the suit. The chairs by the wall, the poplars along the street, we all line up now to lean over the table, stroke the suit with our fingertips, see that it has no faults, no spots, no stains. And it hasn't gone at the knees or elbows either. Our Edgar puts his hand between the legs of the trousers and ascertains that all the buttons are there. Then he takes the jacket and the trousers and holds them up against the light. No, no worn parts! So that, although the suit isn't for sale, we simply must slip into the jacket, stand against the wall, and hold our breath. Then, held aloft by Edgar, the suit comes marching straight toward us. First he holds the trousers—careful now!—against our legs and then we have to slip into the jacket. And then, after he has patted us on the shoulder to calm us down, our Edgar ascertains: yes, it really would fit! True, it's a bit loose here and there, no, not too loose, not too wide, but . . . No, it fits! Except for the sleeves, which may be a bit too long, the suit fits us, he says. Why don't you quickly go, he asks, into the room next door and slip into the trousers? No, no, the widow says, not the other room. But Edgar doesn't hear or else he overhears what she says, or he doesn't want to hear it. Well, off you go, he exclaims, angrily or peremptorily or perhaps he's only meaning to say it and pushes us, not saying anything, toward the door. And before the widow can say: But you don't have to, the suit's not for sale anyway—our Edgar has pushed us into the soft, dark corridor and past the wallpaper stains and into the room next door.

In the room next door, probably a junkroom, the air on the day after our conquest is strangely distinct from that of the Güterhofstraße—noticeably fusty. And into the stagnant air of this room we are now thrust. The moment the door is closed we collide with something which, without knowing what it is, we kick into the corner. These unused next door rooms, how chockablock they always are! And to think that one never knows what one has kicked into their corners! Unlike the window in the widow's room, this one is blacked out, with the result that this room, entered reluctantly in the first place, will stay opaque for as long as we're in it. Yet in the widow's presence, in broad daylight, we can't possibly take our trousers off, in order to put her husband's on. Quite apart from the impropriety of taking our trousers off in front of her, she'd have noticed our wound at once. And while, with outstretched arms, we're looking for something to hold on to in the darkness, we picture at once the scene: her goggling at our wound, mouth open, when she sees we're hurt, her boundless incomprehension. Then her finicky questions, as to the origin, reason, purpose, of our wound, her doubts as to whether it was necessary. But we don't want the whole town to know about our wound! We want our wound to be a secret. Then as we become accustomed to the darkness of the room and, with one hand against the wall, get out of our trousers into Herr Henne's, we suddenly have the feeling that the room isn't empty at all, but is being laboriously breathed into, perhaps it's occupied. And what, we wonder, is breathing into this room? A cat? A bat? Something in a cage? Something behind glass? It's certainly not the widow, for she's sitting in the other room, scratching on the table with her fingernails, but does that mean the junkroom must be un-lived-in? Those, as we hop on one leg, are our thoughts at the moment. Until our gaze eventually assembles in the darkness of the window bay a sagging, lumpy, and darkly grained wooden bed. Yes, there seems to be a bed in here, a heavy piece of furniture. Until, from the door, we realize: Oh my, the bed is occupied! And as we're slipping into Herr Henne's trousers, there's someone looking at us from the bed, someone looking from the depths of the pillows, in the posture of a person dying. That of all the rooms along the soft corridor *this* one should be being breathed into! At once we hold our breath, place our hands over our wound, keep watch, trousers around our knees, now this way, now that. Then it turns out that the laboriously identified wooden bed contains a person, very old indeed, shrunk over the years to the size of a child, long out of circulation, regarded by our mother as dead—the widow's own mother-in-law, old Granny Henne herself, who has probably spent the entire war in this bed, just so that she can now, breathing shallow breaths, look across and see us. And all we'd wanted was to get some *Butterschmalz* and see a few black Americans, and, for our purification, to visit the Amselgrund! So Granny Henne isn't dead at all, she'd simply gone to bed, and soon, surely, she'll speak to us from her bed. Doubtfully we look toward her. As if we didn't remember how mother had exclaimed, when the news of Herr Henne's death went through the town: What a good thing Granny Henne didn't live to hear it. And why not? we'd asked. Ah, she's dead, mother had said. But evidently mother had been mistaken, she hadn't been dead in the least. She'd only gone into the junkroom and lain down in bed. And the younger Frau Henne will have brought her, now and then, a piece of bread and a glass of water. And when the news of Herr Henne's death came, she'll have stooped over her, taken hold of her head, and shrieked the news at her, as she did to the other occupants of the house. And then, pronto, dropped the head back onto the junkroom bed. The room was presumably the only one in the three-story house available for Granny Henne, and it was here that she first waited for her son to come back and then, bit by bit, outlived him. And where, now; with her eyes and ears accustomed to the darkness, she perceives his next-to-new suit on us and will soon ask us about it. Naturally, we turn our back on her, avert our wound from her sight, naturally we button up our trousers, that's to say, her son's trousers, more rapidly. But—too late, she's already drawing a deep breath, she's talking. And she says, out of her pillows, propped in which she'd like to have sat: Sometimes it tastes good, sometimes it doesn't. What do you mean? we ask and stand quite still, our hands over our wound. Yes, she says, that's how it is with me, and she has her hands crossed over her chest, dried-up hands, the color of wood, bygone hands. And us, we say, we're just slipping into Herr Henne's trousers for a moment. And we've already put the jacket on, in the other room though, we say, because she sees we're wearing the jacket. But we'll be taking them off again right away, the jacket and the trousers. Ah, Granny Henne says, my son isn't at home, it's all right with me if you put his suit on for a bit. Yes, we say, but we don't want to go around in it, the suit's much too big, you see. Ah, she says, go around in it for a bit, perhaps you'll grow into it. No, no, we say, we'll not be growing anymore. Yes, yes, she says, you'll certainly be growing. No, no, we say, we've decided . . . Nonsense, she says, come a bit closer, let me just take a look at you. You mean now or later? we ask, because we don't want to appear before her in her son's suit and we're hoping she'll say *later* and then forget it, or in the meantime really die. But she means *now*. Surely you can't see us in this darkness? we say, and we don't feel right at all in the suit, even if the trousers are now buttoned up. So you should come closer, Granny Henne says. How close? we ask, because we'd like to come as little close as possible. As close as possible, she says. Wouldn't it be better if we put the light on? Then you can see us too, without us having to come so close, we say. You mean the light? Granny Henne asks. Yes, we say, so we'll just switch the light on. And now we've found the switch and we switch the light on, but, because there's no electricity today, the room remains as dark as ever it was. What's up? she asks, can't you find the switch? Yes, we say, but it's broken. Yes, that's what they all say, when they want to switch my light on, Granny Henne says, and she chuckles to herself a bit. And she forgets that we're supposed to come closer, also she doesn't need light anymore. Despite the darkness she'll see our wound, even if she won't ask us about it yet. Instead of which she asks us, out of her pillows, if we've come over the bridge. Over the bridge? we ask. Yes, she says, over the bridge. And before we can say yes or no she says that the bridge is new and had probably only been erected last night, which is why she hadn't been able to sleep. Ah, she says, what a hullaballoo! Was it necessary? And that in her time a bridge hadn't been necessary. Instead, people had shouted to one another across the river whatever they had to say to one another, and whatever they wanted to give to one another they'd thrown from one side to the other. And if they hadn't wanted to shout what they wanted to say, and hadn't been able to throw what they wanted to give, there'd been a ferryboat, but small rowing boats had also passed back and forth. Yes, the ferryboat, we say as if we'd heard of it, and we quickly skip the ferryboat, because we don't know a thing about it. And Granny Henne, after taking a quick look toward our wound—now hidden under her son's suit trousers—gropes around with her hands and asks: Did you see the gulls? What gulls? we ask. Ah, she says, what do you mean, what gulls? And that when the gulls had first flown to our town—across so much dry land—and had first been seen down by the river, she'd been eleven years and ten months old. Imagine that, she says, eleven years and ten months old. Yes, we say, you were pretty young then. Yes, she says, I certainly was. And when we ask once more: How do you mean, gulls? she motions with her arms to show us which ones she has in mind. As if she were a gull herself, getting ready to fly. Ah, *those* gulls! we exclaim, and we nod and we even join with her in making some wing beats ourself, although we're certain there aren't any gulls in our town. You know, she now says, on some days I find it very hard to believe. In the gulls? we ask. Yes, she says, and everything else they say I saw once. Ah God, all the things I'm supposed to have seen, you wouldn't believe it either. What, for instance? we ask. Ah, she says, what should I say? I've forgotten most of it, you know, so I'd better not say anything. So you don't always believe it? we ask. Believe what? she asks. Ah, we say, everything. Ah, she says, not everything, perhaps, but there'll have been something. And the gulls, we ask, do you believe in the gulls? Sometimes I do, she says, sometimes I don't. And today, we ask, do you believe in them today? You mean now? she asks. Yes, we say, now. Ah, she says and ponders for a moment and says: Yes, now I believe in them. Then she looks in the direction of our wound and asks if we're hurt. Yes, unfortunately, we say. And where are you hurt? Granny Henne asks. Here, on the leg, we say. Is it painful? she asks. Ah, we say, sometimes it is, sometimes it isn't. So you must have fallen over? Granny Henne asks. Fallen over, we say. On the bridge, wasn't it, because you were running? Granny Henne asks—for whom immediately our wound is no more than a matter of course. Yes, we say, running. And because when you were running you weren't looking at the ground, was that it? she asks. Not all the time, we say. Yes, she says, you have to look at the ground when you're running, especially now, when everything's dark because of the war. Ah, we say, the war's over, hasn't anybody told you? Stuff and nonsense, Granny Henne says, that's mere speculation. Better to look at the ground, then you'll know where you're going. And not end up like me, breaking something in the darkness and having to be put to bed. Why, did you break something? we ask. Yes, she says, a leg. Which one? we ask. The left one, she says, and you? No, we didn't, we say. We've got something, to be sure, but it's higher up and it's not serious. Well then, so you can be going along, she says. Yes, we say, we can. Well then, she says once more, you can be going along. Yes, yes, we say, we can be going along. How do you mean? we ask after a while, having thought about her apparently quite simple statement, how should we understand that? Do you mean go along *now* or *always*? Do you mean that we can walk or that we should be going along now? Should we go along, Frau Henne? we ask. If we should, then we can, you only have to tell us. But Granny Henne says no more, she's silent. For a long time she seems to be looking with slit eyes at our wound still, quite prepossessed by it, but when we ask her if perhaps she'd like to know *whereabouts on the bridge* we fell down, she's silent. And while we're quickly inventing a place where we could have fallen down and about which we could talk with excitement, and while, invisible to us, something heavy trundles past on the Güterhofstraße—instead of black Americans in their tanks our study topic today is pale old Granny Henne in her bed—we see that she has dozed off. Frau Henne, we call, softly at first, then more loud. Frau Henne, we call—but she's silent. Her arms the color of wood, with which only a moment ago she'd wanted to take off and fly or copy for us the motions of a gull or another bird in flight, as well as can be done by someone lying down, rest immobile beside her. Her abruptly and heedlessly hooked nose, her sunken face, her eyes pressed deep into their sockets but still shuttable! Frau Henne, we call and even stamp our feet with impatience, then also we go closer and stoop cautiously over her head which has rolled to one side, but she doesn't hear us. Either she's fallen asleep, or she's dead. Instead of falling asleep over and over again, she has died for keeps. (For she looks the way a dead person does.) And now something quite different. Now, right above her head, the photograph of our town, as we ourself never knew it, but as it presumably once was. Cheek to cheek we turn away from the head and toward the photograph, to study it methodically, as best we can in the darkness. Something immediately noticeable: *our* town is quite different! Our town has in its center a town hall—although it's dilapidated—a Theaterring, and asphalt paved streets, whereas the town in the photograph hanging over Granny Henne's head has no Theaterring and no town hall. And the streets aren't even paved, let alone paved with asphalt. On the other hand, in her town the river is more luminous and clear. What a joy to stand by such a river and call something to the people on the other side! Along this river, on this side and the other, there are many trees standing, varieties unknown to us, their branches softly hanging down, right into the water. Naturally, even just because of the trees, the river looks quite different from our one. But even if you forgot about the trees and shrubs, our river is different. Our river is frequently turgid and dull, it smells bad in summer, and if the sun only shines for long enough it almost dries up and is kept flowing only by the waste waters we pipe into it. Then *our* river, in the ordinary sense, actually ceases to exist. *Her* river, to the contrary, we're thinking, must have been a merry one, with a meadow on either side and flowers in the meadows. What a joy to throw something across such a river to a friend on the other side! Meanwhile *our* river, with its bridge, isn't to be found at all in the yellowed photograph suspended over and retained inside Granny Henne's head. And we see that the river across which people called to one another, with its long-vanished trees and its row of buildings never glimpsed, buildings in all likelihood quickly thrown together, narrow fronted, and now long demolished, belonged for her in *her* town and has no place in *our* town. And there's a dog too, not in the photograph, no, but bodily in the junkroom, where it was lying under the bed, whence it now creeps, quietly snuffling. On top of it all, into the middle of our thoughts about our town, this dog now comes, a live dog! Having crept out, he lays a front paw on our sandal and let us dandle him a bit. Then all at once he tries to get lively, on account of our wound, which he wants not only to sniff but also to lick. But we can't allow that, we push him away. Then he sniffs at our toes a little and, having sniffed his fill, slouches back under the bed. Then we too want to go back. Then we see, as we lay our shirt collar over the collar of Herr Henne's suit, that his collar doesn't fit us, but is much too loose. Hm, to be honest about it, the entire suit doesn't fit. Should we slip out of Herr Henne's suit again? Yes, so we'll take the suit off now, we say, but Granny Henne doesn't stir. All right then, we'll keep the suit on for a while, we say. With our trousers over our arm we stoop over Granny Henne. Well now, you take a little nap, while we keep Herr Henne's suit on for a while, we say. Right, we say and do up all the buttons, tug everything straight, we're off now, hope your leg gets better. And what you told us about the gulls and the rest was very interesting. And we'll leave the light on, shall we? we ask, but Granny Henne doesn't make a sound. That of all the many rooms in the building she should be in the one that our Edgar thrust us into! All right then, we'll leave the suit on, but only for a little while, we say. And we'll leave the light on too, we say, in case the current comes back on. Without further ceremony, wearing Herr Henne's suit, if only for the time being, our eyes on the ground, to avoid breaking anything, we grope at about five o'clock our way on the third floor of Güterhofstraße 83 from the almost empty junkroom on the left, out again into the corridor.

And back in the widow's room, where we are awaited, we have to turn ourself around and around so that Herr Henne's suit, the fit of it, can be studied. A beautiful suit, the widow on her chair says when she sees it hanging from us. Except the collar, we say, is too big. It fits at the back, our Edgar says. Except the jacket is too loose, we say. Yes, the widow says, it's a beautiful thing. And now, we say, we'll take it off again. But where shall we take it off? It can't be done in front of the widow. Do we have to go back into the junkroom? No, that's impossible. Then our Edgar says we should wait a bit before we take it off, and he removes the white letter from our old jacket pocket and hands it to the widow, who opens it at once and reads it and looks across at us and says that we may keep Herr Henne's suit, for the time being, at least. Even if it doesn't fit us? we ask. It doesn't matter, she says. How strange! First she swears to us that she'll not part with the suit, and now she's willing to part with it all the same. Yet we're not all that surprised, we'd been expecting something like this, and we act as if it was quite natural for us to have the suit, for, we're thinking, if we don't have it, someone else will. We're even told we can keep it on now. Because then, at least, the widow exclaims, I shan't have to see it anymore—and she has put a hand over her eyes for a moment, so she won't see the suit anymore. But we could put it in our bag, we say, then you won't see it anymore either. Ah, the widow says, it's all right, keep it on. And now be off with you, before it gets dark, we don't want anything to happen to you in that beautiful suit, she says, and evidently she has separated herself from the suit inwardly now. All right, we say and sigh a bit, then we'll keep it on. The bloodless, half-dead hand which hangs down at the widow's side, as if on a string, and which we have first to grasp by the wrist and then bring it up and bend it straight, before we can shake it! Ah, what could ever happen to us? we say and put our cap on. Then we transfer the blue envelope left in our old jacket to the new jacket. Then the old trousers and the old jacket are slung over our shoulder, which is how we want to carry them. Well then, *auf Wiedersehen*, we say and scuffle a bit with our feet, but cautiously, not wanting to get caught up in our new trouser cuffs. What? the widow asks—again she's lost in her thoughts. Nothing, we say, nothing really. And wearing our cap, with its head smell— ours—and our new suit billowing around us, we walk back down the corridor and through the brown door, and we run down the staircase, with Edgar behind us holding on to the banisters. And don't forget it's hardly been worn, the widow calls after us, and with a slight motion of her housecoat she steps once more to the stairwell, to brandish her right hand powerlessly in the air. Don't you worry, we'll take care of it, we call and climb down the stairs. Our shoulders loosely enveloped in Herr Henne's jacket, his trousers flopping around our legs, we go through the front door turning not to the left but to the right and down the street. For we're meaning to walk not toward the Hindenburg boulevard, but toward Adolf-Hitler-Straße, which, as mother says, will certainly have a new name soon. (What a lot of new names and designations we're going to have to make a note of, and what a lot of old ones we'll have to forget!) And why to Adolf-Hitler-Straße instead of to the Hindenburg boulevard? We take a few steps. The fact is, we won't know how we feel in the new suit until we've seen ourself in it. So before we go to the church, we'll study ourself a bit, wearing the suit, in the big shop windows on Adolf-Hitler-Straße that have survived the war intact, strangely enough, whereas the Hindenburg boulevard—which will probably keep its name— has no shop windows, only low, damp, crisscross, sharp-topped wooden fences in front of their garden villas. Yet we're walking as usual, that's to say our Edgar walks on ahead, fleshless, with pointed knees, though his health has been good until now. And when he feels especially giddy, as he happens to, he simply leans against a house wall and lets us walk on past. Then he's able to see us in our suit from behind. Is anything wrong? we ask and stop. What makes you think it might be? he asks. Ah, we say, because you're swaying so. There you go, you can't stand up straight, even if you're leaning against something, while we can stand up straight even when we're not leaning. Look, we say and walk away from the wall and spread our arms and can't help thinking of Herr Henne, who surely must at one time or another have spread his arms like this and stood in the suit without swaying. And we stand for a while bolt upright and not swaying, but our Edgar doesn't even look. The fact is, we love our Edgar and we don't like Herr Henne, but we're not saying so. Instead, we walk closer to our Edgar and ask him how many times, approximately, he has collapsed. Our Edgar reflects for a moment and says: Twice, and as he says it he straightens his knees, as he needs to do, so as to stand upright, and he props himself up by putting a hand on the wall. And when did you collapse? we ask. Ah, he says, I don't remember exactly. And where was it, do you remember where? Ah, our Edgar says, where might I have collapsed, once on the Theaterring and once in front of your house. And did you just lie there? we ask. Yes, he says, I just lay there. Under a bush? we ask. No, he says, on the footpath. And how is it we didn't see you, if you were lying on the footpath outside our house? we ask. I don't know, our Edgar says, perhaps you just weren't looking. And so you simply collapsed? we ask and shake our head. Yes, he says, just like that. So tell us about it, we say, did it hurt? Not at all, our Edgar says. I just lay there. And nothing else? we ask. No, nothing else, he says. And so you didn't even feel you were lying there? we ask. But how can I have felt myself lying there, our Edgar exclaims, I was unconscious. And if we'd tickled you? we ask. I wouldn't have noticed it, our Edgar says. And if someone had taken a potshot at you? we ask. I probably wouldn't have noticed that either, he says. So you can't remember anything? we ask. No, our Edgar says, not a thing. And didn't anyone even see you lying there? we ask. No, he says, nobody was there. And what did you do, we ask, when you came to yourself again? Ah, I went into the garden shed and lay down, our Edgar says, and for a while we don't ask him any more questions. And when are you going to collapse again? we ask later. Ah, our Edgar says, probably soon. Today? we ask. Possibly, our Edgar says, maybe not until tomorrow. But let's not stand around here, our Edgar then says—who might have become under other circumstances a small-time oddball with the shoulders of an ox—let's walk on now. If you can, why not? we say. But then we walk, after we've searched the suit, new, starchy, and quite alien to us, and have found in it a well-hidden but empty pocket, presumably Herr Henne's secret pocket, and have pursed our lips to whistle—though we don't whistle—not as usual in the gutter, but on the footpath, while this time our Edgar, who usually walks on the footpath, walks in the gutter. And now our one and only concern is the suit, even though we talk about lots of things, because we're arriving at the vacant and darkly draped shop windows on the Adolf-Hitler-Straße. We turn around, look at ourself from the right, from the left, we even stoop to see how the suit looks on us when we're stooping. And in the windows we look as grown-up as our Edgar, if not more so. All the same, we're not feeling good in the suit of Herr Henne, who's dead now. Perhaps this is because he had to be dead so that we could wear the suit. Each move makes us think of him and wonder if that was how he moved in the suit. But something even worse happens. We've hardly arrived at the arcades when we start to smell Herr Henne in the suit. But he'd hardly worn it! Yes, that's true, but all the same. All the same, in the arcades the smell of Herr Henne comes to us out of our suit. Stop, Edgar, we say. Why? our Edgar asks. Can you smell something? we ask, and while walking we hold our sleeve out to him. No, not really, our Edgar says after sniffing at our sleeve. Nothing at all? we ask. No, our Edgar says, can you? We stop, sniff the sleeve. Doesn't it smell of Herr Henne? we ask. Herr Henne, our Edgar says, let me take another sniff. And then, after he's sniffed it again, more carefully this time, he says: Yes, it does smell of him. But he's dead! we exclaim, horrified. All the same, our Edgar says, it smells of him. But can he do that? we ask. Yes, our Edgar says, he can. Even if he's only worn it twice? we ask. That's what she said, our Edgar says. You mean, we exclaim, that he really had it on more often? Otherwise it wouldn't smell so much of him, our Edgar says and ends the discussion. We see our hands in the window, drooping even more like fins and more limply at our sides, whereas our Edgar has his hands in his pockets, probably on the knife. Wash it, mother must wash the suit, we're thinking as we walk along Ritterstraße, where our legs begin to tremble too. We're swaying a bit ourself now, perhaps Edgar is infectious? How glad we'd be to lean against a wall and take a breather and let our Edgar walk past us, up and down. But in May the walls in our town are damp, on account of the changeable weather, while the suit, in spite of all assurances, is simply too big for us. So we wonder if all the time we've been confusing Herr Henne, when we said we knew him, and a much smaller post-office official. To judge by the suit, the real Herr Henne was much taller and sturdier. So we can only hope that mother will not only wash the suit, but also remove some of it at the arms and legs. Yet, even without being shortened, it would fit our Edgar, thin as he is, at least the length would be right. Wouldn't it be? we ask, the suit would be the right length for you? Yes, our Edgar says, it could be. It's a pity we got it, not you, we say. And you need it much more badly than us, because you haven't got anything and that's why you run around looking so quaint, we say and point to his smock, which he's been wearing for weeks now and which they say his father wore while cutting leather. Yes, our Edgar says, but at the moment it's all I've got. At the moment, at the moment! how funnily you talk! we exclaim, the moment is everything, there's nothing else, is there? And we discover once again that it's hard to speak with our Edgar about what he hasn't got, he just won't listen. Fine, our Edgar says, the moment is everything, but I don't want to talk about it. Have it your own way, we say. Otherwise you could just put on Herr Henne's jacket, so at least you could see if it *might* have fitted you. But our Edgar says: No, I'm not going to put it on. And why won't you put it on? we ask and stand in his way, so he can't go on walking. Then our Edgar suddenly yells: No, I'm not going to put it on. And he pushes us with his right hand—who'd have thought he's still got such strength in it?—into the gutter. Then he opens his mouth wide, as if he was going to yell something important at us, but he can't or doesn't want to, and he shuts his mouth again. Let's go, he says. Where to? we ask. Onward, is all he says. So on we go and on our way to the church we pass the confectioner's, Reese's, where Herr Henne also was. Except that he was here with his wife, whereas we're here with our Edgar. But with his limbs guided by the will of the suit, Herr Henne probably made quite similar motions, though sturdier ones, to the more shy and confined motions we're making with ours. And we're thinking that he'll have tugged straight the suit that fitted him like a glove with tuggings presumably like ours, and have seen himself mirrored in the same windows as those we're mirrored in. Until this thought, in our suit, which Herr Henne still inhabits as a smell, gives us goosebumps all over.

Thank God that by the time we reach the "Schöne Aussicht" restaurant everything thinkable about our suit has been thought and that our Edgar leaps onto a large stone in the empty yard behind the restaurant. He's meaning to show us, now, the extent of our war damage, visible from the top end of the Adolf-Hitler-Straße, the point where it forks to right and left, and we have a spacious view, between two houses, out over our town and across the river and the loam fields, far into our upland country and our Saxon sky. Good, we say. Bewildered by the suit we'll follow more patiently than usual the gestures made by our Edgar, who is still quite exhausted from his conversation with the widow, and in spite of the twilight now settling over the rise and fall of our landscape we'll easily be able to see too the ravages on the edge of our town. We absorb the ravages, gazing for a long time, not saying a word: the former Amsel forest, the former clearing in it, the former forester's house, buildings that formerly lined the edge of the forest. Edgar will presumably soon describe the way everything is from his stone. Also he'll speak about his mother, who has been lying beneath the ravages since the eleventh. Admittedly we knew her better perhaps than we knew Denkstein, Frisch, and Ziegel, but we think of her less often, because that's just too horrible. We don't know if our Edgar still thinks of her much, sometimes we believe he's thinking of her when he falls silent in the middle of speaking and topples into something that's inside him, and we want to shake him or call him back to himself or grab him and pull him out of it again. But at other times we believe that he too doesn't think of her. In any case he doesn't speak about her, but inserts this space into his talk and acts as if she hadn't been killed but had never existed. And as we're secretly searching with our fingertips inside the silk lining of the suit for more secret pockets, we're thinking: Ah, his mother! Ah, we hope he won't speak about his mother when he speaks of the ravages! And then, on his high stone, his sandals wide apart, his pale blue gaze launched into the countryside, our Edgar finally starts to speak. Slowly he lets one word after another escape from his mouth, and we with our bare head on a tilt watch out for the words anxiously. But then he doesn't speak about his mother at all, at least not right away, he only speaks in a quite general way and says that since the eleventh he's been asking himself a question. Would you like to know what that question is? he asks us and looks down at us from his stone. Yes, we would, we say, and with our feet we make a dent or two in the intact earth behind the "Schöne Aussicht", why shouldn't we want to? But the question, he says with his hands tucked inside his smock, is philosophical, so to speak. Philosophical! we exclaim and look up at him. Yes, he says. For he's been asking himself why it was only the Amselgrund and the buildings on the edge of it, with very few people really, that were destroyed, while our town center with many people in it and *us too* were unharmed. You mean you're wondering? we ask. Yes, our Edgar says, why only the forest? And he gazes past us with his pale eyes into the ravages which, though only coincidental, are amply visible from where we are. Whether he sees them as clearly as us we can't say, because his eyesight is getting worse and things around him are getting darker every day. Perhaps he can't even see the ravages anymore. Yes, why only the forest, we've wondered about that too, we say and pause for a bit and suppose that he'll come to his mother now, but he still doesn't come to her. Just think, he says and looks over toward our ravages in silence. And he says: Strange. Because, he then explains to us, the bombs had been scattered in broad daylight over our forest, although it would have been easy to scatter them over our town. That's so, we say. And we're thinking: Now, now it'll be his mother! But still she doesn't come. For our Edgar says that the question is now settled as far as he's concerned, he's discovered in the meantime why we were spared. Yesterday, he says, beside the dog kennel, where your Hector used to be. And that it would interest him to know if we'd found the same answer, since we'd been asking the same question. We hesitate a bit. Well, we eventually say, we'd certainly asked the question, but an answer, no, we hadn't found an answer. So you haven't? our Edgar asks. No, we say, but that was a lie, for of course we know the reason, even if we're not telling anyone. All right then, our Edgar says, rubbing the tip of a sandal a few times back and forth over the stone he's standing on, so he'd tell us the reason now. Right, he says, now listen. Right, he says, the reason is simple. And it's this: the bombs trickled down over the forest and not over the city because it was—a mistake. What? A mistake. Aha, we say and look first at Edgar, then at our feet. Why are you looking like that? our Edgar asks. The pilots had made a mistake, that was the reason. True, they'd easily found the town with their expensive equipment and they'd calculated precisely when to drop the bombs, but their ambition had made them *over*calculate it. For the pilots' ambition to destroy our town, spread out so freely and visibly in the middle of our loamy plain on such a fine morning had simply not been enough—they'd wanted more.

Far rather than our little town on the plain they'd wanted to destroy industries essential to the war effort located in the Amselgrund. Therefore they'd dropped their bombs, as long as the supply lasted, on our Amselgrund, where they'd supposed there was an industry, which there hadn't been, and they'd only brushed the edge of the town. You think so? we ask and look at the sky's roof, which certainly won't hold up much longer. Yes, that's what I think, our Edgar says, and with a jerk of his head he turns away from our *flattened* forest, which he perceives in all likelihood only dimly, and toward our almost unscathed town: it was due to a mistake that we'd been spared. So it was a mistake, we say. Yes, our Edgar says. And that without this mistake not the Amselgrund with its trees and the *other thing*, but the town with its houses and *ourselves* would no longer be here. But where would the town be then? we ask. Not here anymore, our Edgar says. And us, where would we be? we ask. Not here anymore, our Edgar says. Like you, when you collapse? we ask and yawn and look along our trouser creases to the ground, on which our Edgar, outstretched like a tree, can lie at any time and be out of reach. Yes, he says, only more permanently. We nod. Rather permanently, eh? we say. Yes, our Edgar says, rather permanently. Yes, we say, even though we know that he's wrong and that our town was only spared because we live in it and our extinction, our destruction, is quite impossible. Yes, we say all the same, and now we turn away from the Amselgrund too, it must have just been a mistake.

9

EXHAUSTED, recognizably so even from far off, we hobble next down the Schilderstraße, past the Sebastian Pfeffer sawmill, now long shut down. Then the Brühlmann and Company distillery, then the vacant lot. In December here a soldier fired a shot in the air, but nobody was hurt. The sky is more heavily curtained by low clouds and accordingly less spacious now. For that reason, as our Edgar exclaims, we must hobble faster, faster and faster, because across the roofs bad weather is coming. And where are we hobbling to? Edgar shows us with a gesture: the church! How stupid to send us to the church, but perhaps it will be shut. At least, the church square is deserted, perhaps because such a wind is blowing around the house-windows sealed with old blankets, pillows, and bits of cardboard. Who'd ever want to leave his well-sealed house toward the end—and soon the end will come—of the first day after our conquest, and go out into such empty streets, such windy ones? And there stands the church now.

Two or three years ago we used to go to church sometimes, but recently we stopped going to church. True, we've walked around it from time to time, but we've never gone inside. For one day we discovered that we don't need the church, and after that we never thought of going there. Also we don't need the pastor, whose name is Herr Meyers, but this is all a family matter, father too can *happily do without him*. Instead of going to church on Sundays, father has recently preferred to sit on the couch and think of the lunch that mother is cooking, alone in the kitchen, or about the factory. Or else before lunch he'd stretch out a bit and thumb through the books that have now all been burned. In which father was always so happy, thumbing his way through them! Why should I need the church, when I've got this, he'd often exclaim, and as he lay there he'd flourish a book so that we could tell from the door what it was. And he'd wanted, in spite of his age, to start studying philosophy after the war, especially Indian philosophy, while mother, because of her headache, is not happy and doesn't expect to be, with church or without it. (The only thing she wants is peace and quiet.) Only very seldom, when father was in Berlin or Dippoldiswalde, did she go to church *without being under any illusions*, or else she made us go. So we went, but we didn't like it, we simply don't believe in it. Our Edgar has never once been to church, except perhaps at Christmas.

So now that we're at the church we hobble around it once, giving it, as our Edgar says, a *tour of honor*. Naturally with our cap on our head, so that if anyone recognizes us he can tell mother that we were *bundled up nice and warm* when we were walking around the church on the first day after our conquest. The church is just as it was before, including the hole torn in the back of it that we always like to look at. Possibly, during the last few weeks, it has become even more dilapidated. Then, because the side entrance is locked, we hobble back to the main entrance, push open the gate, and with Edgar leading the way, we arrive in the little porch. Then we see that this porch, which is meant to shelter the church from the wind, is crammed as high as our wound with boxes and suitcases and luggage. How strange! How many times have we not been here when the porch was not so full! And we start to climb over the luggage, having first hoisted our trousers, in order to get through to the second door, the one leading into the church. No doubt about it—the church is almost inaccessible. The only question is, who can have blockaded our church like this? And it occurs to us, just as we're raising our legs, that it must be the refugees from the east. It's a fact that refugees from the east have been pouring into our town for years, people whom mother has till now been able to *beg off*, though with some difficulty. True, new ones are always being allotted to us and *installed* in our beautiful—even paneled—first-floor rooms, but till now mother has always been able to get rid of them. Herr Schellenbaum has turned out to be *invaluable* in this, but it's only a question of time until he'll not be able to help us anymore. Anyway, the refugees from the east, wherever they've taken refuge, have always brought something with them, which they build up all around them, so as to establish a place for themselves. Even quite large rooms, although empty, are filled up overnight. But there has been no space left in our town for a long time now, so nobody who's not one of our people should spread himself around here. All the same, they've got nothing better to do than spread out everything they've rescued and fill everything up, even the church. Even if somebody else has a wound that he mayn't hit against anything, we're thinking as we climb over the suitcases and boxes. Naturally we'd like to know what's in the suitcases and boxes and we rap on them, but the sound tells us nothing. (Naturally the boxes contain the *Usual Stuff*.) So instead of letting us say a quick prayer for father, people are obstructing us. For a long time we climb over the boxes and rap on them or imagine to ourself in the unrelenting darkness of the porch which refugee belongs with which box, and where this or that refugee, having quickly let his box drop, has run off to, where he's adrift or buried. Until we hear, all at once, coming from inside the church, a noise, a scraping and scratching. Probably a refugee, we're thinking, and he's dragging his box farther inside the church. With this noise in our ears, this gasping and groaning, we arrive at the door—once paneled with frosted glass, but now a sheet of cardboard is glued over it—and we discover that this door into the church is locked. Oh well, our Edgar says. Let's go back, we say.

Outside—the church-square wind blowing full blast takes our breath away. All at once a voice from above: Hey! What are you doing here? Holding our breath, leaning into the wind, the suit flapping about our limbs, we look up. And see it's only the pastor, who is poking his head out of the little window that our church has in its nave. Strange, nobody has ever talked down to us from the window before, the pastor is the first. Ah, it's only us, we call, and we look upward. And what do you want? the pastor calls—he's somewhat red in the face. Ah, we call, we wanted to go into the church, but unfortunately it's closed. Oh, the pastor calls, and then he pokes a naked arm also out through the window, as if he wanted to take hold of us, and where have you been? Ah, everywhere, we call and point with our hands straight ahead, as well as behind us, just now we were on the Güterhofstraße. And we take a little look past the large-cheeked face of the pastor at the church roof, which lost many tiles last winter and has got many bare patches now. The wall is heavily rain-stained too. And where did you go after the Güterhofstraße, the pastor calls and shakes his arm a bit, without directly threatening us. Into the porch here, we call, but we're leaving now. And we're meaning to swing our shopping bag around a little, only we don't dare to. No, stay where you are, the pastor suddenly calls from his church, which, from our standpoint, he seems to be carrying on his back like an enormous snail shell, and where he has probably been busy with some not altogether clean work, for he looks rather dirty. Also he isn't wearing his surplice, by which he's usually to be recognized. No, we've never encountered the pastor before in a shirt like that and divested of his surplice. Also we're wondering how he ever got up to such a high window. True, our church has an organ, rather a shrill one, built high up into the roof beams, but it has no gallery. Yes, but are you standing on a ladder? we ask, but on account of the wind the pastor doesn't understand us, and he calls: Yes, I'm coming now. Ah, you needn't come, we're leaving now, we call. No, wait, he calls, I'm coming. Ah, take your time, we'll wait if we're supposed to, we call. So promise you'll wait, he calls. But of course, we call—while the pastor's head, which has the fewest hairs of all the heads we know, rapidly disappears and we really have to wait for quite a long time in the church-square wind. But we make good use of the time, tug our cap straighter and arrange the shoulders and arms of our new suit. The pastor, who wants to approach us in his usual form on this first day after our conquest, seems to have put on his surplice and to have slipped into his black robe while still in motion, that's why he's so out of breath. Well now, he exclaims from a distance still, and with his rather bulging eyes he looks at us as if he's somewhat relieved, what are you doing out on the streets on a day like this? Ah, we say, we're not afraid, if that's what you mean. And what is it you wanted here? the pastor asks, snuggling up against his church, because of the wind. Ah, what did we want? we wanted to pray. Really, the pastor says—he hasn't forgotten, of course, that we haven't been inside his church recently, and because we don't need him, he doesn't like our whole family—and whose idea was it all of a sudden to pray? Not ours, unfortunately, we say, it was mother's idea. Really, all of a sudden, the pastor says and settles himself, facing half into the wind, half toward us, against his church wall. And for whom did you want to pray? he asks. Mainly for our father, we say, but for the others too. And him, we say, pointing at our Edgar, he was going to pray only for his father, actually, because his mother's already dead and he's got nobody else. Really, the pastor says, and so he thinks that because his mother is dead he doesn't need to pray for her and think of her anymore? But he thinks of her all the time, we exclaim. Don't you, Edgar, you're constantly thinking of your mother, aren't you? But our Edgar, instead of saying Yes, I think of her, only blushes and shrugs his shoulders. Ah, now and then, he eventually says. But surely it's not just now and then, but always, isn't it? we exclaim. Ah, not always, more like now and then, our Edgar says, and he's only embarrassed by our question, because he doesn't like to admit to anybody that he thinks of his mother a lot. Well, the pastor says and raises a hand in the air as if to silence us, he must decide for himself how often he thinks of his mother, but he can also pray for her. Even though she's dead? we ask. Yes, indeed, the pastor says. All right, we say, if you say so, then from now on he'll pray for her too. When did you last hear anything of your father, the pastor then asks, and he smiles at us pointlessly. In January, we say, he's missing, but he'll definitely come back. And because your mother is afraid he perhaps might not come back, you should pray for him, is that it?

he asks. Yes, we say, probably that's it. So it was all of a sudden—when for months there has been no sign of any of you here, even though you could have been a great help to me, the pastor says, and at last he has found a hollow in the church wall in which to shelter a bit from the wind. I happen to have made a note of it, although unfortunately I haven't got my little book with me now, he says. The last time you attended my church was on the third Sunday in February, February last year, not this year, he says and smiles again. And then you didn't only come late, you also left before the blessing, so I had to inscribe you as being unexcused. For months I had to inscribe you as being unexcused. Until I lost patience, nobody could hold that against me, and I simply crossed out your names in my little notebook. Crossed them out? we ask. Yes, he says, crossed them out. And, he asks after a short pause, haven't you got anything to say about that? Well, we say, if you crossed us out . . . Yes? the pastor asks. Well, we say, we'd been thinking it was something like that. Thinking! the pastor exclaims. Well, we say, fearing. Yes, the pastor says, but you needn't have had any fears. No, we say, probably that's so. And what shall I do about you now? the pastor asks after a short pause, and he makes a peevish face, because in this wind he'd much rather be inside his church and strolling around his altar a bit. Yes, we say, we don't know either, if what you've done is cross us out. Well, in any case, your mother did send you to church, the pastor says in rapid summary of everything, so as to get on with it. That's right, we say, and then we had a few other things to do in the town. What things? the pastor asks—he'd like to be quickly inside the church again, but he also wants to know about everything precisely. Well, for instance, we went to the slaughterhouse, we say and ponder how much we should tell him, and how, about the slaughterhouse. To the slaughterhouse! the pastor at once exclaims, and he raises his eyebrows. Yes, to the slaughterhouse, we say. And since we don't want to tell him everything and don't want to conceal everything either, we make a few changes and say we'd been there to ask for some pork dripping, but that it had been sold out already. What? You mean there was pork dripping at the slaughterhouse? the pastor at once shouts into the wind. Yes, we say, but only very early in the morning, while we were still asleep. We didn't hear the shouts either. What shouts? the pastor asks. Ah, the ones in the morning, we say. Frau Kohlhund heard them. But how can there have been any pork dripping at the slaughterhouse, without my knowing it? the pastor exclaims. Yes, that's what Frau Kohlhund said too, we say, but that's something we don't know either. And so your mother sent you to the slaughterhouse, just like that, the pastor asks. Yes, just like that, we say. And we're about to say that she had another headache and had to lie down, but we say instead that because of a *back*ache she'd had to sit in an *arm*chair, and that was why she sent us. It's a pity but the thing with the pork dripping didn't work out, we say, and now the thing with the prayer won't work out either. The thing with the prayer, as you express it, always works out, just so long as one really wants to pray, the pastor says in a voice that's suddenly transformed, so much so that if we hadn't been looking at him we probably wouldn't have recognized it as his. Up till now he'd been speaking in a quite everyday and natural way, at an average speed, but now he's speaking much too slowly and altogether unnaturally. Why he's not speaking as he ordinarily does, the way he spoke, for instance, while he was in the window, we haven't the slightest idea. Also he keeps repeating himself now. And keeps coming back, although we've long since understood what he says, to the *provisionally locked church door* and saying that such a *provisionally locked church door* needn't dishearten us and be considered by us as an insuperable obstacle, for such a *provisionally locked church door*, if it were only knocked on, could quickly be reopened. And besides, there's a reason for locking such a door for the time being, a quite practical reason too, he says while straightening himself up a little against his church wall because he wants to keep a steady eye on everything he's saying, and he looks at us through the wind in a quite practical sort of way. Yes, we say, we know the reason, we've seen it. And what, the pastor asks, pressing his robe closer to his body, what have you seen? Ah, we say, the suitcases and the boxes are what we've seen. And then once more we ask if he was standing by any chance on a ladder when he spoke from the window. Of what ladder do you speak, children? the pastor asks, and he simply won't tell us. Ah, let's drop the subject, we say, we don't have to know everything. And then actually he doesn't tell us. Instead he asks if we know what day it is today. Yes, we say, roughly we do. And whether on this day that is so important for us, a day that would terminate a shameful era in the lives of us all and inaugurate a new era, we had done a goodly work? And please, no evasions now, the pastor exclaims, just yes or no. Which day do you mean, exactly? we ask, because we aren't sure if he means today, when we went to the slaughterhouse, or if he's talking of yesterday, when we were conquered, true enough, but actually did no more than stand at the window and imagine ourselves, by artifice, into our theater. But the pastor means *today*. I speak, he says, of this present day and its task of liberation, which God, to punish us all, has for so long delayed. Do you know, he asks, of what task of liberation I speak? Yes, we say, roughly we do. And of what task do I speak? he asks. Ah, we're free again, our Edgar says without much enthusiasm, because he doesn't quite yet believe in the freedom the pastor has in mind, or else he can't yet picture it. So you mean today, although it's almost over? we ask. How do you mean, over? the pastor asks. Well, at least in our opinion it is, we say, but perhaps you think as Edgar does. Well, how about the goodly works? the pastor asks, without saying whether or not, in his opinion, today is over. Well, if that's a question and we're supposed to answer this question, we say, and we resolve to watch every word very carefully now and we reflect for a long while and look at our Edgar too, though he only shrugs his shoulders. Well, we say, actually we've been to the slaughterhouse. And that, the pastor asks, is supposed to be your goodly work on such an important day? Yes, we say, probably. And you've done nothing else? the pastor asks, and he gives us a piercing look. Nothing that helps man and drives the sweat through the pores? No, we really haven't done anything that drives the sweat through the pores, we say—even though at the slaughterhouse and in Wundenplan we actually sweated quite a lot. Well, the pastor says, then I'll now give you an opportunity to do a goodly work, so that at last I can inscribe your names in my little black notebook again. And before we can tell him that we're not altogether sure we want to have our names in his little notebook again, and besides, we still have to visit Herr Schellenbaum, he has turned around and goes, as he came, keeping very close to his church, back to the main church door, and of course we have to follow him.

On the way to this door, at the border of the Old Graveyard, with the pastor leaping on ahead of us in earnest, we bump into his old housekeeper, Frau Selma or Thelma is her name. In her wide black dress which long ago—we still went to church in those days—used to hang around her like a sack and now seems to have stuck to her—she floats out from behind a tombstone, glides through the open graveyard gate, and stands in our path. Are you going, she exclaims, to the funeral? Us? we exclaim with a twinge of guilt, pointing to ourself. Who else? the housekeeper asks, nobody else is here. A funeral, we exclaim, why, is there one? There will always be funerals, she says. And she asks if one of them is our *grandfather* and which group of mourners we might be looking for. One of whom? we ask and look around, as if we were looking for our group of mourners behind the ancient elm or against the graveyard fence. Ah, one of them, she says and points to the church where they're probably laid out. Strange, how different a church is, the moment you know there are dead people in it! However, we don't display our changed outlook, we act as if the church was the same as ever. And we say that we didn't have a grandfather and couldn't remember one, and ask if the funeral will be today. Yes, the housekeeper whispers, in half an hour, and not just one, but two. And that she, though a mere weak woman, had just dug *the double grave*, even though God hadn't made her and the pastor didn't employ her for such tasks, and—it hadn't surprised her— as usual there'd been nobody near to help. Look, she says and holds out to us her presumably work-worn and earth-encrusted hands, so we say: Just look!—although in the twilight we hardly see the hands. Yes, you could have helped me with the grave, she says, but now it's too late. Many people might have been able to help her with the grave, but none had. Only the pastor had come by once to call in on her down there, asking if she'd soon be finished, but he hadn't lent a hand. Only once had he fleetingly touched the shovel and shown her how one has to do it, and pushed away a few stones *from the surface,* but she'd had *to stand in the grave and scratch in the earth.* And then softly, cupping a hand to her mouth: You see, there aren't any graves anymore, all the space is occupied. You mean? we say. I mean, the housekeeper says, that they both go into the same hole, back there, at six o'clock today. And she points into the depths of the Old Graveyard, in which people are being buried again now, because the New Graveyard in our town was also flattened on the eleventh. So the hole she'd dug was for two: for old Herr Pietsch from the Könnitzerstraße and for one of those folks from the east, whom nobody here knew, however, and whose name was Szczepanski or Stepanski. Did you know old Herr Pietsch? the housekeeper asks us. No, we say, sorry but we didn't. He was a carpenter, she says. Even then, we didn't know him, sorry, we say. And the other one, did you know him? No, we say, not him either. Yes, that's how it is, she exclaims, nobody knows him. Anyway he'd come, the other one had, the day before yesterday in a horse-drawn wagon from the east, and it was still winter there, and while fleeing, with the wagon moving fast, as people had told her, he'd kept opening the flaps, jumping off the wagon, he hadn't wanted to leave. While jumping he'd broken and crushed this or that part of himself, but he'd survived it all. But he'd only just arrived and reached safety and had been raised up and laid on a sort of bed, when he'd all of a sudden died, so now one had to bury him, *even if all the places are taken.* So I simply made the grave of Herr Pietsch a bit wider, she says, it was just about due. I didn't tell anyone. Wider? we ask and giggle a bit, while the pastor at the church door is shifting from one foot to the other in his impatience. It's the same thing, the housekeeper says, as with all these new-fangled experiments, you don't ever know if it's going to work out right. You mean? we ask. I mean burying them both together and inviting the bereaved all together, the housekeeper says. But if you don't belong with them, you won't know, of course. No, we say, we don't belong with them and we don't know anything. And now, we say, we've got to go into the church. Yes, off you go then, I'm going to lie down for a bit, the housekeeper says, and she flits—her sack billowing around her—through the open graveyard gate and back behind her tombstone. Meanwhile, in all our finery, we go now for a third time to the church door and climb over the pieces of luggage, for the pastor, who has a funeral at six, is standing already at the inside door. But it's locked, we exclaim, standing with our wound among the suitcases. But here's the key, the pastor calls back to us, and he pulls a key from his robe on a silver chain, and it fits. So we climb after him to the door and step into the church behind him, having put our cap in our shopping bag, keeping our heads down and cringing a bit, because we haven't been here for so long and we don't deserve church and have been crossed out in the little black notebook, while our Edgar, to whom it's all the same, walks as he always does and perhaps even has his hands in his pockets.

Our church, like our slaughterhouse, is much larger than it need be, especially inside. When it was built probably more people went to church than nowadays and now it's mostly empty. Or in those days they built such a large church hoping that once it existed more people would come, but they were wrong. Also many of us have been killed and so are absent from church, and the emptiness, which was always large, is now larger still. Only when we enter it do we see how large the church really is. Far and wide our footsteps echo through the tall building, into which we can hardly see, it's so dark, and we can hardly detect the main altar, which is smoke-blackened, patched together with cardboard and wooden slats and poorly maintained—on the eleventh an aisle toward the back was ripped open by a small bomb. We can also hardly detect the pulpit, which no longer has a canopy, either the canopy fell in on the eleventh or it was stolen afterward. Even a person with good eyes looking from the entrance can only guess whereabouts the pulpit and altar are. For our Edgar, with his eyes, they're presumably just not there. But in spite of the darkness the pastor knows his way about in the church. When he pushes his way sideways through the chairs, he knows where he's going. Come on, he calls and is far ahead of us. Yes, we're coming, we whisper—for we don't want to speak loudly in the church. And in the darkness—it's good there's no wind here, at least—we allow ourself to be waved onward into the depths of the church by his small, white, and seemingly powdered hands. Slowly we grope our way through the benches, then down the side aisle. The first side nave is empty. The pictures that used to hang here once and the candlesticks that once stood here with their tall white candles have vanished. Either they've been stolen or the pastor has taken them down into the church cellar. When we reach the second side nave we see that it too is full of suitcases. But instead of the single articles being put side by side as in the porch, they've been put on top of one another, to save space. Right up to the window the boxes and suitcases are piled, so that they'll be out of the way. Well, that of course explains a lot. Obviously it was the pastor himself who gasped and groaned while we were standing outside. Probably he was hauling a particularly heavy suitcase through the church or lifting it up on the pile. And as he stands on top of the pile, he hears us talking outside the church, and since he is so close to the window he at once pokes his head out. No wonder he didn't understand us when we asked about a ladder, for he was standing all the time on the pile of suitcases. And he doesn't need his robe and surplice, but is in shirt-sleeves, because robe and surplice would only have hindered him in carrying and lifting. Well, he now exclaims from the side nave, where he has again taken off his robe and surplice and thrown them over a little prayer stool and has just rolled his sleeves up, now you can help me. Very well, we say, although we'd have preferred to say a quick prayer and then gone straight to Herr Schellenbaum, but that's no longer possible. Right, the pastor says, and suddenly he has a long white candle in his hand and is taking a few steps toward us, shining the flame in our face. It was a question, he tells us, of the belongings of some fellow citizens of ours from the east, who had only just managed to save themselves from the *jaws of Moloch,* and which had been deposited here. These belongings had simply been dropped outside the church yesterday, they were blocking the entrance and had to be moved quickly, because at six o'clock . . . There's a double burial, isn't there? we ask and nod. Yes, the pastor says, how did you know? Ah, we say, we just thought so. Well, the graves have been dug, the pastor says. It's a double grave, isn't it? we say. And the deceased, the pastor continues, have been laid out. Where, we ask, at the back there? Yes, indeed, the pastor says and points to the main altar. On the other hand . . . , he says and points with a sigh toward the entrance door. And during the few hours that the personal effects of people from far afield had lain outside the church, they'd been twice broken into and presumably various items had been pilfered. Also he didn't want the impression to arise that his church door was *ever* shut. Before the obsequies take place, the pastor says, gazing after his words which are lost in the space close to the bier behind us, this whole pile of luggage must be here in the side nave, where I can keep an eye on it from the altar, and you've got to help me. To keep an eye on it? we ask. No, to move it, the pastor says. Oh, move it, we say, and since we now know that we're not alone in the church with the pastor, but that Herr Pietsch and Herr Szczepanski are there too, we sneak another look at the main altar, where the two of them—because now forever they belong together—are presumably laid out on a double bier, but unfortunately we can't see them, the main altar is plunged in gloom. Then we look once more up the mound of suitcases illumined by the flickering candlelight, take a deep breath, and draw our arms in to our sides, for now, we're thinking, we'll have to watch every word we utter to the pastor. And then, in our new suit, which he presumably hasn't noticed yet, we say: Well, if it's help you want! Yes, the pastor says and indicates to us with his free hand how he imagines we'll help him. That is, by picking up the suitcases, carrying them through his church—empty but for us and the other two—and then, with his help, hoisting them up onto the pile. But take care, he says, not to pull them so as to scratch these old flagstones of mine. Yes, we say, we'll take care. And where, we ask, do the obsequies take place? In the main nave, the pastor says and points once more into the gloomiest part of his church. Just a moment now, he says and hesitates. And the burial, where will the burial be? In the Old Graveyard, he says. Just a moment now, he says again, because his candlelight has evidently fallen on us at a certain angle. So they've already been laid out? we ask, because naturally we're afraid the pastor might be expecting us to help with the laying out. Yes, they're laid out, the pastor says. And then he asks us, completely out of the blue: What are you wearing there?

And he narrows his eyes a bit, presumably because he doesn't see well without his glasses. You mean this, we say and spread our arms, so that he can also take a good look at our new suit in the flickering candlelight. And we explain to him that it had only recently become available and had been a sort of gift to us. But who from? the pastor asks and comes closer with his candle. From somebody, we say, who had it in their attic, because it wasn't needed anymore. But it doesn't even fit you, the pastor exclaims and tugs a bit with his free hand at our sleeve, which is of course very wide and loose, and we admit that it doesn't. Yes, we say, but it doesn't matter, we'll grow into it. Now just a moment, the pastor says again and even walks all around us with his candle, to see our suit from all sides and even to feel it a little. First he feels under the arms, then the collar, then the sleeves. But you haven't had this suit for long, he then says. No, we say, that's correct. We've walked once around the church in it and a bit through the town. Hm, the pastor says, through the town. And then he asks us if we could tell him where and from whom we'd got the suit and when we had first *slipped into it*. But we'd be glad to tell you, we say, and we swivel around a bit along with the pastor, who is still circling us with his candle. Well, we slipped into it about one hour ago, and then to make everything simpler we kept it on. That was at 83 Güterhofstraße, in a junkroom, where, in addition to a dog, Granny Henne is, though she's asleep most of the time. So nobody saw you slipping into the suit, the pastor asks. No, we say, only the dog. And you say that was an hour ago, the pastor says and looks at his watch. Yes, we say, about an hour. In any case you already had the suit on when you came here from the Güterhofstraße? the pastor asks—he's standing so close to us now that we can't see the outline of his face anymore.

Yes, that's so, we say. And it wasn't here, perhaps outside in the porch, that you first put the suit on? he asks. Where such a suit might certainly be found, amid all that unguarded luggage. Are you thinking that we didn't put the suit on in the Güterhofstraße at all, but stole it here? we ask. But still the pastor wouldn't go so far as that. No, no, I wouldn't go so far as that, he says, and because he wants only to know the whole truth about our suit and doesn't think he's going to learn it from us, he begins now to smell at our suit. Holding the candle well away from him, so as not to set us on fire, he lowers his head a bit and smells at us carefully, first on the right side, then on the left. It smells, doesn't it? we ask, and since we've got nothing to hide we hold out to the pastor each part of the suit he'd like to smell, first our right lapel, then the left one, then one shoulder, then the other, finally the middle of the suit and the back of it. Strange, the pastor says, it smells as if you haven't worn it for long. But that's just it, we haven't worn it for long, we exclaim. But it smells, the pastor says, and he sets his candle down in a corner of the side nave so as not to let it drip on his church, as if it had just come out of a suitcase. From a wardrobe, we exclaim, a wardrobe! On the other hand it smells, the pastor says, and he ponders for a while, but before he can say what or who in his opinion it smells of we exclaim: It smells of Herr Henne! Who wore it before us, but only twice, mostly he only looked at it, and now it's too late. Well, the pastor says, and he has no further ideas regarding the suit, I confess that recent experiences have made me mistrustful. Perhaps too mistrustful. The suit for instance would not be the first ever to be pilfered. Everything was disappearing, everything. First the candles disappeared, then the candlesticks, then the cloth they stood on, then the tabletop on which the cloth had been spread, everything was disappearing, everything. But let's drop the subject, he says. We're about to tell him the name and address of the suit's previous owner, but he stops his ears and exclaims: No, I just don't want to know. And he beckons us away from his side nave and back into the porch, where the suitcases and the boxes are.

We don't know how long we spend tidying up in our much-too-large church under the eyes of the pastor, who at six has a double burial and thinks we're suit thieves, or how long we spend carrying luggage from the front door into the side nave. All this time, Herr Pietsch and Herr Szczepanski, though invisible, are beside us. We don't know how many hundredweights or *tons* we lift that evening, shifting, dragging, pulling, shoving, and thrusting them into the hands of the pastor who stands on top of the pile. All to ensure that the double obsequies will start at six. And our wound? After it has reopened and bled and stained not only our underpants but also the trousers of our new suit inside, it goes quiet. The pastor sends us back and forth so often that it settles down quietly. In any case, we forget it. What our Edgar does or doesn't forget we can't say. True, we see him, but we don't think of him, or only very much in passing, because we're incessantly thinking of Herr Pietsch and Herr Szczepanski. Where exactly are they? we ask the pastor after thrusting a gigantic suitcase into his hands. Who? the pastor asks—building our suitcase into his pile. Ah, we say, the ones that are going to be buried. They're over there at the back, the pastor says. And we bring the next suitcase. And when exactly does the burial begin? we ask and shove a fresh suitcase at him. In half an hour, the pastor calls from up on his pile. But they are laid out, aren't they? we ask. Yes, the pastor says, they're laid out. So we needn't help to lay them out? we ask. No, the pastor says, you needn't help to lay them out. And now, he says, the next one. We keep wanting to sit down for a breather or at least to lean against something, but he's always calling out to us: And now the next one! Or: And now the basket! Or: Cheer up now, the worst is over! Or: Careful, my flagstones! His side nave is getting fuller and fuller, emptier and emptier the space by the door. And when we've passed up to the pastor the last one, a suitcase held together by a thick leather strap—like the ones father takes for making his whips—and he has stowed it away high on his pile, he climbs down again. Well then, he says and lays a hand on our shoulder, now you can sit down, but not for long. *Danke schön*, we say. And side by side we sit down on one of the church benches that are intended for children or dwarves, benches now surrounded by luggage, and for a few minutes we breathe in and out the air that's amply available in the much-too-large church, more air than we'd breathe during an entire day in our room. We also sweat a lot. Then the pastor admits that he'd been thinking a lot about our suit while up on his pile. True, his mind was not altogether at rest regarding its provenance, but he didn't think we were thieves. Many people nowadays would simply be pocketing things that didn't belong to them, or taking them away or eating them or wearing them, without necessarily being thieves. Also in such cases there was a simple remedy for what one had done: simply to take the suit off again, fold it up, and take it back to the place one had taken it from. You mean back into Frau Henne's wardrobe? we ask. I mean the suitcase the suit was in, the pastor says. And since he now has to turn his thoughts to those who are lying on the bier, and since he has no more time for us, he wouldn't be seeing what we might do, so in his presence we needn't be ashamed, we were alone with our conscience. That would be the best opportunity to give back something, if we had something to give back, and had we understood him? Yes, we say, we've understood you all right, and we'd gladly give the suit back, but it really had belonged to Herr Henne and it really does belong to us now. Well then, the pastor says, if you think you have a right to the suit. Ah, we say, whether or not we have a right to it is hard to say, of course, but in any case it belongs to us. Well then, he says, if it belongs to you let's not speak any more of it.

So the pastor pushes us into a niche bordering on the side nave and here, bowing our head, closing our eyes, folding our hands, and going very close to the wall, we say our prayers now, while the pastor goes away, because he has the funeral. Where we stand the wall is so thin that we can both hear and smell the rain falling in the church square. (But then it doesn't rain at all.) Good, so we pray. First, as promised, for father, then for mother, then for our relatives in Pommerania, then for the Hüttenrauchs in Berlin, though probably they're all dead, as well as for the many other relatives we have and whom we can't remember individually, because they're scattered everywhere. We stand there and bow our head and pray that everyone may be well and we wish for them that, like us, they've survived everything all right. Finally we pray for our Edgar and for ourself and our house, that it won't fall to bits anymore but will soon be repaired. And we pray, after praying for everyone we can think of *in particular*, in a *general* way somewhat, for instance for our town or what's left of it, in general for our country or what's left of it, in general finally for the rest of the world likewise. Until, as the first mourners arrive—one can tell that they're arriving by the wiping of feet at the entrance door and the shuffling down the central aisle—we pray once more that particular things may be granted to particular people. Thus, for instance, for our Edgar, that he may be adopted soon and be able to eat more and see better, for mother's left leg, so that she can get up again and go to the slaughterhouse herself, for father, that he may never have been in the vat room during the night in May, also that he never will be in one, and, when he comes back to us, he'll have no wounds, or only a small one, perhaps on his thigh. And then, while the first mourners, presumably those belonging to Herr Szczepanski, for we don't know them and they look somewhat eastern, to judge by the shapes of their faces, by their caps and furs, come hesitantly down the central aisle and the pastor, who has long ago rolled down his sleeves again and put his surplice around him and his black robe on, is lighting the two candles for the dead, we pray a little bit longer, until we can't think of anything more. Certainly there'd still be a lot that we could pray for and wish for us and for father and mother and our Edgar and the Hüttenrauchs and our country and the world, but it doesn't come to our mind at the moment. So we stop praying, because it really comes to nothing and we aren't even certain that we're praying right, still we don't know how else we should pray, we've never learned any other way. Eventually we lean our head against the church wall, because we're trembling so much from dragging suitcases, while our Edgar, who's also exhausted, of course, curiously enough isn't trembling but is quite cheesy-looking in the face, and his temples and cheeks are even more transparent than before. And he keeps swaying before his piece of wall, against which he might topple. We don't know if he's praying only for his father or for his mother too, and he hasn't got any other relatives, because his family has always had a tendency to die out. But also perhaps he's not praying at all, only hoping that he won't fall over. Briefly: our forehead is pressed to the wall, because we're so tired and now we let ourselves go, because the pastor is busy with his mourners, separating them with his seemingly powdered hands into two groups, one for Herr Pietsch and the other for Herr Szczepanski, and leading them up to the common bier and not making any distinction between the local people and the strangers. No, because all of them are frail, dawdling people draped in furs and dragging their feet in the church, he takes people in both groups by the arms and supports them and holds them upright and speaks to them from his small mouth words of hope and encouragement. Yawning or with teeth chattering we look across to the mourners, who, because in the nick of time the boxes and suitcases have been moved into the side nave, can now stand around the bier and quietly sing something. But because we see neither the mourners nor the dead people—in such a large church two candles aren't enough for that—and because we're so tired and don't even understand what the pastor is saying, we soon walk down the central aisle and out through the front door, cross the church square, and are on our way.

10

Before long, looming out of the twilight because it stands against the sky, our theater, the town theater. Over which, to catch the eye, in golden letters set probably in a gigantic steel frame, the words ART FOR THE PEOPLE can be read. But what's become of our glorious though quite small theater during these last weeks? What's become of the fine words which, being so close to the sky, always shone in the sun? Was it really blast from the bombs that knocked the letters crooked, as mother says? Or has the upkeep of the letters been so neglected that they've finally lapsed into the form we're familiar with? The fact is: the words ART and PEOPLE have been hanging every which way for a long time, the gently sloping flowerbeds leading up to the theater are overgrown, the glass panes of the vitrines have been smashed, the door handles unscrewed and carried away, and the stucco is crumbling from our theater's exterior walls. Ah, our beautiful theater! Which, in spite of the many swing doors set in its long nave, has been shut since the winter. In which, however, on the first evening after our conquest, visible even from a distance, suddenly as we're on our way to Herr Schellenbaum, one door stands open. Yes, the stage door, which was locked, is all at once open again, there's a candle set up beside it, throwing a dim luster across the sidewalk. Can the theater have been reopened? Shoulder to shoulder, with our Edgar between us, we station ourselves facing the light and we hear and see everything for a while out of a bush, a forsythia bush, though its flowers have now faded. Several oldish men are standing around the door and at once we can see they're artists. They're actors, who, as late as last fall, were standing on the stage for our benefit, in the most variegated roles—until, when the winter came, they were thrust into uniforms, and after a gun (a real one!) and a few grenades (real ones!) had been put into their hands, they had gone in a column of three, led by a band, from their assigned Siechendorf quarters to the railroad station square. (True, winter sun gleamed on all the trumpets, but because of the way they marched we thought for a long time that their procession was just one more act.) After standing around on the station for a long time—we stood with them, at a distance—they were packed into empty wagons and dispersed in the direction of Hungersleben, so as to defend us, but not for long. Due to the fact that there was no fighting at all out there, they must have flung their guns and grenades away, taken their uniforms off, and, we're telling ourselves, stolen back into our town under cover of darkness. Anyway, there they stand, as usual, at the stage door, and they're talking to one another, and even from inside our bush we can recognize them. And how do we know them in the darkness? Naturally by their wide-brimmed hats pulled well down over their ears, hats that'll have been the first thing they took out of their wardrobes on their return and restored to their heads. But also we can at once distinguish from all other ways of walking the artfully placed, quite particular footsteps with which they walk so well across the stage and march, as father says, so abominably. And then, naturally, by their mellow, well-trained actor's voices, which even if they're only whispering on the stage can still be understood effortlessly up on the balcony. Our Edgar, who knows the actors, waves to them at once, of course. We wave too, but hesitantly, because we're exhausted and we want to spare our suit. We don't know the actors personally either, at most from the stage or the newspapers. One of them, who has donned a tilted, wind-sleek, velvet cap, is probably not an actor at all, but a scene painter, for he has a paintbrush in his hand and even as he walks along is painting something in the air. Then as soon as he's inside the theater he'll be able to leap on the stage for us and rapidly design a scene for a new play, one we don't know. With the piece of scenery he's carrying under his arm—a half moon that transforms for us with its radiance the whole region—he disappears through the black stage door, but the next artist is already coming up. And what luck! It's an actor, a real actor! With the proper bearing, gestures, hat, haircut, and voice. So he doesn't just work in the theater—however artistically employed—even though that would be important too, no, this person is, well, he's an actor. Although of course not one of the greats, who only appear in the big cities and aren't to be found at our stage door, he's just one of the middling and heretofore minor actors, who, however, if nothing interferes, can always develop into greater actors, if not very great ones. The fact is, we don't actually know much about this actor, or about any of them, although we've studied them for a long time from a distance. Also we've never yet had a chance to ask them a few questions. For instance, which theaters have they played in, how long their longest applause lasted, what sort of people they've been while acting and helped by costumes, how they hit on the idea of theater as a solution at all and then made it through to the theater, and if they always know in advance what they exclaim or sing on the stage, suddenly everything at once, or if memorizing it takes months and months. Or whereabouts in them or near them are the many persons they portray, when they themselves aren't on the stage—in the morning, for instance, or after a performance? But who knows if the actors would ever have answered our questions, or, if they'd done so, would they have told us the truth or merely put on an act? Anyway, the actor we see at the stage door on the first day after our conquest, and who, in addition to his artist's hat, is wearing a thick sheepskin, woolly-side-in, and felt knee boots fastened with large buckles, is a real actor, in fact he's the one who acted in the play *The Princess Safe and Sound* the part of the wolf or of some other wild animal (from the stalls we couldn't clearly identify his head with its fangs). But perhaps we also know him from our school, where on April 20 he performed for us unending ballads about our blood and native soil. Yet perhaps we're wrong here too, for the actor reciting the ballads wore glasses, and besides, we were sitting at the back and could only see, hear, and understand bits and pieces of him. (Also our Edgar had brought a frog into the school hall, and while the actor was speaking up at the front we at the back had to stroke the frog's behind.) Briefly: it's not certain that the actor at the stage door is the one from the school hall, but he's very like him. Certainly he played the wolf or hyena in *The Princess Safe and Sound*. Now he's walking, hat on head and with a piece of scenery under his arm that might be even larger than the painter's, toward our stage door. Hallo, he calls to us, what are you doing around here? Is it you, or isn't it? he says, turning to our Edgar, shielding his eyes with a hand as if in too glaring a light—maybe he speaks excellently, but his eyesight might not be so good anymore—aren't we colleagues? Yes, yes, it's me, our Edgar exclaims—he really did once act with him and in a last act carried a train, as a page—and he takes a single small step out from our bush, are you opening again? Yes, the actor says, soon we are. Do you want to watch? May we? our Edgar asks. Why not? the actor exclaims. Ah, everything else is always *verboten,* our Edgar exclaims. Not with us, the actor replies, with us everything is *permitted.* Well now, that would certainly be something else, our Edgar exclaims. We'd like to watch, for sure, if we weren't so tired. Tired, at your age? the actor exclaims, and, as in the play *The Enchanted Elephant,* in which he was just a smaller animal, a mouse or a rat, he shakes his large artistic head, which is quite flattened by his hat. Ah, our Edgar exclaims, we've been out and about since midday. And where have you been? the actor asks. Back there, our Edgar says and points in any old direction, because the word Amselgrund probably doesn't occur to him, or else he can't find a way to say it. Did you see tanks? the actor asks. No, our Edgar says. So there haven't been any clashes? the actor asks. Oh, none at all, our Edgar exclaims. Well, you needn't make such dismissive gestures, the actor says, there have been clashes elsewhere. Possibly, our Edgar says and yawns. And has there been any shooting? the actor asks after pondering a bit and drawing his felt boot sole over the ground, if I might just pop that question too? No, our Edgar says and sways a bit, it was all quiet. And they didn't give away sweets and chocolate either? the actor asks. Unfortunately they didn't, our Edgar says, they simply drove on through. All the same, you might easily have been mistaken for something else and shot or hanged, the actor says, and he looks for a suitable place to put his piece of scenery down. On a day like today children would do better to stay at home. You mean because a new era is beginning? our Edgar asks. Of course, the actor says, and he makes an important-looking face. And you, our Edgar says, shouldn't you have stayed at home too? Ah, as artists we have a special pass, the actor exclaims and pats the breast pocket of his sheepskin, where he has probably put his pass. So you've been drifting around in the town since midday? he asks. Yes, our Edgar says, sort of. And realizing that there's going to be quite a lengthy conversation after all and not wanting to speak so loudly on the street, he spreads his arms and walks out of our forsythia bush. And he begins to enumerate the places where we've been: to the slaughterhouse, which was empty as a barley crib in spring, to the church, where we tidied up, to the Amselgrund, which is *partly flattened*, by the river, where the water is murky, and visiting a widow. A widow too? the actor asks, and what were you doing there? Ah, our Edgar says and points at us, they had things to do. And you, Herr Müller-Königsgut, what have you been doing these days? Ah, the actor says, I was supposed to fight but it was a complete washout. And instead of letting myself be taken prisoner I simply walked home and changed my clothes. Yes, we noticed right away that you'd changed your clothes, our Edgar says. And what are you doing now? I'm bringing this back, the actor says and lifts up slightly his piece of scenery, which depicts a portion of sky on a fine day. All of us, he exclaims and points all around him, even though at the moment there's nobody but ourselves near the stage door, we're all bringing our pieces of scenery back. And then we'll have a discussion. It's beginning again, he exclaims and brandishes his free arm in the air as a sign of small triumph. And what's beginning again, if one may ask? our Edgar asks, finding the actor's answer too general. What's beginning again? the actor exclaims, what a question! Everything's beginning again, he exclaims and points all around him, far and wide, but probably he just means the theater, beyond which he can't see, even today, because he's so obsessed. And what's the discussion about, if one may ask? our Edgar asks. About our repertory, of course, it has to be completely revised, the actor exclaims and points to show where the new repertory will be performed—at our theater building, slightly elevated against the evening sky and now slowly dissolving into the darkness. Has it been settled, the repertory? our Edgar asks. No, the actor says, otherwise we wouldn't have to discuss it. But even if it had been settled I wouldn't be allowed to talk to you about it, because for the time being it's secret and must first be agreed on. But I can tell you this much! Mainly we'll be acting the old plays again, though in a new way. For instance, we'll . . . , he says, but our Edgar interrupts him. No, he exclaims, if it's a secret and, what's more, not even decided on yet, then we don't want to hear anything about it. So we'd better talk about something that isn't secret. For instance? the actor asks. For instance, our Edgar says and ponders for a while. About the pieces of scenery, he then exclaims and points at the portion of sky that the actor is still holding under his arm. How is it, he asks, that there are suddenly so many pieces of scenery here? Where have they been all the time? Everywhere, the actor says, everywhere. At his place, he says and points at the scene painter who, to see if anyone else is coming, is just then poking his head through the stage doorway, at my place, at all our places. Besides, the stuff isn't very heavy, you know, but it's damned unwieldy, he then says and sets his portion of sky down for a moment on the sidewalk after all. Naturally we didn't want to throw it away, we were far too fond of it for that, and we couldn't leave it in the storeroom, that was too much of a fire hazard.

The least stray bomb—and immediately everything would have been lost. I hope you haven't forgotten what happened in our town on the eleventh? he asks. No, I certainly haven't, our Edgar says, we were just talking about it. Well, you see, the actor says, without asking what we'd actually been saying about the eleventh. But the bomb falling on the theater was only an accident, wasn't it? our Edgar asks, and there was nobody killed here, was there? Accident or not, it was enough for us artists, the actor says, and he doesn't go into the question whether anyone was killed on the eleventh. Just look, he exclaims, lifting his piece of scenery up a bit so that we can also see it. And actually it does look a bit singed, at least at the edges. Is it damaged? our Edgar asks and narrows his eyes a bit, because he should wear glasses, of course, only there just aren't any to be had. But of course it's damaged, even a blind person could see that, or perhaps not, the actor exclaims, and he raises the piece of scenery higher now, this time exclusively for us to see. Since it's us being addressed now, we extract our head from our suit and nod, visible from afar. Yes, we exclaim as with one voice, we can see it! And what do you see? the actor asks, wanting to know exactly if we're seeing the right thing. Well, of course we see some damage, we exclaim from our forsythia bush. Quite correct, the actor says. And then he tells us about it: it is, as we've probably noticed, a portion of the sky that appears in most plays, at least it's hinted at, and therefore it's needed for any decent performance. Unfortunately, the sky had been in the backstage area and, what's more, in precisely that corner where there'd been a fire, so that it was charred a bit now, at the edges. But the scene painter who'd examined the pieces of scenery thought that the marks left by the flames could easily be scratched away or painted over. In any case, the actors had taken the eleventh as a warning, and each of them, so as to reduce the risk, had taken home with him as many pieces of scenery as he could carry and accommodate. The company had simply divided among its members the entire sky, with clouds, the sun, the moon, and the stars that are also important for some plays, and taken it home, so that none of it should be destroyed. And right now it's all coming back again, the actor says to our Edgar and points toward a weary old actor who's also wearing a slouch hat and who, loaded with *two* pieces of scenery, is just now walking up the Theaterring and past us. Anyway there'll be plays again soon, the actor says, summing everything up, and he takes a short step back, so that the old actor with the pieces of scenery can pass by him easily. Yes, exclaims the actor who played the wolf—and he rubs his hands—soon we'll be beginning again! Perhaps we'll put on a play about serfs and boyars first, anyway that will be my proposal. Then I can go onstage just as I am, he says, and together with his portion of sky he turns around so that we can see his sheepskin and felt boots from the back too. Will you be a serf or a boyar? our Edgar asks politely, though it's probably all the same to him. I don't know yet, the actor says, in any case much more than we'd hoped was saved, so don't be anxious. But we're not anxious at all, our Edgar says. So much the better, the actor says. But instead of bowing his head, as the old actor did, and disappearing through the stage door with his portion of sky to discuss the new repertory with the other actors, he leans with both arms on his singed and fragile piece of scenery and begins to enumerate for us all the things that were saved. Well, he exclaims, brandishing in the air his right hand with its clawlike fingers so as to count off on them each single piece of scenery saved. Well, for instance, the forest inhabited by animals, the small but agitated portion of sea, the whale for a biblical play, the graveyard for a mournful play, etcetera. And when one considers the state our *real* town, our *real* forest, etcetera, are in! But the actor isn't at all interested in those things. Instead, as long as nothing else occurs to him, he flourishes his hairy claw above his head and exclaims that nature as such has been almost entirely preserved. You remember that nature we used to act in? he asks our Edgar. You mean that autumn nature? our Edgar asks. Yes, the actor says, that play really was the purest nature play. Some plays were acted, after all, only on account of the scenery. Even if it's mere scaffolding? our Edgar asks. It makes no difference, the actor says. For actors in any case viewed the world as a figuration, a representation, everything in it a cipher, even though people in the audience almost always forgot this, the actors offstage sometimes too. Anyway, he says, nature has been preserved, at least part of it. That's fine, our Edgar says, and having the impression that much in the backstage area has been preserved, he finally walks across the street to the actor. Edgar! Where are you going? we call—but he doesn't even turn around. We too now step out from the forsythia bush, but we don't yet venture across to the actor— even though the candle is still shining brightly, everything around is getting darker all the time now. Also we're bored by the enumeration of the many pieces of scenery that have been preserved. Even our Edgar, who knows the actor well, exclaims: Amazing, how fond you are of that stuff! Yes, I admit it's a foible of mine, the actor exclaims proudly, and he tilts his head right back for a while, as if at any moment he were going to howl with emotion. I don't understand you, he then says to our Edgar, you've been on the stage yourself, after all, even if only briefly, and you ought to know how important the scenery is for us artists. And what if it had been destroyed by fire, our Edgar asks—and he's meaning to torment the actor a little. Yes, the actor says, that would have been the worst that could have happened to us. Well, it might have been bad, but surely not the worst of things? our Edgar asks. Yet the actor insists: No, it would have been the worst thing imaginable, he exclaims. Worse than the Amselgrund being destroyed? our Edgar asks. Yes, the actor says, much worse. But surely not worse than the town itself being destroyed? our Edgar asks—but the actor won't change his opinion. The worst thing, the worst thing, he exclaims again and shakes his artistic head. But since the scenery hasn't been destroyed by fire and even our town is still intact, except for some damage here and there, we needn't talk about it anymore. So let's talk about something else. Who, for instance, is that? he asks and points across the street in our direction. Naturally we startle and shrink deeper into our suit again. They're acquaintances, our Edgar says. Of mine or of yours? the actor asks. Ah, only mine, our Edgar says, and he makes a dismissive gesture. And they don't know me? the actor asks and draws himself up a little higher behind his portion of sky. But of course they know you, our Edgar says. Really! the actor exclaims joyfully and tugs at his sheepskin, which is all skewed by the wind, straightening it a bit. But that's not surprising, everybody knows you, our Edgar says. Yes, probably, anyway many people do, the actor says and looks down at himself. But how do *they* know me? Ah, from the stage, of course, our Edgar says. True, they're not very big yet, but they're already admirers of yours. Yes, they're not very big yet, you're right, the actor says and stretches a hand out with thumb and forefinger extended, to measure our size from the distance. And why haven't I met them yet, if they're admirers? Because they haven't been around much, our

Edgar says, mostly they stay at home. And why don't they come over to me now, at least, when they'd have a chance to speak with me? the actor says, are they afraid of me? It's not that they're afraid, our Edgar says, just that they've got a new or almost new suit that doesn't quite fit them and makes walking difficult for them, that's why they'd rather stand, at the moment. A new suit, the actor exclaims, looking sharply across at us, who did they get it from? Ah, our Edgar says, from an old acquaintance. Well, doesn't he need the suit himself? the actor asks. No, our Edgar says, not anymore. Strange, the actor says, and the suit was new? Yes, our Edgar says, almost. True, it's too big for them, but since it's theirs now they put it on. Well, the actor says, taking another quick look at us and our suit across the street and stroking his own shabby sheepskin, it's probably all right as an emergency suit. Do you think he might have another suit, your acquaintance? No, our Edgar says, that was the last one and it wasn't at all easy to get at it. It was hanging in the attic, that's why it's so stiff and starchy. And is that why they won't come over to me, because their suit is so stiff and starchy? the actor asks. I'd have liked so much to feel it. Or do they think I'd gobble them up? Of course they don't, our Edgar says, there's another reason too, why they're not coming over. And what would that be? the actor asks. Ah, our Edgar says, they don't like it to be talked about. Not even with me? the actor asks. Ah, perhaps with you, you'd certainly notice it in time, our Edgar says. Then he pauses for a while and says softly: They have a wound. A wound! the actor exclaims, so were they shot at? Oh no, our Edgar says, it's not a bullet wound, something quite different from that. Well, the actor says, it's a wound all the same. Where have they been wounded? In the leg, our Edgar says. Low down on the leg, the actor asks, or high up? More like high up, I think, our Edgar says. And why is it the leg that's wounded and not somewhere else? the actor asks, and he looks us over from inside his skin. They fell over, our Edgar says. Fancy that, the actor says, and he gives a little whistle, really they should have a poultice put on it, best of all one made of baker's dough. The dough is put over the wound, then sprinkled with flour, and hey presto!—they'll be well again. Yet there isn't any baker's dough to be had, no flour either, what a pity. But joking apart, you're right, they do look rather pale. Where did they fall over? On the bridge, our Edgar says. Which bridge? the actor asks. Ah, our Edgar says and points behind him, the one with the gulls. Gulls? the actor asks, you've seen gulls here? Well, not exactly, our Edgar says, but we've talked with somebody who saw them about a hundred years ago. Really, the actor exclaims, I've known the river for a long time, true, but I've never seen gulls there, actually. And then having turned to us he calls: Hey, you casualties, can't a person even admire you close up in your new suit? I'd gladly walk across to you, he says, but I've got this thing here, he exclaims and lifts his portion of sky up somewhat. Also I must go to a discussion very soon, he says and points at the stage door. Do you mean us? we call and look all around. Who else? you're the only people here, the actor calls back and points first to the right, then to the left, up and down the deserted street. Do you know me? Yes, we exclaim, we've known you for a long time. And how do you know me, if one may ask? the actor asks, although of course he knows precisely how we know him. Oh, we say, and now we walk, leaving behind us the forsythia, out of the darkness it diffused, we know you from the stage. Just that? the actor asks and beckons us closer. Oh, we say and step onto the street, we liked it, of course. Hear that? the actor asks and nudges our Edgar, your friends liked me. And now, he asks, and he's speaking to us again, don't you like me anymore now? Yes, we say, we still like you now. And what do you like about me? the actor asks and stands very upright behind his portion of sky, so that we can get a fuller view of him and find more easily something we like about him. My sheepskin, do you like my sheepskin? he asks. Yes, we say, we like your sheepskin. And my hat? the actor asks, taking his hat off for a moment and waving it back and forth a few times, don't you like my hat? Of course we do, we say, we like your hat as well. Well then, the actor says. And you recognized me right away? he asks. Yes, we say, right away. Hm, the actor exclaims, and with his portion of sky he takes a short step forward, now you've made me curious, now you must tell me *everything*. What play did you see me in? Oh, we say, many. So you've probably seen me, the actor asks, as Hamlet? No, we say, sorry but we haven't seen you as Hamlet. And why haven't you seen me as Hamlet? the actor asks. Because at that time, we say, we still weren't allowed to go to the theater. Was it such a long time ago then? the actor asks. Yes, we say, unfortunately. Well, you've done yourself a great disfavor, not seeing me as Hamlet, the actor says. Everybody agreed that as Hamlet I was very good, you see. And as Franz Moor, he asks, did you at least see me as Franz Moor? No, we say, sorry but we didn't. Not even as Franz Moor, the actor exclaims and stamps his foot a bit with chagrin. But when you played Franz Moor, we say, we still weren't allowed to go to the theater. Still not even then, he exclaims—as if peeved. And why not? Because we were still too young, we say. Too young, too young! One is never too young for art! the actor exclaims, and in the meantime everything gets forgotten. A few more years and there'll be nobody left who saw me as Franz Moor. Either they'll all have died or they still weren't allowed to go to the theater. Ah, we say, there'll be a few people left. Yes, a few, but that's not enough for me, the actor exclaims, and yet again he stamps one boot a bit. How could you say you're admirers of mine if you never go to the theater and haven't ever seen me? he asks after a pause. Ah, we say, if we'd had our way we'd have gone, but father wouldn't allow it. He doesn't like going to the theater himself, he calls it a bladder of a building. A bladder of a building, how strange, the actor says and thinks about the unusual expression for a while. Well, he's certainly strict, your father, isn't he? he then asks. Yes, we say, fairly. And where is he now, the actor asks and looks around as if father might be hidden nearby, perhaps behind one of the artfully ornamental columns that surround our theater. Ah, we exclaim, he isn't anywhere here, he's missing. Missing? the actor asks, and you're sure he hasn't come back in the meantime, while you've been bumming around? We're certain, we say. Well, anyway, you haven't any right to say you've seen me on the stage, when in fact you've only heard people talking about me. You've obviously got no idea what I can be on the stage. And that's a pity, a great pity, he says after a pause and shakes his head gloomily. But we do have an idea, we exclaim, we've seen you in *The Princess Safe and Sound.* And what is that? the actor asks—he obviously doesn't remember the play at the moment. It's a play, of course, we exclaim. Hm, the actor says, and I'm supposed to have been in it? But yes, yes, we exclaim. And what role did I play in it, in your opinion? the actor asks. The wolf, of course, we exclaim as with one deep common voice. A wolf, the actor says and puts a hand to his forehead, so as to remember better. But if I did play the part of a wolf, he says after a brief pause, it must have been a matinée, mustn't it? Yes, it was, we exclaim, it was. But as a wolf, now I remember, he exclaims, I was quite terrible, it was a frightful role. I was only allowed on for a moment in the last act, to hurl a few threats at a few little children who'd got lost, so people would have someone to laugh at. Yes, of course, I do remember, it was an abominable play. But it wasn't, we exclaim, we liked it. As a wolf, we exclaim, you were magnificent. But he makes a dismissive gesture. No, no, no, he exclaims and stamps his feet again, both of them this time. Well, he says and stretches up to overtop his portion of sky, I must tell you something important, so be sure to listen well. Now, he says, I'd like you to forget immediately everything you saw, heard, and perhaps have remembered of me as a wolf, all right? I want you to sweep quickly everything left in your head about that performance, sweep it into a heap, as it were, and, well, burn it. You see, it's not the real me. If you say so, we say. And, the actor goes on, I'd like you not to speak to anyone about that matinée and my role as a wolf, whether they've seen the play or only heard or read about it. I'd like it all to be forgotten as quickly as possible, and so completely forgotten that it's as if I'd never been in the play. If you say so, we say. Instead you must, now that you're big, he then says and places against our cheek his hand, which is cold, hard, smoky, and, so to speak, calloused from carrying so many pieces of scenery around, even if you're still beardless—but that will come— that will come. Hm, well, he then says and ponders what he'd been meaning to say, and, yes, he remembers what it was, and he says that from now on we must only go to the theater in the evenings and that we must attend precisely to how he is. Yes, we say, attend precisely to how you are. Right, the actor says, and to make us take notice even more he places his paw, after drawing us a little closer to him—only the little portion of sky stands in the way of perfect union—on our shoulder, then, before we can do anything to prevent it, branches his clawlike forefinger off from the other fingers and tickles our ear a bit, as he continues to speak. Right, he says, when the theater is reopened, study the repertory carefully and note well the plays I'm in and whom I'll be portraying. And then, when you've found the right play, buy a ticket, go straight in, and applaud for all you're worth. Afterward you may come to me and tell me how much you liked me and, if you so wish, congratulate me and perhaps make a mental note of everything—for later, for your grandsons and great-grandsons, and so forth. Perhaps you could then talk to other people about me, just as you please, but only the evening performances, all right? You'll recognize me on the stage, won't you? he then asks. Certainly we will, we exclaim. But sometimes, he says, I'm fairly hard to recognize. No problem, we say. And how would you recognize me? he asks and winks at our Edgar. Oh, we say, for instance by your nose. But I might go onstage with a different nose, the actor says and takes hold of his nose. I could put a strange nose over my own nose. Well, we say, in that case by your ears. But I could have other ears too, he says and takes our hand and places it on his ear, the right ear, well covered with his long hair, also it's well warmed, probably quite large, in any case very soft. Well, by your voice then, we say. And what if I disguise my voice? the actor asks—suddenly he speaks in a very deep voice. No problem, we say. Good, the actor then proceeds in his normal voice, in any case you should always look at the program in advance, to see if I'm in the play, so that you won't be wasting your money. Only buy your ticket if you see my name on the program. But if you only *think* it's me on the stage and my name isn't on the program, you'll probably be mistaken. Then it's not really me but someone else, and then you needn't clap either. All right, we say. And now, he exclaims, finally letting go of our hand and lifting up his sky scenery again and pointing to the stage door: Let's go inside. Inside where? we ask. Inside the theater, of course, the actor says. Yes? Are we allowed in? we ask. How do you mean? the actor asks. Are we allowed in too? we say. And who's going to stop you, the actor says and looks all around. Well, nobody actually, we say—because as far as we can see there isn't anybody at or in the stage door entrance who could stop us from going inside. Well then, the actor says. And he leaps—after uttering just once, we don't know why, a wolflike howl—ahead of us all through the stage door, our Edgar following behind, who's probably giddy again, at least he steadies himself against the wall as he walks. Then, slowly, slowly we go on in (for we're entering our theater with mixed feelings of dread, delighted anticipation, curiosity, timorousness, longing, forsakenness, comfort, and so forth). The best thing would be for us to hold hands, the actor quickly exclaims, and all we see of him for a while is a piece of sheepskin walking ahead of us, or we wouldn't be the first people to get lost on the way to the stage and to disappear forever among the scenery in the perilous air of the theater. All right, the little ones first, he exclaims, pushing our Edgar back, after all you know your way around here.

Impenetrable darkness reigns over the theater in all directions the moment we enter it, just as it did in the church. Till now we'd only imagined the interior of our theater—behind the curtain—imagined it, and how!—but now we enter this darkness really and we can see nothing whatever, so we have to guess at everything. For the light of the candle left behind us at the stage door is far too weak and any moment, as we step into the interior of the theater, it will be lost from sight. For the corridor we're in at the back of our theater winds and twists and turns, so the little candle flame can't follow us for long. Why didn't they place candles for people wanting to step inside, we wonder as we walk on, and we tell ourself that it wasn't possible, because there aren't any candles to be had. Pulled along by the actor, crowded upon from behind by Edgar with his knees or his head, no wonder we constantly bump against walls. Also our wound, almost forgotten while we were at the stage door, is troubling us again, we feel the blood, feel how it's bleeding. Until, after we've climbed up a few more stairs and down some more and have also passed several dressing rooms that have been left in disarray, or at least poorly tidied up, we arrive at our goal, shining toward us from the distance. Because someone in this vast theater building must have found a second candle after all and lit it and placed it for us, now that everything is brighter again we know where we are—on the stage. (Yet we've come to it from behind.) Yes, indeed, we're standing—after the actor has quickly pushed open one more iron door and pulled us through it—in the center of our temporarily closed, small to middling size theater's stage, which, since it has no scenery and the dark red stage curtain isn't dropped but up, is very wide and deep, thus very spacious (one could really get lost on our stage!) and entirely deserted and a bit like the loft of farmer Schmidtchen's barn in Oberherrndorf. (How many times we've acted our own and other roles in the Oberherrndorf barn!) There's even no sign of the scene painter. If he's really working on the new scenery already, he must be in the quiet backstage area or in the cellar of our theater, for a theater interior like this is quiet, of course, when plays aren't being staged and when one comes into it from outside. A person like us coming into a stillness like this will find it almost impossible to believe that he was conquered only yesterday with such a hullaballoo. Well, the actor exclaims, breaking the stillness, and finally, having pressed our hand quickly once more and, because nothing else is available, wiped with it his sweating forehead, and—perhaps he's looking for something?—moved it around a bit beneath his warm sheepskin, he then lets it go. Well, he exclaims, here we are. That, he exclaims, striking a stageworthy pose beside us, thus with his legs apart and thoroughly conspicuous, also pointing out into the empty but layered darkness, that is the auditorium, which you probably recognized at once and where you actually belong. But I belong here, he exclaims and stamps his feet on the stage floor with such vehemence that dust billows up all around us. So do I need to ask you, he asks, where we are? We are, we exclaim, on the stage. Yes, on the stage, the actor says, and he nods his artistic head contentedly and props his small portion of sky against a stage chair with the candle on it that illuminates the whole stage, diligently if not extravagantly, right up into the cloud machinery. And around this chair, which has been set up on the stage as its sole prop, or which has been forgotten there, the actor, having unbuttoned his sheepskin and opened it somewhat, will now walk for a long time, with firm and elastic strides—real theater strides. Well, how do you like it here? he asks and traces with his arm a big circle embracing the whole interior of our theater from the candelabra, now cooled and darkened, down to the trapdoor. Oh very much, we exclaim and stand as close to the chair as we can, but only so that the actor can walk around it without bumping into us. Then we look outward, then upward, not seeing much, however, because—just as in the church—the little candle flame's light simply doesn't reach far enough. Amazing, we've never gone so far inside a theater and never before has an actor walked around us at such close quarters! No wonder we're amazed. Well then, the actor exclaims, noticing of course our amazement, what questions do you want to ask? Do you know your way around here? we ask. Yes, the actor says, I have to, do I have any choice? As an actor I'm obliged to know my way around here. Well, he asks, what do you want to know? Everything, we exclaim at once. Hm, I can't explain everything for you, of course, he says, at least not in a single evening, but that thing over there, since we have to start somewhere, is, for instance, the prompter's box, empty at present, of course. And he interrupts his walk around the chair, deviating from his track to walk quickly over to the prompter's box and tap it with his foot. And from it there really does come a hollow sound. Yes, we exclaim, you can hear it's empty. And that? we ask, pointing upward into the theater sky. That, the actor says, and he too looks up for a moment, that's the fly space. And if you mean the other thing as well, that's the operating gallery. And who operates the operating gallery? we ask, since today it's empty, of course. Well, who do you think? The stage hands of course, the actor says. But recently they'd been off fighting and were still on the way back. And what's that? we ask, and we stand on tiptoe for a moment, completely still, and instead of pointing to something we hold our forefinger to a nostril, drawing the actor's attention to a faint noise, which, if one listens the right way, can faintly be heard through the stillness of the theater. Ah, the actor says, what can that be? It's the theater mice. The theater mice! we exclaim and burst out laughing, partly because of the phrase *theater mice*, partly because of the thing itself. Yes, the actor says, and other theater animals too, which have spread all over the theater during its long closure. Before anyone can even consider reopening it, they must be exterminated. Exterminated? we ask, but why? Because, the actor says, they eat the props and are terribly disruptive generally. Can you imagine an evening performance, even a relatively successful one, with all that scuffling going on? No, we say, actually we can't. Well then, the actor says. And during the more exciting and sensitive moments of a performance, when the nerves and feelings of the audience were tautened to the limit in any case, such a scuffling and crackling and gnawing was altogether unbearable. Yes, we say, that's not very nice during the exciting moments. Not very nice, well! listen to you now! It's abominable, the actor exclaims, and again he interrupts his walk around the chair, to stand and take a deep breath and to stamp his feet a bit on account of the theater mice. You can't imagine what it means when one's up here on the stage and into that sort of gnawing one has to deliver one's best lines, to which one has been looking forward for hours and for which the entire play was actually written. No, no, he says, it's pointless otherwise, they have to be exterminated, but that won't be simple. They aren't keen on being exterminated? we ask and laugh a bit at the thought of the theater mice retreating deeper and deeper into the foundations of the theater to escape from their pursuers. No, the actor says, unfortunately they aren't. But then the theater would anyway have to be thoroughly cleaned before one could consider reopening it, there was dust everywhere. Here, he exclaims and runs diagonally across the stage, then tweaks at a side curtain, out of which erupts a dense dust cloud, as if it had been ready and waiting to do so, and makes us cough, close as we are to our theater chair, and for a long time the cloud doesn't settle. Then you probably sleep here too, if you know your way around so well? we ask once the dust has settled and the actor has stood before us again, once more to begin walking around us. Well, I don't really sleep here, he says, even though as an old theater creature I do naturally have a small couch in my dressing room and sometimes it happens that in the evening after the performance, if I sit down at my mirror to remove my makeup, I might doze off and leave the theater much later than I'd meant to, perhaps even toward daybreak. Yet that suits me fine, actually, I'm grateful for every minute I can spend in the theater, even if it's only on the couch. When I was a young man, even then, yes, actually about your age, I was determined to spend as much of my life as possible in a theater, or at least close to a theater, for instance in a theater café. And in fact I've never been much farther than, let's say, five or six minutes away from a theater in all my life, and I'm no spring chicken. Not only so that I could be reached at once, if anyone needed me in a hurry, but also in case I myself had had enough of everything else and suddenly needed the theater to take refuge in and quickly forget about everything else. In your theater, then, you probably forgot about the war? we ask. Yes, the actor says, up till these last weeks. Imagine, I've even installed a little cooking facility in my dressing room. So I can cook without leaving the theater, not large and heavy dishes, of course, but at least something small and light, a nice omelet, or a zesty soup. And why don't you cook your soup at home? we ask—we haven't quite understood why he has to cook in the theater too. Because the theater is my home, the actor exclaims, and I make every effort to do as little as possible outside it. Then you haven't got a family? we ask. No, the actor says, I haven't. Unless everyone who's dedicated to acting, like me, belongs to a big family living in a theater or else in many theaters. And a wife, have you got a wife? we ask—but then the actor gets impatient. Ah, he says and wags his head a few times from side to side, what a question again, you just aren't listening to me. What should I do with a wife when I've always got so many performances and rehearsals, I've just told you I do my own cooking. True, I did have a wife once, actually, but that was a mistake. Besides, it was such an age ago that I've long forgotten all the details about that wife and her various soups. But you do have a key, don't you, so that you can always come into the theater and leave it? we ask. A key, the actor exclaims, I've got almost all the keys. And he flings his sheepskin open, plunges a hand deep into his trouser pocket, and pulls out a heavy ring of keys, which he then throws to us, through the candlelight, and which we catch. For a long time we study the individual keys that are still warm from the actor's legs, then we give them back to him. Yes, they're very interesting, thank you very much, we say—we can't think of anything else to say about the keys. Yes, they're interesting, the actor says, and he puts them back into his pocket. And you, he then asks, and no doubt from habit he's speaking so clearly that someone high up in the balcony could probably understand him, wouldn't you like to work here? Yes, we exclaim, very much. Yes, I thought as much, that you'd like best to get off the street and find a home in the theater. But lots of people would like that, the actor says. Instead of wandering around in the rubble outside, you'd certainly prefer to walk about on the stage every evening in a well-made play, perhaps in the pretty costume of a page, eh? Best of all, he says—coming fairly close to us and scrutinizing us for a while—it should be blue. And it would have to fit you, of course, better than this supposedly new suit here, in which you look perfectly awful, I mean no offence. No, no, we say, we aren't offended. Well, the actor says, narrowing his eyes to look before him into the candle flame, in any case wearing your costume you'd have to bow deeply then to the king, which is the part I'd have, and kiss his hands, first the left one, then the right. That'd be quite something, wouldn't it? The page's costume would naturally have to be made to measure, so as to fit you properly, but that wouldn't be a problem, because the theater tailor is a good friend of mine. True, he lost a leg in the army but he's back now and starting work again, I've already had a word with him. I could take you to him myself and explain to him what you need. He'd make you stand before his big mirror and he'd measure everything, the actor says. Is his mirror intact? we ask—because after the slaughterhouse and Frau Henne and the church we can't think of anything to say about the theater tailor. Yes, the actor says, it's still intact. And he has the material? we ask. Yes, the actor says, he uses remnants. And then he stands before us for a moment and suddenly, as if he were the theater tailor himself, drops to his knees in front of us and takes our measurements. First the shoulders, he murmurs—as if he had a dozen pins in his mouth—then the sleeves, the waist, the legs. Yes, the legs, they're important, he murmurs and passes his hand over them, but so gently that we hardly feel his fingers, even when he comes close to our wound. Then out of sheer high spirits he pinches our calves a bit. Ouch! we exclaim—but he seems not to hear us, so deeply immersed is he in portraying his friend the tailor. We certainly don't want, he murmurs—placing his hands on our calves and running them up and down again and again— we don't want the beautiful costume trousers to drag along the ground like these dreadful suit trousers. We want these trousers to be elegant and casual in the way they fall. No, he suddenly exclaims and gets up off his knees, I'll not make long trousers for you at all, but short ones that leave the calves exposed. Well, how would that be? Ah, it really doesn't matter if the trousers are long or short, the main thing is for us to go on the stage sometimes, we say. No, no, the actor says, it does matter. Precisely these external things are what one has to watch, if one's an artist, where would we end up, otherwise? Yes, he murmurs—and then resolutely, now as his friend the tailor again, he simply snips our new trousers off short, using two large, long-haired, slightly bent, clawlike fingers. Yes, now it looks quite different, he exclaims, and he's still snipping, when, all at once—we stand there dumbstruck and rigid—a mighty crash of thunder comes from behind the stage. As soon as he hears the thunder, the actor startles, drops the pins from his mouth, his face blanches immediately, he puts a hand to his heart, and leaps up from the floor. And then he clenches a fist and brandishes it in the direction from which the thunder came: Stop that, do you hear me! he shouts toward the back of the stage. Then he pauses a little while and listens for an answer. And then, when all is quiet except for the scufflings of the theater mice, which are moving back and forth like gigantic armies deployed to and from the fly space: I won't stand for that! he roars and brandishes again a threatening fist, though one can't say at whom. What was that? we ask and straighten our trouser legs which have been all skewed and jumbled by the actor's hands going up and down them. Ah, what do you think, the actor says after standing there in confusion for a while with shoulders drooping, the theater thunder, of course. Some little rascal or other has taken the liberty of playing a trick on me and stirred the thunder up against me! And how do you know it was a rascal? we ask. I always know when it's a rascal, the actor says. Even if you don't know him well? we ask. Yes, the actor says, even then. And us, we ask, are we rascals? No, the actor says, not you. And then he shouts with his well-trained voice, once more shaking his fist toward the back of the stage: Stop that, you sons of bitches! Do you hear me? And when our Edgar who went pale in the face when the thunder came and is swaying more than usual puts a hand on our shoulder to steady himself, the actor asks: What's the matter with him? Ah, he's giddy because he hasn't had anything to eat, we say. Hm, the actor says, and with part of his mind he's probably thinking about the thunder and perhaps wondering if only one person is involved or several, and why hasn't he had anything to eat? Ah, we say, he lives with an aunt in Herrnburg and she hasn't got anything. Nothing at all, the actor asks and raises his eyebrows. Nothing at all, we say. And when, the actor asks—and since our Edgar began to sway he's become far more interested in him—when did he last have something to eat? He says it was two days ago, we say. And what did he eat two days ago? the actor asks. Ah, we say, he eats just about anything. In summer he eats windfall fruits or raw potatoes, which he discovers in ditches. He even eats earth sometimes, if there's nothing else and as long as it's reasonably fresh. Earth, the actor exclaims, he shouldn't eat that! Yes, we say, that's what we say too. And what, the actor asks, did he eat two days ago? Ah, we say, a piece of bread. Bread with what? the actor asks. Nothing, we say, a piece of bread with nothing. Nothing at all, the actor asks and looks at our Edgar. How else? we say. Or wasn't it? we ask, turning to our Edgar. We know anyway and you can tell him, we say and point at the actor, but our Edgar only shakes his head. No, he'd rather not say anything. You know, we say, he doesn't like to talk about what he eats, especially with people he doesn't know well. Even us, he doesn't tell us everything. Sometimes he's eaten nothing for days, without saying a word to us. Perhaps we wouldn't notice it, if he didn't sway so much. So he sways, the actor says, that's what I thought. Yes, we say, he sways. And the actor, after he's taken a few steps back to obtain a clearer view of our Edgar and stood then firmly with his legs apart on the stage floor and has studied for a long time our Edgar who isn't holding on to us anymore, then exclaims: It's really true, he sways! Who'd have thought it, and at his age, and even when he's standing still, he exclaims and shakes his large head. Can he walk at all? Mostly he can, we say, today for instance he walked to the Amselgrund and back, but with us. If his giddiness gets worse, then we can prop him up. And if it gets very bad, he leans against a house or simply sits down. And where does he sit? the actor asks. In the gutter, we say. Strange, the actor says, and he never feels faint? No, we say, but he has collapsed a few times. How often? the actor asks. Twice, he said, we say, but perhaps it was more often. And when he's collapsed, the actor asks, what happens then? Then he stands up again, we say. Well, the actor says, it's all right, as long as he stands up again. But even then, even then. And after placing the back of his hand on the spot where Edgar presumably has his heart, he says that our Edgar would probably be too proud to accept anything from him. Yes, we say and sigh, you're right, he is proud. So he is, isn't he? the actor says. And besides, he goes on, Edgar also seemed to like bread best, but he had no bread, unfortunately, he didn't eat it much, he couldn't digest it on account of an old ailment of his. And you, he asks, can you digest bread? Oh yes, we can digest it, we exclaim. Yes, he thought so, the actor says, at the same time he was sure that if Edgar ate more, then some things would change for him. Certainly he'd have more color in his face and not look so pale anymore, and he'd show more interest in the things of life, artistic things too, like us, instead of standing around so silently and swaying so terribly, he'd join the conversation. But what can we expect? he says and spreads his arms. Could we expect, after such a war, bread and liver sausage to grow on trees for idiots like ourselves? Have *you* got some bread, or do you sway too? he asks us, looking us keenly in the eye. Ah, we say and stand there quite especially steady, it's all right for you to look at us, we won't sway. And when did you last have something to eat? the actor asks. This morning, we say. And what did you eat? he asks. Also just a piece of bread, we say. With what? he asks. Bread with bacon, we exclaim. Aha, so you had bacon, the actor says and smacks his lips. And you could digest the bacon? he asks. Easily, we say. Did you hear that? the actor says to our Edgar, your friends here eat bacon. They can digest it too, it doesn't trouble them. Ah, they've told me all about that, our Edgar says, and he makes a dismissive gesture. And *you* don't have to bother about them, they're looked after. Whenever they come home and have washed their hands, their mother gives them a piece of bread with facon bat. What? the actor asks and raises his eyebrows. Yes, our Edgar says. Bread with what? the actor asks. Ah, with facon bat, our Edgar says and notices he's said something wrong, and immediately he blushes and tries to put things right. With . . . , he says, and we look at him expectantly and we're counting on him saying the wrong word again, but our Edgar hasn't the courage to try the word again, he only says: I mean bread with something on it. I mean, he says and blushes a bit more, with what I was trying to say on it.

We laugh. We wink at each other. We nudge each other. And we look eagerly at the actor, wondering what he'll say now. You mean *bacon fat*, the actor says with his deep, quiet voice, after waiting for a while. Yes, our Edgar says, that's what I meant. But you just said *facon bat*, twice even, the actor says, we all heard it. Didn't we? he asks us, you heard it too, didn't you? Ah, our Edgar says sadly, I know. And why did you say facon bat, the actor asks. Can't you say the other words? Ah, our Edgar says, mostly I can't. That's how it is! we exclaim, and laughing still we hold tight to one another a bit, mostly he says facon bat. Altogether he often makes mistakes, if he doesn't altogether forget what he was going to say. Strange that he always says facon bat, the actor says, and, as in *The Enchanted Elephant*, in which he was a rat, he stands there pensively with his legs apart in front of Edgar, can't you say bacon fat then? he asks and applies to the word, which isn't always so easy for us either, all his elocutionary art. And then our Edgar, after making a great effort, exclaims: Well, that's how it is. Sometimes he could say the word, but sometimes, he didn't know why, he mixed it up without even noticing. That's right, we say and nod, and, close together, head to head, even cheek to cheek, we tell the actor a few more things. That our Edgar for instance in the Amselgrund always said *dub* instead of *bud* and didn't even notice, but simply went on talking, passing over the wrong word. But then our Edgar argues that he did notice it and remembered perfectly well how the wrong word came out of him inadvertently, and that he'd been very startled by it, yet in the Amselgrund, as soon as he came to notice, he'd only been able to say the one word (*dub*) and not the other one (*bud*), and what could he do about it? And then, after some thought, crestfallen, he softly says: we were right, sometimes he didn't notice anymore what he said, or said wrong, or couldn't say at all. We say nothing, sheepishly pass our fingers over our head a bit and then shift our feet on the floor. And how is it that you can't say a simple word like bacon fat, do you think? the actor asks very earnestly after a while. At once our Edgar says that he doesn't know. Then think about it, think about it, the actor exclaims and stabs his paw high into the air as an incitement for Edgar to think. And after Edgar has put a thoughtful hand to his forehead—just as we've seen it done several times today, by the actor, also by the pastor, and by the smaller of the two slaughterhouse men—our Edgar says: Perhaps it's like this. Perhaps it came from his giddiness, from which the swaying came too, evidently his giddiness and his putting the words together wrong when speaking them were connected, they happened at the same time, they . . . Do you need boys here at all? we suddenly ask, simply interrupting our Edgar from behind the theater chair, which, as we see on looking more closely at it, is almost unusable. To tell the truth, we've been bored with his giddiness for a long time. Four times today he's been leaning, three times sitting in the gutter. And his talk about his words bores us even more. What? the actor asks—he hasn't heard our question, because he keeps looking at Edgar. We're asking if boys really are needed in your theater, we say. Boys? the actor says and bares his teeth, but of course. You need only ask your friend here if boys are needed, he says, and to give himself something to do he takes the candle off the theater chair and places it on the stage floor, so as to sit on the chair himself, being still somewhat pooped by the thunder. Yes, yes, that's right, our Edgar says, sometimes they need some, but not often, actually. For in most plays, unfortunately, an awful lot of adults appeared, but no boys. And one hardly ever had a new costume, he certainly never had one. At most, if one was lucky, an old or altered one. Well, the actor says—he's looking now and then from his chair toward where the thunder came from—that's one of the things that are going to change now. From now on, new costumes will be used not only for the great artists but also for the supporting cast. From when on? our Edgar asks—he doesn't seem to trust the actor much. From today on, the actor says. And then after glancing quickly at his wristwatch: I mean from tomorrow on, he says. Well, our Edgar asks, perhaps from tomorrow on there really will be new costumes for boys, but why do so few people come to the theater always? Why do so few people come to the theater still? the actor asks, and he tucks his chin firmly against his chest to defy Edgar's question, because he's had enough of his grumbling. Ah, our Edgar says, when I was acting the theater was almost always empty. Absolutely empty? the actor asks, and he's unwilling to believe him. Well, our Edgar says, at least almost empty, don't you remember? No, I don't, the actor says. I didn't notice the theater was so empty. Probably because while I was acting I didn't always look down into the auditorium, but was immersed in my role, as one should be, with everything I'd got. How many people were there then, do you think? he asks. Thirty at most, our Edgar says. Not more? the actor asks and seems to be even a bit more startled. No, not more, our Edgar says. But then I must have been playing to an almost empty theater! the actor exclaims. That's what I keep telling you, our Edgar says. All the magic of the scene is a waste of effort. Well, that will change, the actor exclaims, from now on the magic will return. You mean from tomorrow on? our Edgar asks. Yes, the actor says, from tomorrow on. You think more people will come then? our Edgar asks. Certainly more will come, the actor exclaims. How many then? our Edgar asks. Oh, the actor says, perhaps three hundred. On a single evening? our Edgar asks. Yes, the actor says, on a single evening. As many as that! our Edgar exclaims—he's still not quite convinced. At least as many as that, the actor says. And you think that boys will be needed too? we ask. I don't only believe it, the actor says, I know it. And you believe, we ask, that we'll be needed too and given a role to play, so we won't be on the street? Why not? the actor exclaims—and settling down comfortably on his chair (the thunder's now forgotten) he stretches out his legs, which may be somewhat the worse for wear after all his marching. Talented people, he adds—since he has the impression he should say something more—are always needed in the world, especially in the theater. And you believe that we're talented? we ask. Well, whether you're really talented or not I can't say for sure, after such a brief conversation, the actor says and proceeds—he's already stretched himself out— to yawn and at once to contradict himself. Also in the theater the question isn't whether one is talented or not, he says. The main thing is to have someone in the administration who'll sponsor you. And if you haven't got anyone in the administration to sponsor you? we ask at once. Then you can't count on getting a position here, the actor says. But honestly we'd like so much to work in the theater, we exclaim. Well, the actor says after giving the matter some thought, if you'd really like so much to work in the theater, I could recommend you to the administration. Then of course everything would look different at once. Everyone I recommend to the administration is always given a position straight away. Really, we exclaim, and you'd recommend us? Well, if that would be doing you a favor, the actor says. But of course you'd be doing us a favor, we exclaim, and a very big one too. You see, we've always wanted to be in the theater, even though we've never told anyone. Hm, the actor says, and why? Ah, we say, that's a long story, and for us at least a fairly complicated one. And we don't like to talk about it, because it's so important for us. One of the reasons was probably that people in the theater were so different from people outside. And we'd always wanted to get away from the people outside. And then, we say, we've always wanted to depict things on the stage. What, for instance? the actor asks. For instance, the ocean, we say— unable to think of anything else at the moment, but the actor is satisfied even with this. Yes, the ocean, he says, and he's lost in thought and pauses for a moment, to picture the ocean to himself, for during the last several days he'd probably quite forgotten about it. Have you seen it? he asks. Do you mean really or in the theater? we ask. Really, the actor says. No, we say, unfortunately we haven't. But we've heard a lot about it. And we've read too that it has to be depicted in the theater sometimes. By boys, is that true? we ask. Yes, the actor says, that's true. And how can boys depict the ocean? we ask. Well, the actor says, one needs a large tarpaulin, preferably a blue one, of course, or, if one wants a stormy ocean, a gray one, even a black one, and a bellows for the wind, a . . . Ah, he then says, I can't tell you everything about how to depict the ocean, my time's too short. Why not tell me, instead, since when precisely have you wanted to be in the theater? Oh, we say, we've always wanted to. Always? the actor asks, is that true? Well, we say, always is perhaps a bit of an exaggeration, but it really has been a long time. And about how long? he asks, and it didn't matter whether it was one month more or less. Well, we say, at least since father was drafted into the army, but actually it has been longer. Hasn't it, Edgar? we exclaim, you remember, don't you? Yes, our Edgar says, as soon as their father was drafted they wanted to go into the theater, they told me so. Of course, I don't know either if they're capable of moving properly on the stage, or even of carrying the train of a robe. We did actually try it once, behind the garage, but it was rather a flop. Edgar, you rascal, how can you! we exclaim and shake our fist at him, because he'd promised never to tell anyone about our effort behind the garage. And then, without even being asked, he goes and tells the actor, who now, of course, has fresh misgivings. Well, he says and rolls his heavy head from side to side, of course they must be able to move properly on the stage, that's the least I could ask. But honestly we can move properly on the stage, we exclaim. Yet mere protestation isn't of course enough for the actor. Well, he says, to move properly on the stage isn't so easy and simple, he says, particularly for children. And of course it's children on the stage who attract particular attention, and of course every wrong step a child takes is at once sharply criticized. Once I recommended a boy, he was about your age. For months he tried to acquire the right sort of stage movements, which have to be on the one hand perfectly theatrical, and on the other hand quite natural too, but it was no good. The poor boy, although his movements were quite right in reality, on the street for instance, at every step he took onstage he kept looking at the floor, because he didn't know how to place his feet, the right one first or the left one. And what's more he was supposed to play the role of a man of the world, the sort of person who walks, of course, in a quite different way. No wonder the public lost confidence in the play, on account of the way he'd walk, and eventually people stopped coming. And yet he was fairly talented, all in all. Well, we exclaim, you needn't be anxious about us, we're quite different. We walk on the stage quite naturally and we don't look at the floor. Are you certain? the actor asks—he's not going to believe us. Yes, certain, we say. And your father, the actor asks—he isn't setting his doubts about our stage movements aside, he's only reserving them—what will your father say, if you suddenly want to go into the theater? Ah, we say, but he's missing. And if he suddenly comes back? the actor asks. Ah, we say, he won't come back for a long time, perhaps he never will. And your mother, the actor asks, what'll your mother say if you suddenly want to go into the theater? Ah, we say, she's ill. She's had a headache for weeks now and does nothing but lie in bed. All right then, the actor says after he has thoroughly reconsidered our plea and weighed carefully all the pros and cons, I'll give you a chance and recommend you. I'll put in a good word for you with the new administration, which will certainly be appointed soon, and I'll see that you get the position, just as soon as one is open. Not because I'm convinced you're really talented—I don't know you well enough for that—but because then we can be together often and have talks. Yes, that would be nice, we exclaim, and out of sheer excitement, us too, now we walk rapidly around the theater chair on which the actor is sitting. Wouldn't it be? the actor says, I think so too. You like to talk with me, don't you? Yes, we exclaim, very much. Fine, the actor says and seems to be thinking again, for he's put his hand to his forehead again. Of course, I'll have to take good care, he says out of the midst of his thoughts, that you always act in the same plays as me, otherwise we'd still not be together and couldn't have talks. If that happened, you might be onstage at weekends and me on the other days, or vice versa. For as regards our new repertory we have great plans. In times like these, people are naturally mad about theater, certainly there'll be a play every evening. But don't worry, I'll see to it that we can always act in the same plays, at least in the coming season. And what if there aren't any roles for boys in the play you're in? we ask. Then we'll just write the roles in, the actor says, rubbing his hands a bit. Only not into the plays in which you may not act under any circumstances, he then adds rather earnestly, because he's probably had a further misgiving and has to think it over methodically in the most various ways. At the same time he keeps grinding his teeth, in preparation for more talk. You must know, he then says, which plays I mean? No, we say, which ones? Well, those ones, the actor says, and grinding his teeth he looks up into the teasers. And after a pause: Those ones. Ah, we see, we exclaim. And why, we ask after a slight pause, mayn't we act in them? Because, the actor says and smiles rather more vigorously, revealing to us a few black gaps between his front teeth, because those plays aren't for boys. Ah, if that's the reason, we say and make a dismissive gesture. It's all the same whether we act in them or not. No, no, it's not all the same, you may not act in those plays, the actor exclaims with severity, and only now, noticing our interest in his teeth, does he shut his mouth. You mayn't even go to those plays, he says—but now he isn't smiling. Well, then we won't and that's that, we say, we'll only act in the others. Yes, the actor says, assuming . . . That they'll take us? we ask. There need be no doubt about that, the actor says, once I've put in a word for you. No, assuming *you*'ll do *me* a small favor now and then. Oh anything, we exclaim. You only have to tell us. Well, at the moment you needn't do me any favors, the actor says, we don't yet know one another very well. But I'll tell you, when the time comes. But what you can do now, he continues and looks at us attentively, now you could, since we're sitting here together, be sweet and friendly to me, I need that very much. But we're always sweet and friendly to you, aren't we? we exclaim, and out of the depths of our new suit we smile at the actor, but he's still not satisfied. Ah, if only one could know that you mean it honestly, the actor says. But how else? we exclaim. All right then, the actor says, I'll believe you. And then he does believe and he hopes that he's not wrong about us and that we're as nice and friendly as we look, and always pay attention when we're in school and won't give him any trouble. But how can we pay attention in school and not give you any trouble when school has been shut since December? we exclaim. All the windows are broken, there just can't be any classes. Ah yes, the war, I'd almost forgotten about it, the actor says and clutches his forehead again. What? You forgot about the war? we exclaim and shake our head a bit, because he could forget the war, though he's living in our very midst. I mean, the actor says—and now he's feeling a bit awkward too about forgetting the war—what I'd forgotten was that the school is shut. But certainly it would soon be opened again, he then says, now that we've been conquered, because it was fairly important, school, along with the theater. So then we could show him how well we'd been paying attention and what we had in us. When he'd been at school, he says and ponders for a moment . . . No, he then exclaims, forget it, you really wouldn't understand that. And why wouldn't we understand that? we ask. Because, he says, it was so long ago that it's just not true, as they say. And why isn't it true? we ask. Because, as I just said, the actor says, it's so long ago. But isn't what was true once always true? we ask. No, the actor says, unfortunately it isn't. So then he doesn't tell us the thing about his school, although actually we'd like very much to hear about it, and now we must talk of something else, but please not about him. You tell me, he says, something about you. All right, we say, what shall we tell you? And we ponder a bit, but the longer we ponder the more we're convinced there's nothing to be told about us, because it won't interest anyone. Well, the actor says, meaning to help us ponder and give us a few ideas, I can remember for instance, when I was about your age, I had a little girlfriend. Do you have a little girlfriend, he asks and winks at us. Oh yes, certainly we have a little girlfriend, we exclaim—though we haven't ever had one yet and the thought of obtaining one has never occurred to us either. But we're not telling him that, since we don't want to disappoint him. Certainly we've got one, we exclaim—as if it were a matter of course. Then you're no longer, the actor asks with some concern from his theater throne, no longer innocent? Innocent! we exclaim, how do you mean? Well, the actor says, just as I say. Ah, so that's what you mean, we say. And then we exclaim: Us, innocent? but of course we're not innocent anymore! And we laugh and traipse with grand strides—as best our suit allows—back and forth before him over the empty stage, which makes our shadows look twisted, like cripples. Oh well, it's a pity actually, but I'd been thinking you weren't innocent anymore, the actor says, and he does seem rather disappointed. Since when? he asks. Ah, we exclaim, long ago. Actually, we say—because the actor seems to be waiting for a more precise answer and presumably wants to know for how many years and months and weeks we haven't been innocent anymore, yes, we say, actually since forever. Or rather, we add—because he seems not to believe that we haven't been innocent anymore the whole time—since father was drafted. Aha, the actor says, so you've made the most of his absence? Yes, we say, of course. Well, the actor says and seems even sadder—perhaps not wanting to say another word—but then he changes his mind and winks at us impudently and asks: Well, and how do you like it? Oh, it's nice, of course, we say and grin and walk up and down before him in our suit even more limberly. Have you got one girlfriend or several? the actor asks. Oh, we exclaim, and since we want to please him and be like he was in time immemorial, we say: Several, of course. And then, just as we're meaning to ask him how many little girlfriends he himself has, something terrible happens. Just as we're hanging on to his chair, standing on the edges of our feet to keep our balance and meaning to ask him how many he has, a loud voice suddenly calls from behind the stage, whence came the thunder: Müller, you pig, stop that! Hearing his name called, the actor startles in his chair. Also he at once puts his hand to his heart, to feel if it's still beating. Then when he feels, yes, that it is, and when he has recovered himself again, he turns around in his theater chair to face the backstage. Then, since someone must be among the curtains, even if we can't see him, he collapses in his chair, sinks deeper into his sheepskin. We're annoyed too by the many interruptions in this apparently empty and quiet theater interior. And that, what was that now? we ask and scrape a sandal over the floor a bit. That, the actor says, was a human voice. And what did it want? we exclaim. Ah, what indeed, the actor says and makes a dismissive gesture. Then he explains to us that it was probably a *so-called friend*, who, out of cheek or envy or high spirits and because today was the first day after our conquest, had taken the liberty of playing *a little trick*. This *so-called friend* knew, for instance, that he, the actor, was a highly sensitive and very vulnerable being, inwardly as well as at the edges, and unable to endure such tricks, even his doctor had warned him about them. Another trick or two giving you a fright and you've had it, my good fellow, the doctor had told him. And that was precisely the reason why this *so-called friend* had picked on him as a victim. Yes, the actor exclaims—slowly bringing his head up out of his sheepskin again, into which he had put it when the fright first came—quite loudly so that he'll be heard everywhere: Some people ought to have their heads bashed in at birth, straight off! Do you really mean that? we ask. Well, throttled, at least, the actor exclaims, that would be the best thing for the lot of them. Am I right, yes or no? he asks. Probably, we say. Well then, he says contentedly, and he tugs a bit at his trouser belt. I've passed hundreds, no, thousands of sleepless nights wondering why I don't just bash in the heads of these *so-called friends*. Nobody would miss them, quite the reverse, a sigh of relief would pass around the globe. Because they're superfluous, the world can manage perfectly well without them. And with people like that, just imagine, I'm supposed to discuss the repertory! No, even worse, he exclaims, I have to go onstage with them, share scenes with them. And then we have to take our Edgar between us, because he's swaying so badly again, and walk right up to the theater throne and give the actor our hand, look him in the eye, and vow never, not even if we live to be a hundred, to play such tricks on other people, or shout names unexpectedly, when nobody's anticipating it, from behind the stage, or to make thunder, but always to respect and be kind to one another, because otherwise it's not friendship, but the opposite. And in friendship, even if not everyone knew it or most forgot it, he says and holds our hand tightly in his own, lies the only happiness. The only happiness? we ask and try to extricate our hand. Yes, the actor says, the only happiness. And he recommends us to have dealings only with people, as far as possible—on the stage or off it—whom one could call *friends*, but not with friends in quotation marks, only with ones without them. Though there are of course others, he suddenly roars into the backstage, who won't allow one a moment's peace, even if one is a wounded veteran with an official disability pass. There are such people too, he exclaims. So are you a disabled veteran, Herr Müller-Königsgut? our Edgar asks. Yes, I am, the actor says. Where are you disabled, if one may ask? our Edgar asks—because the actor has no visible disability. Ah, the actor says, lots of places, but mainly in the leg. And then he points at us and says: An injury like theirs, only a bit farther down and much more serious, of course. That's why I was no use in the war, not even for marching, but had to spend all my time chairborne in the theater. Really? our Edgar asks, but you don't have a limp. You simply don't keep your eyes open wide enough, the actor says. And yet, as you've quite rightly observed, I don't always limp. Sometimes I do and sometimes I don't. But then, our Edgar says, you don't limp, for instance, when you're on the stage, do you? Onstage, the actor says, I seldom if ever limp, but then onstage I'm another person. Yet the fact that he limped in one place and not in another and sometimes couldn't even walk, but also couldn't lie down, he says, stretching his legs right out over the stage, needn't surprise us, for life is after all an irregular arrangement and full of contradictions. Is it, if one may ask, the right one or the left one with you? we ask. The left one, the actor says. And that in life, as he'd explained, the only consolation was to spend as much of it as possible in company with persons one can trust, respect, esteem, and like, even love. Whom one esteemed and whom one loved was really neither here nor there, the main thing . . . But here again he makes a dismissive gesture. How slandered I've been because of these ideas that I'm putting to you so simply, he exclaims and sits up very straight in his chair. What haven't I suffered for them in the offices of magistrates and in lockups! But what am I doing, he says, loading you with a cargo of ideas still too heavy for you, with your youth, in which of course a magic dwells? It's still too much for you to carry. But mark one thing: it's wrong to find the feelings of other persons laughable just because one has none oneself, and to frighten with sudden noises backstage or otherwise the people who have imagination, just because one has none of one's own. Yes, Herr Müller-Königsgut, we say. Will you promise me to mark that? he asks and reaches out for our hand again. Yes, we say, we promise. Good, he says, I believe you. Now you see, he says, and having let go of our hand after a while and allowed a long gloomy pause, he turns in his theater chair and, with legs outstretched and twisted neck, he exclaims in the direction from which his friend's voice and the thunder had come that it's impossible in this accursed place, even on this day, to exchange a friendly word with good friends. This place is not only full of rodents that have recently crept right into the dressing rooms, but also full of human rascals who creep into the dressing rooms too and are only lurking around to hear such friendly words and pounce on them. So we shall have to speak more softly in future, as is always the case with such friendly conversations, even in the world of antiquity, so that people can't hear us, the actor says, and he turns back to us again. So come closer and speak more softly, best of all into my ear. Which ear? we ask and come a little closer. The right one, the actor says and extends it toward us. And why mayn't anyone hear us? we ask and stand on tiptoe around his right ear, which apparently has hairs even inside it. Because what we have to say arouses envy, the actor says. And from now on we mean to be together as often as possible. And shall be, the actor says, for nobody can stop us, however loud he shouts. If there's thunder again or someone shouts again, you needn't be startled. You know who it is now. Yes, we say, it's a friend. Well, the actor says, in any case you know that you needn't be afraid. But we're not afraid, we say. Not at all? the actor asks. Not at all, we say. Fine, the actor says. And you needn't worry about your position, I'm very popular here. All the same, he then says, we'd better not stay on the stage, because people can hear us. So let's get up and go somewhere else, however difficult we find it, he says and stands up from his theater chair laboriously—it seems there really is something wrong with his leg—and he takes us by the hands again. I hope the roaring hasn't frightened you so much that you've had enough of the theater, he says. Not at all, we say. Fine, he says and walks a few steps. And where are we going now? we ask. Ah, we'll go a bit farther in, the actor says and stops, and—since we're not certain if we're supposed to follow him—he pulls us closer to him on the flickering stage. Then he reaches for our head, to tuck it casually under his arm. So we're going farther into the theater? we ask. Yes, the actor says, where do you think?

And he leads us, as nobody else ever has, putting his warm hand under our arm and sort of propping us up, past our Edgar, who presumably knows the interior of the theater already, or else he's feeling weak and doesn't want to go with us, but prefers to stay beside the theater chair, and so we walk diagonally across the stage and through the hangings on the left of it. God, what a lot of things are suspended from the fly space, who'd have thought it! Who'd have thought of all the things that go on in the theater, and so in the world too! If only one could get a better view of it. But unfortunately everything is getting darker all around us at every step we take. Edgar! we call and look back one more time and can just see him, sitting now on the theater chair and waving to us out of the gathering darkness. Let him be, he can wait, the actor says and pulls us onward. What if he wants to go home? we ask. Then he can go, the actor says. And what, we ask, if he gets giddy again? Then he should rest a bit in my chair, the actor says. And where are we going now? we ask again. I've told you, the actor says. We're going backstage. And why are we going backstage? we ask. Because now we're going to look at a few of the old bits of scenery that one really has to have looked at before going on the stage here. These ones, for instance, he says and leads us past a series of canvas and cardboard scenes, lined up or shuffled, scenes that must come from a tragedy, because they stand there so gloomily and joylessly. Or perhaps they're just so old that they've lost their color and brilliance. What do they depict? we ask, because we can hardly distinguish their shapes in the darkness, let alone the figures painted on them, and they're so lackluster that actually they depict anything you please. Ah, all sorts of things that happen on earth and have to be presented in plays, the actor says—he knows his scenery so well that he doesn't even have to look anymore. Bit by bit everything comes to be depicted in the theater. Well, we say, that may be so, but what part of the world do they depict? That one there, the actor says, looking up briefly as he walks along and pointing up at a piece of scenery, was once the forest in a freedom play, a forest in which the heroes of freedom always met. You can still see the tree trunks and branches, anyway the thicker ones. But they aren't green anymore, we say. That's true, the actor says, the color has suffered, but it's always the color that suffers first. And what's this, we say, scratching a little at another scene as we pass by. That *isn't* anything yet, it still has to *become* something. You mean it's still being worked on? we ask. It was being worked on and then the war came and work had to be stopped, the actor says. And what will it be, when it's finished? we ask, because we can see for ourselves that the piece of scenery hasn't been glued and fitted together, let alone painted on. One can't tell yet, the actor says, and he goes somewhat closer to a corner of it, narrows his eyes, and scratches at it a little. In any case, he says, taking our head and pressing it into his sheepskin, people won't hear us now and we can have a good talk. And it'll be even better in the storeroom, which we'll be looking at in a moment, because we can shut the door behind us and nobody will hear anything at all. Even if we talk louder? we ask, for we're still speaking very softly. That's right, the actor says, not even then. Are we only going into the storeroom so that nobody will hear us talking? we ask, or is there something we can see there? There's something to be seen in the storeroom, the actor says. And what can be seen in the storeroom? we ask. Everything in a theater worth seeing that isn't backstage or on the stage itself, the actor says, and with his good foot, to show us what he means, he kicks a large piece of scenery—evidently a graveyard—so vigorously that the bigger graves wobble furiously, and the small ones tremble for a long time afterward. And what's worth seeing? we ask, and the actor enumerates a few things rapidly: the masks, the costumes, the cavalry uniforms, for instance those of the Pappenheim regiment, their helmets, lances, shoulder pieces. Yet, yes, we say rather impatiently, but what's the use of it all? But then the actor falls silent again. The fact is: he himself doesn't know what use it is, and nor do we. And we're astonished that someone should be taking us, on the first day after our conquest, into our theater storeroom and showing us the props, because, for a day like this, much too little is *real* (outside there's Edgar's mother, who is really dead, and here there's the actor, who only shows and tells about everything). For instance, the props needed when an especially solemn mood has to be created in a play and has to spread through the auditorium, props that often have to be silver and gold. You've no idea how many solemn occasions have to be celebrated over the years on a stage, even on a small one like this, he says. Yes, yes, we say, that may well be so, but . . . Especially at the end of a play, when all the conflicts the playwright thought out and the action of an evening too are coming to a close, he says, even if, of course, the objects on the stage, as people in the auditorium seldom notice, are always just theater gold and theater silver, out of which the actors eat and drink and which they clink together, making believe that everything is real and really precious. Yes, yes, we say, that's true, but . . . Also there were musical instruments in the storeroom . . . Backstage or actually in the storeroom? we ask. Both, the actor says. And on these musical instruments the actors in the plays had sometimes to play, or at least make believe that they were playing, also on instruments that didn't even exist, except in the theater. May we play the musical instruments? we ask. On the stage? the actor asks. No, in the storeroom, we say, when we get down there. If we shut the door, nobody will hear us. Ah, you can't play them, the actor says and makes a dismissive gesture. But we could make believe, we say, pretend that we're playing them, like you on the stage. All right, if you want, the actor says. And then, he says—and he's still describing what's in the storeroom—there were also various appurtenances, but one couldn't enumerate them all. What, for instance? we ask. Well, for instance the theater fruits, he says, which shine so appetizingly when you see them from the auditorium, so much so that when we bite into them up on the stage, though we're only making believe, the mouths of people in the audience water, because they can see the juice squirt out and run down our chins, even if in reality the theater fruits are only made of glue and papier-mâché. Lots of things and not only the theater fruits, of course, haven't got any fresher or juicier over the years, and because they have to be brought out again and again and used afresh and doughtily gnawed on, they've become worn out and battered, yet still they're worth seeing. Yes, the actor exclaims, you'll be amazed, I promise you that. And when will we get to this storeroom? we ask, because we've been walking much too long for our liking, though the actor talks in an interesting way, through the backstage area, which is quite useless, though it has come safely through the war. It's right there ahead of us, the actor says, and he quickens his pace. You mean back there? we say. Yes, the actor says, and now he's pulling us along by our sleeve, not by our head, into the storeroom.

Which we really don't want to visit now, because it's so dark here and the air sepulchrally stagnant, also we're missing our Edgar, but what can we do? It's too late to go back, it seems we're standing now at the entrance, and the door is flanked—as we can just manage to see in the flickering and diminished light of the distant candle—by two life-size gilded statues, probably water sprites, which must have played an important part in some bygone play, probably set on the ocean. Yet perhaps they don't come from a play at all, they might come from reality, but from a reality long past and now no longer true, an unimaginable reality, a theatrical one, in which such extravagances could still be paid for and thought of. Anyway, so soon after our conquest the golden statues stand out in our theater as being far too grand to be believable. Also the entrance, probably for security reasons, is blocked like a bank vault by an iron door, which turns out, however, to be unlocked, for with his good foot the actor kicks it open easily. How dark it is on the other side of the door! True, pulled by the actor we're taking a few tiny steps into the storeroom. True, we're finding our way, as we grope around a lot, past the closets full of costumes and props, into the interior, without knocking against the edges of anything or getting caught up anywhere or treading on articles scattered around on the floor or placed upon it, for it isn't completely dark, there's a little ground-level window with several real (!) stars in it, but even then, even then! (Even then: we notice right away that our theater storeroom is one of the vaguest places we've ever known.) In such darkness how could the actor, even if he wanted to, ever let go of our hand and leave us here to our own devices? Of course, he can't. Briefly: we're going into the storeroom with a premonition. And we have to put our hand on the actor's shoulder, so that he'll feel we're with him and we won't get lost among the props and things. Meanwhile he's standing in front of us with his legs apart and, by way of showing us that he's told us the truth so far, pulling single costumes from the closets and at once identifying each one and greeting it with loud cries and holding it up before our eyes in the sepulchral air. Also, aided by his memories, he gives us an account of every single one. Right, he says, fishing out one costume after another—and he spreads them before us and waves and turns them about and then simply tosses them to the ground—there they are: the costumes. This one, for instance, he says, is a king's robe from this or that century, used in this or that play, unforgettable to all who saw it, and worn by this or that actor. Yes, you can touch the robe, the actor exclaims and guides our hand first over the buttons, then over the lapels. And now come on, come on, he exclaims, and he's meaning to pull us, talking or silent, past the now gaping prop closet still deeper into the storeroom interior, where he says there are even lovelier costumes, but now we take our hand from his shoulder and say we've seen enough. Enough, the actor exclaims, what do you mean? We've only just started! Put your hand back where it was. No, no, we say, that's enough. And instead of going to him again and placing our hand on his shoulder, we take a step back. And we say we've come far enough into the storeroom and the costumes here are quite lovely enough. Besides, we say as we edge bit by bit back to the door, we'd forgotten the candle and couldn't see much without it, unfortunately. But the light's much brighter farther on, he exclaims, though that's a lie, because we're certain everything is even darker farther in. And there are the musical instruments too, he exclaims, I thought you wanted to play them. Ah, but we can't, we say, we've never learned how. And if only you'd brought at least a flashlight, we exclaim, to light all this old stuff up. Ah, the actor says, we don't need light here. And where's our Edgar? we ask, because we're missing our Edgar, cramped as it is in here. We don't need him, the actor says, pulling a crown off a shelf with much emotion. And a chair to sit on? we ask— and before the actor knows it we've got one foot outside the door. Not necessary, he exclaims, not necessary at all. And that if we wanted to sit down, we should simply sit down on the floor and imagine it was grass we were sitting on. But we've already sat in the grass today, we say, because our head is full of ideas as we stand in the storeroom doorway. Have you? the actor says, but where? In the Amselgrund, we say. Well, it makes no difference if you sat on the grass in the Amselgrund, the actor says, you can sit on the grass twice in a day. Just think of all the plays I've been in where I had to sit on the stage and proclaim it was grass, he says, and with the crown on his head he subsides among the hangings and pulls us down with him onto the dusty backstage floorboards. Just think, he says, what an excellent exercise it is to sit like this on the floorboards of the stage and close your eyes and think it's grass you're sitting on! Have you noticed now that it's grass? he asks us. No, we say, actually not. Because you aren't closing your eyes, the actor says, that's why you can't imagine the grass. Do you feel it now? he asks after we've closed our eyes. Yes, now we can feel it, we say—so that he'll finally shut up, though of course we still can't feel the grass. See what I told you? the actor says. And do you notice how it prickles? Yes, we exclaim, we notice how it prickles, though on the floorboards, level and smooth as they are, of course it *can't* prickle. But it's a pity so few people come to the performances still, we say. Yes, the actor says, it's a scandal, but that will change. The majority of the public hasn't been coming recently, but now it will come again. But surely not in this darkness? we exclaim, because sitting here we can't see the least thing before, behind, or beside us, but have to organize and *imagine* for ourself everything we want to see. Sh! the actor says, not so loud. But surely not in this darkness? we whisper. Yes, yes, he whispers, yes, yes. But, we whisper, surely people in the auditorium wouldn't be able to see us sitting here? That doesn't matter, the actor says. Right, he says and stretches out his legs a little, where were we? Ah, it was the grass, we say. No, before that, long before that, the actor says, when we were still on the stage.

You mean when your friend interrupted us? we ask. Yes, the actor says, how far had we got? Ah, we say, it was school. That's it, the school. And the little girlfriends who have such lovely soft hair and lovely slender fingers, the actor says. And who, once you know them, aren't really so nice as they're made out to be at all, isn't that so? Yes, we say, they're not nice. You see? the actor says, and because he's sitting so close to us he puts his hand on our knee. And suddenly he begins, while moving his hand up and down our leg a little, to repeat again and again the phrase about the soft hair and slender fingers of the girls, to repeat it *in whispers*. The girls' lovely soft hair and the girls' lovely slender fingers and the girls' lovely soft hair, he whispers rather breathlessly and moves his hand up and down our leg. Herr Müller-Königsgut, we say, and he doesn't hear, but his crown is quite askew on his head and his gaze is turned away from us, immersed in a side curtain. Herr Müller-Königsgut, we whisper and then pause a while and then call out to him and hit him with our elbows and hands and we feel how starved, thin, and hard the actor's ribs are, but he seems not to notice us at all, he simply goes on talking about the lovely soft hair and the lovely slender fingers and the lovely delicate collarbones of the little girlfriends we've invented for him. Until all at once his soft hand hits on our wound, all at once it goes into our wound. Ouch, we exclaim, ouch. Then he stands up—perhaps we shouted too loud or hit him too hard—and walks away, vanishing in all his blackness behind a side curtain. Hey, Herr Müller-Königsgut, we call and hope it's really his name and we're not mixing him up with someone else, where are you going? But the actor doesn't answer and he doesn't come back either. And of course the curtain is much too thick for us to see through. For a long time now we sit alone in the darkness on this first day after our conquest, on the hard backstage floor of our theater, which is supposed to be grass, and we aren't sure if the actor is still standing behind the curtain and perhaps looking down at us, or if perhaps he's gone back into the storeroom without us, to play the musical instruments alone. Or perhaps, being peeved with us, he's already left the theater again by a side entrance and he's got all the keys. And we can't tell if he's still got the crown on his head, or if it fell off when he stood up, or if he took it off, or if it took itself off, when he realized that we wouldn't be going any deeper into the storeroom with him. Herr Müller-Königsgut! we call one more time, but all's quiet behind the side curtain. A good thing that at this moment our Edgar appears again from the hangings, even though he's swaying. Edgar, we call and stand up, a good thing you're here again. Where were you all this time? Where do you think? our Edgar says, on the stage, of course. You simply left me stranded. But we didn't mean to, we exclaim, he was pulling us. And you needn't have stood either, you could have sat on the theater chair. And what good would that have done me, our Edgar asks, sitting all alone on a chair in the middle of the stage, while God knows where you'd got to? But he's left us, we exclaim, just like that, and we don't know where he's gone either. He'd put a crown on his head, then he disappeared. And now he doesn't answer, though we've been calling all the time. Ah, our Edgar says, that's nothing strange, he'll be back. So does he often disappear like this? we ask. Yes, often, our Edgar says. Funny, perhaps he felt sick because of all the dust, or because he was sitting too close to us on the floor, we say. Ah, our Edgar says, he *is* a bit funny. He certainly is, we say, did you hear him talking just now? Yes, our Edgar says, a word now and then, not everything, of course. A pity, we say, you really missed something. You should have heard what he was saying about the little girls and their hair and fingers, it was interesting, maybe. And what did he say? our Edgar asks. Ah, we say, nothing special, but he kept on saying it. Yes, our Edgar says, I heard part of that. And why did he keep on saying the same thing? we ask. Ah, our Edgar says, it was probably from a play he'll be in and he had to rehearse it. But always the same thing, we say, and now that we've stood up we're feeling that we really have taken on too much for this first day after our conquest. It's not only that we're constantly yawning and have to keep putting our hand to our mouth, also our wound is hurting us again, because the actor's hand went into it. We're also worried about the letter for Herr Schellenbaum that we're carrying in our breast pocket. True, it crackles all right when we reach for it, but can we be certain it's not already too late for the letter? Yes, sometimes he does disappear, our Edgar says once more, and he's about to give us a big explanation, but then he lets the matter drop, because he too has tired himself out with talk today. You know, Edgar, we say after a while—during which a lot of thoughts are passing through our head—probably we don't so very much like this place. Don't you? our Edgar says, why not? Ah, we say, it's just that you have to repeat a thing so often in rehearsal. We're also not really so confident about the theater anymore either, what with the art of acting in general and the scenery in particular, but that's not something we say. All right, then, our Edgar says, so tell him you've given the idea up. You mean we have to tell him and can't simply not show up? we ask. Yes, our Edgar says, you have to tell him, he won't just forget it. And when should we tell him? we ask. Best of all right away, when he comes out from behind the curtain, our Edgar says. And when will he be coming out from behind the curtain? we ask. You can't ever know, with him, our Edgar says. Well, we say, so we'll wait. And we stand by the curtain and wait a bit and while we wait we can feel our wound bleeding. And we imagine how much simpler it'd be to leave the theater right away, without first speaking with the actor. Oh well, we'll take a little walk up and down by the curtain, we say after we've waited for a time and imagined very clearly the theater exit. And when we've walked back and forth long enough, with many side-glances into the curtain—also many side-thoughts and side-fears, our footsteps echoing loud over the wooden backstage floorboards—the theater mice keeping up with us, great squadrons of them on the march in the theater attic—the actor returns.

We see at once that he's in more of a hurry than he was before he disappeared. Before, he'd had time to sit down facing us and tell us about the theater, now he hasn't got this time anymore. We also see that he's in a very bad mood. The crown he had on his head is missing, he's holding it behind his back and is wearing again his wide-brimmed actor's hat, and even that hat is askew. And his warm sheepskin coat, which isn't handsome, true, though it's practical, has suffered from all his creeping among all the bits of scenery, it's hardly recognizable. Yes, the actor has changed, and he's letting us feel it. When he sees us, instead of signaling his joy by raising his arms as before, he threatens us with his fist while still far off. Before too, when he smiled—it isn't long ago at all—we could see down his throat, but we can't do so now, because he's so earnest. So we realize to our horror that most of what we've thought or said about the actor till now has been quite wrong. Unbelievable, we never imagined his return would be like this! Why are you goggling at me like that and standing around so oafishly? This is a stage, he exclaims to us from the curtain, closing the flaps of his sheepskin, as if from modesty. This, he exclaims, is the stage of a temple consecrated since time immemorial to art! Here the immortal becomes spoken word, it's not a place to sprawl around in. So be off with you, get out! he exclaims. And he walks, with the flaps of his sheepskin now closed, his hands thrust into his pockets, with firm, deliberate strides up and down before us. But it's us, Herr Müller-Königsgut, we exclaim, because we've almost vanished inside our suit and perhaps he hasn't recognized us yet in the darkness. Well, do you expect me to burst into song on that account? the actor exclaims—and he stations himself frighteningly before us, thin, but with his legs apart and his arms drawn in tight to his sides. But you were just saying we should sit down, here in the grass, we say and point to the floor. What grass? the actor asks uncomprehendingly, and with a few movements of his hand he starts to drive us back toward the front of the stage. Can't you see, these are the boards of a stage? he exclaims and stamps around on them, stirring up their familiar thick dust. Grass? are you trying to make a monkey of me? he exclaims. Oh no, not at all, we exclaim, darting repeated glances at him because we don't dare anymore to look into his eyes and into his face, rather pale as it is and furrowed by the agonies of playacting, and shaven with difficulty smooth. All right, then don't contradict me, the actor exclaims, and amid some further trampling he utters a few more hollow sounds that we recognize, however, from his matinées. But out you go, this way now, stop sniveling, and get out of this theater, at once! he exclaims and claps his hands. Yes, Herr Müller-Königsgut, we say, but we've got to tell you something first. We've been thinking about the position here, we think that acting is probably not for us after all.

What are you talking about? I've no idea, the actor says, turning to Edgar and again he's speaking so loud that his friends backstage can certainly hear every word. But, Herr Müller-Königsgut, don't you remember? we exclaim, and we hold hands again, so as to take a better—though of course illusory—stand against the actor. The position you promised us, for when the theater is reopened, we exclaim. Unfortunately we can't accept it, for one thing because of our wound. What's this wound you're talking about? the actor asks—though just a moment ago he himself was handling our wound and surely he must remember. Ah, it's their leg wound, of course, our Edgar says, it makes it so difficult for them to walk and they'd prefer not to take on the position here because of it. And who, the actor asks, who promised them a position here? You did, so they say, our Edgar says. Me? the actor exclaims and puts his forefinger to his chest. But how could I have offered them a position, I'm hardly countenanced here myself. And who knows if this damned place will ever be opened again? But didn't you say just now that you'd recommend us to the administration? we ask—but, in view of the changed situation, we ask it in a subdued voice. Me recommend them? the actor exclaims to our Edgar, but I don't even know them. I've never once seen them on the stage, not in the tiniest role. And then, still talking to our Edgar: How did they get in here? Well? I must know at once. Now tell me the truth, he exclaims, starting to rattle a bit the ring of theater keys he has in his pocket, meaning to frighten us. How come the moment one turns one's back to attend to one's business in the storeroom, they're suddenly on the stage talking about a position? Was a door left open? Or did you bring them in with you? Would you kindly give me an explanation? Ah, our Edgar says, they'll have seen you on the street and then have simply walked in behind you. Into the theater? the actor asks. Into the theater, our Edgar says. And how come I let them walk into the theater? the actor asks, advancing on us again, meaning to drive us farther toward the front of the stage. Except that in his agitation he makes a crass mistake and drives us not toward the stage stairs but back among the sets and hangings, thus backstage, where we'd certainly get lost and be gone forever. Ah, our Edgar says, swaying along behind the actor, with all those new plans going around in your head, you probably didn't notice they were walking behind you. You simply didn't pay any attention to them, since you've got so much to think about. So then they exploited the darkness, the actor exclaims, to creep along behind me. Yes, of course, I remember hearing slight footsteps. But since I'm not a suspicious sort of person I simply didn't pay attention, but thought they'd go away of their own accord. And now they're here trying to exploit the situation and not leave the place but blackmail me, the actor exclaims in such a loud voice that everyone must be hearing him. But no, we exclaim, we're not trying to blackmail you, we're leaving right away. So you're trying to blackmail me, the actor exclaims once more, as if he hadn't heard us. And he takes a long step back, as if to take a run at us and stampede us off the stage once and for all, not noticing in his temper that we'd leave of our own free will, if only he'd let us. Admittedly, it's harder for us to cross the stage than it is for him, admittedly it takes us more time. For each time the actor takes a single stride with his almost storklike legs, very long ones at any rate, we with our short legs have to take two strides, if not three. And now and again we stop, of course, to catch our breath and rest a bit or listen to him. Or we simply stop because he stops and then we prefer not to run—not defying him, but because we can't think what else to do. Besides, to tell the sorry truth, he's driving us in the wrong direction. But we're leaving! we exclaim over and over again, can't you see? I certainly hope you are, the actor exclaims—fetching meanwhile the crown from behind his back and shaking it at us, playfully at first. Who talked them into asking about a position here? he asks, turning toward our Edgar. Ah, our Edgar says, they think it was *you* who made them an offer of that sort. Me? the actor asks incredulously and points at himself. Yes, you, our Edgar says. But how could I make them an offer of that sort when I don't even know them? the actor exclaims, and he takes another stride toward us. Ah, it doesn't matter in the least what we'll become or make of ourself, Herr Müller-Königsgut, you needn't worry about it at all, we quickly exclaim—taking advantage of his pause for breath. It isn't a question of whether we go into the theater now or not. We can go somewhere else, for instance to the station or the slaughterhouse. Yes, the actor exclaims, assuming the slaughterhouse will take you. And he stands erect in his tracks, like a stork, with his rump held in tight, and he looks at everything, as is the way with artists, from his own standpoint. For him it would certainly be difficult to find any occupation outside the theater, even in the slaughterhouse, but for us too? Besides, we don't want to say good-bye to the theater for all time, only provisionally, just so long as the actor is there. What can one say to people, he says to our Edgar, who are so deluded they think I meant to foist my profession on them and draw them into the theater? Doesn't that almost mean I wanted to foist myself on them? I, who stand so high above them that they couldn't even look up to me if they stood on the tips of their filthy little toes and dislocated their skinny necks! Who am so far above the reach of their sweaty little paws. As far above as the fly space! he exclaims after a moment's thought, and he points upward, shaking himself with disgust. And on a day like this too, just after our conquest. What cheek, to walk behind my back and simply follow me onto the stage on a day like this, when I should have been sitting long since with my friends and deciding on the repertory. And to fling at my feet—the cheek of it!—beyond all comprehension!—an offer I never made them, would never have dreamed of making them. Why haven't they gone away, why are they still here? he exclaims and drives us across the stage, but in precisely the wrong direction, of course, as we'd like to inform him, but will he let us? Only when he realizes himself that he's driving us into the wrong corner of the stage, the one without any stairs, the one we couldn't leave the stage by, even if we wanted to—except by toppling into the orchestra pit—only then does he hesitate for a moment and let his arms drop, but immediately he starts stamping his feet again and shaking his behind, meaning to drive us into the opposite corner, where there really is a staircase. Who are they to talk to me like this? he meanwhile exclaims—but his long walk and many reproaches have by now deprived him of breath enough to talk. Why do I even bother with them? Why don't I just tell their father the whole story, so he'll come and fetch his offspring from the theater himself? Ah, our Edgar says, he can't. And why can't he? the actor asks. Ah, our Edgar says, he's missing, you know. I don't care, the actor exclaims, who is he? Ah, our Edgar says, his name is Imbach and he owns the whip factory in Wundenplan. What's that? It's that man with the whip factory! the actor exclaims, and now he stops driving us onward and suddenly takes a step back from us. When he hears who our father is, the look on his face is really furious. So they're the little Imbachs! Yes, that's correct, our Edgar says and gives a shrug. Out of politeness we give one too, but only a slight one, of course. To think that even if we almost forget it ourselves we're incessantly being father's children! Anyway, as soon as he hears who we really are and who's been hiding inside Herr Henne's suit, the actor takes a step back and stretches his arms out, as if to banish us, then he slowly retreats from us. From the way he retreats we can see that he knows our father, or at least has heard of him, and that he detests him. Get out at once, get these rascals down off the stage at once! I don't want to see any more of them, he exclaims and makes with his arm a motion as if to purge the whole stage space of us forever, including the wings, with one single vigorous stroke. Get rid of these little industrialist's boys, they've got no business here, he exclaims and starts to wave his long arms, so as to sort of sweep the stage clear of us. If I'd known who was hidden behind their innocent masks, he exclaims . . . Bit by bit they grew to be the way they are! we exclaim. Quiet! he shouts. And then he suddenly seems to realize how he can rid his theater of us in the fastest possible way. He begins, that's to say, while standing his ground, to stamp his feet in a steady rhythm, meaning to scare us off with the thumping, which he skillfully modulates from louder to softer and gradually makes to sound more and more menacing. And truly this noise on the quiet stage—the thumping of a fighting machine—is hard for us to take. But we're leaving right away! we exclaim and tighten our grip on our shopping bag. We'd have left long ago, if you hadn't driven us into the corner where there aren't any stairs, we exclaim. Well then, *auf Wiedersehen*, we say and tighten our grip on our old trousers and old jacket, which we're carrying over our shoulder. A pity that . . . , we say. But the actor doesn't want to see us or hear us. Get out! he simply shouts, raising an arm high above his head, as if pronouncing a curse. As he does so, we see that under his arm there's a gigantic and sweaty hole. And how old he really is! All over his mottled cheeks he hasn't so much a beard as downy gray hairs, no, white hairs that we study with frank disgust. As for his throat and the back of his neck, the darkness of the stage makes it hard to see them, but very probably they're covered with an old man's shrunken skin, the breadth of his shoulders is contrived artificially by his sheepskin, under which there lurks presumably a wizened, senile body, and even if his legs are long they're probably difficult to lift. Suddenly too it's obvious that one leg is injured. But whereas with us the right leg is injured, with him it's the left leg, and whereas our wound is fairly high up, his is fairly low down. And his well-trained voice is already cracked, or at least quavering, in the upper registers. Yet from now on he doesn't say much, he's just harassing us in silence and is content to dismiss us without much noise, down the stage stairs into the stalls and then through the auditorium into the corridor and through an iron door into the dark theater passageway. While doing so, he signs to us from the stage, so that we won't go astray again at the last moment and instead of making for the exit stumble perhaps back into the theater interior through a side door, directing our movement first right and then left with a pointed forefinger. And even while we're fleeing into the corridor he continues, from the now deserted stage, to send us his signals. Outside—through the stage door, which is open—the external world, dark now, with the Theaterring and the upward sweep of the terraced staircase, and our flowerbeds all overgrown, and the smashed vitrines. On the other hand: the freedom of the evening air, with the candle shining in it, apparently real.

11

Ever since we can remember, Herr Schellenbaum has been a strong man, tall and robust, after all he shovels coke, and he has so much sheer muscle that he'd often burst the seams of his trousers, shirts, and jackets, especially after meals. But for a long time now he's been only a shadow of himself, shrunken by the food shortage. We used to enjoy studying his belly and shoulders, chin and jaws, but we've scarcely been able to recognize him recently. My God, is that Herr Schellenbaum? My God, what's become of Herr Schellenbaum, he used to be so robust? How inanely, all of a sudden, his thick head has begun to flop around on his shoulders! And look how awkwardly he dodders around the corner with his trouser legs flapping! Twice already his poor wife has taken his trousers in, but they're still too big. (Especially around Herr Schellenbaum's thighs, which used to be so powerful.) Even his boots, which have come to clatter much less dashingly down our streets, seem too big for him. Only his voice, when a little breeze carries it toward us across the street, still reminds us of the earlier voice and of the way he used to shout over our heads or shout us down. But nowadays Herr Schellenbaum even restrains his voice. Suddenly—our conquest was in the offing—he went very quiet, and after he'd cleaned out his office and locked

it up—our Edgar calls it Herr Schellenbaum's Brown House—
he meekly disappeared from our streets, went back home
to his garden and dug in it a little, because gardening, as
mother says, never harmed anyone. And he didn't wear his
uniform anymore, he wore his old singlet, which had probably been kept in his attic, like the suit in Herr Henne's
house. Now he thrashes around in his shrubbery, wearing
his singlet, we saw it ourselves on a Wednesday afternoon.
Do you remember, we ask our Edgar, how Herr Schellenbaum got stuck inside his elder bush? Yes, our Edgar says,
I remember. And how he saw us and stooped a bit lower
and looked away, pretending he was searching for something
under the bush? we ask. Yes, our Edgar says, have you got
the letter? Yes, we say and put our hand on the breast of
our suit, it's here. That's all we say to one another on our
way from the theater to Herr Schellenbaum, going this time
not through the town park but outside and alongside it.
Never suspecting anything, we walk through the early night-
time out of our theater and along the strangely twisting park
road, which lies open, upward, to the stars, on our way to
the flimsy house, intending to hand over the blue letter to
Herr Schellenbaum, who will be standing in his double
window, so we imagine, quietly and all stitched up, thus
with seams in his shirt, his mouth, and his trousers. Never
suspecting anything, we're walking into a trap, a *death trap*.
Once we've gone up the crunchy garden path and the level
steps to the front door, we're surprised beneath a quince
tree—soon it will have to break into flower—to find the
door wide open. (As the door usually is in apartments and
houses where there has been a disaster—to let the air used
by the disaster escape quickly.) But what a fright we have
in store when we go in! As in all houses in new develop-
ments, the hallway is narrow, dank, and dark. Here, as we

recall, there should be a chest with a mirror, and over it, to hang a few hunting hats from, some antlers sticking out of the wall. In fact, as soon as our eyes are accustomed to the darkness of the hallway, we do see the antlers, and the chest is there, as we'd pictured it. All the same, we sense that the hallway is different from the one we've got in our heads. *It's not so empty.* Yes, in Herr Schellenbaum's hallway there are lots of people standing. In long shabby coats and dresses, shiveringly drawn over chest and shoulders, with hats and hoods on their heads and scarves around their necks and starved throats, they've come into Herr Schellenbaum's hallway to talk with one another on this first evening after our conquest. Yet, as we listen more closely, we find that nothing is being said, all the people seem to be mute, and they only give one another, with eyes, head, and hands, speechless signals that we can't understand, because we don't know what they refer to. For instance, the people look up at the ceiling and seem to repudiate it, then down at the floor, but they disapprove of the floor, then they look into this corner, then into that corner, but they don't agree about either corner, and then all they do is shake their heads. The whole house seems not to suit them, perhaps they find it too cramped. Someone in the farthest corner even taps on a wall, which he presumably finds too thin. Quietly—best walk on tiptoe—our arms outstretched—we grope our way—here and there just a glint of light thrown our way by the moon—past the dark shapes, soon finding them no longer strange, for gradually we come to recognize them. There in the pale moonlight stands large-mouthed Herr Stubenrauch, there's bony Frau Reichmann, there's Herr Pelikan with his heart disease, Frau Hoppe, Frau Steinweg, Herr Kurz. They're all pale, bled white by the moonlight, as if all around them decay was floating, with many folds and wrinkles on their whispering and sighing throats and faces, and with hair growing out of their heads, but also out of their ears. Evidently they've been roused out of their beds, perhaps from sleep, for they've got their night attire on under their coats. Many keep tugging at their caps and hats, take them off, put them back on, don't know where to put them, whether to carry them in a hand, under an arm, or on a head. Us, too, we take our cap off, but we have our shopping bag to put it in. From between the shoddily built, peeling walls of their mistakenly spared houses all of them have come here tonight, emaciated with hunger and worn with care, they've all walked through the streets of our town to the low-ceilinged and cramped oblong of Herr Schellenbaum's hallway. Where they now jostle one another, but why? *Guten Abend*, we whisper. And why doesn't anyone return our greeting? It's as if greetings had been abolished in Herr Schellenbaum's house. Yet the door to the parlor is open, a black hole in the wall. In our suit that smells of Herr Henne—we're bringing the smell to Herr Schellenbaum—we stop, letter in hand, by the mirror, which is also black, and we catch our breath a bit. And we look at our Edgar, who, intimidated by the neighbors, tugs at his belt, with a jerk of his loins pulling his trousers up. Then he walks, summoned and restrained by no one, with three, four strides quickly through the throng of neighbors and into the parlor, where he's never been before, while we, who follow him, know the parlor already. Yes, this is Herr Schellenbaum's house, this is his headquarters! It doesn't only look like Herr Schellenbaum's house here, it smells of him. The darkness follows us, persisting, for there's no chance of light here, except that the ceiling and a strip of wall are bathed in moonlight. A good thing the moon is still there. Good too that we're now in the parlor, for there can be no doubt about that. And here in Herr Schellenbaum's parlor, which suddenly seems to us, with a sense of foreboding, emptier and more theatrical and in an eerie way more momentous than before, we see beside an ornamental plant, which shoots up from a flower pot in a window corner, Herr Schellenbaum himself, sparsely moonlit, sitting on his sofa, waiting for our letter. (Probably our Edgar, because of his eyes, can only guess that he's there.) His legs, the legs of an agèd farmer, are clad in working trousers, recently taken in, and his old singlet, which we know from the elder bush and which now looms up before us and seems to balloon out around his belly and his chest, is clamped to his body by a pair of suspenders embroidered in a folksy fashion. Yes, that's Herr Schellenbaum, this must be Herr Schellenbaum, who, shortly before our conquest, so as to become a different person, slipped out of his uniform and into his previous costume. And now, dressed in this way—though we recognize him—he has sunk into the right-hand corner of his sofa, because we've been conquered, with a look of finality about his mouth, and he has rested on his knees his heavy hands, still soiled from gardening, and has propped the large back of his head— with light falling on the top of it—against the back of the sofa, where this head, which has lolled to the side somewhat, has now found repose. Herr Schellenbaum's rather astonished eyes, like those belonging to someone who's hard of hearing, gaze up at the ceiling, where he's making an effort to stare himself into something, perhaps a crack. We tiptoe close, waving our letter. *Guten Abend*, we say, it's only us. And we cling close to one another, as we did at the slaughterhouse, no, even closer. And think or say or are about to say and then perhaps don't say that we've been delayed, in the church and in the theater. And before that we were arrested at the slaughterhouse, though only provisionally, because he got sick by the calf-killing slab, we say or think and point at our Edgar, who's standing under the plant in the corner, where, to pass the time, he's about to get himself entangled in the curtain cord. Our Edgar, who has probably eaten earth again today behind his garden shed, so that he's feeling sick now, and he'd certainly have collapsed if we hadn't held him up. And this is the letter, we say and hold mother's letter out to Herr Schellenbaum. But Herr Schellenbaum has settled himself so deeply into his corner of the sofa that he doesn't notice us yet, he goes on goggling up at the ceiling, as if we weren't there at all. Feeling a bit ill at ease we step up beside him and join him in looking upward, but we can't detect any pattern there, or any crack. Perhaps Herr Schellenbaum isn't even looking, but listening, perhaps, at something inside the walls that eludes us, because our ears are smaller. He'd like to hear more from us too before he takes the letter and puts it in his gardening trousers, and then he'll speak. Yes, we say or think, it's dark here, outside it's dark too. Well, what a day it's been! And then we think about the day and say or think to ourselves that all in all it was disappointing. True, we've been to the town, true, we even went across the river, but we haven't seen much, only the usual things. When you think of all the things that have happened, but not here. And that a new era is beginning, but not here. We haven't even seen any dead people, though we know where they are. Certainly we've obtained a suit, we think, and spread our arms and remember Granny Henne and how she copied the gull. And this is from mother, who sends her best wishes, we say, and for a long time we've been holding our letter out to Herr Schellenbaum, and we're meaning to go on talking or thinking, but first we pause, because someone calls to us through the cloud of cigarette smoke in the hallway that Herr Schellenbaum is dead. Dead? We lower the blue letter, we stand straighter. What does that mean? Well, he isn't alive anymore. But wasn't he creeping under his bush when he saw us on Wednesday? Yes, but now he's dead. And so very dead—poison, it's even to be seen trickling out of his mouth, if you look long enough—that he ought to be buried right away. Fancy, he's as dead as that, we think. Behind us, but also behind the dead Herr Schellenbaum, at whom our inquisitive neighbors keep staring from the smoky hallway—the windowpanes are softly touched by the light and shadow of the moon. Beside them the rubber plant, which, at a moment like this, naturally has something poetic about it. Then a chair, which certainly isn't a theater chair, though it could be. Then our Edgar, who's getting more and more violently entangled in the curtain cord, he's so very ill at ease. And beneath the sofa one can see, if one is feeling embarrassed and prefers to lower one's eyes, Herr Schellenbaum's boots, which, like two tamed animals, are waiting for the return of familiar conditions in the parlor. Over them, again, Herr Schellenbaum himself, his thighs, his belly, his head, features that seem even more important now that we know he's dead. (Later, when we're in our beds again, we'll be able to see and describe everything better.) Outside, dark night, an earnest wind blowing between our houses and over them and away. It's May, for us here too. There's a little warmth mixed into our air, though you'd hardly notice it. In the house a stillness, perhaps horror, at all events incomprehension. We stand there, with our limbs cautiously taut, skin thinned, hair on end or anyway slightly lifted up, but we don't stand like that for long. We hardly have the time to see and absorb this and that, so as to carry it away with us, out of this room, which, if one listens more closely, seems distinctly to be creaking now, to be sighing, we think. For instance, the strange light on the furnishings, not falling on them from outside but coming out of their interiors, as if drawn forth by fingers. It's true, the furnishings here, which we've known—their lower extremities—since childhood, glow from inside, especially the closet. Or the rods for the blinds, all of them hollow and empty. How strange, we're thinking, and we'd like to go on looking, but then everything is over. Fingers are pointing at us from where the neighbors are in the hallway, fists threaten us, as if we were guilty of this death and of their uneasiness. Then we're forbidden to go any closer to the body that Herr Schellenbaum has left us, or to walk around it or even to study it a bit from a distance. We're not even allowed to go behind it, from one piece of furniture to another. Instead, we hear in the stillness—who'd ever have thought such a stillness could exist outside the theater—voices saying: Get the children out of there! Quickly, already on our way out, we take Herr Schellenbaum in, the whole magnitude of him. Since we've known he's dead, he looks quite different. Head and body and hands and face, which till now had been held together by our gaze, are dissolving. We take in the unbearable corpse eyes too. They look very shocked. And on closer inspection we see they're not looking up at the ceiling but have turned around in their sockets, to look into Herr Schellenbaum himself. Then we're taken by the shoulders, our Edgar is taken out of his cord, and with a few rough shoves we're driven away from Herr Schellenbaum, out of his parlor. As we're leaving, in the hallway, under the antlers, which have nothing to hang from them today, we mingle with the neighbors talking beside the chest. Here's Frau Hoppe, here's Herr Schimmelpfennig, but nobody notices us. Only Herr Pelikan gives us a wink, as if to say: How stupid of this Schellenbaum person! Well, a good thing he's gone now. Finally, here's our Edgar standing behind us and looking at Frau Hoppe—she's chewing something. Did she bring it with her or did she find it on her way here? While she's swallowing it, our Edgar licks his lips with his tongue. Well, let's go now, we're thinking. Let's go, our Edgar says.

So now we're outside the house in our suit, blue letter in hand, and night is all around us, above us too, night into which we've been given a push. Then along the park street and along Lindenstraße, the last stretch of our way under the stars. Boring, the way one has to place one foot in front of the other, while walking in darkness! So as not to be seen by someone and shot, we have to keep our heads down. Heads down? we ask. Yes, our Edgar says, keep your heads down all the time. But we are keeping our heads down, we say and keep them down and walk with our heads down through the night. Can't you keep them farther down? our Edgar asks—and he's much taller than us. No, we say, because of our wound. All right then, our Edgar says, just keep them down as low as you can. And you, we ask, aren't you keeping yours down?—because he isn't. No, he says. I don't care if they see me. And if they shoot you? we ask. Ah, our Edgar says, it doesn't matter. It does matter to us, we say and keep our heads down as low as we can, with our wound. And can't you walk any faster either? our Edgar exclaims later, although we've arrived at the Meistersingerstraße in such a short time. Even faster? we ask. Yes, he says, the stars are going away. The stars! we exclaim, startled. Yes, our Edgar says, take a look for yourself. And he points upward, after taking his hunger stone from his pocket and putting it in his mouth. It's true, as we look up into the sky, heads down, twisting around, there aren't so many stars as before. The moon is vanishing too. What if we can't walk any faster? we ask. Then it'll be dark when you get home, our Edgar says. All right, let it be dark then, we say, and we're thinking of Herr Schellenbaum again and would like to think—the poison was an accident!—but our Edgar shakes his head. And then, fighting back his nausea—he must have eaten some earth—he tells us—now we're walking up our Laubgasse—all about it. While he's telling us, we notice how impetuously our Edgar speaks when he has the stone in his mouth. Yet perhaps it isn't the stone in his mouth, perhaps it's a piece of paper. And we're meaning to ask: Have you got a stone in your mouth or is it paper? but we don't ask it, because our Edgar doesn't like to say what he's chewing on. Do you swallow it, when you've finished? is all we ask. Depends what it is, he says. And if it's paper? we ask. Yes, he says, then mostly I swallow it. And the stone, we ask, do you swallow that too? No, he says, not the stone. But what do you do with the stone? we ask. Ah, he says, what do you think? But he doesn't tell us. Perhaps he puts it back in his trouser pocket, when he's finished, and saves it up for later. Briefly, several times tonight when Edgar is chewing on something we wipe threads of his spittle off our suit jacket and our face. Then his very voice and the clatter of his teeth make him quite strange to us. Briefly, soon he's walking between us again and telling us everything. That Herr Schellenbaum will have to be buried in a sitting position, because, having sat for such a long time in the corner of his sofa, he can't be stretched or pulled straight. Sitting! we exclaim and look up at our Edgar and purse our lips to whistle. Yes, sitting, our Edgar says. The idea of stretching or pulling Herr Schellenbaum straight, while he's dead! We say nothing and shake our head. On the other hand, the idea of burying him in a sitting position! We nod: but of course.

Later then, at home in the kitchen, when we've got used to the idea and have given the letter back to mother, who has been standing for hours at the window looking out for father and for us as well, and when we've copied for her the way Herr Schellenbaum sits on the sofa and doesn't want the letter, and have also told her how we were pushed out afterward into the night and got lost around the park and that's why we're so late and the slaughterhouse was empty and there wasn't a chance of getting any *Butterschmalz* and she has kept on pulling us to her and pressing us and kissing us and licking us clean and exclaiming with her arms in the air that it was so late in the night and she'd never let us go again and has finally knelt before us and taken off our shoes and is meaning to take our trousers off, because we belong in bed and everything is dirty . . . The trousers! we exclaim, putting our hands to our wound, no, not the trousers! Quiet, mother exclaims, no back talk. Don't you know how late it is? No, we say, what's the time? But then she doesn't tell us. So we'll never know what the time was when we came home on the first day after our conquest. But she stands up full-stretch before us and exclaims: Be quiet now! You'll do as I say in this house as long as father's not here, do you understand? And then she even wants to light a fire, using the old apple crates from the cellar, and to wash our feet, but she can't find the crates. At least stand against the wall, so I can take your trousers off, she says. No, not the trousers, we exclaim, but she won't let us go. Up against the wall! she exclaims. And you, Edgar, take the pail and go bring some water. Yes, Frau Imbach, our Edgar says, and he goes off with the pail. And then, as mother comes closer and pulls at the trousers, which are stuck because of our wound, at several points: Keep still now and don't dither, mother exclaims and pulls at one trouser leg. Don't pull, we exclaim, please don't! And as mother goes on pulling all the same and our wound comes to light and mother doesn't see it, but feels something vaguely about us, and we also look down and can only make guesses about our wound, which is bleeding warm blood, suddenly we can't help crying. My God, as if that were necessary. But it's no wonder either. It's a fact, our leg is hurt, we're hurt all over. Again and again, in the flickering candlelight—our Edgar behind us, pail in hand, sucking on his stone—the longer we look the more we cry. As she kneels down and surveys the extent of our wound, mother can hardly believe her eyes. My God, my God, she exclaims again and again, and she puts a hand in her mouth and doesn't want to look at the wound but looks outside to see the trees. And when her curiosity forces her to look at our wound, she just can't comprehend at first how we've been carrying such a wound around with us and have been all the way to the slaughterhouse with it. Of course, she wants to know at once how we came by it and if it was an accident or whatever else, but we're not telling her, we just look down at ourself and cry again. And of course our Edgar, who isn't crying, isn't telling her either, but sucking around with his stone, standing there with his legs apart. My God, mother exclaims, you poor children! My God, why does all this have to happen? But we can't tell her that either, it just came to be that way, bit by bit. Later, when we've finished crying, she asks us if we're hungry. Yes, very, of course. And you, have you had anything to eat? she asks our Edgar, who has the pail, not needed now, between his feet. No, he says, actually I haven't. And why not? mother asks, and she goes to the kitchen closet, where she put the two-pound loaf this morning, or what was left of it, didn't your aunt give you anything? No, our Edgar says, I haven't been there for a week. And nobody put anything outside your garden shed for you? mother asks. No, our Edgar says, I don't think so. What do you mean: I don't think so? mother asks sternly, and she takes the half loaf from the closet, didn't you look? Yes, our Edgar says, I looked this morning. And what did you find? mother asks. Nothing, actually, our Edgar says. And what did you have to eat yesterday? she asks. A piece of bread, our Edgar says. Our bread! we exclaim. And we wrap our legs in the old dog blanket and sit down on the bench at the table, upon which, through the Golden Pearmain tree, the last moonlight is falling. Edgar meanwhile sits with his pail far from our table and hardly visible to us, probably on the coal box or on some old box or other. Well then, no wonder you sway, mother says, and she cuts three, then four slices from the old loaf. Humans, like other animals, have to be regularly fed, even if only with slush, they need it, particularly their brains do, from which everything comes and without which nobody can either think or move his limbs—one slice of bread, mother says, over two or three days, that won't get us far. Particularly this bread, she says and holds up our loaf, which, it's no secret, has to be baked in tin molds, otherwise it would fall apart, because of all the water in it. It isn't that we don't want to help you, she says, but look, we haven't got anything, and she points to the empty closet again. Considering all the thoughts that pass through your head, haven't you sometimes wondered what Frau Imbach lives off? mother asks. Yes, I've wondered, our Edgar says. And what do I live off? mother asks. I really don't know, our Edgar says. It's a mystery to you, isn't it? mother says. Yes, she says, and you're not the only person it's a mystery to, it's a mystery to me as well. When a person eats as little as I do and has so many troubles at the same time, he could easily have been dead and buried a long time ago. Yes, our Edgar says, I know. Well, I'll tell you why I'm not dead and buried and what I live off, mother says, and she leans against her old cooker. I live off tea from the herbs and berries I pick behind the house. And off my hope which I'm not going to let anyone take away from me, my hope that all of this is only a bad dream, from which we'll wake up one day. Now do you know what I live off? Yes, our Edgar says, off your tea. And then, after she has put the slices of bread on a plate and set the plate on the table, she asks him if he had another headache today. Yes, our Edgar says. And where did it hurt you today? she asks. About the middle, our Edgar says on his box, and he puts a hand probably to his head, where the middle is. Mine's over my eyes, mother says and puts a hand to her forehead. Did you faint today? she asks then. No, our Edgar says, not yet. Things went a bit dark once, but there was still a flicker of light. Well, mother says, just so long as there's a flicker. And how do you feel now? As if you might still faint today? It's hard to say, our Edgar says after attending to his thoughts for a bit. Well, mother says, probably it's too late to be fainting today, first the night has to come. You must realize that first the night has to come, for all of us. Yes, Frau Imbach, our Edgar says. And take this and eat it, mother says and picks up a slice of bread from the plate. But eat it slowly and don't gobble it like the last one, chew it well and draw the pleasure out, I haven't got any more, you see. I know, Frau Imbach, thank you very much, our Edgar says and stands up from his box and goes to mother and takes the bread and looks at it awkwardly and then puts it behind his back, so that he won't see it anymore. Also he doesn't sit down with it at our table, but walks around the table a bit, sort of flutters around it. And don't think so much anymore, mother says, but go to your garden shed and lie down. Yes, Frau Imbach, our Edgar says, I'll go and lie down now. And what's he supposed not to think about anymore? we ask from our bench by the window. Ah, mother says, it'd be best if he didn't think about anything anymore. Nothing anymore? we exclaim. Yes, she says. But how can he not think about anything anymore, everyone thinks about something, we say—but mother isn't going to get involved in a question like that. The best thing, she says, and she's talking to our Edgar again, would be simply for you to lie down and not think about anything anymore. Yes, our Edgar says, I'll lie down and not think about anything anymore. And he's standing now with his slice of bread, which one can't see, at the back door, with one foot on the threshold. Well, *auf Wiedersehen*, Frau Imbach, he says. Yes, yes, all right, mother says. And lie on your right side, because the heart's on the left and you mustn't strain it. Yes, our Edgar says, I'll lie on my right side. And now too he takes the stone out of his mouth, because, as soon as he's out in the yard, as we know, he'll cram the bread into his mouth and gobble it up at once in two or three big mouthfuls. Take care, Edgar, we say and again wonder why he hasn't starved to death yet, though that could still happen. And we wave to him a little out of our moonlight, even if only with a forefinger. See you tomorrow, our Edgar says, and he doesn't wave, but vanishes in an instant with the bread.

Now the kitchen table is quickly laid, there's a sort of supper. Mother has hidden another piece of bacon in the *Kachelofen*. But it's such a trifling and brief piece that it couldn't possibly have been shared with Edgar, and now we eat it alone. Crouching over the table we cut it into strips, which, as mother looks on, we thrust deep into our throats. Rapidly we shred it with our pointed teeth and crunch it to pulp and swallow it. Was that all? we ask and look around the cold kitchen, knife and fork in our fist. That was all, mother says. Well, if that was all, we say. So then the table is cleared again and Herr Henne's suit comes in for study, which, as mother says, not only fits us but also suits us well. Only we must gradually get accustomed to it, since we haven't worn such a new suit for a long time. Even if it smells? we ask when we're up in our room and have taken the suit off and mother has hung it on the outside of the closet, so that we can see it from bed. Ah, mother says, what's it supposed to smell of? Of Herr Henne, we exclaim loudly. Ah, mother says, he's far away and buried deep in the ground and his little bit of smell, even if it's really there, will soon fly away. No, we say, you've got to wash the suit. Wash it! she exclaims, and me with nobody to help me and my leg and no soap? All the same, we say, you've got to wash it. Oh well, mother says and pulls the blanket up to our chin, then I'll wash it, and we fall asleep. Later, after the things that were slightly disturbed in our room that night have been returned to their places and we've grown accustomed to our suit—mother has drawn a chair up to the window, but still it's springtime—later, after our Edgar has again collapsed on the Adolf-Hitler-Straße and lain there a long time before Herr Pelikan and a bakery man picked him up and put him on a cart and trundled him across Denkstein, Frisch, and Ziegel to be fattened up again in the internal medicine wing of the town hospital on the Wikingerhalde, where nobody's allowed to visit him, and we still haven't heard from father, even though we're determined to go on waiting for him and if necessary to leave the factory and quit the house, which is now full of refugees who, during the cold nights, because there's no fuel, saw the boughs off the fruit trees, and, on account of our father, who as a manufacturer of small leather goods was always, as mother says, an industrialist, to go with the Americans if they abandon our town to the Russians, as mother fears they will, and for that reason have already packed three big suitcases and two rucksacks and put them under the stairs tied to the banisters with leather straps, on account of the refugees, who are people from the Sudetenland now, and we're only waiting for a signal from father, however secret it might be, and are constantly standing among the suitcases, especially in the evening, testing the straps, yet still we have no news from him . . . But Edgar's father was killed in action near Dessau and Granny Henne suddenly died and was buried next to the Pietsch-Szczepanski double grave. (If she really did die and get buried at all, so people tell us much later, which is how things around us tend to be, so probably we'll never know what really happened, what was said and done and not said and not done, in L., our town, during the day after our conquest.) As for Herr Schellenbaum's poor wife, she was also found in their flimsy house, like her husband, but in the cellar. We finally *tormented* our mother into telling us this. Now mother lets us out, to walk around the house or into the town, if not all the way to the slaughterhouse. Since we mostly go out at noontime, our shadow goes with us. With one bound our shadow leaps through the wrought-iron gate into the middle of the Laubgasse. Mute, it squeezes through the fresh green leaves. And creeps past the houses of Frau Reißer and Frau Wittke and Dr. Grünfeld—*the nails*—and it dwindles outside our theater, and behind the church, where the stray bomb fell, it becomes mostly very small, very small. On the Adolf-Hitler-Straße, where Edgar was lifted onto the cart—it's now called Helenenstraße—it seems to be trying to melt away. For a long time it jitters up and down before us, because we stand here for such a long time and trace with our feet pensive lines across the place where Edgar lay. And as for Herr Schellenbaum's wife, who was found in the cellar—also poison—she was found in a *quite indescribable state* and lying, not sitting. So that we ourself, easily identifiable as casualties in Herr Henne's suit, which we still don't like—long, thin, insubstantial snail tracks, soon to condense, traverse our sky in those days—from now on we make a wide arc, our shadow shivering at our side, around Herr Schellenbaum's house. Even if the stench that comes from it is probably something we imagine.